W9-BVU-686

TRANSFORMERS

THE IDW COLLECTION • PHASE TWO, VOLUME 5

Collection Cover Art by Marcelo Matere
Collection Edits by Justin Eisinger and Alonzo Simon
Collection Design by Chris Mowry
Publisher: Ted Adams

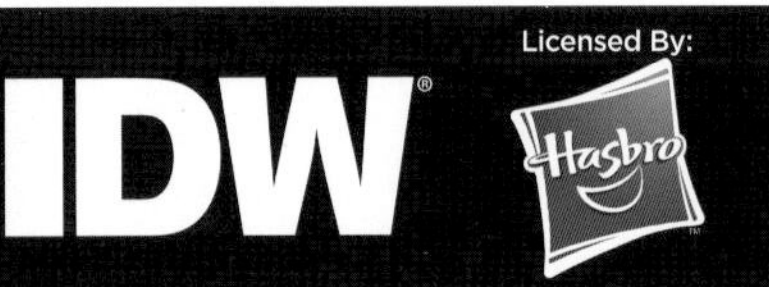

Special thanks to Hasbro's Ben Montano, David Erwin, Josh Feldman, Ed Lane, Beth Artale, and Michael Kelly for their invaluable assistance.

For international rights, please contact licensing@idwpublishing.com

Become our fan on Facebook **facebook.com/idwpublishing**
Follow us on Twitter **@idwpublishing**
Subscribe to us on YouTube **youtube.com/idwpublishing**
See what's new on Tumblr **tumblr.idwpublishing.com**
Check us out on Instagram **instagram.com/idwpublishing**

ISBN: 978-1-63140-844-1 21 20 19 18 2 3 4 5

Originally published as TRANSFORMERS: PRIMACY issues #1–4, TRANSFORMERS: ROBOTS IN DISGUISE issues #19–22, and TRANSFORMERS: MORE THAN MEETS THE EYE issues #17–22.

PRIMACY

STORY BY **CHRIS METZEN** AND **FLINT DILLE**

ART BY **LIVIO RAMONDELLI**

LETTERS BY **CHRIS MOWRY** EDITS BY **JOHN BARBER**

ROBOTS IN DISGUISE #19-20

WRITTEN BY **JOHN BARBER**

ART BY **DHEERAJ VERMA** AND **ANDREW GRIFFITH**

COLORS BY **JOANA LAFUENTE** AND **PRISCILLA TRAMONTANO**

LETTERS BY **CHRIS MOWRY** AND **SHAWN LEE**

EDITS BY **CARLOS GUZMAN**

MORE THAN MEETS THE EYE #17-21

WRITTEN BY **JAMES ROBERTS** ART BY **ALEX MILNE**

INKS BY **ALEX MILNE** AND **BRIAN SHEARER**

COLORS BY **JOSH BURCHAM**

ADDITIONAL COLORS BY **JOHN-PAUL BOVE** AND **JOANA LAFUENTE**

LETTERS BY **TOM B. LONG** EDITS BY **JOHN BARBER**

ROBOTS IN DISGUISE #21-22

WRITTEN BY **JOHN BARBER**

ART BY **ANDREW GRIFFITH** (PRESENT DAY) AND **LIVIO RAMONDELLI** (PAST)

COLORS BY **PRISCILLA TRAMONTANO** (PRESENT DAY)

AND **LIVIO RAMONDELLI** (PAST)

LETTERS BY **SHAWN LEE** EDITS BY **CARLOS GUZMAN**

MORE THAN MEETS THE EYE #22

WRITTEN BY **JAMES ROBERTS** ART BY **JAMES RAIZ**

COLORS BY **JOSH BURCHAM** LETTERS BY **TOM B. LONG**

EDITS BY **JOHN BARBER**

THE SOUND OF BREAKING GLASS

WRITTEN BY **JAMES ROBERTS**

PRIMACY #1 COVER A
by **LIVIO RAMONDELLI**

CYBERTRON.

THERE WAS AN *EXODUS*.

AND A *CATASTROPHE*.

THE RAMPAGE OF A COLOSSAL, PRIMORDIAL *HORROR*.

THERE WAS A MOMENT WHERE THE MOST DANGEROUS CYBERTRONIAN ALIVE... *SAVED* THE *WORLD*.

NOW ALL IS *QUIET*.

BUT THE *PEACE*... CANNOT LAST.

...THE CONCLAVE OF REPRESENTATIVES' REPORT ON THE CRISIS IN HARMONEX IS HERE.
THE REPORT CLAIMS THAT THE PRIME AND HIS AUTOBOTS DEFEATED THE CREATURE NAMED TRYPTICON... BUT WE STILL HAVE NO DIRECT LINE TO ANYONE IN HARMONEX.
SOME HAVE CLAIMED THAT THE MEDIA IS BEING KEPT AWAY FROM THE AREA...
IN OTHER NEWS, THE CONCLAVE HAS DENIED MEDIA REQUESTS TO REVEAL THE TOTAL NUMBER OF 'BOTS WHO FLED CYBERTRON DURING THE RECENT EXODUS...
WELL, HOT ROD—YOU JUST GRADUATED FROM THE AUTOBOT ACADEMY. WHAT DO YOU MAKE OF ALL THIS? YOU REALLY THINK WE CAN TRUST THE GOVERNMENT?
I DON'T KNOW ABOUT THE CONCLAVE, OR WHATEVER. BUT I BELIEVE IN OPTIMUS. HE'S THE REAL DEAL.
I LEAVE IT TO YOU, VIEWERS—ARE WE LOOKING AT A TOTAL INFORMATIONAL BLACKOUT?
ARE WE BEING LIED TO?
IS OPTIMUS' BURGEONING ADMINISTRATION JUST AS BAD AS ALL THE OTHERS?
WHATEVER.
I DON'T KNOW. SOUNDS LIKE THEY BRAINWASHED YOU AT THAT ACADEMY.
CAN'T IMAGINE WHY YOU'D WANNA GO OFF AND JOIN UP WITH THOSE CLOWNS.
BETTER THAN THE ALTERNATIVE. THE DECEPTICONS JUST WANNA SEE EVERYTHING BURN.
WHAT DO YOU CARE?
I'VE SEEN ENOUGH THINGS BURN.

OUTSIDE, MOMENTS LATER.
WELL, NOW I'VE SEEN EVERYTHING.
THAT CAN'T BE OL' HOT ROD WEARING AN AUTOBOT SYMBOL ON HIS CHEST?
WHO'S THERE? SHOW YOURSELF!
WHAT'S THE MATTER, HOT ROD...?

...DON'T RECOGNIZE YOUR OL' PAL, SLINGER?
MAN, IT'S GOOD TO SEE YOU! BUT...
...YOU LOOK DIFFERENT.

I AM DIFFERENT!
EVERYTHING'S DIFFERENT SINCE YOU BLEW UP NYON*!
KRONK
WEARING THAT BADGE IS A DISGRACE TO EVERYONE WHO DIED THAT DAY!
*SEE TRANSFORMERS: AUTOCRACY.

DON'T YOU JUDGE ME, SLINGER!
YOU WERE RIGHT THERE WITH ME! ZETA PRIME WAS CONSUMING OUR PEOPLE—THEY WERE DEAD EITHER WAY!
IT HAD TO BE DONE AND YOU KNOW IT!

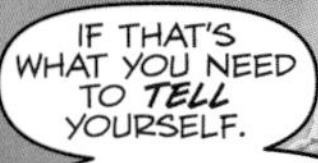
IF THAT'S WHAT YOU NEED TO TELL YOURSELF.
ME, I SEE THINGS DIFFERENT NOW. I THREW IN WITH THE REAL "PEOPLE'S MOVEMENT."
THEY FIXED ME UP. MADE ME A FIGHTER. THEY'RE THE REAL POWER, NOW.

SO FROM HERE ON OUT—YOU BETTER WATCH YOUR BACK.
AND TELL YOUR AUTOBOT PALS... THEIR DAY IS DONE.

THE GRAV–HARAAN GLACIER. SOUTHERN POLAR REGION.

UNFORGIVING **PLASMA STREAMS** HAMMER AGAINST PRIMORDIAL GLACIERS OF **SOLID ORE** THAT HAVE STOOD FOR **FIFTY MILLION YEARS.**

THE WIND SHRIEKS AS IF ALIVE... **ELECTRIC**. VENGEFUL.

YOU SURE PICKED A **HELL** OF A **VACATION SPOT**.

WHEN YOU SAID YOU WERE TAKING A **SABBATICAL**, I PICTURED SOMEPLACE A LITTLE LESS...

REMOTE?

DANGEROUS.

I SWEAR, **PRIME**—YOU'RE THE ONLY 'BOT I KNOW THAT **REHABILITATES** AFTER A **BATTLE** BY PUSHIN' HIMSELF EVEN **HARDER**.

I FIND THE WILD, OPEN SPACES **PURIFYING**. TESTING MY LIMITS AGAINST **CYBERTRON ITSELF**.... PUTS EVERYTHING INTO PERSPECTIVE.

OUT HERE, I'M NOT A **PRIME**. JUST... MYSELF.

THE ONLY BURDEN TO BEAR IS **SURVIVAL**.

WELL, DON'T YOU WORRY ABOUT ME, BOSS.
I CAN CARRY MY OWN WEIGHT.
KREEESH
OH, FRAG...
YOU WERE SAYING?
YEAH. YEAH.

THE SUMMIT AT LAST.
JUST LOOK AT THIS GRANDEUR, IRONHIDE. I'D TAKE THIS MAJESTY OVER THE CONSTANT BUSTLE OF IACON ANY DAY.
THERE'S PURITY IN THIS DESOLATION. THINK ABOUT IT—NO 'BOT HAS SET FOOT ON THIS GROUND FOR MILLIONS OF YEARS.
I DUNNO.
YA SEEN ONE POLAR WASTELAND, YA SEEN 'EM ALL...
I'M NOT SO SURE ABOUT THAT, BOSS.
I'M DETECTING SOMETHING OUT ON THE HORIZON LINE. THE LINES ARE ALL WRONG FOR GLACIAL FEATURES.
IT'S BIG.
COULD BE AN OLD OBSERVATION POST. MAYBE A RESEARCH FACILITY?
WHATEVER IT IS, IT'S GIVING OFF A SERIOUS ENERGON SIGNATURE.
WE'RE NOT ALONE OUT HERE, OPTIMUS.
LET'S CHECK IT OUT. BUT STAY ALERT.
ANYONE DESPERATE ENOUGH TO SEEK THIS KIND OF ISOLATION COULD BE CAPABLE OF ANYTHING.
YEAH...
...JUST LIKE US.
I HEARD THAT.

METROPLEX, IACON CITY CENTER.
WHAT'S THE STATUS IN THE MED-BAY, KUP? THIS... EXPERIMENT SHOULD HAVE BEEN WRAPPED UP HOURS AGO.
IT'S A COMPLEX PROCEDURE, MAGNUS. HAVE SOME PATIENCE.
RATCHET AND WHEELJACK ARE DOING EVERYTHING THEY CAN IN THERE.
I KNOW. IT'S JUST THIS WHOLE BUSINESS MAKES ME... UNEASY.
WHAT BUSINESS? WHAT'D I MISS?
'BOUT TIME YOU SHOWED UP, HOT ROD... ISN'T PUNCTUALITY ONE OF THE FIRST THINGS THEY TEACH YOU AT THE ACADEMY?
SORRY. GOT HELD UP.
AT ANY RATE, THE SCIENCE TEAM'S FLOODED THE CONTAINMENT CHAMBER WITH VAPORIZED IONIUM. IT'S THE FINAL STAGE OF THE ENERGON-PURIFICATION TREATMENT...
PURIFICATION... FOR WHO? CAN'T SEE ANYTHING IN THERE.
GRIMLOCK. HE'S THE LAST OF THE DYNOBOTS TO UNDERGO THE PROCESS.
RIGHT—TO BREAK THE CURSE OF THEIR CORRUPTED ENERGON!
WELL, HAS IT WORKED?
SO FAR, SO GOOD, LAD. BUT THEY'VE HAD THE MOST TROUBLE WITH GRIMLOCK.
THE CORRUPTION RAN DEEP WITHIN HIS CIRCUITS. IF THIS DOESN'T WORK...
THIS IS RATCHET. WE'RE PREPARING TO VENT THE CHAMBER.
EVERYONE KEEP YOUR DIODES CROSSED.

KEEEEEE-SHHHHHH
WELL, GRIMLOCK— HOW DO YOU FEEL?
GOOD AS NEW, AUTOBOT. BETTER EVEN.
YOU'RE SURE? YOU'RE NOT EXPERIENCING ANY HEIGHTENED PULSE-SURGES OR AGGRESSIVE COMPULSIONS?
NOT YET. BUT THE DAY IS YOUNG.
HUMOR. THAT'S GOOD. YOUR VITALS LOOK STRONG. NO ANOMALIES IN YOUR ENERGON PROFILE. I THINK WE DID IT.
HMM.
AND YOU'RE WELCOME.
SO WHAT ABOUT THE DYNOBOTS' UNCONTROLLABLE DRAGON MODES? ARE THEY STILL A DANGER?
NOT ANYMORE. ALONG WITH THE ENERGON TRANSFUSIONS, WE RE-ENGINEERED THEIR ORIGINAL ALT-MODES.
FOR ALL INTENTS AND PURPOSES, THE DYNOBOTS ARE BACK TO THE SHAPE THEY WERE AS PART OF THE PRIMAL VANGUARD.
THAT'S FANTASTIC! CONGRATULATIONS, GRIMLOCK!
I'VE HEARD ALL THE STORIES ABOUT YOU GUYS AND I'M LOOKING FORWARD TO KICKING SOME DECEPTICON TAIL WITH YOU!
DON'T TALK TO ME LIKE YOU'RE A SOLDIER, BOY. FRESH OUT OF THE ACADEMY, RIGHT?
JUST BECAUSE WE WEAR THE SAME BADGE DOESN'T MEAN WE'RE THE SAME.
YOU GOTTA LOT TO PROVE BEFORE YOU EARN MY RESPECT... OR MY TRUST.

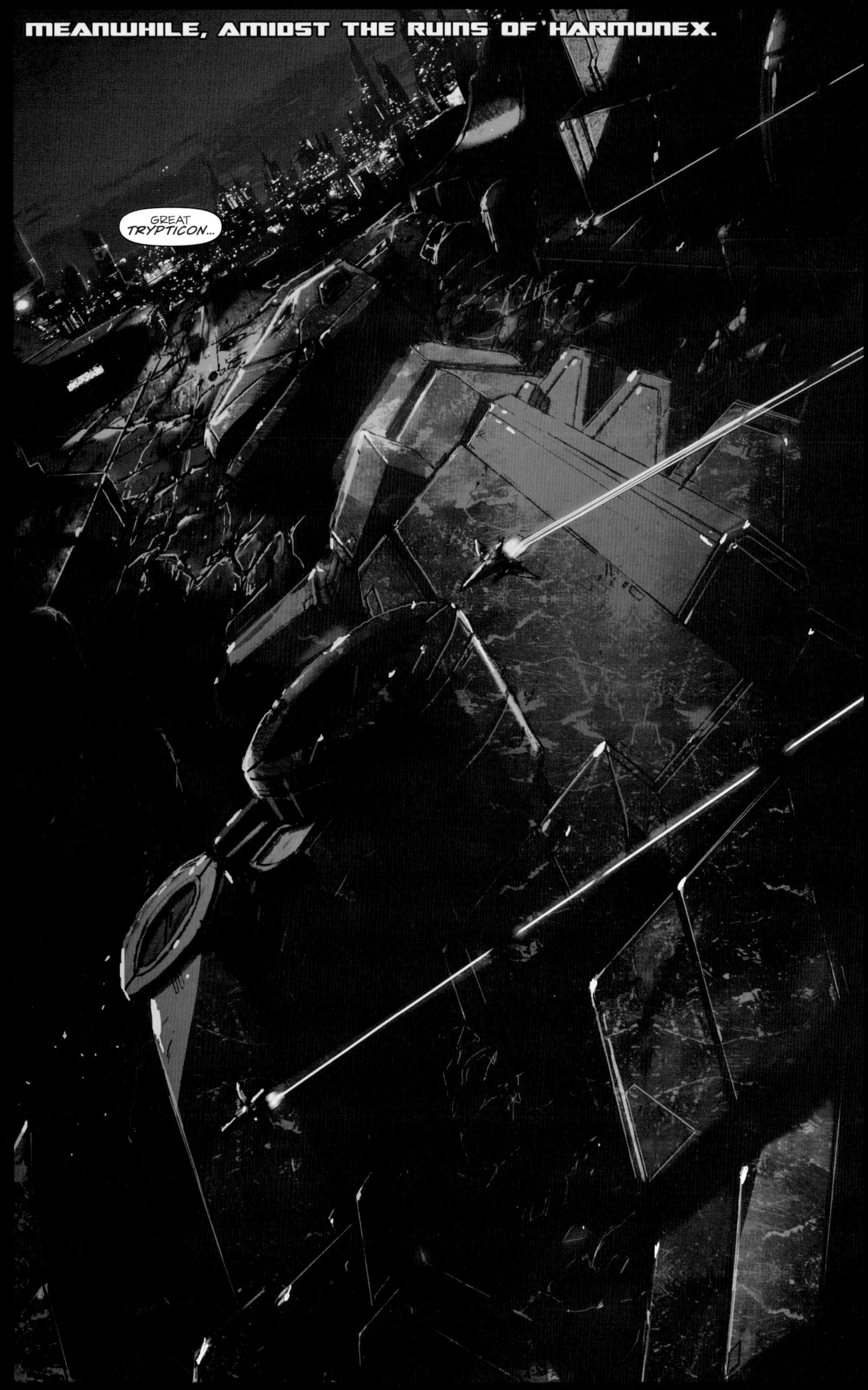
MEANWHILE, AMIDST THE RUINS OF HARMONEX.
GREAT TRYPTICON...

...YOU HAVE *SLEPT* LONG ENOUGH.

DOWN THROUGH THE *LONG AGES* OF THIS WORLD... YOU HAVE DREAMED *TERRIBLE DREAMS* OF *DESTRUCTION.*

OF *RUIN.*

THAT CYCLE HAS *COME 'ROUND* ONCE AGAIN.

I SEE NOW MY *TRUE PURPOSE.*

AND *YOURS.*

IN HIS PRIDE, *SCORPONOK* SOUGHT TO UNLEASH YOUR *PRIMAL FURY*; HE BELIEVED YOU TO BE A *MINDLESS BEAST*—AND THAT THE UNBRIDLED CHAOS YOU WOULD WREAK WOULD CULL THE *WEAK* FROM THIS *WORLD.**

*SEE *TRANSFORMERS: MONSTROSITY.*

ON *BOTH COUNTS*, HE WAS MISTAKEN. IT IS NOT *CHAOS* THAT WILL TRANSFORM THIS WORLD...

...BUT *CONTROL.*

NOW, AS THE *VILE SPARK* I PLACED WITHIN YOU STIRS TO LIFE, WE WILL *RISE* TOGETHER—AND BRING RUIN UPON ALL THOSE WHO OPPOSE US.

THIS DAY—THIS *WORLD*—SHALL BE OURS.

SO SWEARS *MEGATRON.*

I FEEL IT... COURSING WITHIN MY FRAME—REMNANT TRACES OF THE SPARK WE NOW SHARE.
POWER ENOUGH... TO WAKE THE DEAD.
GREETINGS, WANDERER. I KNEW WE WOULD MEET AGAIN.
PENTIUS?
NO.
AND YES.
I AM MORE THAN TRYPTICON NOW—AS YOU ARE MORE THAN THE MEGATRON YOU ONCE WERE.
AND YOU ARE CORRECT—WE HAVE A GREAT WORK TO DO. TO BREAK A WORLD... AND FORGE A MORE PERFECT ORDER FROM ITS HUSK IS NO SMALL THING.
DO YOU HAVE THE WILL TO SEE SUCH A THING TO ITS CONCLUSION, GREAT MEGATRON?
TRY ME.

THE GRAV-HARAAN GLACIER.
KEEP UP THE PACE, IRONHIDE! WE'RE NEARLY THERE!
RIGHT BEHIND YA, AS USUAL, BOSS!
BUT I'M STARTIN' TO THINK MAYBE THAT THING AIN'T A STRUCTURE AFTER ALL.
WHAT ARE YOU... YOU'RE SUGGESTING IT'S A CYBERTRONIAN?
HEY, WE'VE MET OUR FAIR SHARE OF HUGE 'BOTS, RIGHT? I THINK I REMEMBER YOU RAISING SOME KINDA SUPER-TITAN FROM THE GROUND ONCE...
WELL, WHATEVER IT IS, IT HASN'T SO MUCH AS TWITCHED SINCE WE'VE BEEN HEADING TOWARD IT.
MAYBE ITS INERT? SOME OL' HUNK OF IRON STANDIN' THERE, ALL FROZEN-LIKE.
I DON'T THINK SO, IRONHIDE.
LOOK AT ITS POSE... ITS BODY LANGUAGE.
IT'S STANDING WATCH.
OPTIMUS, TAKE A CLOSER LOOK.
DO YOU RECOGNIZE THE SHAPE OF THOSE SHOULDER SECTIONS?
THE HEAVY PARTICLE CANNON ON ITS ARM...?
I RECOGNIZE IT, IRONHIDE...

...IT'S AN OMEGA SENTINEL!

THE RUINS OF HARMONEX.
YOU QUESTION MY RESOLVE, TRYPTICON—BUT IF YOU ARE TO SERVE ME IN THE CONFLICT TO COME, I WOULD KNOW MORE OF YOU.
YOU ARE MASTER HERE, MEGATRON. WHAT WOULD YOU ASK OF ME?
I WANT TO KNOW HOW MUCH OF PENTIUS... STILL LIVES WITHIN YOU.
MY MEMORY IS A JUMBLE OF SCATTERED IMAGERY. DARK FLASHES OF AGES LONG PAST.
I REMEMBER... CRUELTY.
MALICE.
AN UNQUENCHABLE HATRED.
HATRED FOR WHOM?
ALL WHO LIVE.
YOU VEX ME, TRYPTICON! HOW AM I TO TRUST THAT THESE ARE HIS MEMORIES AND NOT YOURS?!
HOW AM I TO TRUST YOU?
CLEAR YOUR MIND... AND I WILL SHOW YOU WHAT I HAVE SEEN.
THEN... DECIDE.

"I SEE...
"...I SEE YOU STRIDING ACROSS VAST FIELDS OF DESOLATION...
"...A LIFELESS, PRIMORDIAL LANDSCAPE...
"WAIT, I... I SEE ANOTHER WORLD ADRIFT IN THE VOID...
"...BROKEN...
"...AND THE BIRTH OF SAVAGE MONSTROSITIES.

"...THERE WAS A... A WAR?
"A BATTLE OF GODS?
"IS THAT... IS THAT CYBERTRON?!
"...ITS PEOPLE, ITS DREAMS AND ASPIRATIONS SCATTERED ACROSS THE CELESTIAL WINDS...
"... AND DEVILS.
"I SEE DEVILS THAT PREY UPON ENTIRE CIVILIZATIONS...
"...I SEE THE DEATH OF RACES.
"BUT... IT'S NOT JUST ONE WORLD. I SEE THOUSANDS OF WORLDS.... ALL BURNING.
"OVER AND OVER.
"CYCLES WITHIN CYCLES..."

...ENOUGH!
I HAVE SEEN ENOUGH!
THERE IS NO SHAME IN *TURNING* FROM THESE *VISIONS*, MEGATRON. YOUR SPARK CANNOT PROCESS THE *ENORMITY* OF SUCH *DEPTHLESS EVIL*.
NOT *YET*, AT ANY RATE.
DO NOT SPEAK TO ME OF *EVIL*.
THE VISIONS... MERELY *CONFIRM* WHAT I'VE KNOWN *ALL ALONG*: IN THIS UNIVERSE—THERE EXIST THE *WEAK* AND THERE EXIST THE *STRONG*.
WHATEVER *MEMORIES* YOU HOLD—AND WHATEVER ELSE YOU MAY BE—YOU ARE CERTAINLY THE *LATTER*.
SERVE ME *WELL*, TRYPTICON.
RISE.
AS YOU WILL, LORD MEGATRON.
SHALL WE *DEPART*?
NOT QUITE YET.
THE *DECEPTICONS* ARE COMING.
RRUUMMMBLE

GRAV-HARAAN.
GREETINGS, FRIEND!
WE ARE TRAVELERS IN THIS WILDERNESS AND WE'RE VERY SURPRISED TO FIND YOU OUT HERE!
WILL YOU SPEAK WITH US?
OTHERS. AFTER ALL THESE LONG AGES...
YOU ARE NOT MEANT TO BE HERE!
I WAIT FOR THE PRIME—AND NONE MAY DISTURB MY WATCH!
WAIT! WAIT!
I AM THE PRIME!
THERE'S NO NEED FOR VIOLENCE!
YOU ARE NOT NOVA! HOW DARE YOU CLAIM TO BE PRIME!
PLEASE, MIGHTY ONE...
...LET ME SHOW YOU.

YOU BEAR THE ***MATRIX.***

BUT... WHAT OF ***NOVA?*** I VOWED TO ***REMAIN*** HERE—AND WATCH FOR THE RETURN OF HIS ***ARK.*** HE WAS TO HERALD A ***GRAND NEW ERA*** FOR OUR PEOPLE.

WATCHING... ***WAITING*** FOR HIS RETURN... WAS MY ***ONLY PURPOSE.***

NOVA AND HIS EXPEDITION WERE LOST ***MILLIONS OF CYCLES*** AGO, FRIEND. HAVE YOU BEEN STANDING HERE, WAITING, ALL THIS TIME?

IT WAS... MY ***DUTY.***

I ***UNDERSTAND.*** BUT MUCH HAS ***CHANGED*** SINCE THE TIME OF ***NOVA PRIME.*** OUR WORLD IS ***VERY DIFFERENT*** FROM THE ONE YOU REMEMBER.

I THINK YOU SHOULD COME ***BACK*** WITH US.

HE'S BEEN OUT HERE A ***LONG TIME,*** OPTIMUS. MAYBE HE'S NOT ***READY*** FOR—

YOUR LONG WATCH IS OVER!

RETURN TO CIVILIZATION WITH US, AND I WILL GIVE YOU A ***NEW*** MISSION—A NEW ***PURPOSE.*** SERVE THE PEOPLE OF CYBERTRON ONCE AGAIN!

IT SEEMS THERE IS ***NOTHING*** FOR ME HERE, ***YOUNG PRIME.*** I WILL FOLLOW THE ***MATRIX-BEARER*** WHEREVER HE ***LEADS.***

NOW, ***PLEASE...*** ALLOW ME TO SHIFT INTO A MORE... ***PRACTICAL*** MODE...

GRAAGH... IT'S BEEN ***QUITE*** SOME TIME SINCE I LAST ***DID THIS...***

CHEE-CHUUUR-CHAAA-TRONG

CLIMB ABOARD, YOUNG FRIENDS—AND I WILL SEE YOU SAFELY HOME.
THANK YOU. BUT, WHAT SHALL WE CALL YOU?

SUPREME.
I AM... OMEGA SUPREME.

HARMONEX.

WAR IS COMING, MY DECEPTICONS!
THE HOUR OF OUR FINAL VENGEANCE DRAWS NEAR!
BUT MANY OF OUR FORCES WERE SCATTERED WHEN THE AUTOBOTS RETOOK IACON FROM US.*
MANY OTHERS ABANDONED OUR CAUSE DUE TO SCORPONOK'S UNTIMELY REIGN. IN SHORT, OUR NUMBERS ARE TOO FEW TO LAUNCH A FULL-SCALE ASSAULT AGAINST OUR ENEMIES.

*SEE TRANSFORMERS: AUTOCRACY.

RRRHUUMMMBLE

SO NOW, WITH THE AID OF MIGHTY TRYPTICON, WE WILL DEPART CYBERTRON FOR A TIME.
WE WILL MUSTER OUR FORCES. GATHER OUR FULL STRENGTH.

AND BRING OUR LONG-LOST BRETHREN BACK INTO THE FOLD.

ABOVE TORAXXIS.
GENTLEMEN, WE'LL REACH THE OUTSKIRTS OF HARMONEX IN A FEW MOMENTS.
ROGER THAT, SKY LYNX.
MAGNUS WANTED A REPORT ON TRYPTICON'S CONDITION. PRESUMING THAT MONSTER'S STILL TAKING A NAP, WE SHOULD BE IN AND OUT.
ROGER THAT, HOT ROD.
THE NEW MEGA-REFINERY IS A REAL FEAT OF ENGINEERING.
IT CAN DRAW THE RAW ENERGON FROM THE CAVERNS BENEATH TORAXXIS AND PURIFY IT AT AN ACCELERATED RATE OF PRODUCTION.
THERE'S FINALLY ENOUGH POWER FOR EVERYONE!
YEAH. RIGHT.
EVERYONE THAT'S LEFT AFTER THE EXODUS, YOU MEAN.
WHAT IS IT WITH YOU TODAY, GRIMLOCK? YOU'RE EVEN MOODIER THAN USUAL.
YOU MEAN APART FROM BEING PAIRED WITH YOU ON THIS OP?
YEAH, APART FROM THAT.
I DON'T LIKE TORAXXIS, KID.
NOT EVEN JUST FLYIN' OVER IT. NOTHIN' BUT NIGHTMARES FOR ME HERE.
I... LOST MY BEST FRIEND DOWN IN THOSE CAVERNS. AND THAT DAMNED ENERGON TURNED ME INTO A FRAGGIN' MONSTER.
YOU LOOK DOWN THERE AND YOU SEE A REFINERY.
HOPE.
POWER.
I LOOK DOWN THERE AND SEE ONLY HELL.
BUT YOU DYNOBOTS ARE BETTER NOW. YOU'VE GOT A NEW START!
HOLDING ON TO ALL THAT PAIN AND GUILT'S JUST GONNA BURN YOU UP INSIDE.

WHO THE HELL DO YOU THINK YOU ARE, KID?!
YOU THINK YOU CAN ANALYZE ME? YOU DON'T KNOW FRAG ABOUT PAIN AND GUILT.
YOU THINK YOU'RE THE ONLY ONE WHO'S EVER GONE THROUGH ROUGH TIMES, GRIMLOCK?
GET OVER YOURSELF ALREADY!
DON'T PUSH ME, KID...
OR WHAT, YOU'LL FIND SOME NEW CANNIBAL ALT-MODE AND BITE MY HEAD OFF?
DON'T NEED AN ALT-MODE TO—
SORRY TO INTERRUPT, GENTLEMEN—WE'VE ARRIVED AT HARMONEX...
...BUT I THINK YOU SHOULD TAKE A LOOK OUTSIDE THE VIEWPORT.
SKY LYNX, WHAT ARE YOU—
OH, PRIMUS.
WHAT?
TRYPTICON...
...IT'S GONE.

ALL THE ASTRO-NAVIGATIONAL PREPARATIONS HAVE BEEN MADE, LORD MEGATRON...
...COORDINATES ARE SET. WE AWAIT ONLY YOUR COMMAND.
THEN SET ALL ENGINES TO FULL, SHOCKWAVE.
THE TRACKLESS VOID AWAITS.

PRIMACY #1 COVER B
by **SARAH STONE**

PRIMACY #2 COVER A
by **LIVIO RAMONDELLI**

ALSO KNOWN AS THE *CAULDRON*.
ONCE A WORLD OF AFFLUENCE AND SHINING CITIES, IT'S NOW LITTLE MORE THAN A PATCHWORK OF *BROKEN HIGHWAYS* AND *LAWLESS OUTLANDS*.
THE PERFECT PLACE FOR AN *AMBUSH*.
THIS IS *STRONGBOX* ON EMERGENCY FREQUENCY *NINE-SEVEN-NINE!*
CONVOY, DO YOU READ? I GOT SEPARATED AND I CAN'T FIND YOU GUYS ON MY NAV-SYSTEM!
I'VE GOT *BANDITS* IN PURSUIT! I NEED IMMEDIATE *BACKUP*... DO YOU READ ME, CONVOY?
ANYBODY...?
OH, WE READ YA *LOUD* AND CLEAR, *FRIEND*...
YEAH, WE HEAR YA *SQUAWKIN'*, ALRIGHT.
WHO THE HELL IS *THIS?*
I THINK YOU KNOW THE *ANSWER* TO THAT...
IT'S JUST *YOU* AND *US* ALL ALONE OUT HERE...
...AND WE'RE *REALLY* LOOKING FORWARD TO MEETING YOU.
OH, FRAG.

LOOK, MY CONVOY WAS PAID TO BE OUT HERE! IF THIS IS YOUR TURF, I DIDN'T MEAN TO—
DON'T WORRY, FRIEND—WE'RE JUST AFTER YOUR CARGO. HAND IT OVER AND YOU CAN BE ON YOUR WAY.
THAT'S CRUEL, DRAGSTRIP. YOU KNOW US STUNTICONS NEVER LEAVE OUR MARKS ALIVE.
STU-STUNTICONS?!
OH, NO. WAIT... WAIT!
NICE GOING, DEAD END. NOW HE'S GONNA PANIC.
SO MUCH FOR DOING THIS THE EASY WAY...
KEERUNCHH
YOU DON'T HAVE TO DO THIS!
I'M NOT CARRYING ANYTHING SPECIAL!
WAS A CLASSIFIED HAUL—I WASN'T EVEN TOLD WHAT IT IS!
WELL, FRIEND, IT'S YER LUCKY DAY! WE'RE ABOUT TO FIND OUT TOGETHER!
FIRE THE GRAPPLE LINE! WE'RE GOIN' OVER!
CHAROOOM
NO NO NO!
AAARRRGH!
YEEE-HAH!

YOU'RE INSANE, WILDRIDER! YOU CUT IT WAY TOO CLOSE THAT TIME!
THANKS, BREAKDOWN! WAS PERFECT, WASN'T IT?
YEAH. WAS AWESOME.
EVERYONE SHUT UP WHILE I REEL THIS ONE IN...
...AND WE SEE IF OL' SWINDLE'S TIP PAID OFF.
HERE WE GO. SHOW ME THE MONEY...
I SAID SHUT UP!
NOW, NOW, MOTORMASTER... WHY SO TENSE?
WHAT THE...?
WHAT, YOU WERE EXPECTING SOMEONE ELSE?
THUNDERCRACKER.
WHAT IS THIS?
PARDON THE RUSE, BUT I HAD TO SEE FOR MYSELF WHETHER OR NOT YOU STUNTICONS HAD LOST YOUR EDGE.
WE HAVEN'T.
CLEARLY.
WHAT'S IT TO YOU, ANYWAY? YOUR BOSS, SCORPONOK, DOESN'T HAVE ANYTHING BETTER TO DO THAN WASTE EVEN MORE OF OUR TIME?
INTERESTING. YOU HAVEN'T HEARD. SCORPONOK'S OUT.
MEGATRON'S BACK.
AND HE'S GOT A HEIST IN MIND YOU WON'T BELIEVE.
OH, YEAH? THIS OUGHT TO BE GOOD. JUST WHAT ARE WE STEALIN' THIS TIME?
CYBERTRON.

CANIS TOR.
A LUSH, SAVAGE WORLD—TEEMING WITH VAST, COMPLEX ECOSYSTEMS AND BIOLOGICAL SPECIES OF EVERY KIND.
AT LEAST, IT WAS UNTIL RECENT MONTHS...
...WHEN FIVE STRANGERS ARRIVED IN A STARSHIP.
TO HUNT.
NOW, CANIS TOR IS A LIFELESS GRAVEYARD.
IT'S ONLY DENIZENS... PREDATORS.
GRRRAAAAGGGH
RRROOOOAAARGH
GIVE IT UP, RAMPAGE! YOU DON'T HAVE THE STRENGTH TO BEAT ME!
AIN'T TRYIN' TO WIN, RAZORCLAW. I JUST WANT TO MAKE YOU BLEED.
YOU LED US TO THIS! TRAPPED HERE ON THIS DEAD WORLD WITH NOTHING LEFT TO FEED ON! THIS IS YOUR LEADERSHIP?!
IT WASN'T DEAD WHEN I BROUGHT US HERE! YOU INSATIABLE FOOLS HUNTED THIS WORLD TO THE POINT OF EXTINCTION AND RUINED ANY CHANCE WE HAD OF FINDING A TRANSPORT!
IT SHOULD BE MY FANGS AT YOUR THROAT!
GGRRAAAGH!

I COULD WATCH THE BOSS KICK RAMPAGE AROUND ALL DAY. HE'S HAD IT COMIN' FOR A WHILE.
YEAH, TANTRUM—BUT WITH OUR ENERGON RUNNIN' SO LOW, WATCHIN'S ALL WE CAN DO.
WE GOTTA FIND SOMETHIN' TO FEED ON OR WE'RE GONNA GO INTO PERMANENT STASIS-LOCK...
YOU BOTH KNOW THERE'S ONLY ONE WAY THIS ENDS FOR US.
WHAT'S THAT YER SCREECHIN' ABOUT, DIVEBOMB? YOU DON'T SOUND SO GOOD.
NONE OF US... DO. FACE IT: THE ONLY POWER SOURCE ON THIS WORLD... LEFT TO FEED ON...
...IS EACH OTHER.
FITTING, REALLY. IT'S... THE DECEPTICON WAY. SURVIVAL... OF THE FITTEST—IN ITS RAWEST FORM.
SO WHAT YER SAYIN' IS...
I THINK OL' RAMPAGE... IS ABOUT TO BECOME...
...LUNCH.
UURRK.

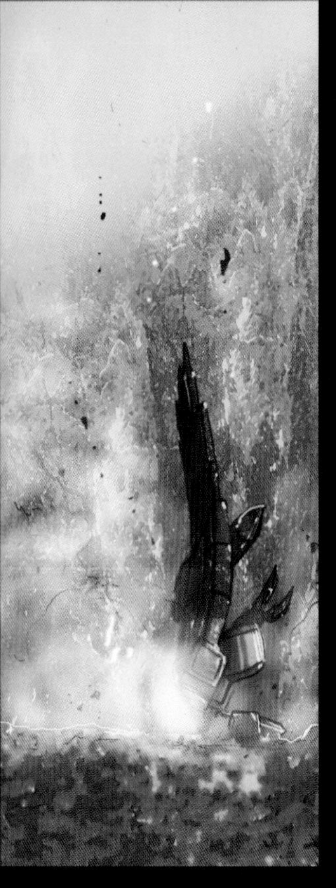

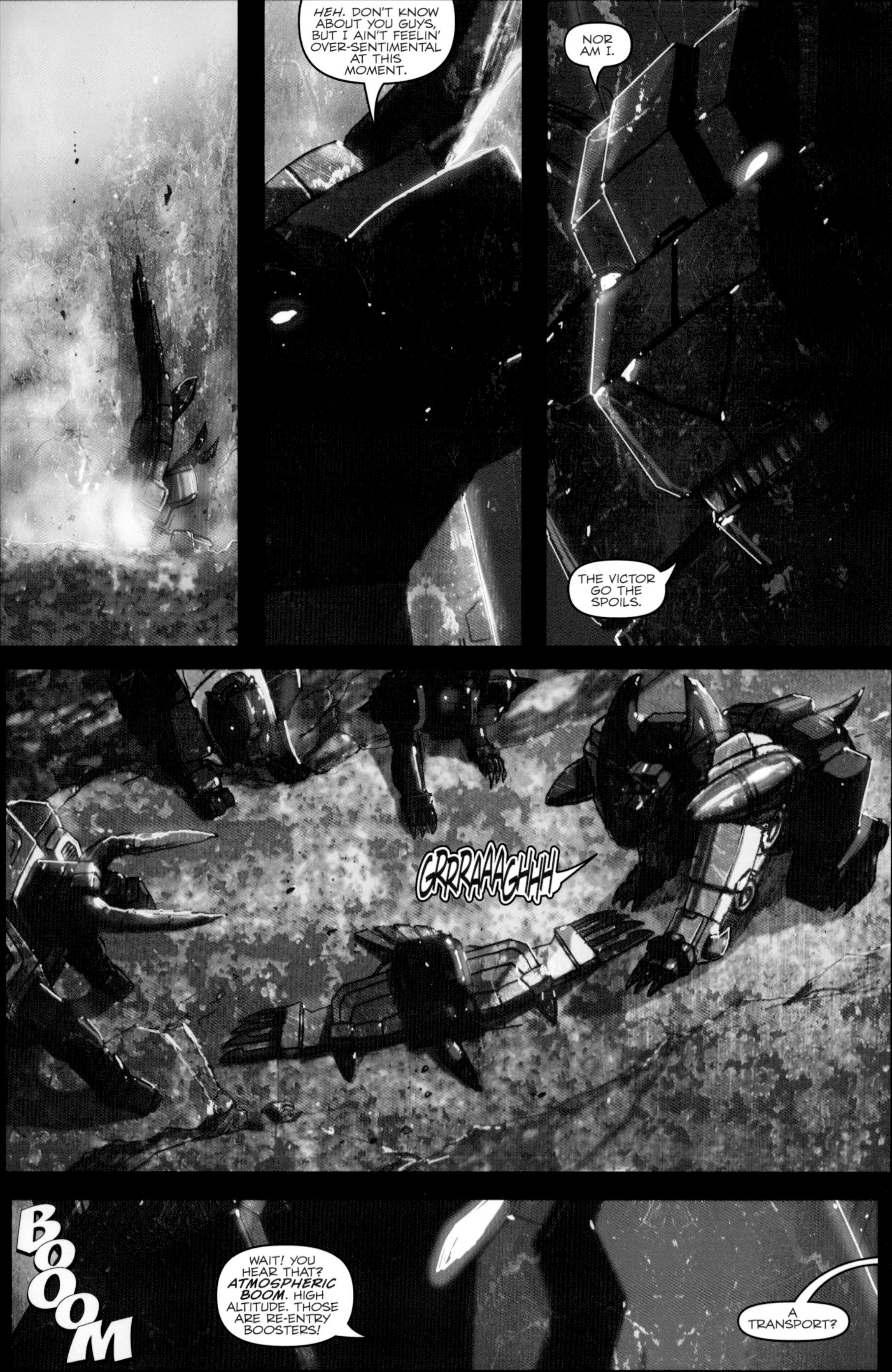

HEH. DON'T KNOW ABOUT YOU GUYS, BUT I AIN'T FEELIN' OVER-SENTIMENTAL AT THIS MOMENT.

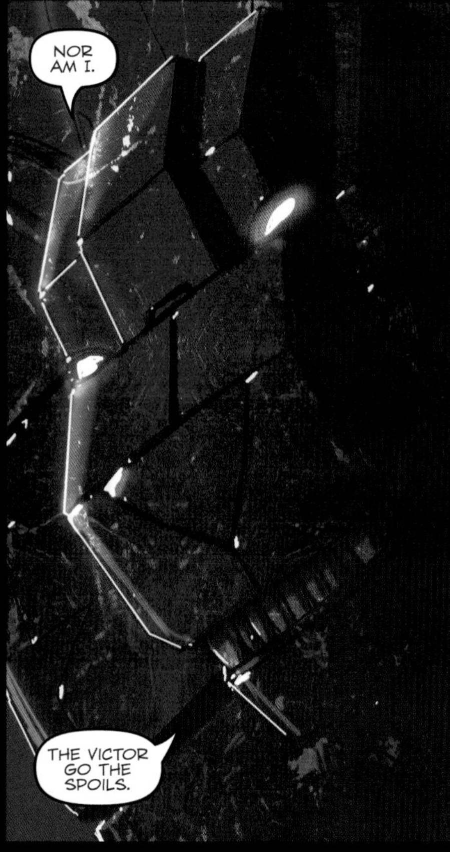

NOR AM I.
THE VICTOR GO THE SPOILS.
GRRRAAAGHHH

BOOOM

WAIT! YOU HEAR THAT? ***ATMOSPHERIC BOOM***. HIGH ALTITUDE. THOSE ARE RE-ENTRY BOOSTERS!

A TRANSPORT?

PREDACONS! WE'VE FOUND YOU AT LAST...
ASTROTRAIN?!
...AND NOT A MOMENT TOO SOON, IT SEEMS.
STARSCREAM. HOW DID YOU FIND US?
YOU PREDACONS AREN'T REALLY THAT HARD TO TRACK.
WE JUST FOLLOWED THE PATH OF MURDERED WORLDS YOU LEFT IN YOUR WAKE.
WHY ARE YOU HERE, STARSCREAM? I TOLD YOU WHEN WE LEFT CYBERTRON THAT WE HAD NO INTEREST IN SERVING SCORPONOK OR HIS VISION OF A SAVAGE NEW CYBERTRON.
WHILE I ADMIT, I DO HOLD WITH MANY OF HIS MORE... PREDATORY VALUES...
...I SWORE MY OATH TO MEGATRON.
EVEN IF IT MEANS I MUST WHITHER AND DIE UPON THIS FORSAKEN WORLD...
I WILL SERVE NO ONE...
HEY, SPEAK FOR YOURSELF.
CHEE-CHU-CHON-CHURNG
...BUT HIM.

THEN IT WILL PLEASE YOU TO HEAR THAT HE HAS *RETURNED*.
YOUR MASTER *CALLS*, RAZORCLAW. THE *HUNT* BEGINS ANEW.
ARE YOU *IN*? OR ARE YOU *OUT*?

AFTER SO LONG... OMEGA SUPREME. WE THOUGHT HIM LOST FOREVER.
I CAN SCARCELY BELIEVE HE'S RETURNED TO US.
HE'S REAL ENOUGH, TRION. BUT HE REMAINS SO DISTANT. BURDENED.
HE REFUSES TO LEAVE HIS POST WATCHING OVER MY QUARTERS. I HAD HOPED THAT BRINGING HIM BACK HERE WOULD...
WOULD WHAT? HELP HIM ENGAGE WITH OTHERS OF HIS KIND? HELP HIM BECOME A HEROIC AUTOBOT?
FACE IT—FOR THE TIME BEING, HIS IDENTITY LIES ONLY IN HIS CHOSEN FUNCTION.
HE STOOD WATCH FOR A MILLION YEARS, OPTIMUS—
—WAITING FOR A SIGN THAT WOULD NEVER COME. HE'LL HAVE TO ACCLIMATE TO THIS NEW WORLD IN HIS OWN TIME.
AND YOU MUST ACCEPT...
...THAT IT MIGHT BE ANOTHER MILLION YEARS BEFORE HE FINDS HIS SOUL AGAIN.

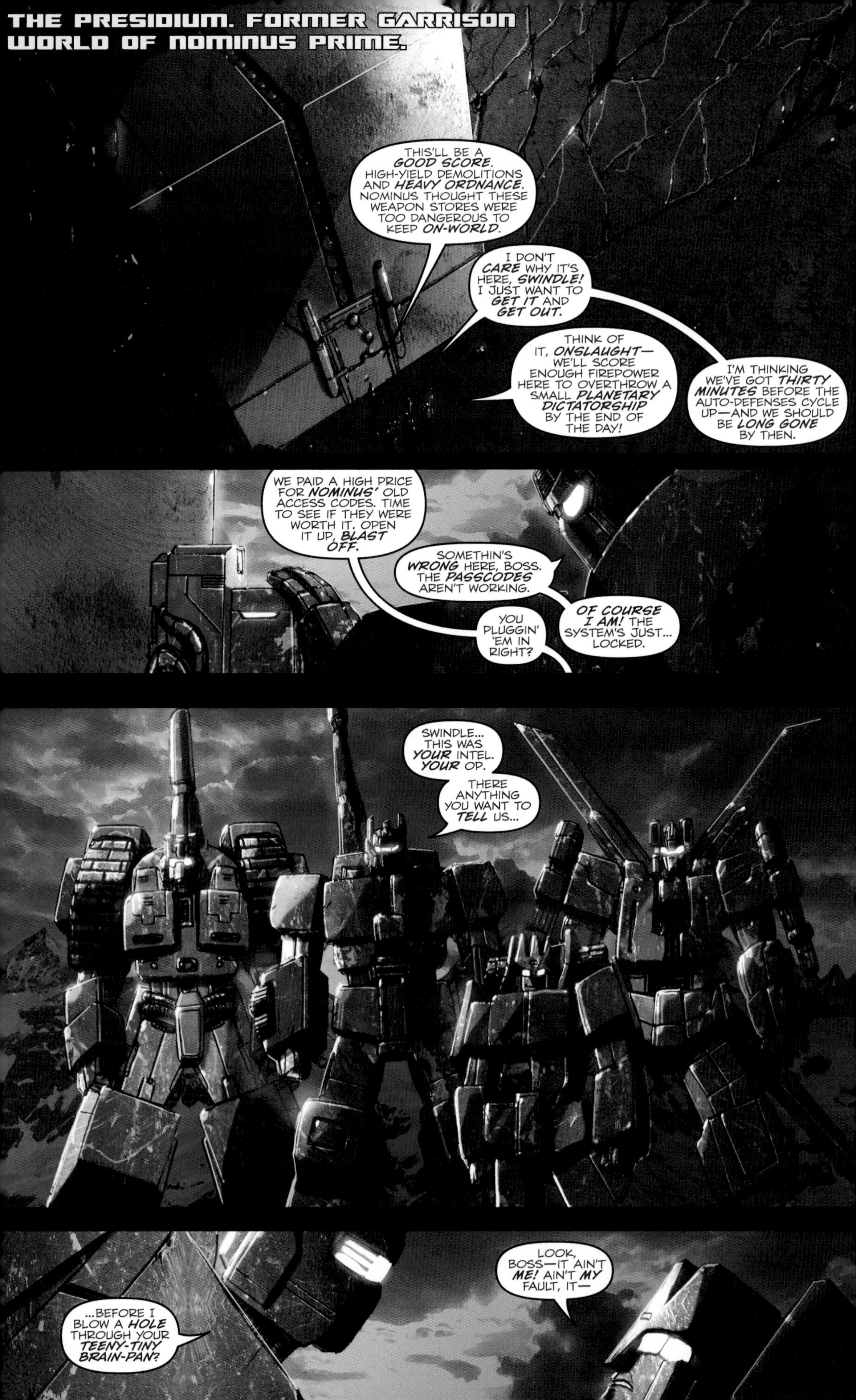
THE PRESIDIUM. FORMER GARRISON WORLD OF NOMINUS PRIME.
THIS'LL BE A GOOD SCORE. HIGH-YIELD DEMOLITIONS AND HEAVY ORDNANCE. NOMINUS THOUGHT THESE WEAPON STORES WERE TOO DANGEROUS TO KEEP ON-WORLD.
I DON'T CARE WHY IT'S HERE, SWINDLE! I JUST WANT TO GET IT AND GET OUT.
THINK OF IT, ONSLAUGHT— WE'LL SCORE ENOUGH FIREPOWER HERE TO OVERTHROW A SMALL PLANETARY DICTATORSHIP BY THE END OF THE DAY!
I'M THINKING WE'VE GOT THIRTY MINUTES BEFORE THE AUTO-DEFENSES CYCLE UP—AND WE SHOULD BE LONG GONE BY THEN.
WE PAID A HIGH PRICE FOR NOMINUS' OLD ACCESS CODES. TIME TO SEE IF THEY WERE WORTH IT. OPEN IT UP, BLAST OFF.
SOMETHIN'S WRONG HERE, BOSS. THE PASSCODES AREN'T WORKING.
YOU PLUGGIN' 'EM IN RIGHT?
OF COURSE I AM! THE SYSTEM'S JUST... LOCKED.
SWINDLE... THIS WAS YOUR INTEL. YOUR OP.
THERE ANYTHING YOU WANT TO TELL US...
...BEFORE I BLOW A HOLE THROUGH YOUR TEENY-TINY BRAIN-PAN?
LOOK, BOSS—IT AIN'T ME! AIN'T MY FAULT, IT—

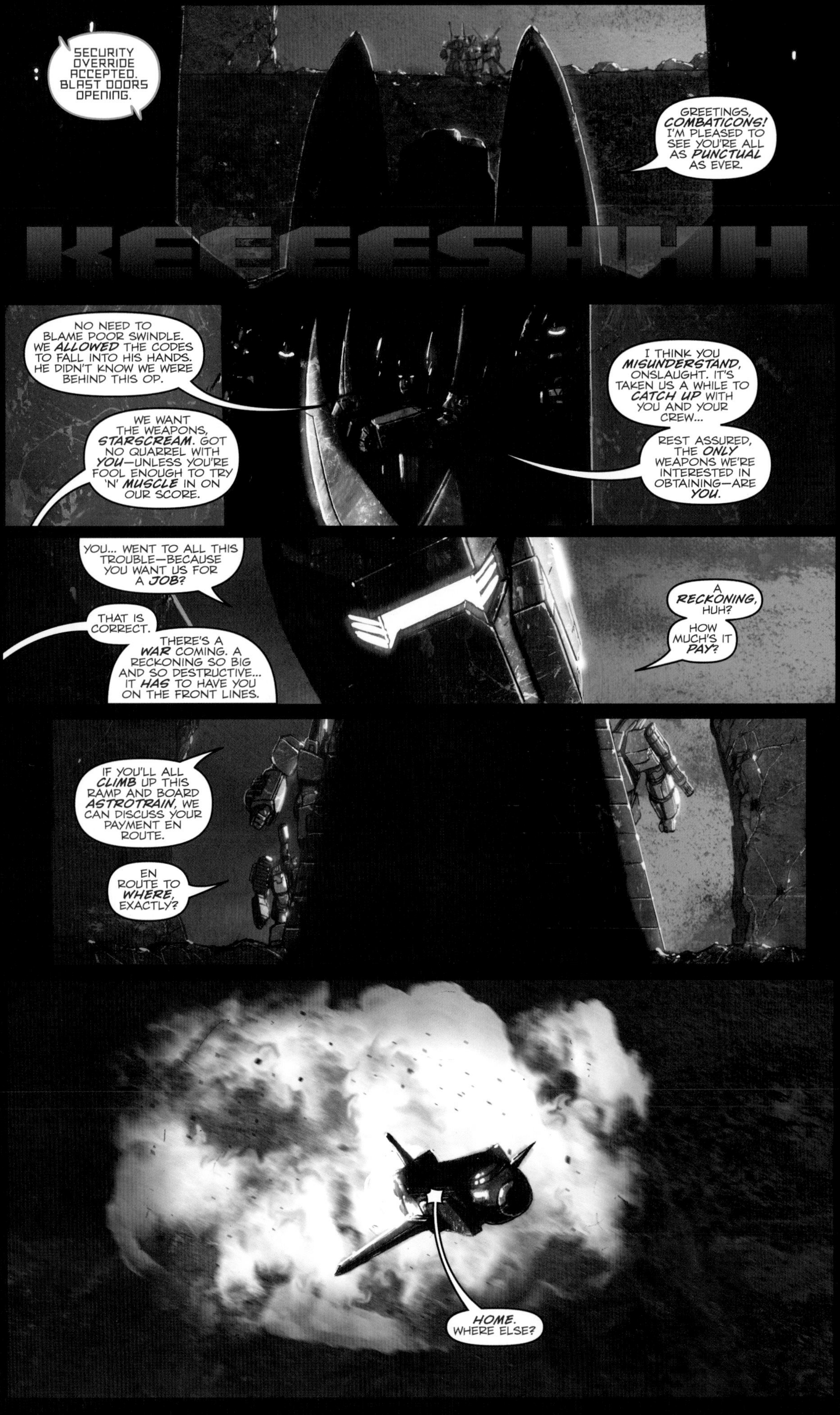

SECURITY OVERRIDE ACCEPTED. BLAST DOORS OPENING.

GREETINGS, ***COMBATICONS!*** I'M PLEASED TO SEE YOU'RE ALL AS ***PUNCTUAL*** AS EVER.

KEEEESHHH

NO NEED TO BLAME POOR SWINDLE. WE ***ALLOWED*** THE CODES TO FALL INTO HIS HANDS. HE DIDN'T KNOW WE WERE BEHIND THIS OP.

WE WANT THE WEAPONS, ***STARSCREAM***. GOT NO QUARREL WITH ***YOU***—UNLESS YOU'RE FOOL ENOUGH TO TRY 'N' ***MUSCLE*** IN ON OUR SCORE.

I THINK YOU ***MISUNDERSTAND***, ONSLAUGHT. IT'S TAKEN US A WHILE TO ***CATCH UP*** WITH YOU AND YOUR CREW...

REST ASSURED, THE ***ONLY*** WEAPONS WE'RE INTERESTED IN OBTAINING—ARE ***YOU***.

YOU... WENT TO ALL THIS TROUBLE—BECAUSE YOU WANT US FOR A ***JOB***?

THAT IS CORRECT.

THERE'S A ***WAR*** COMING. A RECKONING SO BIG AND SO DESTRUCTIVE... IT ***HAS*** TO HAVE YOU ON THE FRONT LINES.

A ***RECKONING***, HUH?

HOW MUCH'S IT ***PAY***?

IF YOU'LL ALL ***CLIMB*** UP THIS RAMP AND BOARD ***ASTROTRAIN***, WE CAN DISCUSS YOUR PAYMENT EN ROUTE.

EN ROUTE TO ***WHERE***, EXACTLY?

DEEP SPACE. TRYPTICON.
SOUNDWAVE— HAVE THE SEEKERS RETURNED?
ARE MY FORCES ASSEMBLED?
NEARLY, LORD MEGATRON. EVERYTHING IS PROCEEDING AS PLANNED.
ONLY ONE WORLD REMAINS.
I HEAR QUESTIONING IN YOUR VOICE, SOUNDWAVE.
SPEAK YOUR FEAR.
THIS WORLD... IT IS DEATH. MADNESS.
ARE YOU CERTAIN, WE—
YOU HAVE ALWAYS SERVED ME FAITHFULLY, SOUNDWAVE. YOU ARE THE MOST LOYAL OF ALL MY SOLDIERS.
BUT YOU QUESTION MY JUDGMENT AT YOUR PERIL.
I AM NOT THE MEGATRON YOU KNEW.
AND I WILL NOT BE DENIED.
NOW... TAKE US DOWN.
AS YOU WILL, LORD MEGATRON.

THE DEATH-WORLD OF JUNKION.
RUUUMMMBLE
OUTCASTS COME...
IN DEATH WE RISE...
EVISCERATE WANDERERS FROM THE SKIES...
SILENCE!
COME NEARER, YOU BROKEN WRETCHES!
AND TAKE A GOOD HARD LOOK.
REMEMBER ME?
STRANGER-DESTROYER.
WRECKAGE-DEMON.
THE RUIN-KING.

PRECISELY.
NOW.
KNEEL BEFORE YOUR MASTER.
KNEEL BEFORE MEGATRON!
GATHER YOUR CLANS.
SCAVENGE YOUR PARTS AND INSTRUMENTS OF WAR. MAKE YOUR WORLD-SHIP READY!
YOU'RE COMING WITH US...
...AND LEAVING THE GHOSTS OF THIS HELL BEHIND.

CYBERTRON. METROPLEX COMMAND CENTER. LATER.
PRIME, WE HAVE AN EMERGENCY!
LONG-RANGE SCANS SHOW SOMETHING HEADING OUR WAY. SOMETHING BIG.
TRANSPORTS, BUMBLEBEE? OUR PEOPLE COMING HOME?
UNLIKELY, SIR. THEY'RE RUNNING DARK—NOT RESPONDING TO HAILS. HOLDING A STRAIGHT LINE TRAJECTORY THROUGH OUR ORBITAL DEFENSE NETS.
LOOK AT THAT MASSIVE ENERGY SIGNATURE! IT'S GOT TO BE—
TRYPTICON. IT SEEMS HE'S FOUND HIS WAY HOME, BULKHEAD. THIS HAS MEGATRON WRITTEN ALL OVER IT.
WHY DON'T WE JUST SHOOT IT DOWN?
THAT WOULD BE CATASTROPHIC, HOT ROD.
DETONATING SOMETHING THAT BIG IN LOW ORBIT RISKS RAINING DEBRIS ACROSS A THIRD OF THE PLANET.
NO DOUBT AN ASSESSMENT MEGATRON'S COUNTING ON.
THE QUESTION IS, WHAT IS HE PLANNING? WHAT'S HIS TARGET?
NO QUESTION ABOUT IT...
KNOWING HIM, GRIMLOCK—HE'LL DROP THAT MONSTER RIGHT ON TOP OF US.

WITH PLEASURE, LORD MEGATRON.

THAT MONSTER'S DROPPING LIKE A STONE.
UNLESS WE SOMEHOW SLOW IT DOWN, ITS IMPACT WILL LEVEL IACON AND EVERY TORUS-STATE SURROUNDING!
THERE'S NO TIME LEFT, THEN...

...TELETRAAN, INITIATE GAMMA DEFENSE PROTOCOLS!
AUTHORIZATION PRIMUS SEVEN-ONE-SEVEN!
AUTHORIZATION ACKNOWLEDGED, OPTIMUS PRIME.
CITY-CENTER ENERGON BATTERIES REROUTING TO PRIMARY TITAN-CORE.

AUTOBOTS, THIS IS OPTIMUS PRIME!
ABANDON THE FACILITY AND EVACUATE TO ADJACENT BLAST BUNKERS!

WE NEED YOUR STRENGTH, MIGHTY ONE...

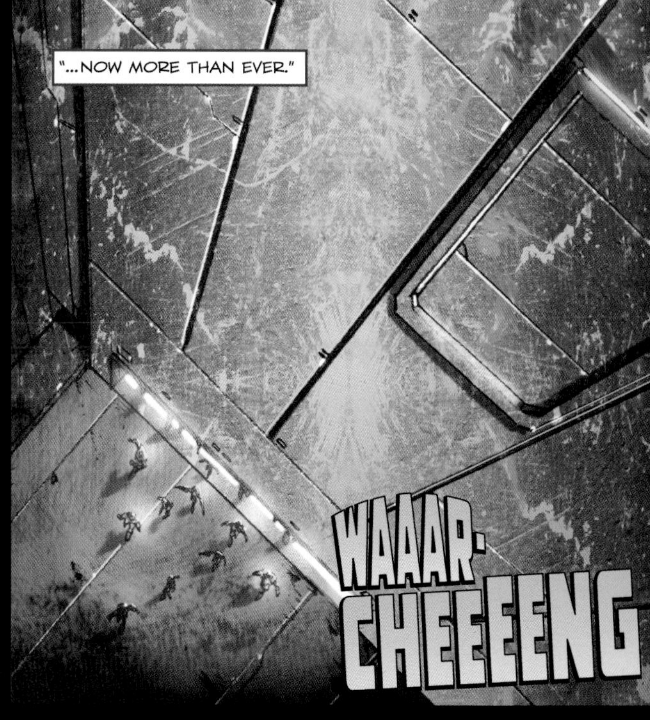

"...NOW MORE THAN EVER."
WAAAR-CHEEEENG

OPTIMUS, FACILITY'S EMPTY! THE LAST EVACUEES ARE GETTING CLEAR!
ACKNOWLEDGED– BRACE FOR IMPACT!

METROPLEX —IT'S TIME!
STAND AND DEFEND!
ORDER ACKNOWLEDGED, OPTIMUS.

DO NOT FEAR.

ALL WILL BE WELL.

DO YOU THINK METROPLEX CAN HANDLE THIS, SIR?
YEAH.
WE'D BETTER HOPE SO, BUMBLEBEE. IF NOT...
TARGET AQUIRED.

DESCENDING AT MAXIMUM VELOCITY.
PROJECTED CATASTROPHIC IMPACT...

...IMMINENT.

IT'S GOOD TO SEE YOU AGAIN, OLD TITAN.
IT'S BEEN FAR...
...FAR TOO LONG.

PRIMACY #2 COVER B

by **SARAH STONE**

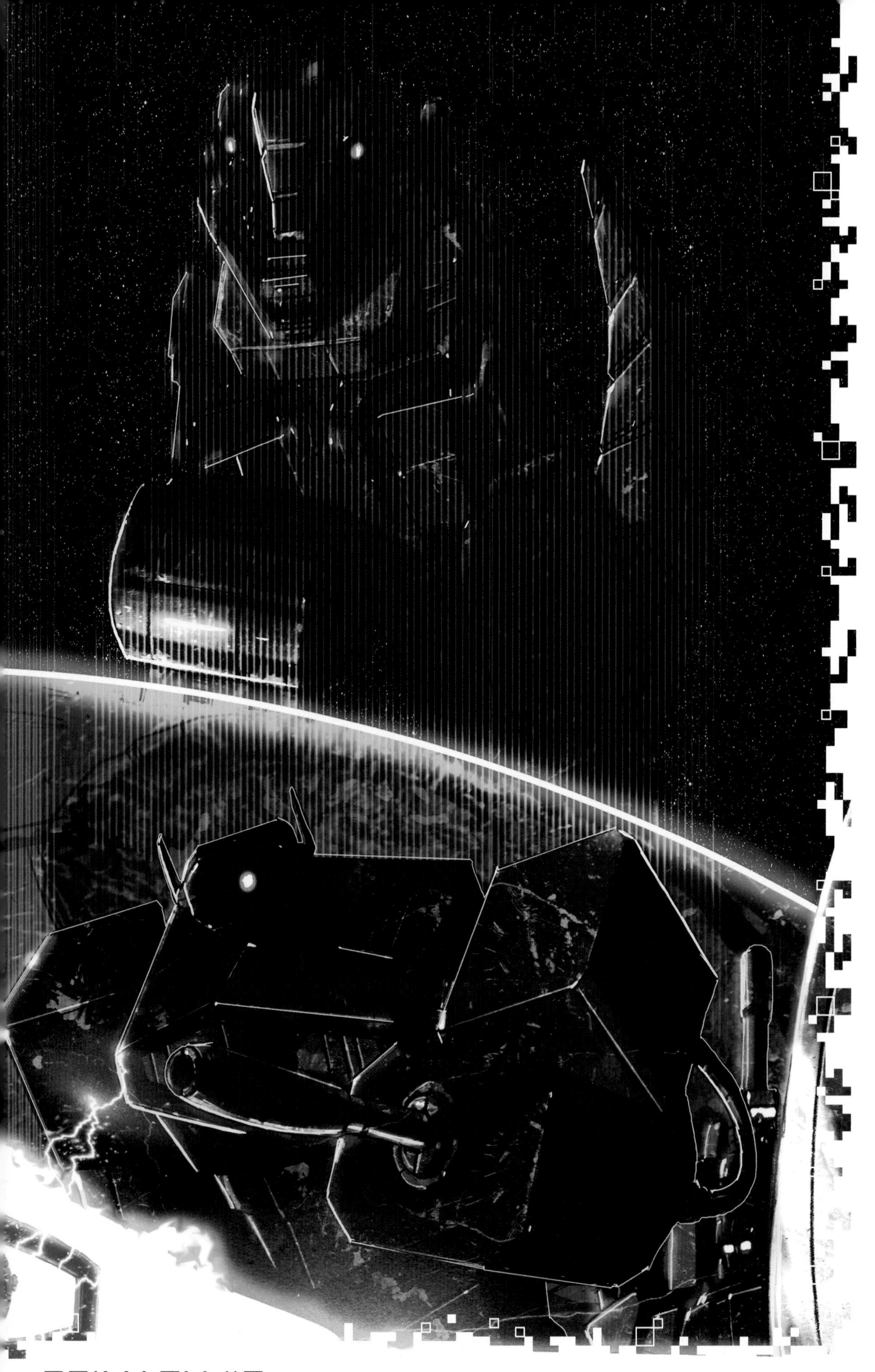

PRIMACY #3 COVER A

by **LIVIO RAMONDELLI**

IACON. CITY CENTER.
BWAAAAAMMM
GIANTS.
COLOSSAL DEMIGODS OF STEEL AND RAGE. THE THUNDERING SHOCKWAVES FROM THEIR BLOWS ARE FELT EVEN IN THE MOST DISTANT TORUS-STATES.
THEIR MELEE AS HORRIFIC AS IT IS DEVASTATING.
AND IT WAS ALL JUST BEGINNING.

YOU, MONSTER. THE BEAST OF PERFECT DARKNESS...
I'LL SEAL YOU BACK BENEATH THE WORLD WHERE YOU BELONG.
THE TERRIBLE VIOLENCE THAT'S BEEN SET IN MOTION CANNOT BE STOPPED—NOT EVEN BY YOU.
IF ALL YOU HAVE FOR ME IS CRYPTIC RIDDLES, THEN YOU'D BEST SAVE YOUR BREATH.
THRAAAWWWWNG
LET ME SPEAK IN A LANGUAGE YOU'LL BETTER UNDERSTAND.
BELIEVE ME, I UNDERSTAND COMPLETELY.
BOOM BOOM BOOM
KRAAABAM
BAM
BAM
TWERG TWERG TWERG

BELOW:

OMEGA SUPREME, THIS IS OPTIMUS. THE CONCUSSIONS HAVE DISRUPTED THE LINK TO OUR ORBITAL SENSOR-SCREENS!
CAN YOU READ THE STATUS OF THE SECOND SHIP ABOVE US?
MY LONG-RANGE SCANNERS SHOW THAT IT'S HOLDING POSITION IN LOW ORBIT, PRIME.
NO WEAPON SIGNATURES DETECTED. IT IS JUST... SITTING THERE.
ROGER THAT, OMEGA. STAND BY FOR FURTHER ORDERS.
VERY WELL, PRIME.
THAT SEEMS CERTAIN. BUT IT FEELS LIKE WE'RE MISSING SOMETHING...
MEGATRON'S WAITING FOR HIS OPTIMAL MOMENT. I DOUBT HE'LL MAKE A MOVE UNTIL HE'S SURE METROPLEX IS DOWN FOR THE COUNT.
"...LIKE HE'S ALREADY SIX STEPS AHEAD OF US."
SOUNDWAVE, PREP SUB-WARP DRIVES TWO AND SIX!
BRACE THE SHIP FOR VIOLENT REENTRY.
AS YOU COMMAND, LORD MEGATRON.
THIS, AT LAST, IS THE HOUR OF OUR ASCENSION, SOUNDWAVE.
TRY TO ENJOY IT.

KRRUUUNCH

BWAAAAM
AAARRRGH!
YOU'RE FAR WEAKER THAN I REMEMBER YOU, TITAN...

BY NOW YOU MUST SENSE... YOU CANNOT BEST ME.
YOU WOULD DO WELL... TO JUST LAY DOWN AND DIE.
KRUUUUNCH

IT'S YOU WHO'LL FALL!
GRONNNNG

FALL!
WAAAR-THOOM
EVEN DOWN... CAN... STILL... SWIPE!

YOU WON'T CATCH ME *THAT* EASILY!
BRAA-CHOOM
BRAA-CHOOM

GRAAAGH!
GRAAAANG-KRAAK
SUCH ARROGANCE.
ALL THESE YEARS... AND YOU NEVER LEARNED TO PROTECT YOUR ***KNEE***, TITAN.

STAGGERING SO SOON? SURELY YOU'RE NOT *TIRING* ALREADY?
NNNG...
NOT ***HARDLY***, MONSTER. ALL I NEED TO END YOU...

...ARE MY BARE HANDS.
KRONNNNG

YOU REALLY HAVE LEARNED NOTHING—MY HANDS ARE SHARPER!
GRAAAGH!
SKRAAANG

GRAHH—MAYBE, BUT MINE ARE BETTER FOR GRABBING.
WAIT, WHAT ARE YOU—
SKRUNCH

THE YEARS DID TEACH ME ONE THING, BEAST... HOW TO STAND—

–EVEN IN PAIN!
CHOOM
BWAAAR-THOOM
GRRRAAAGH!
YOU ARE... VICTORIOUS, TITAN...
BUT YOU... STILL LOSE...
NONSENSE. YOU'RE BEATEN. NO POSSIBLE THREAT TO ME.
HAHAHA...
IT WAS MERELY... MY TASK... TO *DISTRACT* YOU.
WHA—?

AAAAARRRGGHHH!
SHEEEER-KRONNNNG
NO!
I...
...PRIME, I...
WAAA-THOOOM

MOMENTS LATER, WITHIN THE JUNKION SHIP.
TRYPTICON DID WELL. NOW THE STAGE IS SET. THERE IS NOTHING TO STOP US NOW.
DECEPTICONS, READY YOURSELVES FOR BATTLE. GIVE NO QUARTER.
A QUESTION, LORD MEGATRON. WHEN WE HIT THE GROUND, WHAT ARE OUR TARGET PRIORITIES?
YOUR PRIORITY, MOTORMASTER... IS TO KILL EVERYTHING THAT MOVES.
IACON, AUTOBOT COMMAND BUNKER.
WHAT IN PRIMUS' NAME IS THAT THING?
A... SHIP OF SOME KIND. WITH ALL THE INTERFERENCE WE COULDN'T TRACK ITS DESCENT.
WHAT'S THE STATUS ON METROPLEX?!
HE'S OFF-LINE, PRIME. I'M NOT GETTING ANY READINGS FROM HIM AT ALL. IT... DOESN'T LOOK GOOD.
...AT LEAST HE TOOK CARE OF TRYPTICON. IF THE DECEPTICONS ATTACK WITH CONVENTIONAL INFANTRY, WE SHOULD HAVE THE STRENGTH OF NUMBERS TO REPEL THEM.
PERHAPS. MEGATRON'S MADE ALL THE MOVES SO FAR, BUT I DOUBT HE'D TRY TO TAKE THE FIELD IF HE WAS OUTNUMBERED.
ALL THE PIECES ARE SET... THE MOMENT IS NOW.
LET IACON BURN.
WHATEVER UNFOLDS...
...WE MUST PROTECT THE CITY AT ALL COSTS!

READY YOURSELVES—AND ORDER ALL FAST RESPONSE TEAMS INTO POSITION.
THIS MAY BE THE FIGHT OF OUR LIVES!
WHATEVER WE MAY FACE US OUT THERE...
...REMEMBER WHO YOU ARE, AUTOBOTS!
REMEMBER WHAT YOU FIGHT FOR!
THERE! AT THE BASE OF THE SHIP—
—IT'S OPENING!
BRACE FOR ATTACK!
A PERFECT WORLD...
...COLD CRYSTAL SKY...
A KILLING FIELD...
...WHERE ALL MUST DIE!
OKAY... WHO THE HELL ARE THESE YAHOOS?

THE "WHO," IRONHIDE—IT'S THE "HOW MANY" THAT'S GOT ME WORRIED!
AUTOBOTS! REPEL THE INVADERS!
THEY'RE... A LOT MORE RESILIENT THAN THEY LOOK!
OPTIMUS, WE HAVE TO PULL BACK OR THEY'LL OVERWHELM US WITH SHEER NUMBERS!
STAND YOUR GROUND, PROWL! FIGHT!
WE WILL HOLD THE LINE!

OPTIMUS, THIS IS *JETFIRE*.
SIR, ***BE ADVISED***—WE'RE PICKING UP ALARMING ***SUBTERRANEAN ACTIVITY*** BENEATH YOUR POSITION!
WE'RE A LITTLE ***BUSY*** HERE, JETFIRE—KEEP THIS LINE SECURE UNLESS THERE'S—
PRIME, ***STRUCTURAL ANALYSIS*** CONFIRMS THE JUNK-SHIP THAT SPEARED METROPLEX ALSO PENETRATED DEEP INTO ***IACON'S SUB-STRUCTURE!***
THE CITY'S ***PRIMARY COOLANT PLANTS*** HAVE BEEN ***COMPROMISED!***

GAAARGH!
GET TO THE POINT, ***PERCEPTOR!***

SIR, THE SUB-STRUCTURE IS SUFFERING MASSIVE FLOODING OF VOLATILE, UNPROCESSED ***COOLANT!***
YOU HAVE ONLY ***MINUTES*** UNTIL THE CITY CENTER IS ***FLOODED*** AS WELL!

ROGER THAT.
ONE MORE THING, PERCEPTOR... WHAT HAPPENS WHEN THE COOLANT IS EXPOSED TO THIS ION-CHARGED ATMOSPHERE?

KEEEESSSHHHHHH
WELL, SIR, I CAN ONLY THEORIZE AT THIS POINT...

KAAAAA-SHAAAAAAA
BUT THE RESULTANT MIX COULD PRODUCE A CATASTROPHIC ENVIRONMENTAL CHAIN REACTION...
...DENSE CORROSIVE MIST, HYPER-IRRADIATED PARTICULATES IN THE WIND...
HIGHLY-CONCENTRATED ACID RAIN?
YES, SIR—THAT IS A FORESEEABLE POTENTIALITY.
CLEVER, MEGATRON... IT'S AS IF YOU'VE CREATED THE PERFECT HABITAT FOR—
SOMETHIN'S MOVIN' IN THE FLOOD WATERS!
GREAT! MORE FRIENDS TO THE PARTY...
THOSE JUNK-ZOMBIES WERE JUST A FEINT! DEFEND YOURSELVES, AUTOBOTS!

CRUDE AS THEY ARE, THE JUNKIONS AND SHARKTICONS ARE PROVING EFFECTIVE. PRIME'S FORCES ARE BEING WHITTLED DOWN, JUST AS I PLANNED.
THEN WHAT ARE WE WAITING FOR? LET'S CHARGE IN AND FINISH THEM OFF!
PATIENCE, STARSCREAM.
WE'LL LET THIS PLAY OUT A FEW MORE MOMENTS WHILE THE FLOODING AND CORROSIVE CLOUDS HAMPER OUR ENEMIES FURTHER.
OFTEN, THE KEY TO STRATEGIC VICTORY ISN'T THE DIRECT APPLICATION OF BRUTE FORCE, BUT KNOWING WHEN TO HOLD IT IN CHECK.
VERY SOON NOW, WE WILL ENTER THE FRAY—AND WE WILL TIGHTEN THE NOOSE AROUND OPTIMUS PRIME.
GRAAAAAGH!
YOU THINK YOU'RE SAVAGE, BEAST?

SHHRIIIING
...I'LL SHOW YOU SAVAGE!
YEEAAARGH!
IT'S GOT ME! IT'S GOT—
OPTIMUS, THERE'S TOO MANY OF THEM! FIGHTING THESE THINGS HAND TO HAND ISN'T GETTING US ANYWHERE!
WHAT, THIS FIGHT TOO MUCH FOR YOU, BOY?
ENOUGH, BOTH OF YOU!
DON'T YOU SEE—IT'S LOYALTY AND HONOR THAT BIND US TOGETHER! THAT'S THE DIFFERENCE BETWEEN US AND OUR ENEMIES!
"FOR ALL HIS VISION, MEGATRON'S FOLLOWERS ARE MOTIVATED ONLY BY MISTRUST...
"...FEAR...
"...OR BLIND OBEDIENCE."

WE... WILL STAND FOR ONE ANOTHER.
NOW—AUTOBOTS, LAY DOWN FULL SUPPRESSIVE FIRE AT THE SECOND WAVE!
SHOOM
WE READ YOU, OPTIMUS!
SHOOM
SHOOM
CHAA-CHA-KOOOOM
THAT DID IT, PRIME! SECOND WAVE'S FALLING BACK!
LOOKS LIKE WE BOUGHT OURSELVES SOME BREATHING ROOM!
A CLEVER MANEUVER, PRIME... BUT NOT UNANTICIPATED.
ASSAULT TEAMS—PREPARE TO STRIKE AT THEIR CENTRAL POSITION! ARMORED UNITS—ENCIRCLE THE FIELD AND LOCK YOUR ORDNANCE UPON TARGET ALPHA!
MOVING INTO POSITION, LORD MEGATRON!
DO NOT ENGAGE TARGET ALPHA UNTIL I GIVE THE ORDER. IS THAT UNDERSTOOD?
LOUD AND CLEAR, SIR!

AT THE BATTLE'S CENTER.
BIG BAD GRIMLOCK. BEEN A LONG TIME SINCE OUR GLADIATOR DAYS.
BLACKWALL...?

I'VE BEEN WAITIN' FOR A REMATCH WITH YOU.
I HEAR THEY TOOK AWAY YOUR KILLER BEAST-MODE. THAT'S TOO BAD. THAT WAS THE ONLY EDGE YOU MIGHT HAVE HAD AGAINST ME.
WHAT DO YA SAY, "DYNOBOT"...?

THINK YOU CAN TAKE ME?
KRONNNG

GRANNG

GAAAH!
PATHETIC. SOME GLADIATOR, HUH, GRIMLOCK...?

REALLY, YOU AND YOUR DYNOBOTS SHOULD HAVE NEVER COME OUT OF HIDING.

PRIME, GRIMLOCK'S UNIT GOT SEPARATED! THEY'RE TIED UP AT THE CENTER AND DECEPTICON ASSAULT GROUPS ARE CLOSING IN ON THEIR POSITION FROM THE EAST!
WE'VE GOT TO GET OUT THERE AND BACK THEM UP!
THAT'S EXACTLY WHAT MEGATRON WANTS, BUMBLEBEE. IF WE SPLIT OUR FORCES HERE, HE'LL OVERRUN OUR STRONGPOINT.
SO WE'RE JUST GOING TO LEAVE THEM OUT THERE?
KEEP CALM, BUMBLEBEE. I WOULDN'T COUNT THE DYNOBOTS OUT JUST YET. AND WE HAVE YET TO REVEAL OUR GREATEST WEAPON...
ONSLAUGHT, DO YOU HAVE TARGET ALPHA IN YOUR SIGHTS?
YES, LORD MEGATRON. AWAITING YOUR ORDER TO FIRE...
EXCELLENT.
STARSCREAM, DO YOUR SEEKERS ALSO HAVE A LOCK ON THE TARGET?
OF COURSE. HOW COULD WE MISS HIM?
IT'S PAST TIME WE GOT MEGATRON'S ATTENTION.
OMEGA SUPREME—ARE YOU READY TO DO YOUR PART?
WHAT IS IT YOU WOULD ASK OF ME, PRIME?
SET YOUR FUSION CANNON FOR MAXIMUM RANGE! I NEED YOU TO BOMBARD MEGATRON'S POSITION AND SCATTER HIS COMMAND GROUP!
I UNDERSTAND THE ORDER, PRIME... BUT I...

OMEGA, THE TIMING IS CRITICAL! WILL YOU NOT OBEY MY ORDER?
I... I LIED TO YOU, OPTIMUS.
OMEGA, THIS IS NOT THE TIME FOR—
MY EXILE. I DID NOT CHOOSE TO ENDURE COUNTLESS CYCLES OF ISOLATION OUT OF SOME LOYALTY TO NOVA PRIME... I WAITED TO DESTROY HIM UPON HIS RETURN. HE WAS CORRUPT—A DISGRACE TO THE PRIMES I ONCE SERVED.
BUT YOU... I SEE GREATNESS IN YOU.
THOUGH IT GRIEVES ME TO MAKE WAR UPON MY FELLOW CYBERTRONIANS, THESE UPSTARTS HAVE RAVAGED THE WORLD I LOVE.
THEY REMIND ME OF NOVA AND ALL THAT HE BETRAYED BY SEEKING DOMINION OVER OTHERS.
I WILL HEED YOUR ORDER, OPTIMUS PRIME. I WILL BRING JUSTICE DOWN UPON THEM.
NOW, ONSLAUGHT!
NOW, STARSCREAM!
BRING TARGET ALPHA DOWN!
SHOOM
SHOOM
SHOOM
CHAA-CHOOM
SHOOM

GRAAAAGH!
BWOOOM BWOOOM
KRAAA-KOOOM
OMEGA SUPREME!
NOOOO!
THE OMEGA SENTINEL IS DOWN, LORD MEGATRON!
SUSTAIN FIRE! PULVERIZE ANYTHING THAT MOVES!
HAHAHA HAHA...
YOUR FURY IS MAGNIFICENT, WANDERER...
WHA—THAT VOICE... I KNOW THAT LAUGHTER...
PEN... PENTIUS?
NO....
HOW IS IT THAT I HEAR YOUR VOICE IN MY MIND?
AFTER ALL THIS TIME... CAN YOU NOT GUESS, "MIGHTY MEGATRON"...?

FOOLISH LITTLE CONQUEROR.
I LIVE... WITHIN THE REMNANTS OF YOUR HOLLOW SPARK. I AM A PART OF YOU.
AND THROUGH YOU...
...I WILL DEVOUR...
...YOUR PRECIOUS CYBERTRON.

PRIMACY #3 COVER B
by **SARAH STONE**

PRIMACY #4 COVER A

by **LIVIO RAMONDELLI**

ACON CITY CENTER.
THE EYE OF THE STORM.

SKYWARP REPORTING! WE'RE COMMENCING OUR ATTACK, BUT WE'RE IN BAD SHAPE!
STATUS: CLARIFICATION REQUIRED.
OUR INSTRUMENTS ARE GOING HAYWIRE ALL OF A SUDDEN—AND WE'RE IN DANGER OF ENGINE BURNOUT!
PLEASE ADVISE!
HYPOTHESIS: HYPER-ACIDIC ATMOSPHERE RELEASED BY MEGATRON NOW CORRODING YOUR MANIFOLDS AT ACCELERATED RATE.
TACTICAL RECOMMENDATION: ABORT ATTACK!
I DON'T THINK WE'RE GONNA GET THE CHANCE, SOUNDWAVE!
ENGINES ARE CUTTIN' OUT!
HEADS UP, FELLAS—WE'RE DROPPING FAST!
OH, YOU'VE GOT TO BE KIDDING M—
KRAAAKA-KOOOM

AT THAT MOMENT.
THE ENEMY IS SURPRISED AND IN DISARRAY. IT'S TIME WE SEIZED THE INITIATIVE!
TRAILBREAKER'S FORCE-SHIELD PROTECTED US FROM THE DECEPTICONS' BOMBARDMENT! THIS IS WHERE WE PUSH BACK!
OMEGA SUPREME, ARE YOU FIT FOR DUTY?
MERELY SINGED, OPTIMUS.
I RETURNED WITH YOU TO PERFORM MY FUNCTION—TO FIGHT FOR MY PEOPLE.
THAT IS WHAT I WILL DO.
VERY WELL, THEN...
LOOK! THROUGH THE SMOKE—THE AUTOBOTS ARE REGROUPING!
THE PRIME... ANTICIPATED THIS. HE DREW US OUT AND NOW...
...AUTOBOTS, ATTACK!

I ALWAYS KNEW I WAS STRONGER THAN YOU, GRIMLOCK.
IT DON'T MUCH MATTER WHAT HAPPENS AROUND US...
...I'M GONNA WRENCH YOUR HEAD CLEAN OFF AND TAKE THAT FIRESWORD OF YOURS AS A TROPHY.
YOU WANT THE SWORD SO BAD, BLACKWALL...
...YOU CAN HAVE IT!
SHRAAAAAAK

...GZZZZ...
TSSSSSSSRAKKKKK
YOU MAY HAVE BEEN STRONGER, BLACKWALL...
...BUT I FIGHT DIRTIER.
DECEPTICON COMMAND POINT.
AUTOBOT COUNTER ATTACK BREAKING FORWARD LINES! PREDACONS ADVANCING THROUGH EASTERN GRID—BUT OVERARCHING TACTICAL ADVANTAGE ERODING RAPIDLY.
HOW COULD I HAVE BEEN SO BLIND, SOUNDWAVE?
I MUST REACH TRYPTICON WHILE THERE'S STILL A CHANCE TO UNDO WHAT'S BEEN DONE. IF I COULD JUST... TRANSFER THE SPARK...
...MAYBE THEN WE COULD...
...IF I FAIL TO REACH TRYPTICON, SOUNDWAVE—I WANT THE REST OF YOU TO PULL BACK... AND BURN IACON TO THE GROUND.
THESE ARE YOUR ORDERS?!
BURN IT ALL.

ELSEWHERE.
PRIME, THIS IS HOT ROD! THE EASTERN GRID'S COLLAPSING AND THERE'S MORE DECEPTICONS BEARING DOWN ON OUR POSITION!
WE NEED IMMEDIATE REINFORCEMENTS!
REPEAT AGAIN, HOT ROD! SIGNAL'S BREAKING UP!
I SAID, WE NEED IMMEDIATE— UNF!
KRRRONG
WELL WELL! HOT ROD OF NYON!
MAN, KILLING YOU'S REALLY GONNA PUT ME ON THE MAP!
ONSLAUGHT—
NO MORE GRUNT WORK FOR ME! I MAY EVEN HAVE A SHOT AT JOINING DECEPTICON HIGH COMMAND AFTER THI—
KWHAAAAM
TZZAAAT
GAAARGH!
SLINGER!
WHAT? YOU TOOK HIM OUT JUST SO YOU COULD BE THE ONE TO END ME?
NO.
I WAS WRONG, HOT ROD. ABOUT EVERYTHING. TAKE A LOOK AROUND...
AUTOBOTS... DECEPTICONS... IT'S ALL BROKEN.
EVERYTHING'S JUST... BROKEN.
NO...

...JUST *YOU*, TRAITOR.
GRRAAAAAAAHHH!
SHHKRAAAAAANG

NO...

HOPE YOU GOT A GOOD LOOK AT WHAT HAPPENED TO YOUR FRIEND, AUTOBOT...
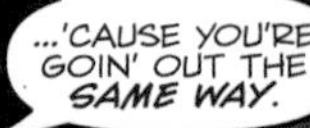
...'CAUSE YOU'RE GOIN' OUT THE ***SAME WAY***.

NEAR THE BASE OF TRYPTICON.
MEGATRON?! DON'T COME ANY CLOSER!
FOOLISH AUTOBOTS...

CHOOOM
YOU SHOULD KNOW BETTER BY NOW.
GROOONG
GAAAH!

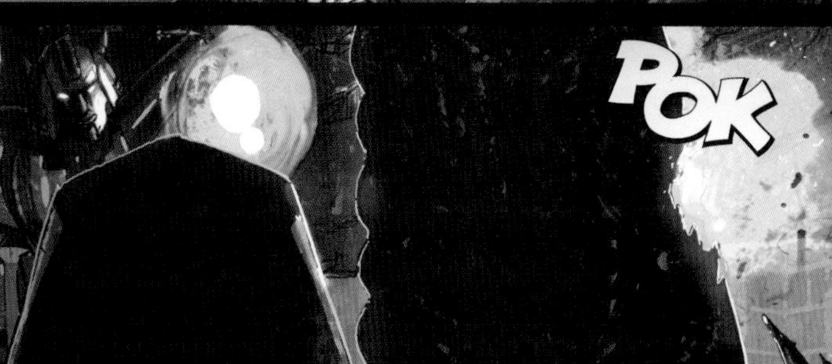
I'M IMPRESSED, BUMBLEBEE. GIVEN THE TORTURE YOU EXPERIENCED AT MY HANDS, I EXPECTED YOU TO RUN.
POK

GRK!
YOU'RE... AFRAID OF SOMETHING, MEGATRON...
...I CAN SEE IT IN YOUR EYES.

YOU HAVE COURAGE, LITTLE ONE. I'LL GIVE YOU THAT.
BUT MY FEARS...

...ARE MY OWN.
SKLUUURCH

MEGATRON...
...WHATEVER HE WANTS WITH TRYPTICON... I DON'T INTEND TO LET HIM HAVE IT!
HOLD THE LINE HERE. I'LL HANDLE THIS MYSELF.
THE ONLY WAY YOU'RE GETTING TO MEGATRON, PRIME...
MOTORMASTER.
...IS THROUGH ME!
FAIR ENOUGH.

KRRRASSHH
STUNTICONS, MOTORMASTER'S DOWN! CIRCLE UP AND FLANK THE PRIME!
WE GOT HIM! HE CAN'T OUTRUN US!
UH, GUYS— WE'VE GOT A PROBLEM!
WATCH YOUR SIX!
YOU WILL NOT TOUCH HIM.
YOU WILL ALL BE ERADICATED!

AT THE EASTERN GRID.
I CAN SMELL THE FEAR ON THIS AUTOBOT.
HE'LL TASTE SWEET—LIKE MOLTEN STEEL. FIRST BITE'S MINE.
IT WON'T BE THAT EASY, PREDACON.
I THINK THEY ALMOST BELIEVED YA, KID.
JUST A THOUGHT—BUT NEXT TIME SOMEONE'S TRYIN' TO KILL YOU, USE YOUR BIG-BOY VOICE.
GRIMLOCK?
THANKS, I'LL REMEMBER THAT.
DYNOBOTS!
FINALLY, SOMEONE WORTHY OF THE KILL!

ATOP THE HEAD OF TRYPTICON.
I DON'T KNOW WHAT YOU'RE SEARCHING FOR HERE, MEGATRON...
...BUT YOU'VE GONE AS FAR AS YOU'RE GOING TO GO.
YOU'VE BROUGHT ENOUGH MISERY AND DESTRUCTION TO THIS WORLD.
YOU SPEAK OF DESTRUCTION, PRIME... BUT YOU HAVE NO CONCEPTION OF THE TRUTH.
THE MADNESS... THE CARNAGE THAT'S BEEN UNLEASHED—IT WON'T END HERE. IT WILL ECHO OUT FROM CYBERTRON—RAVAGING COUNTLESS OTHER WORLDS ACROSS THE MILLENNIA.
THIS WAR BETWEEN US... IT WILL NEVER END.
NO.
IT WILL END BECAUSE IT MUST, MEGATRON.
YOU DAMNED FOOL!
CAN'T YOU SEE WHAT'S HAPPENING ALL AROUND YOU?!
THIS IS OUR FATE! VIOLENCE AND STRIFE UNTIL THE STARS BURN COLD!
NOT WHILE I FUNCTION.
HELP ME STOP THIS, MEGATRON. OUR STORY DOESN'T HAVE TO END THIS WAY.
SHRAANG
SHONNG

KROOONG
GAH!
SHREEENG

I TRIED TO BRING ORDER TO OUR CIVILIZATION!
BUT NOW I KNOW...

"...CYBERTRON HAS NO FUTURE...

"THEN BELIEVE *THIS*—THERE ARE *DEVILS* THAT LURK IN THE DARKNESS BETWEEN THE STARS—AND THEY HUNGER ONLY FOR OUR ANNIHILATION...

"I WAS... *DECIEVED,* OPTIMUS.

OF COURSE IT DOES!
I TRIED TO CREATE A *BETTER WORLD,* PRIME...

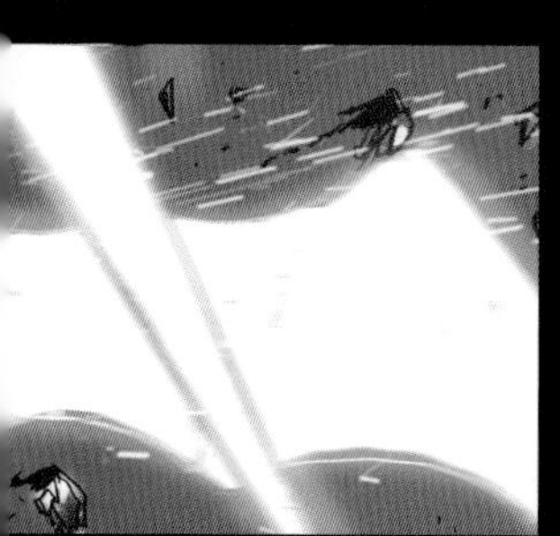

"THERE IS ONLY *DEATH* FOR THIS WORLD."
"I WON'T BELIEVE THAT!"

"I NEVER IMAGINED... IT WOULD COME TO *THIS.*"

WHAT ARE YOU SAYING, MEGATRON?
WHAT HAVE YOU DONE?!

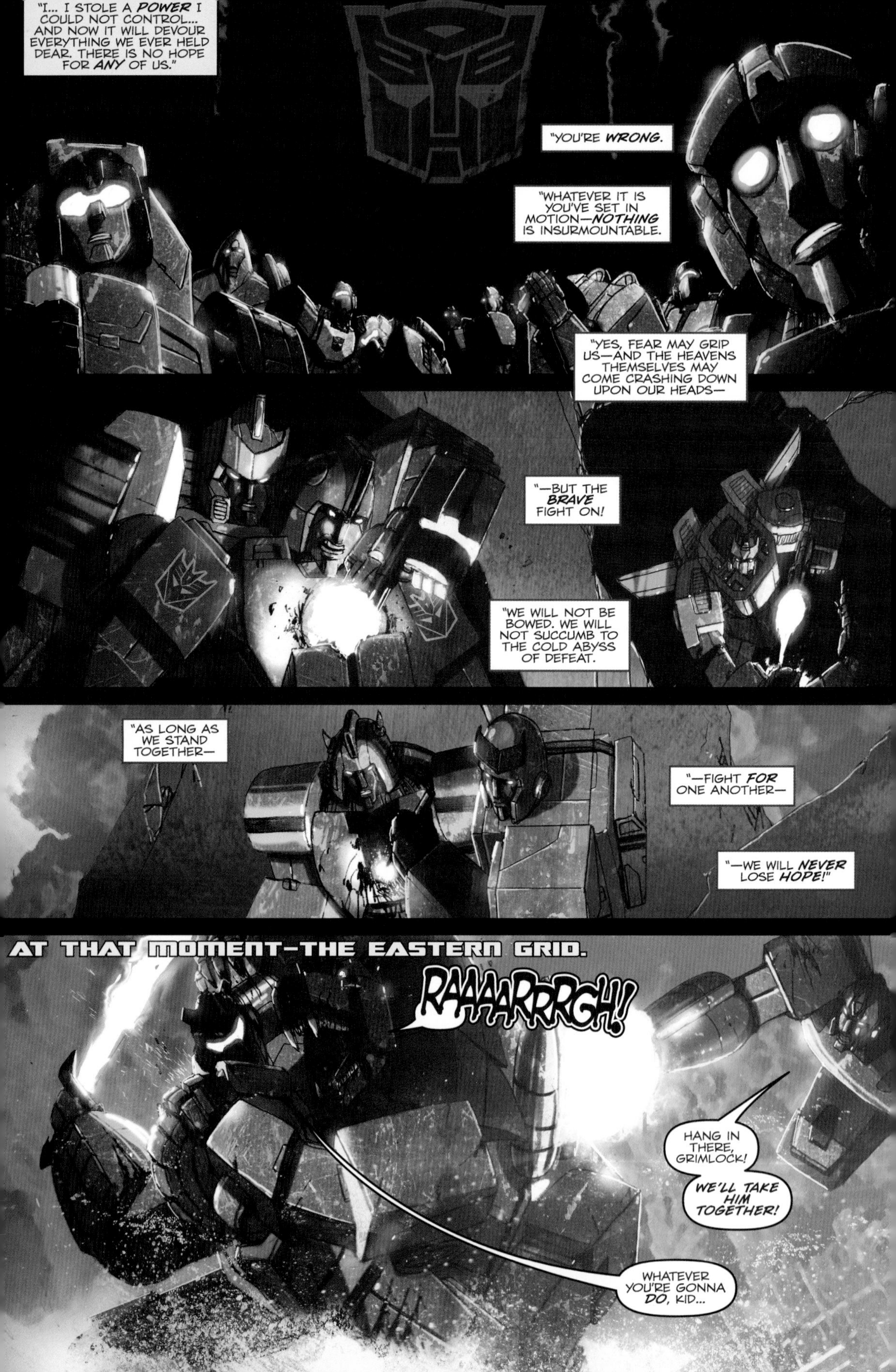
"I... I STOLE A POWER I COULD NOT CONTROL... AND NOW IT WILL DEVOUR EVERYTHING WE EVER HELD DEAR. THERE IS NO HOPE FOR ANY OF US."
"YOU'RE WRONG.
"WHATEVER IT IS YOU'VE SET IN MOTION—NOTHING IS INSURMOUNTABLE.
"YES, FEAR MAY GRIP US—AND THE HEAVENS THEMSELVES MAY COME CRASHING DOWN UPON OUR HEADS—
"—BUT THE BRAVE FIGHT ON!
"WE WILL NOT BE BOWED. WE WILL NOT SUCCUMB TO THE COLD ABYSS OF DEFEAT.
"AS LONG AS WE STAND TOGETHER—
"—FIGHT FOR ONE ANOTHER—
"—WE WILL NEVER LOSE HOPE!"
AT THAT MOMENT—THE EASTERN GRID.
RAAAARRRGH!
HANG IN THERE, GRIMLOCK!
WE'LL TAKE HIM TOGETHER!
WHATEVER YOU'RE GONNA DO, KID...

...DO IT QUICK!
SHRAANG
GAAH!
YAARRGH!
WEAKLINGS! I'LL FEAST ON YOUR SERVOS!
THAT AIN'T GONNA HAPPEN, RAZORCLAW.
GRUUURH?
GET A HOLD OF HIS CLAWS, KID...
I'M GONNA MAKE SURE...
GRAAANNG
...HE AIN'T CHOMPIN' DOWN ON ANYONE EVER AGAIN!
GRA-KAK

ATOP TRYPTICON.
SHROOONNNG
AAARGH!
THIS... WILL BE OUR DANCE, OPTIMUS...
...BATTERING AWAY AT EACH OTHER FOR THE NEXT FEW MILLION YEARS...
...UNLESS...
BWAAAAAM
...YOU CAN KILL ME!
I DON'T WANT TO HAVE TO KILL YOU, MEGATRON.
YOU STOOD FOR JUSTICE ONCE. YOUR PRINCIPLES INSPIRED US TO OVERTHROW CORRUPTION AND FIGHT FOR A BETTER WORLD.
YOU LOST YOUR WAY. BUT YOU CAN STILL BE THE LEADER YOU WERE MEANT TO BE.
HELP ME DESTROY THIS EVIL YOU'VE UNLEASHED!
IT... CANNOT BE DESTROYED, OPTIMUS.
IT IS A... MALIGNANT SPARK. ITS POWER IS BEYOND MEASURE–RESTORING EVEN TRYPTICON TO LIFE. AND NOW... IT DEVOURS ME FROM WITHIN.
THIS ANCIENT MALEVOLENCE... FUSED TO MY CIRCUITS...
IT'S... INSIDE YOU...
ITS VICIOUS LAUGHTER ECHOING OVER AND OVER IN MY MIND...
...TO SAVE CYBERTRON... THERE IS ONLY ONE WAY THIS CAN END.

NO.
IF I'VE LEARNED ANYTHING FROM CARRYING THE MATRIX—FROM BEING PRIME—IT'S THAT THERE IS ALWAYS A WAY.
IF IT'S DARKNESS THAT'S CONSUMED YOU...
...THEN LET THERE BE LIGHT.
THE VILE LAUGHTER... I CAN'T HEAR IT ANYMORE. I CAN FEEL... THE SPARK IS GONE...
YOU DID IT, OPTIMUS—THE MATRIX-FIRE HAS PURGED MY SYSTEM...
THE MALIGNANCY HAS BEEN EXPUNGED, YES...
...BUT WE BOTH KNOW... YOUR SPARK WAS CORRUPT LONG BEFORE THIS.
HAH. PERHAPS.
AND PERHAPS WE'VE JUST AVERTED CYBERTRON'S DARK DESTINY...
...BUT KNOW THIS, OPTIMUS PRIME—I WILL NEVER STOP HATING YOU.

I KNOW.
KRONNG

MOMENTS LATER.
A PRIORITY-ONE TRANSMISSION BEAMS OUT ACROSS THE RAVAGED BATTLESCAPE...
AUTOBOTS.
DECEPTICONS.
THIS BATTLE IS OVER.
WE HAVE ALL SUFFERED. WE HAVE ALL LOST COMRADES TO THIS MADNESS. IT IS TIME TO LAY DOWN YOUR ARMS—AND STAND DOWN.
LOOK AROUND AT THIS RUINED CITY—ONCE THE SHINING HEART OF OUR CIVILIZATION—AND SEE THE TERRIBLE COST OF WAR.
FOR ALL OUR GREAT ASPIRATIONS AND PRINCIPLES, I DO NOT SEE "ORDER" OR "JUSTICE" AMIDST THE WRECKAGE. ALL I SEE IS LOSS.
AND I HAVE HAD ENOUGH OF IT.

MEGATRON AND HIS FOLLOWERS WILL FACE THE CONSEQUENCES OF THEIR ACTIONS.
MAKE NO MISTAKE—THERE WILL BE A RECKONING.

"FOR NOW, WE WILL RESTORE SOME SEMBLANCE OF CIVIL ORDER—AND BEGIN TO REBUILD THIS WORLD WE'VE SACRIFICED SO MUCH TO SAVE.
"WHILE WE CAN NEVER HOPE TO SEAL AWAY THE SINS OF OUR PAST... WE MUST NEVER FORGET THE LESSONS OUR MISTAKES HAVE TAUGHT US.
"TRUE ORDER—*HARMONY*—CAN NEVER BE INSTILLED THROUGH THE THREAT OF TOTALITARIAN CONTROL. THE SOCIETY WE LONG FOR CANNOT BE BUILT UPON THE PILLARS OF DOMINATION AND FEAR.
"IF EVER WE FORGET THE TERRIBLE COST OF OUR VIOLENCE, WE WILL LOSE MORE THAN JUST THE HOPE OF A BETTER FUTURE...
"...ULTIMATELY... WE WILL LOSE OURSELVES."

I WAS AN OFFICER.
A PEACEKEEPER.
BUT I HAVE FOUND A NEW LIFE.
A NEW CALLING.
WITH THE POWER OF THE MATRIX COURSING WITHIN ME...
...I WILL STAND FOR MY PEOPLE...
...FOR ALL THOSE WHO CANNOT STAND FOR THEMSELVES.
WITH MY AUTOBOTS AT MY SIDE, I WILL FIGHT TO THE LAST.
FOR FREEDOM. FOR JUSTICE.
FOR CYBERTRON.
I... AM OPTIMUS PRIME.

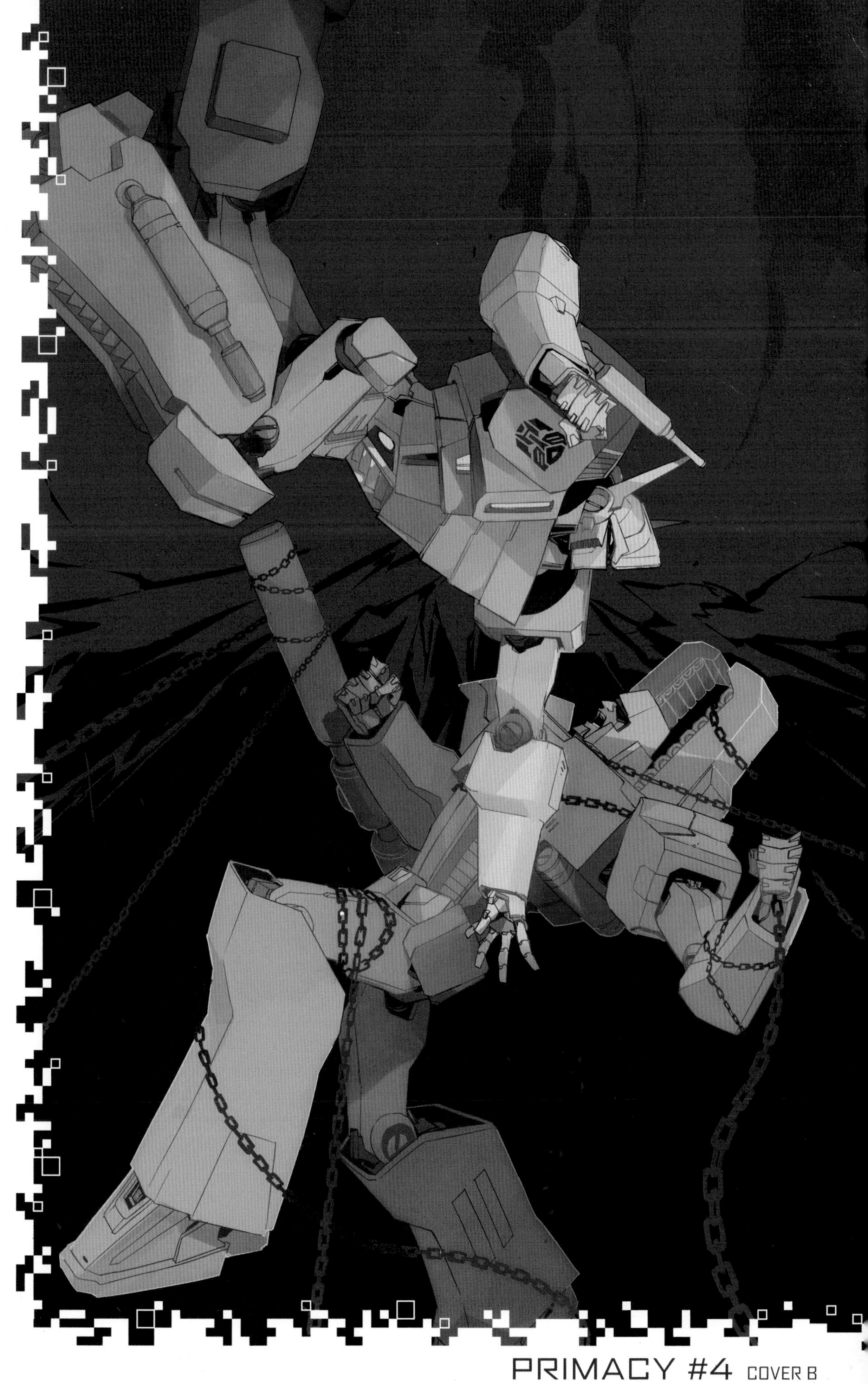

PRIMACY #4 COVER B
by **SARAH STONE**

ROBOTS IN DISGUISE #19 COVER A
by **DHEERAJ VERMA** Colors by **JOANA LAFUENTE**

WASPINATOR DON'T UNDERSTAND WHAT YOU WANT FROM HIM.
YOU ALREADY KNOW WHAT HAPPENED.
IT WAS ZZO LONG AGO...
...WHY WON'T YOU LET WASPINATOR FORGET?
"WASPINATOR WAZZ A HUNTER. YOU KNOW THAT. WE WERE ALL HUNTERZZ...
"WASPINATOR HAD NEVER... NEVER BELIEVED. WASPINATOR THOUGHT THEY WERE MYTHZZ.
"STORIEZZ ABOUT PRIMUS' SERVANTZZZ...
"...UNTIL OPTIMUS PRIME RAIZZED A TITAN FROM THE GROUND OF CYBERTRON."
ARISE.
"AND MEGATRON DEZZIRED ONE...
"...SO WE BECAME TITAN HUNTERZZ.
"REMEMBER HOW LONG WE ZZEARCHED? BUT YOU WERE GONE BY WHEN WASPINATOR FOUND ONE.
"WASPINATOR KNEW HE HAD TO MURDER IT, ZZO SHOCKWAVE COULD HARVEST THE SPACE BRIDGE INSIDE."
AND THEN...
...AND THEN...
...THE WORZZZT THING HAPPENED. THE WORZZT THING THAT COULD EVER HAPPEN TO WASPINATOR, HAPPENED...

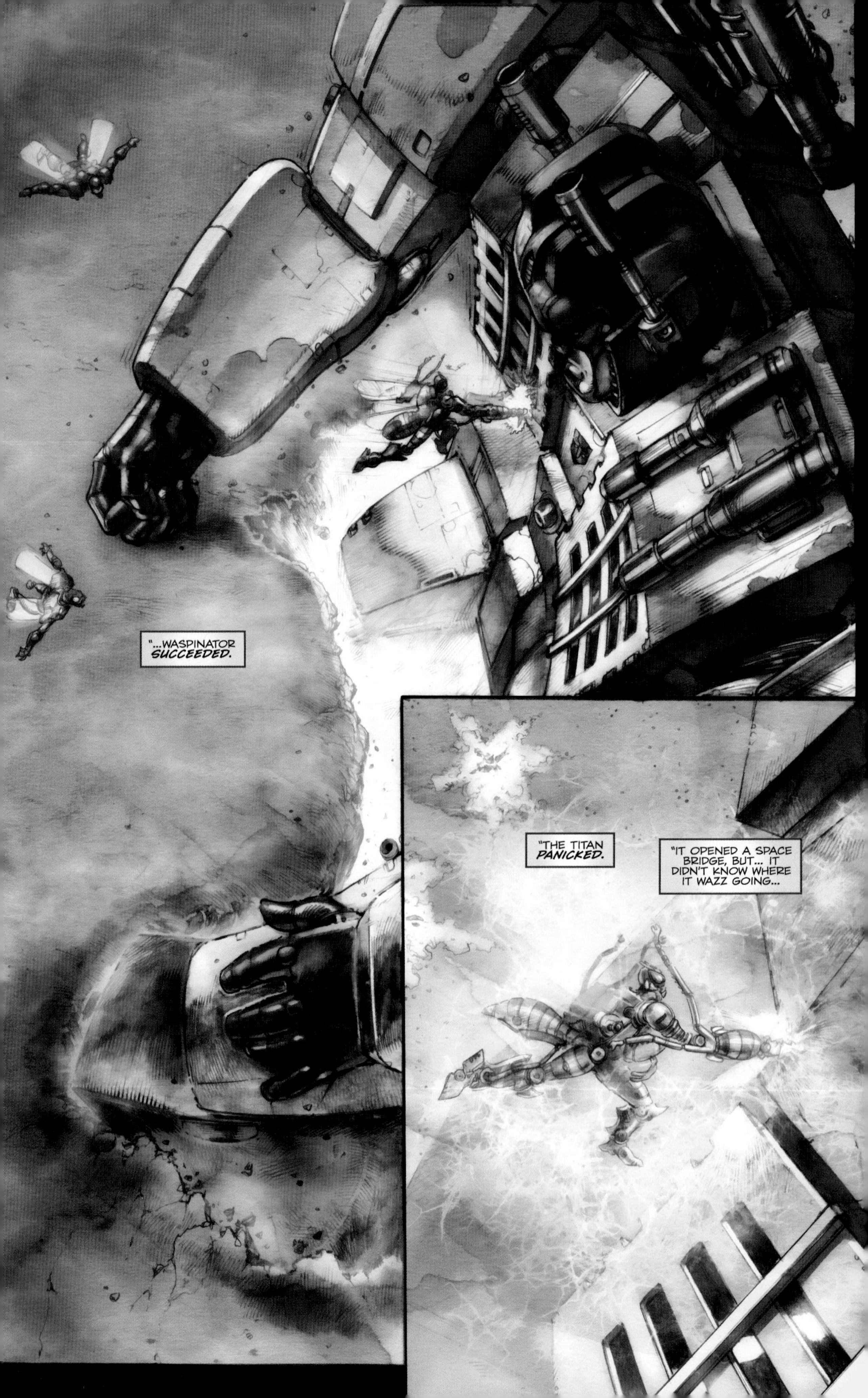
"...WASPINATOR SUCCEEDED.
"THE TITAN PANICKED.
"IT OPENED A SPACE BRIDGE, BUT... IT DIDN'T KNOW WHERE IT WAZZ GOING...

"...AND NEITHER DID WASPINATOR.

"WASPINATOR WAS *PULLED* ALONG, THROUGH *SPAZZE* AND *TIME*.

"EVERYTHING *LOOKED DIFFERENT*...

"...LIKE THE WAY WASPINATOR'S *OPTICZZ* LOOK DIFFERENT WHEN WASPINATOR *CHANGES MODES*... BUT...

"...*BIGGER*.

"WASPINATOR CAN'T *THINK* ABOUT IT ANYMORE.

"THE CREATURE... THE *TITAN*...
"...ITZZ *SPARK* DIMMED... THE DAMAGE WASPINATOR HAD *DONE* TO IT...
"...WAZZ TOO MUCH.

"WASPINATOR WAZZ OUT OF CONTROL... ADRIFT WITH THE TITAN... UNTIL... SOMEHOW... *IMPOZZIBLY*...
"...WASPINATOR CONTROLLED IT.
"WASPINATOR ... *FELT* SOMETHING. ZZOMEWHERE WASPINATOR COULD AIM FOR."

WASPINATOR THOUGHT IT WAZZ *LIFE*—BUT IT *WAZZN'T*.
IT WAZZ *DEATH*. WASPINATOR FOUND *DEATH* ITZZELF.
DEATH, *INDEED*...

...AND WHAT DID YOU SAY TO MY OLD FRIEND?
BLUDGEON. PLEASE.
HE'S JUST GETTING TO THE GOOD PART.
YOU CONTROLLED A TITAN ONCE. TELL ME, WASPINATOR—
—CAN YOU DO IT AGAIN?

HOMECOMING

GORLAM PRIME—AN OUT-OF-THE-WAY PLANET IN THE BENZULI EXPANSE.

THE SORT OF PLANET THAT SHOULD HAVE NEVER HEARD OF AUTOBOTS OR DECEPTICONS, LET ALONE BECOME INVOLVED IN OUR WARS.

BUT GORLAM PRIME DID GET INVOLVED.

AND IT DIED.

THE FRONT LINE OF A WAR WITH ANOTHER UNIVERSE, GORLAM PRIME FELL.

IS THIS OUR LEGACY? IS CHAOS ALL WE SERVE, OR IS THERE SOME MEANING TO IT?

PERHAPS THAT QUESTION MUST REMAIN IN THE REALM OF POETS AND PHILOSOPHERS, NOT OF A WARRIOR.

FOR TODAY—AS EVERY DAY...

...THE UNIVERSE NEEDS ME TO SAVE IT, NOT UNDERSTAND IT.

YOU LIVED HERE.

NICE OF YOU TO FINALLY JOIN US. AND, WHEN YOU PUT IT LIKE THAT, NO...

...I DIDN'T EXACTLY LIVE HERE.
THIS WAS EIGHT, NINE YEARS AGO? JHIAXUS AND THE OTHERS CAPTURED ME, TURNED ME INTO SOMETHING...
NOT ALIVE BUT, WELL, ALSO NOT DEAD— YOUR LIFE IS SO CONFUSING, HARDHEAD.
...UH, YEAH, THANKS, WHEELIE.
ANYWAY, PRIME—I'VE HAD ENOUGH OF WALKING INTO JHIAXUS' TRAPS. THIS IS THE THIRD ONE.
IT'S NOT A TRAP IF YOU KNOW YOU'RE WALKING INTO IT.
I TRY TO IMPRESS THAT ON ALL MY FRIENDS.
FRIENDS? YOU USED TO CALL US SOLDIERS.
THOSE DAYS ARE OVER, HARDHEAD. I'M NOT OPTIMUS PRIME ANYMORE—I'M JUST ORION PAX.
I MAY BE A WARRIOR—BUT MINE IS NOT THE PATH ALL CYBERTRONIANS SHOULD FOLLOW.
HAH. YEAH, RIGHT.
THIS PLANET. THIS DEAD WORLD... HOW DID YOU STAND IT, HARDHEAD?
IT WASN'T ALWAYS DEAD.
FIRST TIME I CAME HERE, IT WAS FULL OF PEOPLE. LIKE THOSE LITTLE... WHAT ARE THOSE LITTLE THINGS FROM EARTH CALLED?
EARTHLINGS.
HUMANS, GARNAK.
YEAH, PRETTY CLOSE TO THEM. BUT JHIAXUS EXPERIMENTED—TURNED THEM INTO LITTLE VERSIONS OF US.
AND I HAVEN'T EVEN GOTTEN TO THE CRAZY PART YET.

HARDHEAD LEADS US DEEP UNDERGROUND, TO THE CAVE THAT WAS HIS HOME FOR SEVERAL YEARS.
THIS DEAD WORLD'S ENTRANCE TO... THE DEAD UNIVERSE.
A PARALLEL REALITY, DISCOVERED EONS AGO BY THE ARK-1, WHEN NOVA PRIME AND JHIAXUS LED THEIR EXPEDITION AT THE END OF CYBERTRON'S SO-CALLED GOLDEN AGE.
THEY WERE TRAPPED IN A PLANE UTTERLY DEVOID OF LIFE—THEMSELVES DISTORTED INTO SOMETHING EVIL...
...OR MAYBE THEY WERE ALWAYS EVIL. I SUPPOSE IT'S RELATIVE.
NOVA AND JHIAXUS AND THE OTHERS WERE GONE FOR MILLIONS OF YEARS... UNTIL THEY FOUND A PERMANENT PORTAL BETWEEN UNIVERSES. HERE.
YOU KNOW WHAT THE PEOPLE HERE STARTED CALLING THE PLANET, WHEN JHIAXUS TURNED THEM CYBER-ORGANIC?
NO. AND I DON'T CARE. ALL I CARE ABOUT IS WHAT HAPPENED TO THEM...
...AND HOW I CAN STOP IT FROM HAPPENING TO ANYONE ELSE.
THESE ROCKS, BOSS. SOMETHIN'S WEIRD WITH 'EM.
IT'S LIKE WHAT WE SAW BACK ON ARDURIA AND LV-117. I THINK THESE IS ONE O' SHOCKWAVE'S REGENESIS ORES...
AMAZING. I WAS HERE FOR YEARS AND NEVER THOUGHT ABOUT... OH.
THERE'S SOMETHING ELSE. SOMETHING...

"...BIG."
THESE STRUCTURES—THEY'RE CYBERTRONIAN. ANCIENT CYBERTRONIAN.
I CALLED THEM THE CATACOMBS.
YEAH—THAT'S WHAT MADE THEM SO FASCINATING. JHIAXUS MUST HAVE BUILT THEM TO MAKE THE PLACE FEEL MORE LIKE HOME.
HOME. HOME TO MILLIONS OF PEOPLE... THEN GORLAM PRIME BECAME GROUND ZERO OF AN INVASION MADE POSSIBLE BY NOVA... BY JHIAXUS.
THE REST OF US—WE SAVED THE UNIVERSE.
BUT WE FAILED GORLAM PRIME.
THIS STYLE PREDATES JHIAXUS.
THESE TOWERS ARE FROM THE AGE OF PRIMUS. THE AGE OF THE TITANS.
I HAVE SOME... OLD FRIENDS WHO LIVED IN PLACES LIKE THIS.
PRIME'S VOICE RAISED THE TITAN KNOWN AS METROPLEX—WHO JOINED HIS WAR AGAINST THE VILLAINS HE REJECTS.
HUH. YA LEARN SOMETHIN' EVERY DAY.
WHEN I CONFRONTED JHIAXUS ON LV-117—
—BEFORE HE SLIPPED THROUGH MY GRASP—
—HE SAID HE WOULD BRING GORLAM PRIME FROM THE PAST TO THE FUTURE.

DID HE MEAN IT LITERALLY?
HIS SHIP CAN BEND TIME. AND THESE BUILDINGS, OUT OF THEIR OWN TIME...
WHEELIE TRUSTS WHATEVER ORION HAS TO SAY... BUT THIS PLACE IS CREEPY; WHEN CAN WE GO—
—AWAY...
WHEELIE!
YOUR ARM— DISOLVING!
IT HURTS! HARDHEAD, MAKE IT STOP— BEFORE IT SPREADS TO THE TOP!
SORRY, LITTLE BUDDY...
AHHH!
BRAKKA
NOTHING LIKE THIS EVER HAPPENED BEFORE.
WHEELIE, ARE YOU OKAY?
B-BEEN BETTER, BUT AT LEAST NOT DISINTEGRATED. WHEELIE'S GOTTEN USED TO THE LIFE HE'S BEEN FATED.
BOSS... THERE'S MORE—

"—*PROXIMITY ALERT* FROM THE *ARK-27*."

ZZOMEBODY—

—ZZOMEBODY—

—ZZAVE WASPINATOR!

THERE ISN'T ANYONE TO *PROTECT* YOU, TRAITOR—

—NO ONE ESCAPES US!
CHAGGK
AIGGK!

UNNF—
—GET—GET *OFF* OF WASPINATOR, YOU *MONZZTER*—!
KRUMPP

THOOM
YOU'RE *WORSE* THAN A MONSTER...

...BUT THE GREEN FELLOW IS CORRECT.
STAND DOWN, WILDFLY.
YOU—SAY THAT TO US?
YOU KNOW WHAT WE ARE!
I KNOW EXACTLY WHAT YOU ARE.
OPTIMUZZ PRIME—I—PLEAZZE—
—HELP.
WE'LL HELP ANYONE IN NEED—DECEPTICON OR NOT.
THAT'S WHY WE'RE THE GOOD GUYS. GET BEHIND ME—THINGS ARE ABOUT TO GET A LOT WORSE.
PRIME—WHEELIE DOESN'T MEAN TO WHINE, BUT THOSE SIX VILLAINS STARTED TO COMBINE!
YOU KNOW US—
—YOU FEAR US—
—YOU FEAR—

—MONSTRUCTOR!
I AM GETTING REALLY REALLY SICK OF FIGHTING THIS GUY!
WASPINATOR THANKZZ YOU... WASPINATOR WOULD NEVER BE ABLE TO EZZCAPE WITHOUT YOU—
YEAH, I KNOW—AND I'M NOT SAYING I'M GIVING UP...
BRAKKA BRAKKA

RRRRAAHGH!
PINC
PINC
PINC
...I'M SAYING HE'S NOT!
RUUGHHGAAH
KRA-CRUNCHK
THOOOFFF
SO MUCH FOR THE ARK-27... AND OUR RIDE HOME. HEY, PRIME—
—REMEMBER WHAT I SAID ABOUT WALKING INTO A TRAP?
HARDHEAD, HOW MANY TIMES DO I HAVE TO TELL YOU—
—CALL ME ORION PAX!
THOOM THOOM
I DON'T CARE IF HE SAYS HE'S NOT—
FWOOT-KWA-CHOOM
—ONLY OPTIMUS PRIME WOULD EVER BE THAT STUPIDLY HEROIC.

T-THERE'ZZ SOMETHING YOU SHOULD KNOW.
THEY—THEZZE MONSTERZZ—THEY KIDNAPPED WASPINATOR!
BROUGHT WASPINATOR HERE TO DO SOMETHING TERRIFYING.
YEAH, I CAN SEE TERRIFYING AND IT'S BEARING DOWN ON US!
NNNSS NSS SSNN NNSSN SNNNG SNNSS SSNN NSSS SSNSSS SSSSNG!
UH, OKAY, YEH.
I COULD HEAR IT IN MY HEAD—YOU SEE, WHAT IT WAS I SAID—
FWIP
WOOMP
THERE'ZZ NO TIME FOR THIZZ!
DON'T WORRY, MY DECEPTICON FRIEND. I HAVE A PLAN.
THOOM THOOM
NO—THERE'ZZ SOMETHING UNDERNEATH US.
THAT'ZZ WHAT THEY'RE AFTER.
THE ANCIENT CITY?
IT—OH!
WASPINATOR SEEZZ. IT'ZZ IN CITY MODE. YOU—YOU DON'T KNOW WHAT IT IZZ!
PRIME, WHAT'S HE TALKING ABOUT?

OF COURSE.
ANYWAYS, PRIME, THAT PLAN OF YOURS—YOU BETTER DO WHATEVER IT IS—
—MONSTRUCTOR IS RIGHT ON US!
THE LUCK. THE LUCK THAT YOU WOULD BE HERE.
OPTIMUZZ PRIME.
THE TRUE MATRIX-BEARER. YOU CAN FEEL IT, CAN'T YOU?
YOU KNOW ITZZ THERE.
YES. OF COURSE.
ARISE.
RRRRMMMMMBL
UH-OH. GOTTA GO!
STAY CALM, WHEELIE. THIS WILL BE...
R-R-RUM-M-M-B-L-L-L-L-L-L-L-L-L-L-L
...WAIT—YOU CALLED ME "THE TRUE MATRIX-BEARER"?
OH—NOW WHEELIE CAN CLEARLY SEE. GUESS THE BAD GUYS HAD BETTER FLEE.

WELL, MONSTRUCTOR—

—ANYTHING TO SAY?
WAIT...
MASTER. IT IS ARISEN.
YES, MONSTRUCTOR...
...JHIAXUS SEES ALL.
THANK YOU, ORION PAX. THE TRUE MATRIX-BEARER.
I COULD BE SURE YOU, OF ALL CYBERTRONIANS, WERE CAPABLE OF RAISING A TITAN.
EVEN ONE WHOSE FUNCTIONS CEASED LONG AGO.

THE CITY DISINTEGRATES, OPTIMUS PRIME.
THIS PLANET'S EQUILIBRIUM IS WRECKED.
THE ORE MY STUDENT, SHOCKWAVE, PLANTED SO LONG AGO—THE ONE THAT PROVIDED AN OPENING INTO THE DEAD UNIVERSE—
—ORE-2: DEATH, AS I LIKE TO CALL IT—
—NOW IT SPREADS.
YOUR ROLE IS NOT FINISHED, MATRIX-BEARER.
YOU WILL BE DRAGGED TO THE FUTURE WITH GORLAM PRIME.
YOU WILL STAY HERE, ORION PAX, WHILE WASPINATOR PILOTS THE TITAN BACK TO CYBERTRON.
YES, MASTER.

AND WE SHALL FOLLOW, AS QUICKLY AS WE CAN.
GOODBYE, ORION PAX.
GOODBYE, OPTIMUS PRIME.
WASPINATOR OBEYS.
JHIAXUS, YOU VILE...
OH, ONE MORE THING—
—PAX CYBERTRONIA.
THE ARROGANCE.
THAT GETS TO ME. THE ARROGANCE OF IDEOLOGUES LIKE JHIAXUS.

THEY THINK THE UNIVERSE BOWS TO THEIR WILL.
WELL.
JHIAXUS HAS ANOTHER THINK COMING.
BOSS, WE'RE ABOUT TO GET DISINTEGRATED. YOU GOT A DENUVIAN GERI-RABBIT TO PULL OUT OF YOUR SERVO-HELMET?
WHAT?
I DUNNO. YOU GUYS SAY STUFF LIKE THAT.
NO LAUGHING MATTER—GORLAM PRIME TURNS TO RUST! IF THERE IS ANY WAY TO ESCAPE—WELL, WE MUST!
HA.
JHIAXUS PLAYED RIGHT INTO MY HAND.
NO WAY. YOU KNEW ABOUT THE TITAN?
OF COURSE NOT, BUT I KNEW JHIAXUS WANTED ME HERE.
YEAH! AND HE GOT WHAT HE WANTED!
MAYBE. BUT NOW WE KNOW EXACTLY WHERE HE'S GOING AND WHO HE'S WORKING WITH.

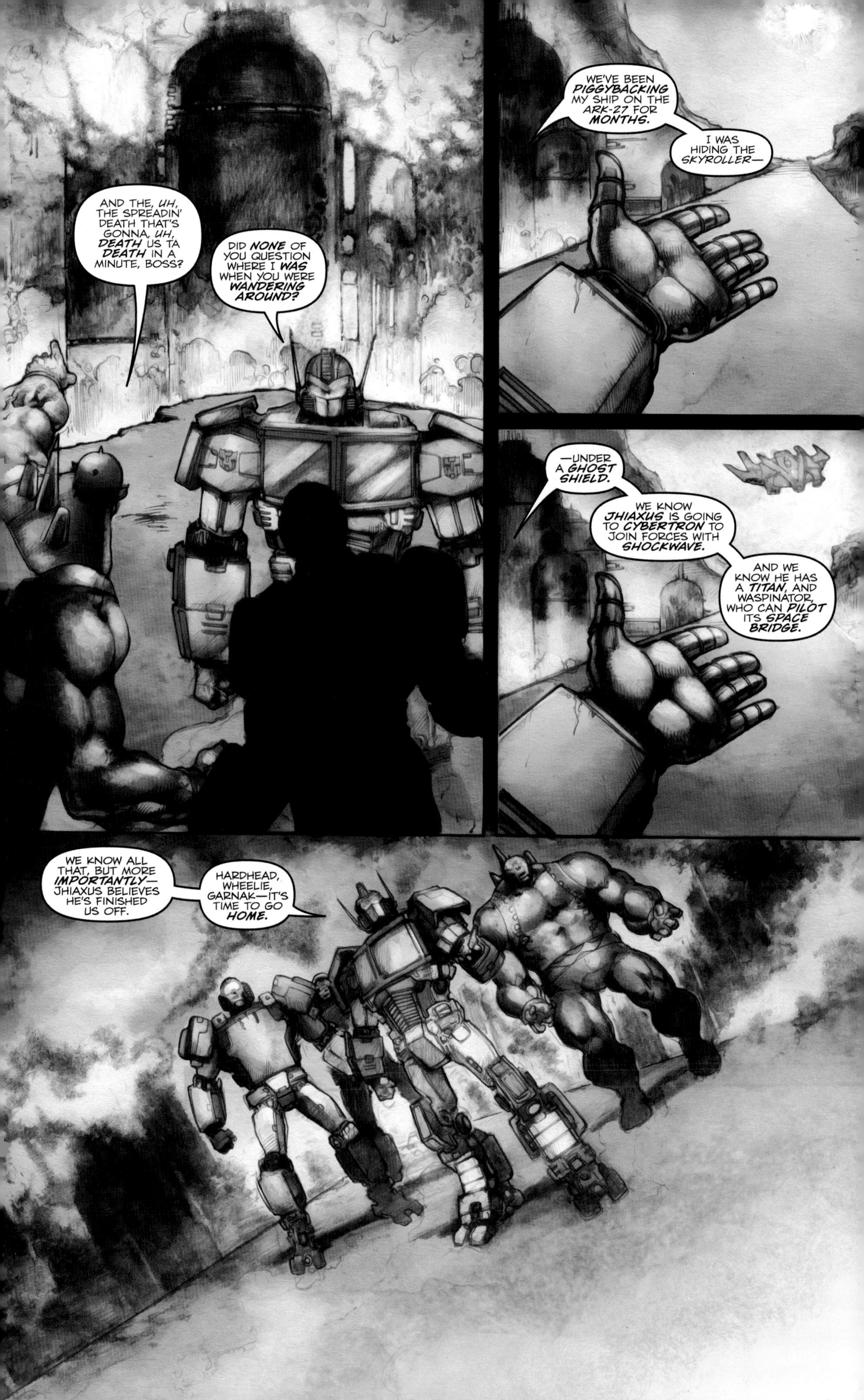
AND THE, UH, THE SPREADIN' DEATH THAT'S GONNA, UH, DEATH US TA DEATH IN A MINUTE, BOSS?
DID NONE OF YOU QUESTION WHERE I WAS WHEN YOU WERE WANDERING AROUND?
WE'VE BEEN PIGGYBACKING MY SHIP ON THE ARK-27 FOR MONTHS.
I WAS HIDING THE SKYROLLER—
—UNDER A GHOST SHIELD.
WE KNOW JHIAXUS IS GOING TO CYBERTRON TO JOIN FORCES WITH SHOCKWAVE.
AND WE KNOW HE HAS A TITAN, AND WASPINATOR, WHO CAN PILOT ITS SPACE BRIDGE.
WE KNOW ALL THAT, BUT MORE IMPORTANTLY— JHIAXUS BELIEVES HE'S FINISHED US OFF.
HARDHEAD, WHEELIE, GARNAK—IT'S TIME TO GO HOME.

THERE'S A UNIVERSE THAT NEEDS *SAVING*...
...AND WE ***WON'T*** LET THIS HAPPEN TO ***ANOTHER WORLD***.

ROBOTS IN DISGUISE #19 COVER B

by **CASEY W. COLLER** Colors by **JOANA LAFUENTE**

ROBOTS IN DISGUISE #20 COVER A

by **ANDREW GRIFFITH** Colors by **JOSH PEREZ**

YOU WERE MY FRIEND, AND I APPRECIATE WHAT YOU DID FOR ME.
YOU GOT ME WHAT I ALWAYS WANTED, METALHAWK,
YOU GOT ME CYBERTRON.
WHEN THE TITAN SAID I WAS THE CHOSEN ONE—THE TRUE RULER OF CYBERTRON...
...YOU WERE THE ONE WHO TOLD ME WHAT IT ALL MEANT.
YOU TOLD ME IT WASN'T ABOUT SERVING MY OWN GOALS. IT WAS ABOUT SERVING OUR WORLD—AND YOU WERE RIGHT.
SO, WELL...
...I'M SORRY I KILLED YOU, BUDDY.
THREE MONOLOGUES
1: LONG NIGHT

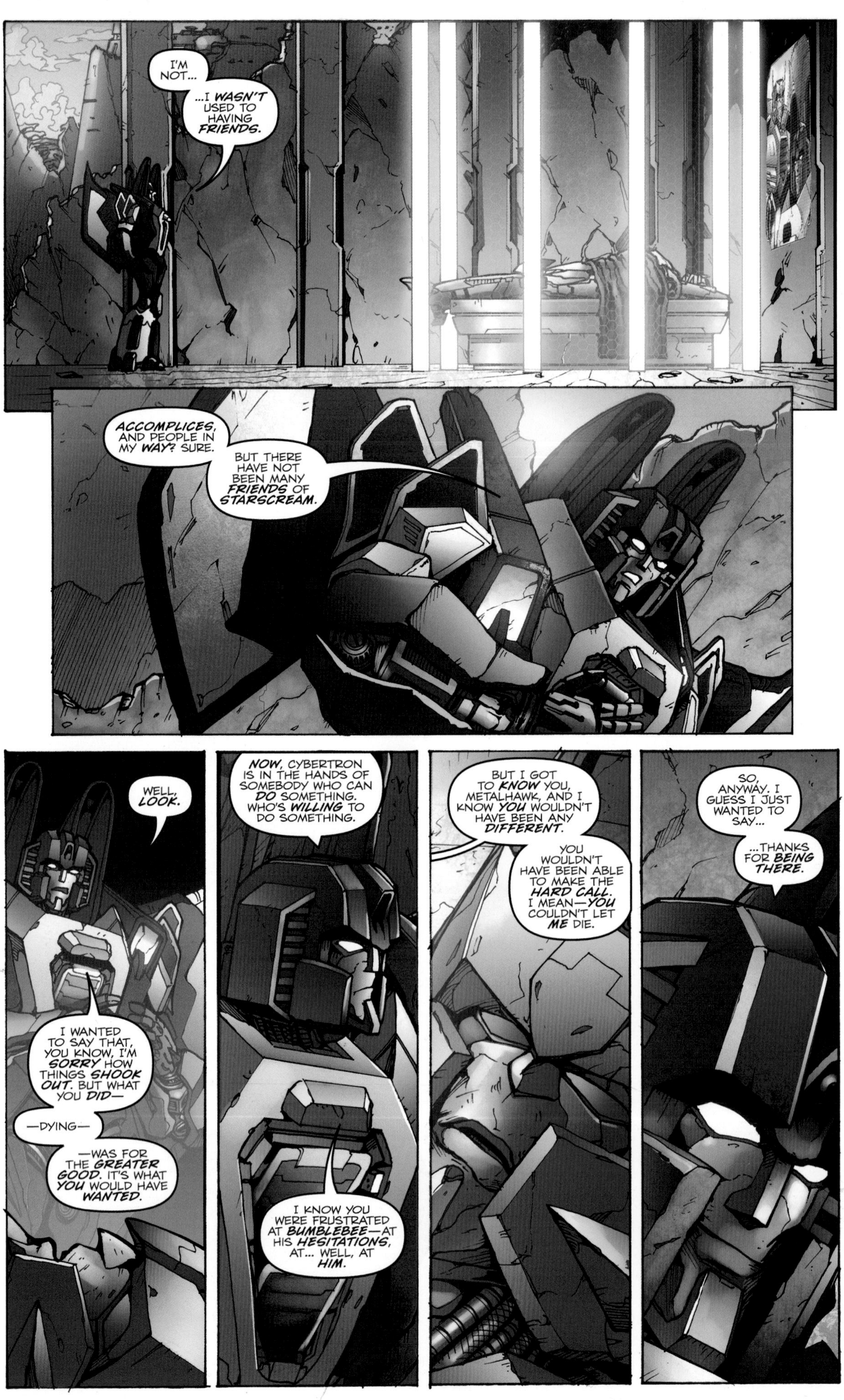

I'M NOT...
...I **WASN'T** USED TO HAVING **FRIENDS**.

ACCOMPLICES, AND PEOPLE IN MY **WAY**? SURE.
BUT THERE HAVE NOT BEEN MANY **FRIENDS** OF **STARSCREAM**.

WELL, LOOK.
I WANTED TO SAY THAT, YOU KNOW, I'M SORRY HOW THINGS SHOOK OUT. BUT WHAT YOU DID—
—DYING—
—WAS FOR THE GREATER GOOD. IT'S WHAT YOU WOULD HAVE WANTED.

NOW, CYBERTRON IS IN THE HANDS OF SOMEBODY WHO CAN DO SOMETHING. WHO'S WILLING TO DO SOMETHING.
I KNOW YOU WERE FRUSTRATED AT BUMBLEBEE—AT HIS HESITATIONS, AT... WELL, AT HIM.

BUT I GOT TO KNOW YOU, METALHAWK, AND I KNOW YOU WOULDN'T HAVE BEEN ANY DIFFERENT.
YOU WOULDN'T HAVE BEEN ABLE TO MAKE THE HARD CALL. I MEAN—YOU COULDN'T LET ME DIE.

SO, ANYWAY. I GUESS I JUST WANTED TO SAY...
...THANKS FOR BEING THERE.

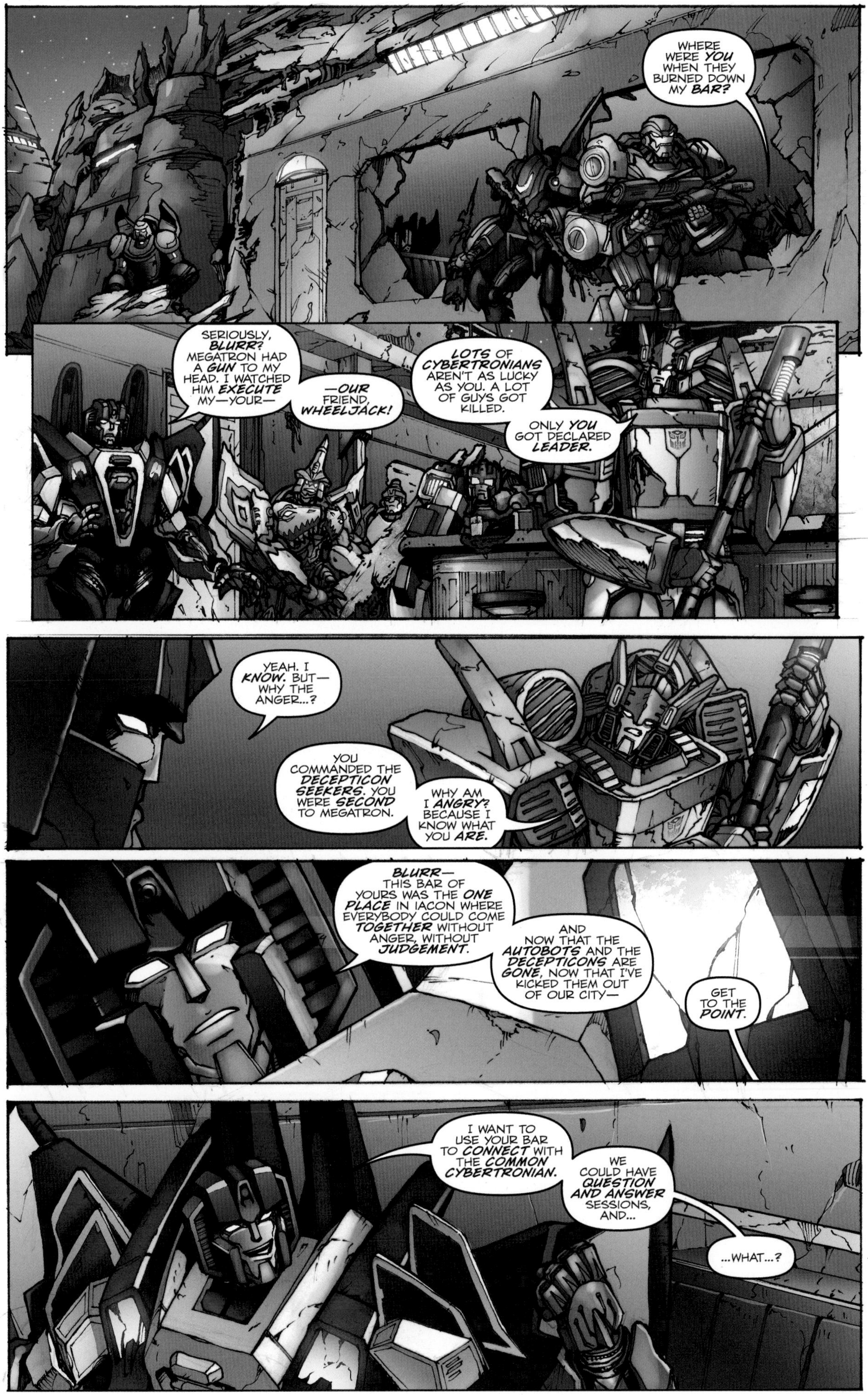

WHERE WERE ***YOU*** WHEN THEY BURNED DOWN MY ***BAR?***

SERIOUSLY, ***BLURR?*** MEGATRON HAD A ***GUN*** TO MY HEAD. I WATCHED HIM ***EXECUTE*** MY—YOUR—

—OUR FRIEND, ***WHEELJACK!***

LOTS OF ***CYBERTRONIANS*** AREN'T AS LUCKY AS YOU. A LOT OF GUYS GOT KILLED.

ONLY ***YOU*** GOT DECLARED ***LEADER.***

YEAH. I KNOW. BUT— WHY THE ANGER...?
YOU COMMANDED THE DECEPTICON SEEKERS. YOU WERE SECOND TO MEGATRON.
WHY AM I ANGRY? BECAUSE I KNOW WHAT YOU ARE.

BLURR— THIS BAR OF YOURS WAS THE ONE PLACE IN IACON WHERE EVERYBODY COULD COME TOGETHER WITHOUT ANGER, WITHOUT JUDGEMENT.
AND NOW THAT THE AUTOBOTS AND THE DECEPTICONS ARE GONE, NOW THAT I'VE KICKED THEM OUT OF OUR CITY—
GET TO THE POINT.

I WANT TO USE YOUR BAR TO CONNECT WITH THE COMMON CYBERTRONIAN.
WE COULD HAVE QUESTION AND ANSWER SESSIONS, AND...
...WHAT...?

HA HA HA HA
"COMMON CYBERTRONIAN"?
YOU ACTUALLY SAID THAT TO ME?

WELL, I—
GET OUT OF MY BAR, STARSCREAM.
DON'T BE LIKE THIS—

WELL. THAT'S NOT GOOD.
YOU WANT THE COMMON CYBERTRONIAN ON YOUR SIDE?
FIX THINGS.

NOBODY PICKED YOU AS LEADER.
WE PICKED NOT BEING KILLED BY THE AUTOBOT/DECEPTICON WAR. YOU WERE JUST THE GUY STANDING THERE SAYING THE RIGHT THING.
YOU DON'T HAVE ANY SEEKERS LEFT TO COMMAND—ALL YOU HAVE IS A CITY FULL OF 'BOTS THAT SEE YOU AS THE LESSER OF A FEW EVILS...

...AND I HAVE A FEELING THAT THIS IS GOING TO BE A LONG NIGHT FOR YOU.

IT'S BEEN A STRUGGLE, BUT WE'RE ***HERE***. THE WAR, THE ***FACTIONS***—ARE ALL ***BEHIND US***.
NOW'S WHEN WE START ***SAVING LIVES***.
THE ***HEROES*** OF LAST NIGHT'S ***BATTLE*** MAY BE ALIVE—BUT THEIR ***LIFE-SUPPORT*** IS RUNNING ON ***EMERGENCY RESERVES***.
BOT SCOOP PLEDGES TO HELP REBUILD IACON AFTER LAST
INN
I—AND MY ***CONSTRUCTION PATROL***—VOW TO ***RISE*** TO THIS ***NEW CHALLENGE!*** WE WILL ***RESTORE POWER*** TO THE CITY... ***TONIGHT!***
SITUATIONS LIKE ***THIS*** ARE WHY WE ***STAYED*** IN IACON, AND ***HELPING EVERYONE*** IS MY ***PLEDGE***.
BRAVE WORDS—***INSPIRING WORDS***—FROM ***SCOOP*** AND HIS ***CONSTRUCTION PATROL!***
THIS IS ***CIRCUIT***, FOR THE ***IACONIAN NEWS SERVICE***, BROADCASTING TO ANYONE RUNNING OFF ***BATTERIES*** DURING THIS ***DARK NIGHT***—
—BRINGING YOU A STORY OF HEROISM, OF A PATROL WHO CARRIED THE SEVERELY INJURED ***AERIALBOTS*** TO IACON'S MAKESHIFT MED-CENTER...
PORTING LIVE FROM IACON HOSPITAL DURI

NOBODY ASKED HIM TO.
WELL, COME ON. THE PEOPLE SEE THE AERIALBOTS AS HEROES.

THEY WERE THE FIRST TO DECRY IACON'S FACTIONALISM, PLUS THEY STOPPED DEVASTATOR AND—
ENOUGH, FLATLINE.

YOUR NEW BODY'S NOT READY YET. COME SUNRISE—
THAT'S NOT WHY I'M HERE. I NEED TO TALK TO THE LAST OF THE SEEKERS...

"...I NEED TO TALK TO DIRGE."
YOU THINK I'D LIFT A FINGER FOR YOU?!
WE SERVED TOGETHER FOR MILLIONS OF YEARS DURING THE WAR. THAT'S GOTTA COUNT FOR SOMETHING.
YOU LEFT ME TO DIE THE SECOND IT WAS CONVENIENT!
MISTAKES WERE MADE.
BUT IT'S NOT ME—IT'S CYBERTRON THAT NEEDS YOUR HELP.
THE POWER'S OUT.
WITH OBSERVATIONS LIKE THAT, HOW DID YOU NEVER TOPPLE MEGATRON?
DIRGE. HAVE YOU LOOKED AROUND? I DID TOPPLE MEGATRON.
I NEED SOMEBODY I CAN TRUST. I MEAN, EVEN IF YOU HATE ME—YOU'RE STILL A SEEKER, RIGHT?
YOU KNOW WHAT?

HUH. I THOUGHT YOU'D AT LEAST GIVE ME A SNAZZY ONE-LINER.
"SEEK THIS" OR SOMETHING.

I COULD KILL YOU, DIRGE.
THERE ARE A THOUSAND WAYS I COULD KILL YOU.
NOT ANYMORE, STARSCREAM. HAVE YOU LOOKED OUTSIDE LATELY?

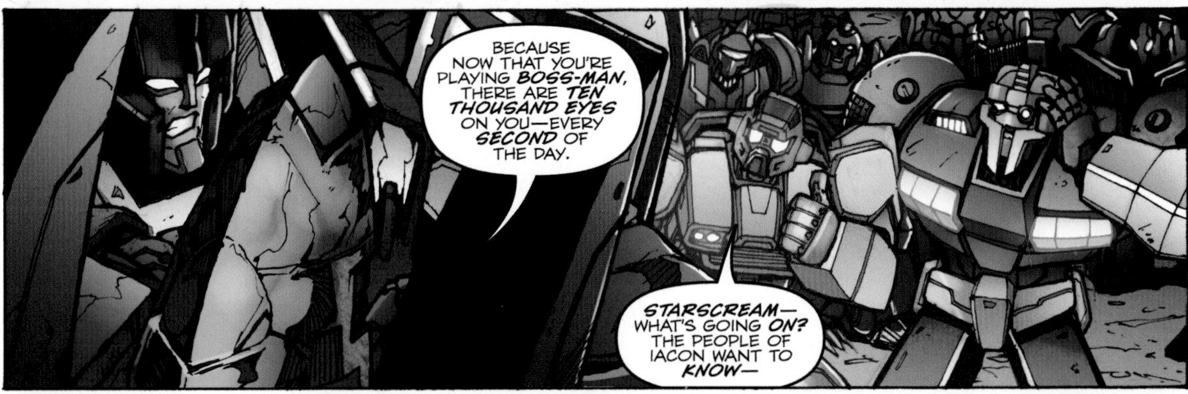

BECAUSE NOW THAT YOU'RE PLAYING BOSS-MAN, THERE ARE TEN THOUSAND EYES ON YOU—EVERY SECOND OF THE DAY.
STARSCREAM—WHAT'S GOING ON? THE PEOPLE OF IACON WANT TO KNOW—

—IS THEIR NEW LEADER ATTACKING WOUNDED CYBERTRONIAN WAR HEROES?
HA. NOT AT ALL.
I JUST WANTED TO MAKE SURE THAT MY OLD FRIEND HERE—AND ALL OF OUR WOUNDED—ARE GETTING THE BEST TREATMENT IACON CAN PROVIDE, EVEN DURING THIS—

—BLACKOUT.
THAT IS SOME TERRIFIC TIMING.
WORD JUST IN—

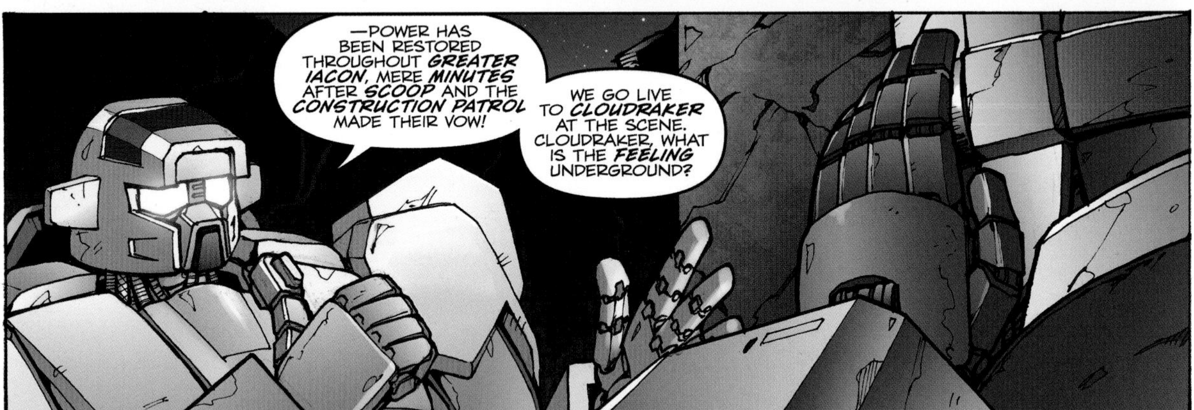
—POWER HAS BEEN RESTORED THROUGHOUT GREATER IACON, MERE MINUTES AFTER SCOOP AND THE CONSTRUCTION PATROL MADE THEIR VOW!
WE GO LIVE TO CLOUDRAKER AT THE SCENE. CLOUDRAKER, WHAT IS THE FEELING UNDERGROUND?

ELATION, CIRCUIT! SCOOP, ANY WORDS FOR A GRATEFUL CITY?
IT WAS NOTHING. JUST NEEDED TO REROUTE POWER AROUND AN OVERLOADED CONDUIT.
NOTHING SINISTER—JUST TOO MUCH STRAIN ON OUR POWER SYSTEM FOR ONE NIGHT.

YES—SCOOP IS A TRUE PATRIOT, BUT WE MUST REMEMBER—
THE MICROPHONE'S NOT ON, STARSCREAM.
...

...I SUPPOSE NOT...
PSST. HEY, UH, HEY DERE...

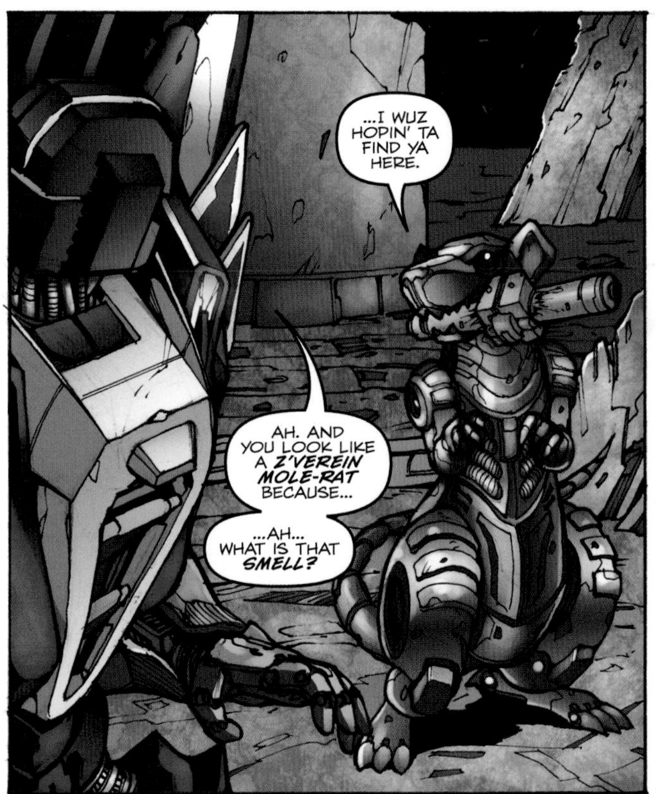
...I WUZ HOPIN' TA FIND YA HERE.
AH. AND YOU LOOK LIKE A Z'VEREIN MOLE-RAT BECAUSE...
...AH... WHAT IS THAT SMELL?

THE NAME'S RATTRAP.
I LOOK LIKE DAT CUZ I SPENT A COUPLE MILLION YEARS FIGHTIN' YOU DECEPTICONS ON Z'VEREI.
AN' WHAT SMELL YOU TALKIN' 'BOUT?

LOOK. I WANTED TA ASK YA. YOU TRUST DAT GUY?
UH.
WHAT? WHO?
SCOOP. CUZ I NEVER DID.

GUY WUZ ALWAYS JEALOUS O' THE 'BOTS WHAT GOT FLASHY JOBS, Y'KNOW?
ALWAYS WANTED MORE.
AND YOU'RE TELLING ME THIS WHY?
MAYBE I SCRATCH YER BACK, YOU SCRATCH MINE. DAT'S HOW THINGS WORK WIT' GUYS LIKE US.

"GUYS LIKE US"? I THINK YOU HAVE ME MISTAKEN FOR—
OH, I GOT YER NUMBER, STARSCREAM. AN' I BEEN SCURRYIN' AROUND HERE LONG ENOUGH TA KNOW WHEELJACK AIN'T GONNA BUILD A POWER GRID WHAT COULDN'T HANDLE THINGS.
Y'SEE DIS? A-276 POWER COUPLING. AN'...

...DAT IS A PHOSPHEX BURN.
WE DIDN'T LOSE POWER CUZ O' AN OVERLOAD. WE LOST IT FROM SABOTAGE.

THEY WORSHIP ME.
IT'S LIKE YOU ALWAYS WANTED, MEGATRON.
EVERY ONE OF THEM LOOKING UP AND SAYING "THANK YOU FOR SAVING US."
AND IT ISN'T JUST BECAUSE OF THE TITAN.
I MEAN, I CAN'T LIE, THAT HELPED—BUT THE THING THAT REALLY GETS THEM IS MY ACTIONS.
I UNITED THE PEOPLE.
I DIDN'T HAVE TO SUBJUGATE THEM. I DIDN'T HAVE TO BETRAY THE PRINCIPLES I BELIEVED IN.
I JUST HAD TO BEAT YOU.
THREE MONOLOGUES
2: YOUNG EVENING

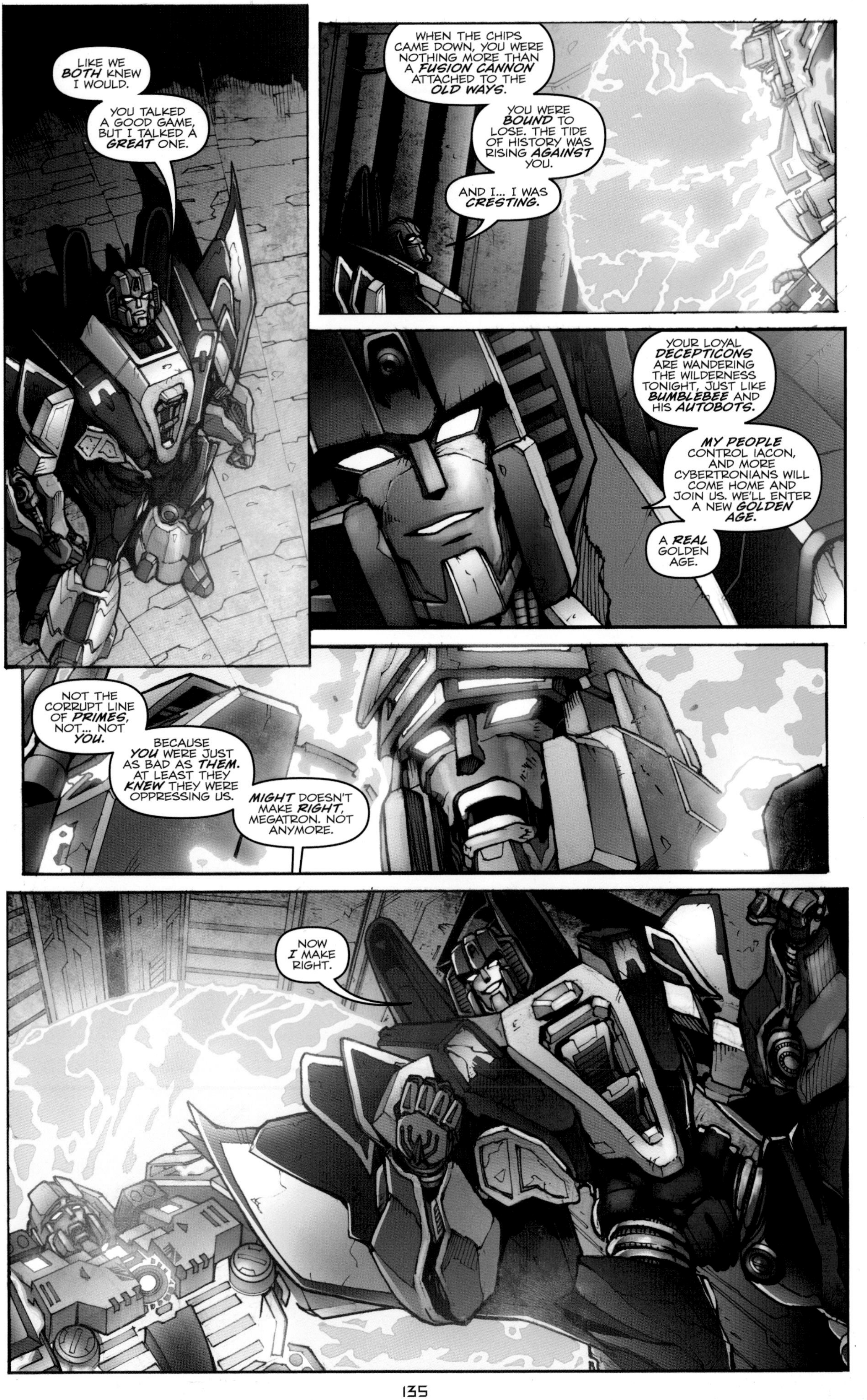

LIKE WE **BOTH** KNEW I WOULD.

YOU TALKED A GOOD GAME, BUT I TALKED A **GREAT** ONE.

WHEN THE CHIPS CAME DOWN, YOU WERE NOTHING MORE THAN A **FUSION CANNON** ATTACHED TO THE **OLD WAYS**.

YOU WERE **BOUND** TO LOSE. THE TIDE OF HISTORY WAS RISING **AGAINST** YOU.

AND I... I WAS **CRESTING**.

YOUR LOYAL **DECEPTICONS** ARE WANDERING THE WILDERNESS TONIGHT, JUST LIKE **BUMBLEBEE** AND HIS **AUTOBOTS**.

MY PEOPLE CONTROL IACON, AND MORE CYBERTRONIANS WILL COME HOME AND JOIN US. WE'LL ENTER A NEW **GOLDEN AGE**.

A **REAL** GOLDEN AGE.

NOT THE CORRUPT LINE OF **PRIMES**, NOT... NOT **YOU**.

BECAUSE **YOU** WERE JUST AS BAD AS **THEM**. AT LEAST THEY **KNEW** THEY WERE OPPRESSING US.

MIGHT DOESN'T MAKE **RIGHT**, MEGATRON. NOT ANYMORE.

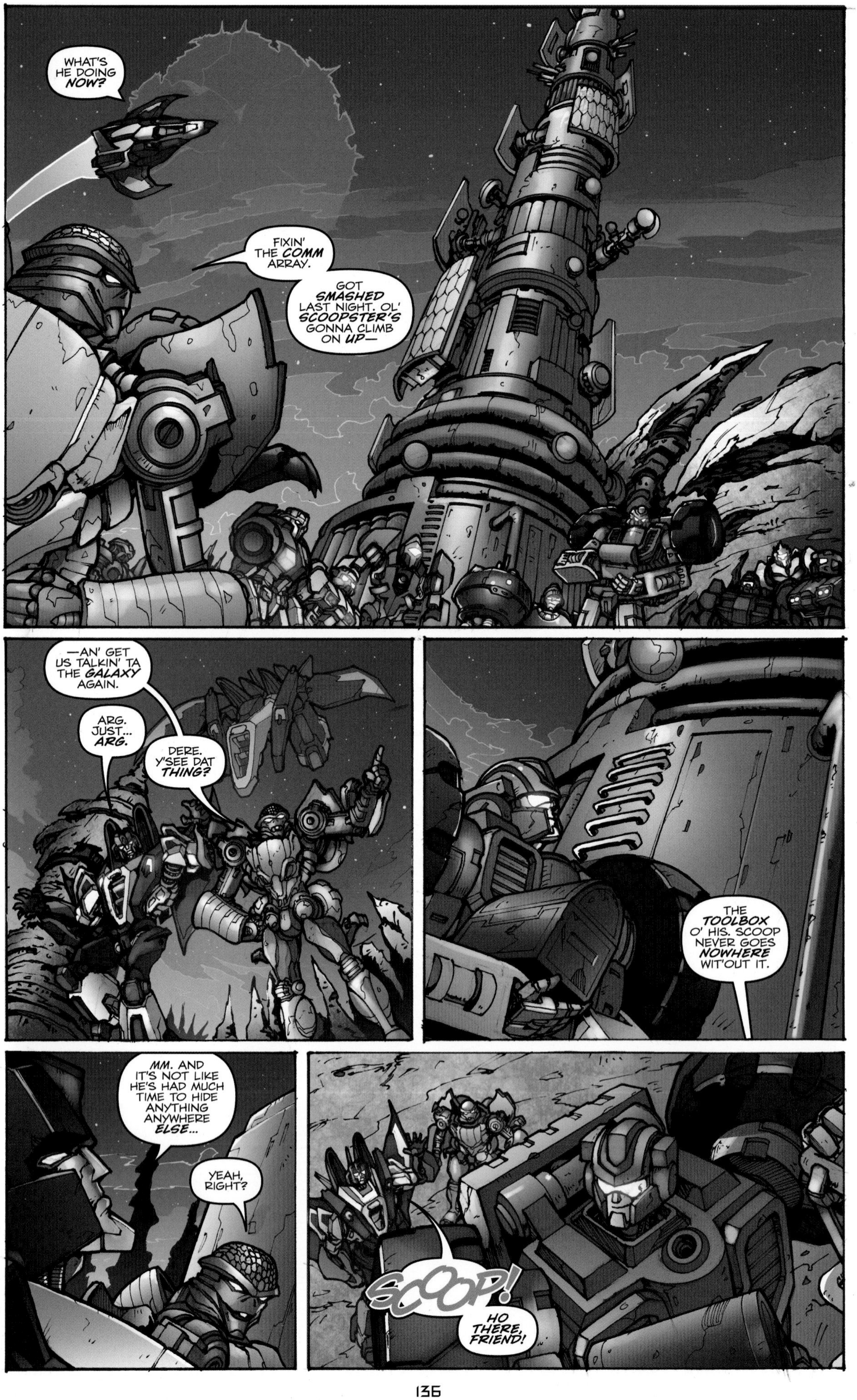

WHAT'S HE DOING *NOW?*
FIXIN' THE *COMM* ARRAY.
GOT *SMASHED* LAST NIGHT. OL' *SCOOPSTER'S* GONNA CLIMB ON *UP*—

—AN' GET US TALKIN' TA THE *GALAXY* AGAIN.
ARG. JUST... *ARG.*
DERE. Y'SEE DAT *THING?*

THE *TOOLBOX* O' HIS. SCOOP NEVER GOES *NOWHERE* WIT'OUT IT.

MM. AND IT'S NOT LIKE HE'S HAD MUCH TIME TO HIDE ANYTHING ANYWHERE *ELSE*...
YEAH, RIGHT?

SCOOP!
HO THERE, FRIEND!

STARSCREAM!
IT IS AN HONOR TO MEET YOU.
WHAT?

I MEAN... SURE IT IS.
GET UP, SCOOP.

YES, OF COURSE.
I JUST... IF I MAY... I WANTED TO SAY WHAT AN HONOR IT IS TO BE HERE, IN IACON, WITH YOU.
OH, DO GO ON.
I... I ALWAYS BELIEVED IN THE TITANS.

BACK WHEN OPTIMUS PRIME RAISED METROPLEX FROM THE GROUND, I KNEW MY CALLING WAS TO BE AN AUTOBOT.
BUT... WORD CAME THAT METROTITAN HAD REAPPEARED AND SPOKEN TO YOU. HAD DECLARED YOU—
—AND THE AUTOBOTS, MY SO-CALLED BROTHERS—LIKE PROWL—WANTED TO KEEP IT SECRET...

WELL, HE WASN'T REALLY PROWL AT THAT PARTICULAR MOMENT, BUT—
IT DOESN'T MATTER.

HAVE YOU HEARD THE PROPHECIES THAT SURROUND THE COMING OF THE CHOSEN ONE?
THE... WHAT? HANG ON NOW.

YOU—YOU AND YOUR MERRY BAND OF BUILDERS—
THE CONSTRUCTION PATROL!
—YOU'RE DOING THIS BECAUSE YOU'RE RELIGIOUS NUTS?!

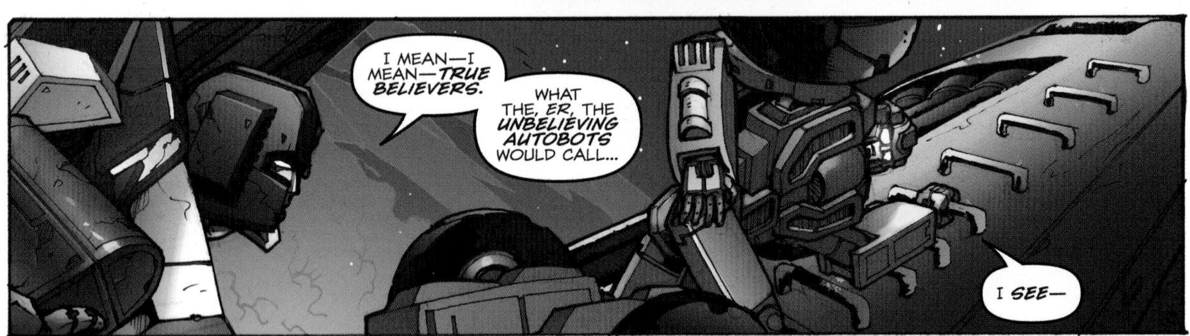
I MEAN—I MEAN—TRUE BELIEVERS.
WHAT THE, ER, THE UNBELIEVING AUTOBOTS WOULD CALL...
I SEE—

—YOU'RE JOKING!
YOU KNOW WHAT IT'S LIKE. WE ONLY WANT TO DO GOOD.
HEY, CAN YOU HAND ME MY TOOLBOX?
REALLY?

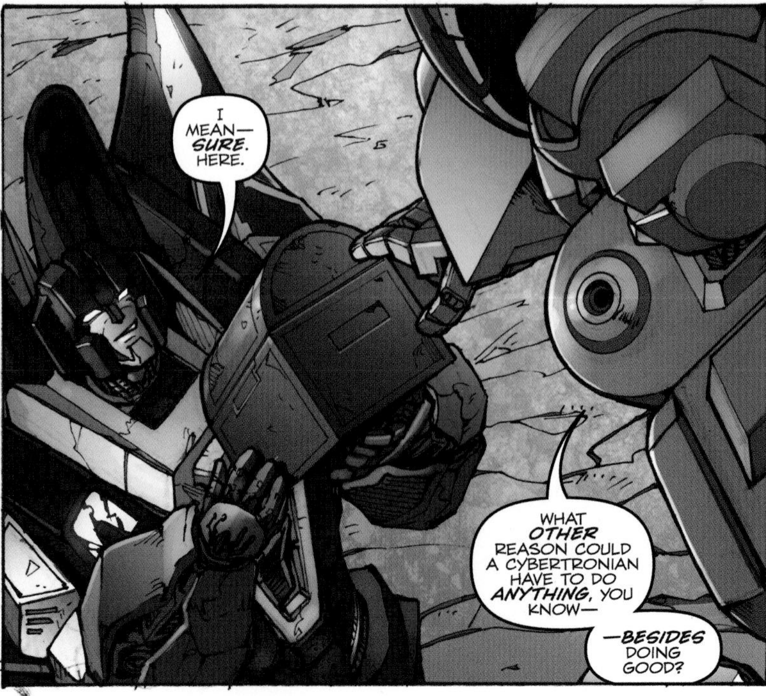
I MEAN—SURE. HERE.
WHAT OTHER REASON COULD A CYBERTRONIAN HAVE TO DO ANYTHING, YOU KNOW—
—BESIDES DOING GOOD?

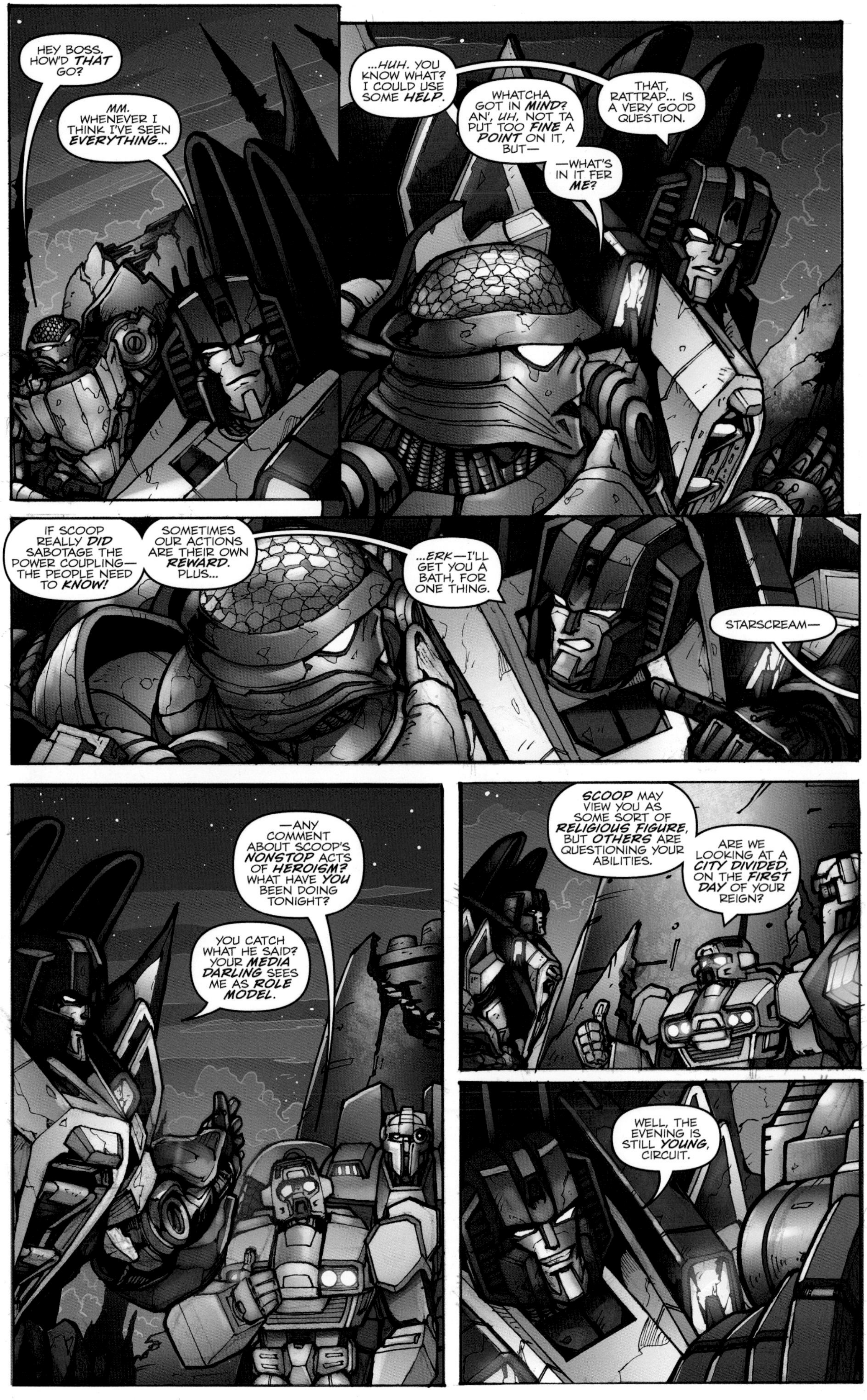

HEY BOSS. HOW'D *THAT* GO?
MM. WHENEVER I THINK I'VE SEEN *EVERYTHING...*
...*HUH.* YOU KNOW WHAT? I COULD USE SOME *HELP.*
WHATCHA GOT IN *MIND?* AN', *UH,* NOT TA PUT TOO *FINE* A *POINT* ON IT, BUT—
—WHAT'S IN IT FER *ME?*
THAT, RATTRAP... IS A VERY GOOD QUESTION.

IF SCOOP REALLY *DID* SABOTAGE THE POWER COUPLING—THE PEOPLE NEED TO *KNOW!*
SOMETIMES OUR ACTIONS ARE THEIR OWN *REWARD.* PLUS...
...*ERK*—I'LL GET YOU A BATH, FOR ONE THING.
STARSCREAM—

—ANY COMMENT ABOUT SCOOP'S *NONSTOP* ACTS OF *HEROISM?* WHAT HAVE *YOU* BEEN DOING TONIGHT?
YOU CATCH WHAT HE SAID? YOUR *MEDIA DARLING* SEES ME AS *ROLE MODEL.*

SCOOP MAY VIEW YOU AS SOME SORT OF *RELIGIOUS FIGURE,* BUT *OTHERS* ARE QUESTIONING YOUR ABILITIES.
ARE WE LOOKING AT A *CITY DIVIDED,* ON THE *FIRST DAY* OF YOUR REIGN?

WELL, THE EVENING IS STILL *YOUNG,* CIRCUIT.

"AND THE CROWD IS THRILLED, AS SCOOP CONTINUES THIS PHENOMENAL NIGHT BY RESTORING COMMUNICATION TO A GALACTIC COMMUNITY—"

—ONE THAT HAS, UNTIL NOW, HAD GOOD REASON TO SHUN US.
YES INDEED, CIRCUIT, TODAY—
WAIT, IT LOOKS LIKE THE HERO OF THE HOUR IS DESCENDING!

WELL, SCOOP— HOW DID IT GO?
IT WENT WELL, MY FRIENDS! COMMUNICATION IS RESTORED!

IF I COULD TAKE THIS CHANCE, TO SAY THAT WE—ALL OF US—
—SHOULD BELIEVE IN OUR LEADERS, AND THANK PRIMUS FOR EVERY CHANCE WE—

—HAVE.
OOPSEY.

MY WORD—
SHATTER

...PRIMUS. IT—IT—
—WHAT WAS THAT ALL ABOUT? AND...

—IT *IS* PHOSPHEX.
THERE WERE— MY *INVESTIGATION* INDICATED THERE WERE *PHOSPHEX* BURNS ON THE *POWER COUPLING* THAT SCOOP CALLED "DEFECTIVE."

YOU... YOU *ORCHESTRATED* THE BLACKOUT FOR YOUR OWN *BENEFIT?!*
I—I DON'T—
HOW—?

SCOOP.
YOU'VE LET US *ALL* DOWN. I BELIEVED IN *YOU*, JUST AS YOU BELIEVED IN *ME*.
BUT I SUPPOSE THE *LESSON* IS THAT NOT *EVERYONE* IS AS TRUSTWORTHY AS THOSE WHOM THE *TITANS* HAVE *VALIDATED*.

COULD SOMEONE TAKE HIM TO A *HOLDING CELL?*
IF THE OLD *AUTOBOT PRISON* ISN'T STILL *FUNCTIONING*... I'M SURE WE'LL FIND *SOMETHING.*
I—*NO!*

WE'LL *HOLD* HIM UNTIL WE CAN ORGANIZE A *TRIAL.* UNTIL THEN, NOT A *PAINT FLECK* WILL BE HARMED ON OUR LITTLE...
NO! THIS ISN'T *HAPPENING!*

...WHAT *WAS* IT YOU CALLED HIM, CIRCUIT? OH, *THAT'S* RIGHT—
—OUR LITTLE *HERO.*
I HAVE BEEN PRESENTED WITH A TREMENDOUS *RESPONSIBILITY*— LOOKING AFTER *EACH* AND EVERY *ONE* OF YOU.

AND I PROMISE YOU, *TONIGHT*— THIS *FIRST NIGHT* OF OUR *FUTURE*—
—I WILL *NOT* LET YOU DOWN.
OCKER! SCOOP INDICTED! STAR
INN

IT'S ABOUT TIME, RATTRAP...
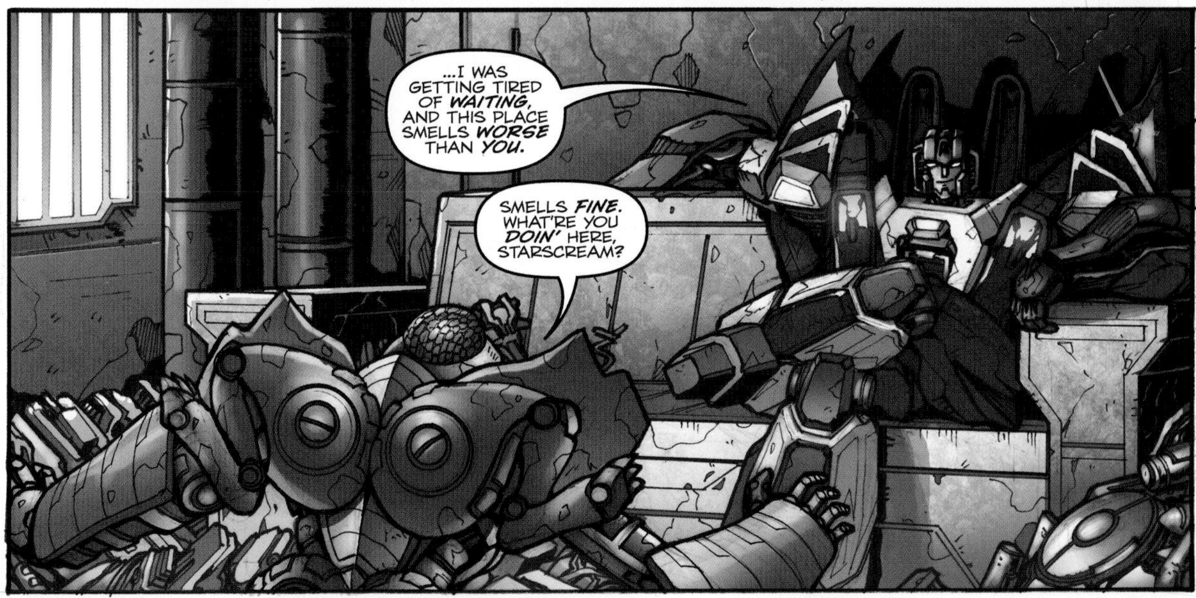
...I WAS GETTING TIRED OF WAITING, AND THIS PLACE SMELLS WORSE THAN YOU.
SMELLS FINE. WHAT'RE YOU DOIN' HERE, STARSCREAM?

I'M A LIAR.
YOU KNOW IT, I KNOW IT, SO THERE'S NO POINT IN DENYING IT.
BUT DO YOU UNDERSTAND THE SPECIAL GIFT BEING A LIAR HAS GRANTED ME?

I CAN TELL WHEN SOMEBODY'S TELLING THE TRUTH.
LIKE SCOOP.
HE REALLY WANTED TO DO GOOD.
SO I PUT TWO AND TWO TOGETHER...

...YOU PLANTED THE PHOSPHEX.
PHOSPHEX

YOU CAN'T—I WUZ—I WUZ JUST—
NO, NO—NO NEED TO EXPLAIN.

I GET IT. YOU'RE ME.
HUH?

YOU WEREN'T DESCRIBING SCOOP, BEFORE.
YOU WERE THE ONE STUCK ON SOME FORSAKEN BACKWATER PLANET WHILE PROWL AND BUMBLEBEE COZIED UP TO OPTIMUS PRIME.
I GET THAT FEELING. I UNDERSTAND IT, I KNOW HOW IT WORKS.

SCOOP... SCOOP JUST WANTED TO DO WHAT WAS RIGHT.
AND ALTRUISM IS UNPREDICTABLE.

SO. UH, WHAT'S ALL THIS MEAN TA ME?
HA. SEE? I TOLD YOU, THAT IS A GOOD QUESTION.

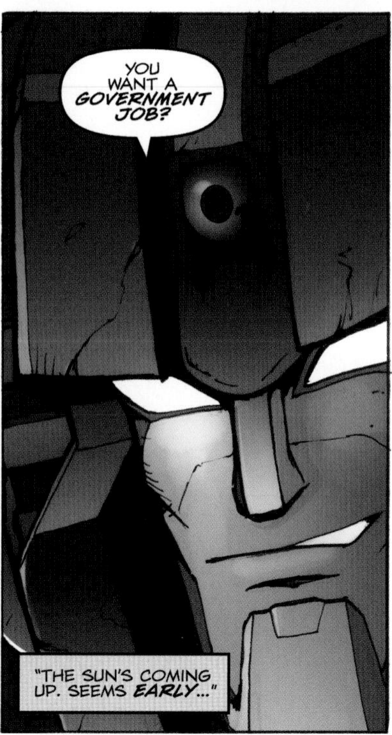
YOU WANT A GOVERNMENT JOB?
"THE SUN'S COMING UP. SEEMS EARLY..."

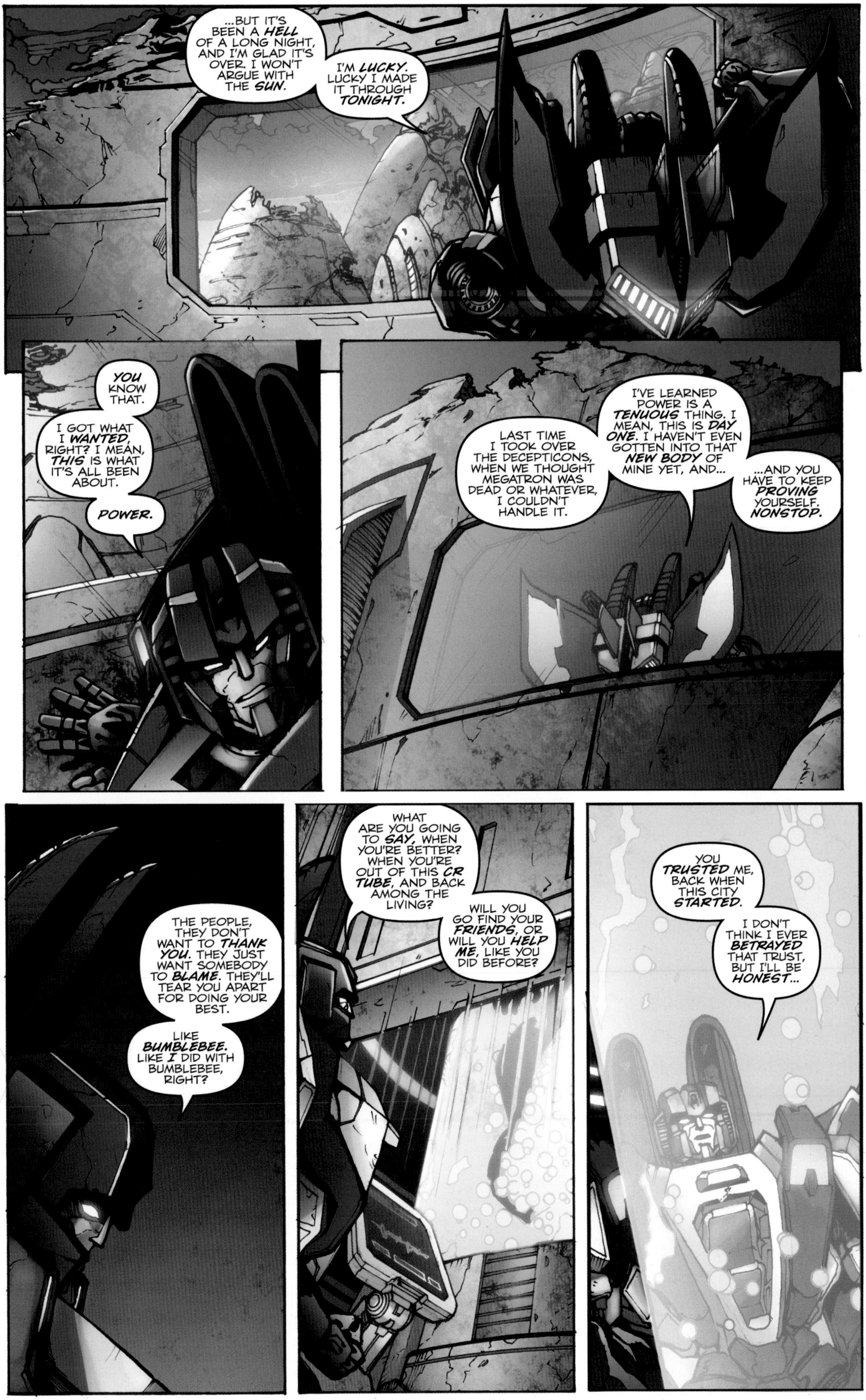

...BUT IT'S BEEN A ***HELL*** OF A LONG NIGHT, AND I'M GLAD IT'S OVER. I WON'T ARGUE WITH THE ***SUN***.

I'M ***LUCKY***. LUCKY I MADE IT THROUGH ***TONIGHT***.

YOU KNOW THAT.

I GOT WHAT I ***WANTED***, RIGHT? I MEAN, ***THIS*** IS WHAT IT'S ALL BEEN ABOUT.

POWER.

LAST TIME I TOOK OVER THE DECEPTICONS, WHEN WE THOUGHT MEGATRON WAS DEAD OR WHATEVER, I COULDN'T HANDLE IT.

I'VE LEARNED POWER IS A ***TENUOUS*** THING. I MEAN, THIS IS ***DAY ONE***. I HAVEN'T EVEN GOTTEN INTO THAT ***NEW BODY*** OF MINE YET, AND...

...AND YOU HAVE TO KEEP ***PROVING*** YOURSELF. ***NONSTOP***.

THE PEOPLE, THEY DON'T WANT TO THANK YOU. THEY JUST WANT SOMEBODY TO BLAME. THEY'LL TEAR YOU APART FOR DOING YOUR BEST.
LIKE BUMBLEBEE. LIKE I DID WITH BUMBLEBEE, RIGHT?

WHAT ARE YOU GOING TO SAY, WHEN YOU'RE BETTER? WHEN YOU'RE OUT OF THIS CR TUBE, AND BACK AMONG THE LIVING?
WILL YOU GO FIND YOUR FRIENDS, OR WILL YOU HELP ME, LIKE YOU DID BEFORE?

YOU TRUSTED ME, BACK WHEN THIS CITY STARTED.
I DON'T THINK I EVER BETRAYED THAT TRUST, BUT I'LL BE HONEST...

...SOMETIMES IT'S HARD TO KEEP TRACK OF THE TRUTH, WHEELJACK.
BUT KNOW THIS— I NEED YOU ON MY SIDE. CYBERTRON NEEDS GREAT MINDS.
AND HONEST SPARKS.
GET BETTER SOON...
...MY FRIEND.
THREE MONOLOGUES
3: EARLY DAWN

ROBOTS IN DISGUISE #20 COVER B

by **CASEY W. COLLER** Colors by **JOANA LAFUENTE**

MORE THAN MEETS THE EYE #17 COVER A

by **ALEX MILNE** Colors by **JOSH PEREZ**

THE LOST LIGHT.
THE BEGINNING OF THE END.

REMAIN IN LIGHT

CYCLONUS?

I'VE JUST HAD SOME STUPID NEWS.

THIS THE ONLY FOOTAGE?
OF THE MEDIBAY, YEAH.
JUST THE CCTV. WHERE WAS THE MEDIBOT, AMBULON?
WATCHING OVER SPOKE AND LOCKSTOCK.
IT'S... TAKEN RATHER A SHINE TO THEM.
PLAY IT AGAIN.

I'M SORRY, BUT I DON'T SEE HOW A COMATOSE ULTRA MAGNUS CAN SUDDENLY SIT BOLT UPRIGHT.
IT'S NOT SO MUCH THE COMA—PEOPLE COME OUT OF COMAS—IT'S THE SPEED.
NO ONE CAN SIT UP THAT FAST.

IF WE CUT TO THE CORRIDOR CAMS WE CAN SEE HIM MAKING HIS WAY TO SHUTTLE BAY 3.
CAN YOU ZOOM IN?
SOMETHING ABOUT HIS SHADOW DOESN'T QUITE—

NO, NO, CLOSER. CLOSE AS YOU CAN.
SOLES OF HIS BOOTS.
THANK YOU.
NOW, IS IT JUST ME, OR ARE HIS FEET NOT TOUCHING THE GROUND?

WAIT—I'VE GOT MAINFRAME IN MY EAR...
THEY'VE GOT SOMETHING.
MAGNUS?
THE SHUTTLE HE STOLE. THEY'VE GOT A TRACE.
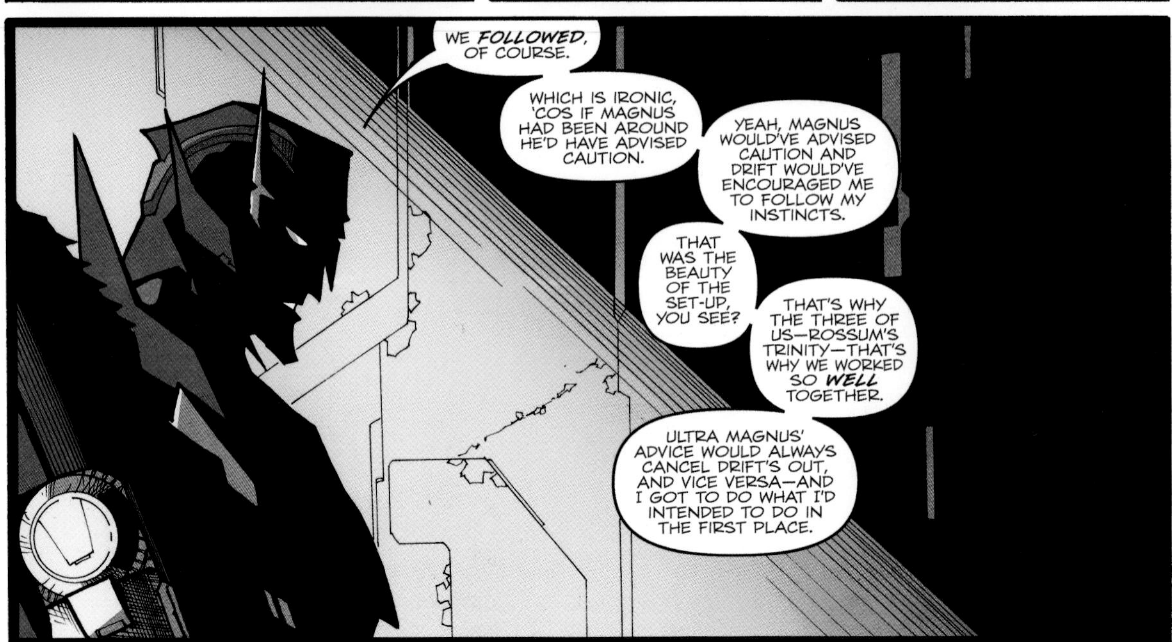
WE FOLLOWED, OF COURSE.
WHICH IS IRONIC, 'COS IF MAGNUS HAD BEEN AROUND HE'D HAVE ADVISED CAUTION.
YEAH, MAGNUS WOULD'VE ADVISED CAUTION AND DRIFT WOULD'VE ENCOURAGED ME TO FOLLOW MY INSTINCTS.
THAT WAS THE BEAUTY OF THE SET-UP, YOU SEE?
THAT'S WHY THE THREE OF US—ROSSUM'S TRINITY—THAT'S WHY WE WORKED SO WELL TOGETHER.
ULTRA MAGNUS' ADVICE WOULD ALWAYS CANCEL DRIFT'S OUT, AND VICE VERSA—AND I GOT TO DO WHAT I'D INTENDED TO DO IN THE FIRST PLACE.

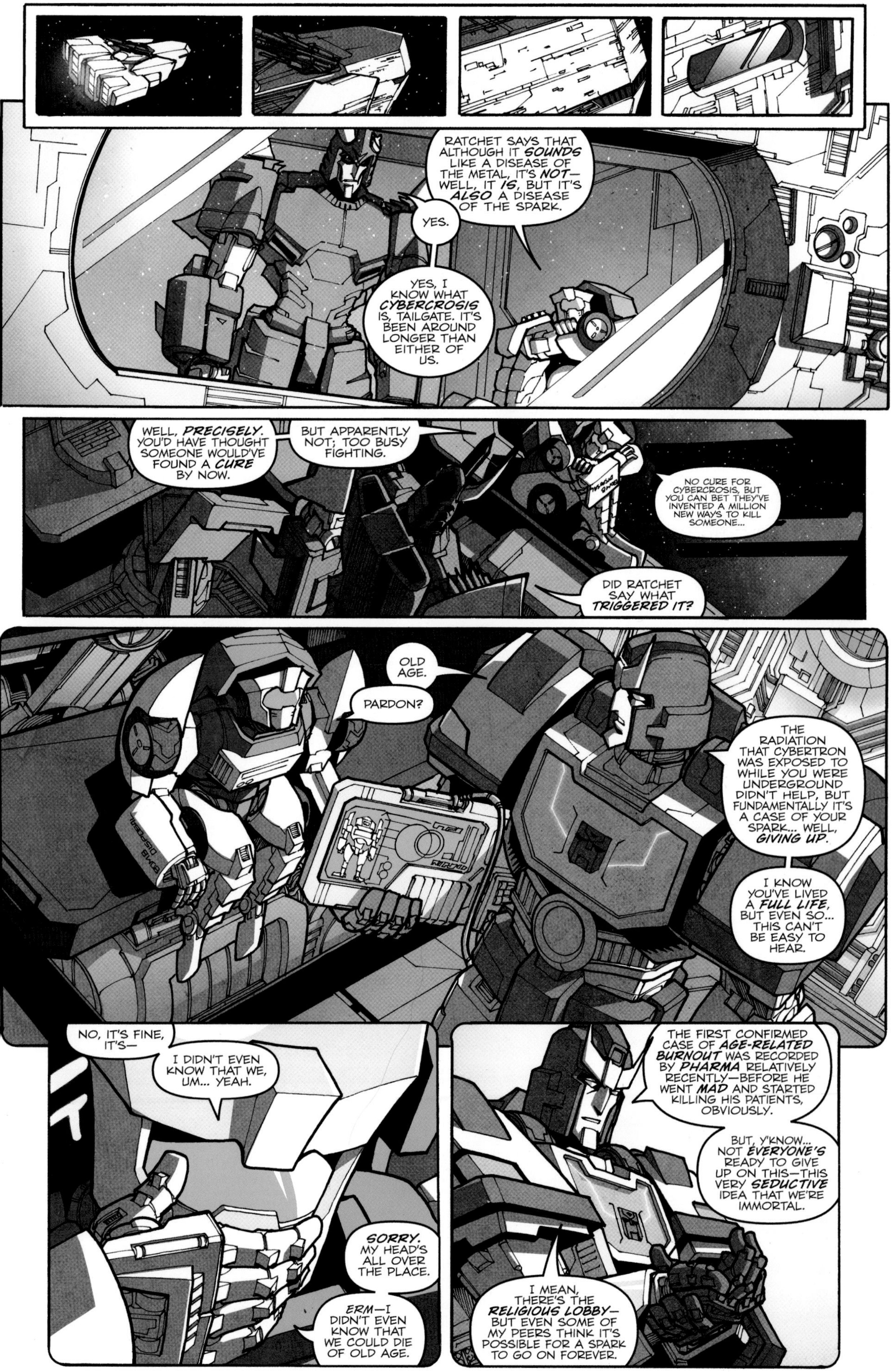

RATCHET SAYS THAT ALTHOUGH IT *SOUNDS* LIKE A DISEASE OF THE METAL, IT'S *NOT*— WELL, IT *IS*, BUT IT'S *ALSO* A DISEASE OF THE SPARK.

YES.

YES, I KNOW WHAT *CYBERCROSIS* IS, TAILGATE. IT'S BEEN AROUND LONGER THAN EITHER OF US.

WELL, *PRECISELY*. YOU'D HAVE THOUGHT SOMEONE WOULD'VE FOUND A *CURE* BY NOW.

BUT APPARENTLY NOT; TOO BUSY FIGHTING.

NO CURE FOR CYBERCROSIS, BUT YOU CAN BET THEY'VE INVENTED A MILLION NEW WAYS TO KILL SOMEONE...

DID RATCHET SAY WHAT *TRIGGERED IT?*

OLD AGE.

PARDON?

THE RADIATION THAT CYBERTRON WAS EXPOSED TO WHILE YOU WERE UNDERGROUND DIDN'T HELP, BUT FUNDAMENTALLY IT'S A CASE OF YOUR SPARK... WELL, *GIVING UP*.

I KNOW YOU'VE LIVED A *FULL LIFE*, BUT EVEN SO... THIS CAN'T BE EASY TO HEAR.

NO, IT'S FINE, IT'S—

I DIDN'T EVEN KNOW THAT WE, UM... YEAH.

SORRY. MY HEAD'S ALL OVER THE PLACE.

ERM—I DIDN'T EVEN KNOW THAT WE COULD DIE OF OLD AGE.

THE FIRST CONFIRMED CASE OF *AGE-RELATED BURNOUT* WAS RECORDED BY *PHARMA* RELATIVELY RECENTLY—BEFORE HE WENT *MAD* AND STARTED KILLING HIS PATIENTS, OBVIOUSLY.

BUT, Y'KNOW... NOT *EVERYONE'S* READY TO GIVE UP ON THIS—THIS VERY *SEDUCTIVE* IDEA THAT WE'RE IMMORTAL.

I MEAN, THERE'S THE *RELIGIOUS LOBBY*— BUT EVEN SOME OF MY PEERS THINK IT'S POSSIBLE FOR A SPARK TO GO ON FOREVER.

WHAT'S GONNA HAPPEN TO ME, DOC?
YOUR BODY'S GOING TO SHUT DOWN. INCREMENTALLY.
YOU'VE NOT LOST ANYTHING ESSENTIAL AT THIS STAGE, BUT YOUR FUEL PUMP'S ON THE WAY OUT, AND WE'LL PROBABLY FIND THAT YOUR INNERMOST ENERGON HAS CURDLED.
AND I'M SORRY, TAILGATE, BUT— YOU'VE PROBABLY CHANGED SHAPE FOR THE LAST TIME.
REALLY?
I'M AFRAID SO. YOUR TRANSFORMATION COG IS... YEAH.
I CAN'T EVEN REMEMBER THE LAST TIME I WAS IN VEHICLE MODE...! IT DIDN'T EVEN REGISTER!
AT SOME POINT OVER THE NEXT FEW DAYS YOUR LIMBS WILL FREEZE UP AND YOUR OPTICS WILL GIVE OUT.
YOU'LL LOSE THE ABILITY TO COMMUNICATE VIA THE HIGHER FREQUENCIES, AND IT'S POSSIBLE—NOT CERTAIN; POSSIBLE— THAT YOU'LL SUFFER MEMORY LOSS.
I'M GONNA GO BLIND? I'M GONNA BE PARALYZED?
AMNESIA?
I'M SORRY, DOC, THIS IS—THIS IS TOO MUCH!
TAILGATE—
HOW LONG BEFORE YOU DIE?
03:10:19:04
I, ER—
WOW. THAT'S PRETTY DIRECT.
UM. ABOUT THREE DAYS.
AND PLEASE—THIS IS BETWEEN YOU AND ME, OKAY?
BOMB DISPOSAL

OH, CYCLONUS. WHAT AM I GONNA DO?
...
MAKE PEACE WITH THE WORLD AROUND YOU—AND THEN FACE DEATH HEAD-ON.
YOU'RE LEAVING?
AS OPPOSED TO...?
...
FINE. YOU GO.
BOMB DISPOSAL
"YOU GO AND DO WHATEVER IT IS YOU SUDDENLY FEEL THE NEED TO DO."

SO YEAH, WE FOLLOWED THE SHUTTLE'S FLIGHT SIGNATURE. WE GAVE CHASE.
IF YOU KNEW ME, THAT WOULDN'T SURPRISE YOU.
WHAT DID YOU TELL THE CREW?
WHAT DID I TELL THE CREW ABOUT WHAT?
WEREN'T YOU DEVIATING FROM YOUR QUEST?
I DON'T THINK I TOLD THEM ANYTHING.
ANYWAY, IT'S IRRELEVANT. ONCE WE SAW WHERE THE SHUTTLE HAD GONE, EVERYONE KNEW SOMETHING WAS UP...
NOW THAT IS WHAT I CALL A PORTAL!
"SWERVE'S."
SERIOUSLY, CHECK IT OUT! THAT—THAT'S JUST—HOW CAN YOU NOT GO INTO THAT?
OH, MAN, THIS QUEST IS TICKING ALL THE BOXES!
YOU KNOW WHAT'S ROUND THE CORNER, DON'T YOU?
OBSTACLES. CHALLENGES. THINGS TO OVERCOME.
YOU'RE NOT EVEN LOOKING...

THE OBSERVATION DECK.
IS ANYONE ELSE GETTING A SENSE OF DÈJÀ VU?
IMPRESSIVE, ISN'T IT?
CONVENTION DICTATES THAT I PUT THIS TO THE VOTE, BUT, TRUTH BE TOLD, I'VE ALREADY DECIDED THAT WE'RE GOING THROUGH THAT THING, AND TO PRETEND OTHERWISE WOULD BE DISHONEST.
SO I GUESS YOU'VE GOT A CHOICE: STAY ON BOARD AND SHARE THE ADVENTURE, OR... DON'T AND DON'T.
ANYONE WANT OUT? NO? IN THAT CASE, HOLD ON...
"...BECAUSE THIS IS WHERE THINGS GET INTERESTING."

RESULT.

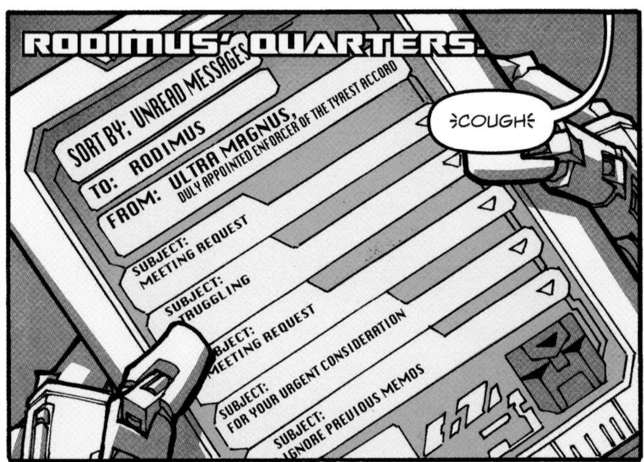
RODIMUS' QUARTERS.
UNREAD MESSAGES
SORT BY: UNREAD MESSAGES
TO: RODIMUS
FROM: ULTRA MAGNUS, DULY APPOINTED ENFORCER OF THE TYREST ACCORD
SUBJECT: MEETING REQUEST
SUBJECT: STRUGGLING
SUBJECT: MEETING REQUEST
SUBJECT: FOR YOUR URGENT CONSIDERATION
SUBJECT: IGNORE PREVIOUS MEMOS
COUGH

WELL?
IS IT LUNA 1?
EVERYTHING WOULD SUGGEST YES.
I KNEW IT.

LUNA 1, PERCEPTOR! THE MIRACLE MOON!
EVERYTHING YOU COULD EVER WANT TO FIND, ALL IN ONE PLACE!
I'M WELL AWARE OF ITS POSITION IN THE POPULAR CONSCIOUSNESS.
THE ANSWER TO EVERYTHING, EVER. AREN'T YOU EXCITED?

VERY.

LONG-RANGE VISUAL.
IT LOOKS DESERTED.
NO OBVIOUS SETTLEMENTS. NO LIGHTS. COURSE, THERE'S ALWAYS UNDERGROUND.
ACTUALLY, SCANS SUGGEST THAT IT'S LARGELY SOLID—MUCH LIKE LUNA 2.

HAVE YOU SCANNED FOR LIFE SIGNS?
I'M RE-SCANNING, YES.
RIGHT. YOU WEREN'T HAPPY WITH THE RESULTS OF THE FIRST SCAN?
NOT PARTICULARLY, NO.

OKAY. SO... HOW ABOUT YOU GIVE THEM TO ME ANYWAY, AND I'LL DECIDE IF I'M HAPPY WITH THEM OR NOT.
WELL, ACCORDING TO WHAT IS ALMOST CERTAINLY A FLAWED FIRST READING...
YES?

LUNA 1 IS HOME TO A BILLION PEOPLE.

RUNG'S OFFICE.
I'M THRILLED, BUT—WHY ME?
AT THE RISK OF INFLATING YOUR EGO—NOT THAT YOU HAVE ONE—I'D VALUE YOUR COMPANY.
IT'S NOT JUST YOU AND ME—THAT WOULD BE WEIRD—BUT YES: I'D LIKE YOU TO COME WITH ME TO LUNA 1.

I WAS AFRAID WE'D FALLEN OUT.
WHAT, YESTERDAY? I'LL BE HONEST: WHAT YOU SAID ABOUT OVERLORD—I DIDN'T WANT TO HEAR IT.
BUT WITH MAGNUS GONE I THINK I NEED SOMEONE TO TELL ME THINGS I DON'T WANT TO HEAR.
WHO ELSE IS COMING?

BRAINSTORM'S WORKSHOP.
SHUTTLE BAY 1.
FIFTEEN MINUTES. DON'T BE LATE.
ALREADY PACKED.

THE SHOOTING RANGE.
YEAH, I HEARD YOU WERE PUTTING TOGETHER A TEAM: RATCHET THE DOCTOR, PERCEPTOR THE SCIENTIST, CHROMEDOME THE... ACTUALLY, I FIGURED THAT WAS KIND OF A SYMPATHY THING.
SO WHAT AM I, THE TOKEN EMPURATA VICTIM?
BIT OF POSITIVE DISCRIMINATION?
I JUST NEED SOMEONE WHO CAN THROW A PUNCH.

HAB SUITE 208.
YOU'LL HAVE TO MAKE IT QUICK, SKIDS.
I'M OFF IN A MINUTE.
SO I HEAR! LUNA 1, EH?
ALL THINGS TO ALL 'BOTS.
"EVERY PROBLEM SOLVED, EVERY QUESTION ANSWERED, EVERY WISH GRANTED."
LET ME GUESS...

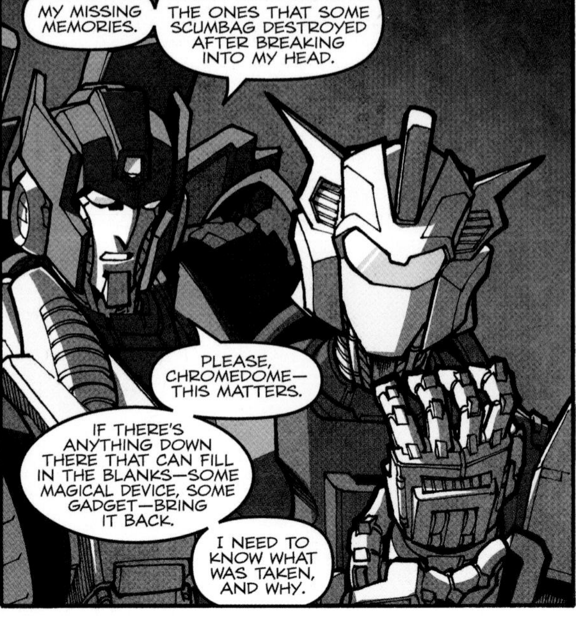
MY MISSING MEMORIES.
THE ONES THAT SOME SCUMBAG DESTROYED AFTER BREAKING INTO MY HEAD.
PLEASE, CHROMEDOME—THIS MATTERS.
IF THERE'S ANYTHING DOWN THERE THAT CAN FILL IN THE BLANKS—SOME MAGICAL DEVICE, SOME GADGET—BRING IT BACK.
I NEED TO KNOW WHAT WAS TAKEN, AND WHY.

HAB SUITE 14.
CHROMEDOME, RATCHET, RUNG, AND WHIRL HAVE ALL SAID YES; SO HAVE BRAINSTORM AND PERCEPTOR.
YOU'RE THE LAST PERSON ON MY LIST.
WHY ME?
BECAUSE LUNA 1 IS PART OF THE CREATION STORY, AND YOU KNOW ABOUT THOSE THINGS.
DRIFT WOULD'VE COME, BUT HE'S GONE AND...
...AND HE'S GONE.

SO— WILL YOU COME?
YES...
ON ONE CONDITION.

SHUTTLE BAY 1.
SORRY, SWERVE, LIMITED NUMBERS.
ONCE I KNOW IT'S SAFE, WE CAN ALL GO DOWN.
BUT IT'S LUNA 1!
THE SEETHING MOON!
I SPENT YEARS SEARCHING FOR IT—WE BOTH DID!
AND ANYWAY— YOU NEED ME!
HOW'S THAT?

I HAVE SKILLS! I'M A METALLURGIST!
FOR THE LAST SEVERAL MONTHS YOU'VE BEEN A BARTENDER.
BUT—
NO.
NO, YOU DON'T GET TO PLAY THAT CARD THIS LATE IN THE GAME.

I KNOW IT'S NOT THE KNIGHTS, BUT I WISH BUMBLEBEE WERE HERE TO SEE THIS.
BUMBLEBEE, PROWL... EVERYONE WHO'S EVER ACCUSED ME OF RUNNING AWAY.
NO ONE'S EVER ACCUSED YOU OF THAT.
NOT TO MY FACE.

EVERYONE BACK HOME THOUGHT THIS QUEST WAS A JOKE, DIDN'T THEY?
BUT REWIND'S NOT LAUGHING; NOR POLARIS; NOR ANIMUS; NOR SHOCK.
PEOPLE HAVE DIED, RATCHET...

"PEOPLE HAVE DIED."
YOU'RE NOT GETTING A SPEECH.
NOT TODAY.
LIFE'S TOO SHORT.
I JUST WANT TO KNOW WHAT HAPPENED TO MAGNUS.
ANYTHING ELSE IS A ***BONUS***.
CYCLONUS..?

CYCLONUS, I'VE BEEN THINKING, AND—
NO.
WHAT?
YOU'RE VISITING LUNA 1 FOR THE ***EXPERIENCE***, NOTHING ELSE. THIS CAN'T BE ABOUT FINDING A ***CURE***.

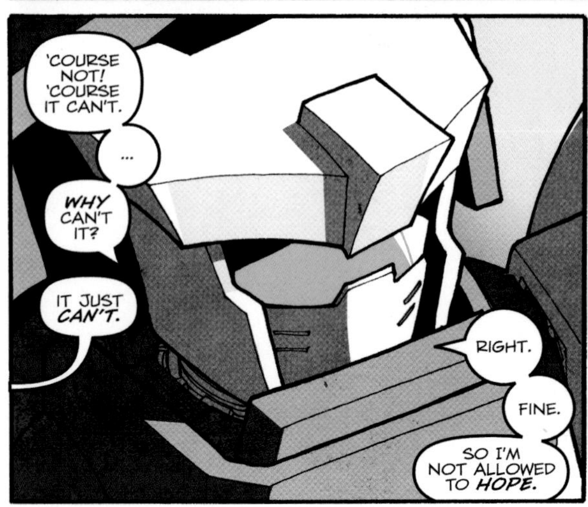
'COURSE NOT! 'COURSE IT CAN'T.
...
WHY CAN'T IT?
IT JUST ***CAN'T***.
RIGHT.
FINE.
SO I'M NOT ALLOWED TO ***HOPE***.

LISTEN TO ME. ***NEVER. HOPE.*** HOPE IS A ***LIE***.

OKAY, SO ACCORDING TO THE SCANNER, MAGNUS' SHUTTLE IS SOMEWHERE NEARBY.
TIME TO BREAK OUT THE M.A.A.B.S AND PLAY "HUNT THE CREWMEMBER."
WAIT— M.A.R.B.S OR M.A.A.B.S?
"M.A.A.B.S OR M.A.A.B.S?" WHAT?
MOBILE AUTOBOT REPAIR BAY, OR MOBILE ANTI-ASSAULT BATTLE-SUIT?
THE ONES THAT TURN INTO— THE COOL ONES. THE BATTLESUITS.
RIGHT.
WE DON'T HAVE ANY OF THOSE.
THEN WHY ASK IF—?
FINE.
IN THAT CASE...
TALK ABOUT BARREN. JUST A MOUNTAIN RANGE AND A LOT OF... FLATNESS.
YOU KNOW WE COULD JUST DRIVE.
SOMETIMES I WONDER WHY WE EVEN HAVE ALT MODES...
CAN YOU HEAR US OKAY, MAX?

LIKE WE WERE SHARING A CIRCUIT SLAB.
ANY SIGN OF THE SHUTTLE?
YES, ACTUALLY. JUST APPROACHING IT NOW.
NO SIGN OF MAGNUS. COCKPIT'S BEEN SMASHED.
FROM THE *INSIDE OUT*, OR—
OUTSIDE IN.
DAMN.
LET'S HAVE A CLOSER LOOK.
VOOM

THE WHOLE MOON JUST LIT UP!
WHAT DID YOU DO?
I DON'T KNOW—
—BUT I THINK WE JUST FOUND OUR LIFE SIGNS.
SPARKS?
YUP.
A BILLION UNBORN CYBERTRONIANS.
YOU SAID THIS PLACE WAS BARREN, TAILGATE; YOU WERE WRONG. IT'S THE OPPOSITE.
IT'S TEEMING WITH LIFE. SEETHING.
WE'RE STANDING ON A GIANT HOT SPOT.
IT'S A HOT SPOT.
A RE-IGNITED HOT SPOT.

BUT WHY NOW? WHY WASN'T IT ACTIVE WHEN WE ARRIVED?
IT'S OBVIOUS. ISN'T IT OBVIOUS?
IT'S NOT OBVIOUS.
YOU DID IT.
THE WHOLE MOON WAS FERTILIZED THE MOMENT YOU STEPPED OFF YOUR M.A.R.B.
SERIOUSLY, YOUR FEET TOUCHED THE GROUND AND—
VOMF!
YOU FEEL OKAY?
I DON'T KNOW. YES.
YOU REALLY THINK I DID THIS? I MEAN, I S'POSE I AM CARRYING THE MATRIX.
WELL, HALF A MATRIX. WELL, HALF AN EMPTY MATRIX.
MAYBE THERE'S A CONNECTION.
I'VE NEVER SEEN A HOT SPOT BEFORE.
NOR ME. NOT UP CLOSE. NOT AN ACTIVE ONE.
BY THE TIME I CAME ONLINE MOST OF THEM HAD COOLED.
YOU WERE CONSTRUCTED COLD?
I WAS, YES.

YOU LOT ARE ALWAYS TALKING ABOUT "CONSTRUCTED COLD."
I THINK THE TERMINOLOGY CHANGED OVER THE YEARS. CONSTRUCTED COLD MEANS YOU WERE BUILT FROM SCRATCH AND GIVEN LIFE USING A SAMPLE TAKEN FROM SOMEONE ELSE'S SPARK.
OH, SPARK SPLICING. YEP, KNOW ABOUT THAT.
ONE OF NOVA'S BIG IDEAS.

WERE YOU CONSTRUCTED COLD?
DON'T WORRY, IT'S NOT A TRICK QUESTION.
I WAS ANTI-APARTHEID. WENT ON THE MARCHES AND EVERYTHING: "EQUAL RIGHTS FOR KNOCK-OFFS!"
EH?
IGNORE HIM— HE THINKS IT'S FOUR MILLION YEARS AGO AND HE'S BEING PROGRESSIVE. SUFFICE TO SAY THAT AFTER NOVA LEFT, CERTAIN CITY-STATES "PROVED" THAT PEOPLE LIKE ME WERE... SUBSTANDARD.

I WAS FORGED— BORN UNDER THE STARS IN A FIELD LIKE THIS ONE.
SOWN AND HARVESTED. NURTURED.
PERFECTED.

RODIMUS?
YOU NEED TO SEE THIS.

WE'VE LOST VISUAL.
RODIMUS?
RODIMUS, DO YOU COPY?
ZZZZZZK
THE TRANSMISSION'S BEING BLOCKED. I CAN'T REACH THEM.
THIS IS DELIBERATE. THEY'RE BEING ISOLATED.
THEM? OR US?

THE OIL RESERVOIR.

FZZZZT

NINETEEN EIGHTY-FOUR.

I'M TELLING YOU, IT'S A POINT ONE PERCENTER.
CAN WE PLEASE NOT JUMP TO CONCLUSIONS.
LOOK AT THE COLOR!
IT'S A SUPERSPARK! WE COULD BE LOOKING AT THE NEXT OPTIMUS PRIME OR ULTRA MAGNUS!
OKAY, YES, MAYBE THE NEXT SCORPONOK OR SHOCKWAVE, BUT...
WHAT ARE YOU—
HARVESTING IT.
NO, BECAUSE HARVESTING TAKES SKILL. AND PATIENCE. AND TIME.
YOU CAN'T JUST—YOU CAN'T JUST DO PRECISELY WHAT YOU'RE DOING NOW...!
I DON'T HEAR RODIMUS TELLING ME TO STOP.
HAVEN'T YOU GOT TO REMOVE A REALLY SPECIFIC AMOUNT OF THE—WHAT'S THE SCIENTIFIC NAME? THE SENTIO METALLICO?
THE STUFF AROUND THE SPARK. I'M SURE THERE'S AN EQUATION...
RODIMUS, PLEASE TELL ME YOU'RE NOT GOING TO LET HIM REMOVE—
WHERE ARE YOU GONNA PUT IT, BRAINSTORM? IN YOUR BRIEFCASE?
I WASN'T, BUT IF I DID...
OH MAN.
YOU'VE JUST BLOWN MY MIND.
THIS IS WRONG.
THE GROUND HASN'T EVEN BEEN CONSECRATED.
THIS DOES MAKE ME A LITTLE UNCOMFORTABLE, RODIMUS.
NOT ONLY ARE WE TECHNICALLY STEALING, BUT WE'RE STEALING LIFE. RAW LIFE.
STEALING FROM WHOM? AND IN ANY CASE, IT'S NOT STEALING, IT'S SAVING: IT WASN'T VIABLE 'TIL I TURNED UP.
SO WHAT ABOUT ALL THE OTHER SPARKS?
ARE YOU GOING TO "SAVE" THEM ALL, OR JUST THE GREEN—
CHOOM!

TRESPASSERS!
WE DIDN'T EXPECT—
THIS SOUNDS STUPID, BECAUSE IT'S BEEN FOUR MILLION YEARS AND—WAR OR NO WAR—WE SHOULD ALWAYS EXPECT IT; BUT WE DIDN'T EXPECT THE DECEPTICONS TO SHOW UP.
I'M LIKE: LUNA 1, HOT SPOTS AND THE DECEPTICONS?
IN ONE NIGHT?!
AND THIS WAS BEFORE WE'D FOUND THE DEAD BODIES AND...
ACTUALLY, I'M SO SORRY. I'VE JUST REALIZED—
WE COULD BE SPENDING THE REST OF OUR LIVES TOGETHER I HAVEN'T EVEN ASKED YOUR NAME.
CALL ME AMBUS.

ALRIGHT, THEN!
LET'S DO THIS!
COME ON!
SHOW YOUR FACE!
NINE-TEEN EIGHTY-FOUR.
NINE-TEEN EIGHTY-FOUR.
NINE-TEEN EIGHTY-FOUR.
NINE-TEEN EIGHTY-FOUR.

"SWERVE'S."
FZZZZT

THAT YOU, TRAILBREAKER?
SORRY, PAL— WE'RE CLOSING. FOR GOOD.
SEVENTEEN TWENTY-ONE.
I *SAID* WE'RE—
AH.

SEVENTEEN TWENTY-ONE.

SEVENTEEN TWENTY-ONE.
SEVENTEEN TWENTY-ONE.
SEVENTEEN TWENTY-ONE.
SEVENTEEN TWENTY-ONE.
SEVENTEEN TWENTY-ONE.

SEVENTEEN TWENTY-ONE.
SEVENTEEN TWENTY-ONE.
SEVENTEEN TWENTY-ONE
SEVENTEEN TWENTY-ONE.
SEVENTEEN TWENTY-ONE.
SEVENTEEN TWENTY-ONE.
SEVENTEEN TWENTY-ONE.
SEVENTEEN TWENTY-ONE.
SEVENTEEN TWENTY-ONE.
SEVENTEEN TWENTY-ONE.
SEVENTEEN TWENTY-ONE.
SEVENTEEN TWENTY-ONE.
SEVENTEEN TWENTY-ONE.
NINETEEN EIGHTY-FOUR.
SEVENTEEN TWENTY-ONE.
SEVENTEEN TWENTY-ONE.

DON'T ENGAGE! THERE'S TOO MANY OF THEM!
HEAD FOR THE MOUNTAINS AND FIND SOMEWHERE TO HIDE!
ARGH!
CH-KOOM
THAT WAS A NASTY FALL, RATCHET.
PHARMA?
NEED A HAND?
1 of 5: THE FECUND MOON

MORE THAN MEETS THE EYE #17 COVER B

by **SEAN CHEN** Colors by **TOM CHU**

MORE THAN MEETS THE EYE #18 COVER A

by **ALEX MILNE** Colors by **JOSH PEREZ**

THE LOST LIGHT.
HEY— CAN'T YOU *READ?*
NO GUNS
NO SWORDS
NO BRIEFCASES
AND DON'T SAY, "*I'VE GOT NO EYES IN THE CONVENTIONAL SENSE.*"
EVERYONE SAYS THAT.
SEVENTEEN TWENTY-ONE.
OKAY, NOT EVERYONE SAYS *THAT*.
BRAKATATATATATATATATA
HEY!
HEY!

BRAKATATATATATA
I MET AN ASSOCIATE OF YOURS LAST YEAR— HE WAS CHASING MY BEST FRIEND.*
YEAH, I NEVER FORGET AN UGLY FACE, ESPECIALLY WHEN—
OKAY, SO YOU'RE JUST GONNA KEEP ON FIRING.
FINE.
CONSIDER THAT ESTABLISHED.
*SKIDS, IN ISSUE #2
BRAKATATATATATA
AND I'VE ONLY JUST HAD THIS PLACE REDECORATED.
WHIRL WENT ON A THREE-DAY COCKTAIL BINGE—OVERDOSED ON BERZERKER BUTTONS AND FLIPPED OUT WHEN SOMEONE ASKED HIM THE TIME.
KER-CHUNK
I HAD BRAINSTORM INSTALL SOME SECURITY, AND YOU KNOW WHAT?
K-CHUK
K-CHUK
K-CHUK
HE DID A BANG-UP JOB.
CHOOM CHOOM CHOOM

to: SWERVE from: BRAINSTORM

NOW, I DIDN'T SAY IT TO *FORT MAX*—

AND I DIDN'T SAY IT TO *WHIRL*—

AND I DIDN'T EVEN SAY IT TO *CYCLONUS* WHEN HE HAD HIS *DEAD UNIVERSE FLASHBACK.*

MY FIRST BLASTER™

BIG GRIP FOR LITTLE HANDS

BUT YOU, MY FRIEND—

—TO YOU I SAY:

MY FIRST BLASTER

CH-CHUK

GET THE HELL OUT OF MY BAR.

MY FIRST BLASTER
HOORAY! YOU SCORED A DIRECT HIT!

REMAIN IN LIGHT 2 of 5: HOUSE OF AMBUS

FORTRESS MAXIMUS AND BLASTER.
REPEAT, THE LOST LIGHT IS UNDER ATTACK.
OUR DEFENSES HAVE BEEN BREACHED BY UNKNOWN AGGRESSORS.

FIRST AID AND AMBULON.
"EVERYONE BE ON YOUR GUARD...

HOUND, GEARS, AND HUFFER.
"...WE DON'T KNOW HOW MANY HAVE TELEPORTED ON BOARD, BUT IT'S POSSIBLE—

SMOKESCREEN AND INFERNO.
"—IN FACT IT'S VERY POSSIBLE—

TRAILCUTTER, DIPSTICK, AND HOIST.
"—THAT WE'VE BEEN OVERRUN."

SKIDS.
I DON'T KNOW WHAT I DID TO MAKE YOU LOT SO INTERESTED IN ME, BUT I CAN SPOT A CONNECTION A MILE AWAY.
THE LAST TIME I DANCED THIS DANCE SOME PIECE OF SCUM HAD JUST DESTROYED MY MEMORIES.*
I WOKE UP WITH A BLOWTORCH IN MY HAND AND NOTHING IN MY HEAD, AND YOUR FRIENDS WERE ALL OVER ME.
SO YOU'LL FORGIVE ME IF I PUT TWO AND TWO TOGETHER—
*ISSUE #2
—AND MAKE FIST!
THWOK
OKAY, THAT DIDN'T REALLY WORK, DID IT, THE WHOLE "TWO AND TWO" THING.
IT SHOULD BE "FOUR"—YOU'RE EXPECTING ME TO SAY "FOUR," BUT I SAID...
'COS IT COINCIDED WITH ME PUNCHING YOU, YEAH?
FORGET IT.
THUD
LOOK, BEFORE THIS GETS INFAMOUS, YOU SHOULD KNOW THAT I'M WHAT THEY USED TO CALL AN OUTLIER.
IN MY CASE, THAT MEANS I'M A VERY FAST LEARNER.
I LEARN ALL THE TIME. I LEARN INDISCRIMINATELY. I LEARN FASTER THAN YOU CAN TEACH—AND YOU'RE TEACHING ME RIGHT NOW.
THE WAY YOU FIGHT TELLS ME HOW TO FIGHT BACK.
EVERY TIME YOU CHOOSE FIST OVER SWORD, EVERY TIME YOU LEAD WITH ONE SHOULDER AND NOT THE OTHER... EVERY TIME YOU EXERCISE DISCRETION, YOU BECOME MORE PREDICTABLE.
EVEN MORE OF YOU?
OKAY, I DIDN'T SEE THAT COMING.

LUNA 1.
RATCHET.
LOCKDOWN? IT'S PHARMA.
HM? YES, YES, "MAD DOCTOR PHARMA."
VERY CLEVER.
VERY WITTY.
LISTEN—I'VE JUST PICKED UP MY PRESENT AND THE EXCITEMENT'S GOT THE BETTER OF ME: I'M GONNA TAKE HIM HOME AND OPEN HIM.
I'LL TELL OUR LORD AND MASTER THAT YOU'RE STILL PLAYING CHASE WITH THE OTHERS—DON'T STAY OUT TOO LATE!
PHARMA, WE REALLY MUST SIT DOWN SOME TIME SO I CAN EXPLAIN WHY WE ALL HATE YOU.
WE'LL START WITH YOUR PERSONALITY AND GO FROM THERE.
WHIRL AND CYCLONUS.
SO THIS IS WHAT RUNNING AWAY FEELS LIKE?
I'M NOT KEEN.
IT'S LIKE—IT'S LIKE FIGHTING IN THE WRONG DIRECTION.
RODIMUS TOLD US NOT TO ENGAGE.
HE DID, YES, HE ABSOLUTELY DID.
AND I'M GOING TO INTERPRET THAT AS A VEILED ORDER TO ATTACK.
CARE TO JOIN ME?
I SAID, RATCHET ISN'T BEHIND US!
MAYBE NOT, BUT FIFTY ANGRY DECEPTICONS ARE, AND WE CAN'T RESCUE RATCHET IF WE'RE DEAD.
WE HIDE, WE TAKE STOCK, WE RE-ESTALBISH CONTACT WITH THE LOST LIGHT, AND THEN WE LAUNCH AN EPIC COUNTER-ATTACK.
RODIMUS AND TAILGATE (AND THE REST).
IT'S CALLED A PLAN. AND THE SECRET OF A GOOD PLAN IS TO KEEP ONE STEP—

—AHEAD.
I TAKE IT YOU'VE HEARD OF THE TITANS—MASSIVE, SUPERPOWERED CYBERTRONIANS WHO ONCE CARTED THE KNIGHTS OF CYBERTRON AROUND THE GALAXY.
I'M... FAMILIAR WITH THE STORIES.
RIGHT. SO ON THE OTHER SIDE OF THE MOUNTAIN WAS—IT WAS ESSENTIALLY A TITAN GRAVEYARD.
A HUNDRED DEAD BODIES, SHOT TO BITS. RUSTING IN THE SUN.
WE'D BEEN AMBUSHED BY THE DECEPTICONS, THE HOT SPOT HAD COOLED—I WASN'T, Y'KNOW, STANDING ON IT ANYMORE—AND WE'D FLOWN INTO THIS—INTO THIS NECROPOLIS.
SO WHAT DID YOU DO?
WHAT DID I DO?
WELL, AMBUS, DEPENDING ON YOUR RELIGIOUS BENT, WHAT I DID WAS EITHER SENSIBLE...

"...OR SACRILEGIOUS."
WE'RE GONNA FLY INSIDE THEM?!
THEY'RE MASSIVE AND THEY'RE COMPLICATED AND THERE'S NO WAY WE'LL BE FOLLOWED.
JUST NEED TO FIND A WAY IN. CRATER OR SOMETHING.
WE'RE GONNA FLY INSIDE THE CORPSES OF OUR ANCESTORS?!
TAILGATE, YOU REALIZE THAT WHENEVER YOU TRY TO SOUND AWESTRUCK YOU ACTUALLY SOUND CRITICAL AND INCREDULOUS.

THEY'RE GAINING!
YEAH? LET'S SEE HOW THEY LIKE—
—THIS!
THEY— THEY SEEM TO LIKE IT.
IN THAT THEY'RE STILL CHASING US.
AND NOW THERE'S A DEAD END UP AHEAD.
GREAT.
PUT YOUR ARMS AROUND MY NECK AND HOLD ON TIGHT.
BOMB DISPOSAL

!!!

KAVROOM

02:09:48:57

IF I STILL KEPT A JOURNAL OF ALL MY MOVES—

—*THAT* WOULD BE ON THE FRONT COVER.
EXCELLENT, EXCELLENT EFFORT.

IT'S JUST A SHAME NONE OF YOUR FRIENDS ARE AS MUCH OF A SHOW-OFF AS YOU ARE.

YEAH, WELL, NONE OF MY FRIENDS HAVE FLAMES ON THEIR CHEST.

IT'S A LOT TO LIVE UP TO.

THE CELL.

AND THEN THEY BROUGHT YOU STRAIGHT HERE?

YES.

...AND NO.

SEEING AS HOW EVERYONE ELSE IS TOO COOL TO ASK, *I* WILL—
—WHERE ARE YOU TAKING US?
IS THIS WHERE WE MEET YOUR CRAZY BOSS?
WHAT MAKES YOU THINK I HAVE A "BOSS"?
GIVE US *SOME* CREDIT, LOCKDOWN. LUNA 1 AS YOUR OWN PERSONAL MOONBASE?
A THOUSAND ACRES OF DEAD TITANS?
HOLOMATTER INHIBITORS AND *MODE LOCKS* AND COPYCAT GUARDIAN DROIDS?
THERE'S NO *WAY* YOU CAN PUNCH *THIS* FAR ABOVE YOUR WEIGHT.

WHAT THE—
MAGNUS!
MAGNUS, OVER HERE!
HEY!
DID ANYONE ELSE—?
IT WAS ULTRA MAGNUS!
HE IGNORED ME...!
I'LL ADD IT TO THE LIST OF THINGS THAT MAKE NO SENSE.
DON'T WORRY, DEFENDANT...
...I PROMISE TO MAKE SENSE OF EVERYTHING.
TYREST?!

CHIEF JUSTICE TYREST.
YOU WANT TO AVOID A SLAP? HERE'S HOW—
YOU TELL YOUR PET 'CONS TO STAND DOWN. YOU TAKE OFF THESE CUFFS. YOU LET ME SPEAK TO MY SHIP. AND YOU CONVINCE ME THAT RATCHET AND MAGNUS ARE SAFE.
AND THEN— AND THEN— YOU WATCH ME REPORT YOU FOR ABUSE OF OFFICE.
OH, SHUT UP.
"SHUT UP?"
SHUT UP OR BE HELP IN CONTEMPT.
YOU'RE IN NO POSITION TO DEMAND ANYTHING OF ANYONE. LEAST OF ALL ME.
HM?
LEAST OF ALL ME.
LOOK OVER THERE, BRAINSTORM...
I SEE IT. SOME KIND OF SPACE BRIDGE.
AN OLD SPACE BRIDGE. EXCEPTIONALLY OLD.
PROTOTYPE OLD. BUT WHERE DID TYREST FIND IT?
TELL YOU WHAT, PERCEPTOR, I'LL ADD IT TO THE LIST OF—
OH, FORGET IT.
AS CYBERTRONIAN CHIEF JUSTICE AND PRIMARY LAWMAKER I HEREBY CHARGE YOU—ALL OF YOU—WITH CRIMES AGAINST CREATION.
ANYTHING YOU DO AND SAY WILL BE USED AGAINST YOU.
MY LEGISLATORS WILL ESCORT YOU TO YOUR CELL, WHERE YOU WILL AWAIT TRIAL.
ANY QUESTIONS?
JUST ONE: WHY ARE YOU SUCH A—
"AND THAT'S WHEN I STARTED SWEARING."

HM.
NOT MY PROUDEST MOMENT.
MAYBE MY LOUDEST...

I HAVE TO ASK— IS IT JUST "AMBUS"?
NO, ACTUALLY. MY PRIMARY IDENTIFIER IS MINIMUS.
MINIMUS AMBUS. RIGHT. THAT... MAKES A LOT MORE SENSE.
YOU THOUGHT I WAS SOMEONE ELSE?

UM—YES. IT WAS THE— Y'KNOW. ON YOUR FACE.
YOU'RE THINKING OF MY SPARK BROTHER, DOMINUS AMBUS.
THE HOUSE OF AMBUS HAS A VERY DISTINCT FACIAL INSIGNIA... BUT DOMINUS IS LONG GONE.

YOU'VE HEARD OUR STORY, AMBUS.
IF I MAY TURN THE TABLES FOR A MOMENT... WHY ARE YOU HERE?
I'M A TRADER. ENERGON DERIVATIVES.
I WAS ARRESTED BY ULTRA MAGNUS YEARS AGO.
HE'D INTERCEPTED ONE OF MY SHIPMENTS AND FOUND TRACES OF ENRICHED NUCLEON.

AH, ENRICHED NUCLEON...! THE MAGIC INGREDIENT!
TWO DROPS TURNS A HAND GUN INTO A BANNED GUN.
YOU REALLY SHOULD STOP AND LISTEN TO YOURSELF SOMETIMES.

I LODGED AN APPEAL AGAINST MY SENTENCE— A THOUSAND YEARS IN GARRUS 9—AND WAS TOLD TO WAIT FOR THE RETRIAL.
I'M STILL WAITING.
YOU'RE AN AUTOBOT, I PRESUME?
I AM, YES.
I BECAME SEPARATED FROM MY BADGE.

HERE.
NO, NO, I REALLY—
I NEVER WEAR IT. PLEASE.
IT'S TOO BIG FOR ME.
THAT'S NO EXCUSE. YOU SHOULD PUT IT ON.

HEY, AMBUS, HAVE YOU EVER—
OW!
HAVE YOU EVER TRIED TO ESCAPE?
I'D RATHER WAIT AND WIN MY APPEAL. JUSTICE CAN'T BE RUSHED.

THAT'S NO GOOD TO ME. I NEED TO GET OUT.
WE CAN'T WAIT FOR CYCLONUS AND NUTJOB TO SAVE US.
DON'T DO ANYTHING RASH.
ESCAPE ATTEMPTS ARE OFTEN CONSTRUED AS EVIDENCE OF GUILT.
YEAH? I PREFER TO THINK OF THEM AS FORCEFUL EXPRESSIONS OF INNOCENCE.

BRAINSTORM! HOW ABOUT COBBLING TOGETHER SOME KINDA SUPERWEAPON OUT OF— OUT OF THE CEILING OR SOMETHING?
YOU'RE ALWAYS TELLING US WHAT A GENIUS YOU ARE...
I DON'T RESPOND WELL TO PRESSURE.

WELL, WHY NOT JUST OPEN YOUR MAGIC BRIEFCASE AND MAKE ALL THE NAUGHTY PEOPLE IN THE UNIVERSE DISAPPEAR?
DON'T.
MOCK.
THE BRIEFCASE.

THEY LET YOU KEEP THE CASE?
THERE'S AN ATTENTION DEFLECTOR IN THE HANDLE.
UNLESS YOU KNOW THE CASE EXISTS, YOU DON'T REALLY NOTICE IT.
SCIENCE-Y STUFF. YOU WOULDN'T UNDERSTAND.
YOU'D BE SURPRISED.

WHAT ABOUT YOU, DOMEY?
THE LEGISLATORS ROUND THE CORNER— COULD YOU EXTEND THE NEEDLES IN YOUR FINGERS FAR ENOUGH TO REACH THEIR NECKS AND BRAINWASH THEM INTO LETTING US GO?
SHORT ANSWER: NO.
LONG ANSWER: NO, DON'T BE AN IDIOT.
AND DON'T EVER CALL ME "DOMEY."

FANTASTIC! SO WE'RE STUCK HERE FOR THE REST OF OUR LIVES!
TURN IT DOWN, TAILGATE.
BEFORE WE DO ANYTHING WE NEED TO FIGURE OUT WHAT TYREST'S UP TO.
THERE'S A BIGGER PICTURE HERE, AND WE'RE NOT SEEING IT.
AND BESIDES...

...WHAT'S THE RUSH?
02:03:57:30

RATCHET...?
RAAAAT—CHET...?
...
IT'S ME, PHARMA.
COME ON—I WANT TO PLAY A GUESSING GAME.
YOUR FACE: OFFICIALLY THE VERY LAST THING I WANT TO WAKE UP TO.

OUCH. TONGUE STILL SHARPER THAN A SCALPEL.
AND TO THINK—WE USED TO BE BUDDIES!
THE DELTARAN MEDICAL FACILITY, REMEMBER? WE WERE INSEPARABLE!
YEAH, YOU HEAR THAT? IT'S THE GLORIOUS SOUND OF THE PAST TENSE.

IT DOESN'T MATTER, ANYWAY: I'VE OUTGROWN YOU. I'VE GOT A NEW BEST FRIEND NOW. HE FOUND ME SLEEPING IN THE SNOW AND SHOWED ME HOW TO WORK MIRACLES!
CALM DOWN, PHARMA. YOU'RE BUZZING.

I AM NOW.
YOUR HANDS...
WHAT ABOUT MY HANDS?
THEY'RE STUPID.
ACTUALLY, THEY'RE VERY CLEVER. THEY CAN TURN INTO ANYTHING.

THEY WERE A GIFT FROM ONE GENIUS TO ANOTHER.
SPEAKING OF GIFTS...

TA-DAH!
NOW, ABOUT THAT GUESSING GAME...

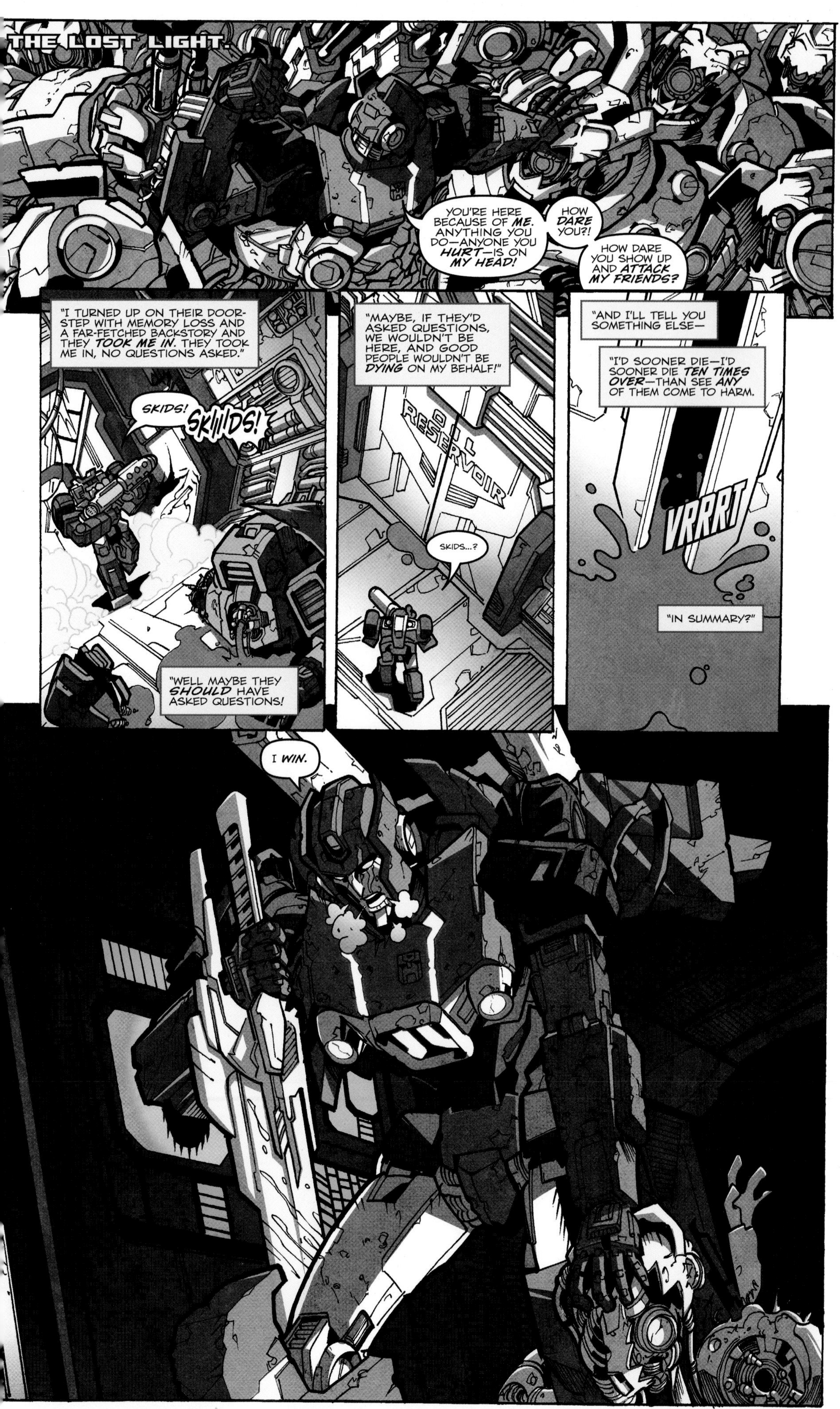
THE LOST LIGHT.
YOU'RE HERE BECAUSE OF ME. ANYTHING YOU DO—ANYONE YOU HURT—IS ON MY HEAD!
HOW DARE YOU?!
HOW DARE YOU SHOW UP AND ATTACK MY FRIENDS?
"I TURNED UP ON THEIR DOOR-STEP WITH MEMORY LOSS AND A FAR-FETCHED BACKSTORY AND THEY TOOK ME IN. THEY TOOK ME IN, NO QUESTIONS ASKED."
SKIDS!
SKIIIDS!
"WELL MAYBE THEY SHOULD HAVE ASKED QUESTIONS!
"MAYBE, IF THEY'D ASKED QUESTIONS, WE WOULDN'T BE HERE, AND GOOD PEOPLE WOULDN'T BE DYING ON MY BEHALF!"
OIL RESERVOIR
SKIDS...?
"AND I'LL TELL YOU SOMETHING ELSE—
"I'D SOONER DIE—I'D SOONER DIE TEN TIMES OVER—THAN SEE ANY OF THEM COME TO HARM.
VRRRT
"IN SUMMARY?"
I WIN.

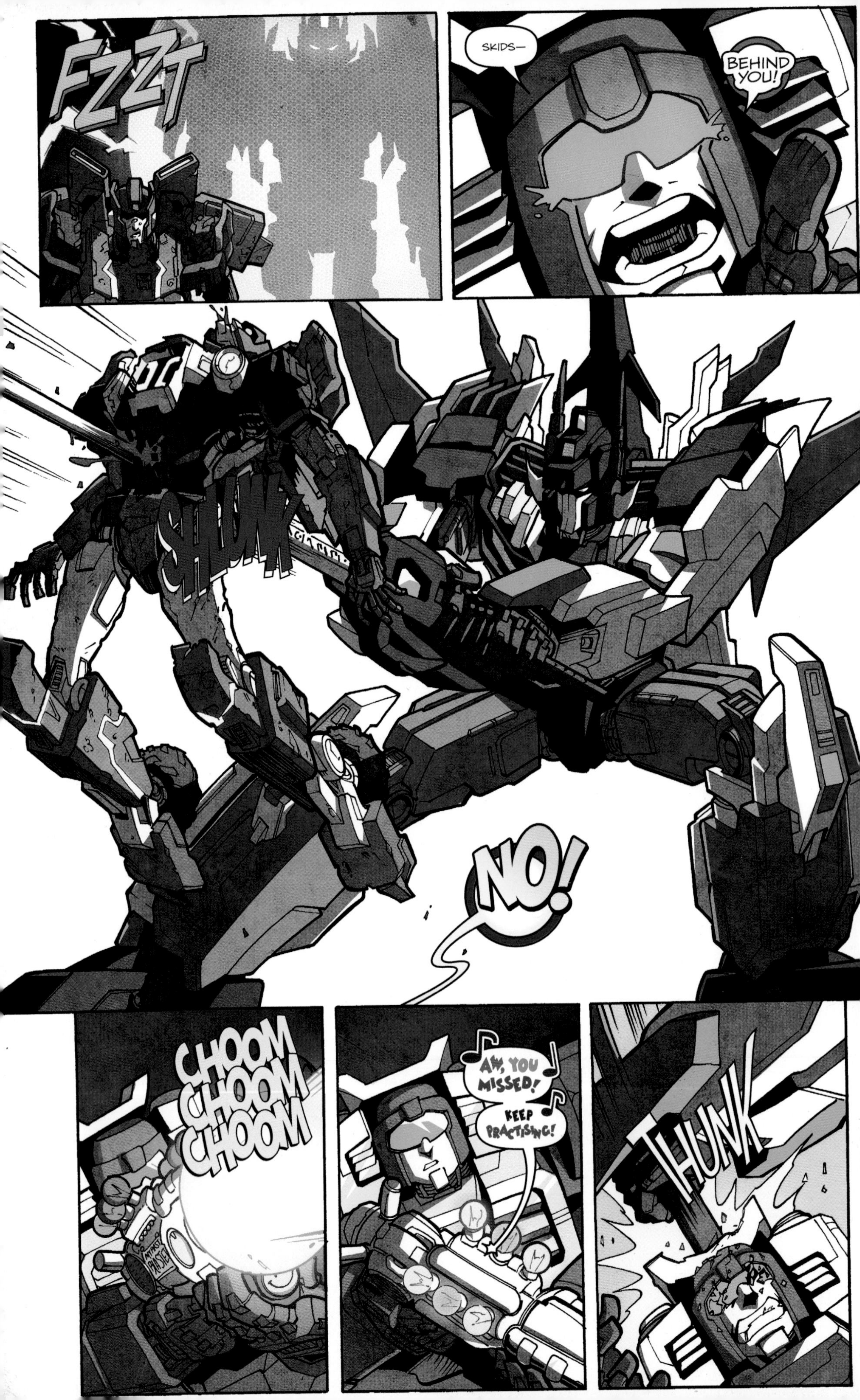
FZZT
SKIDS—
BEHIND YOU!
SHLUNK
NO!
CHOOM CHOOM CHOOM
AW, YOU MISSED!
KEEP PRACTISING!
THUNK

I'M DONE WITH THIS, PHARMA.
I GIVE UP, OKAY?
BUT YOU HAVEN'T EVEN HAD YOUR FIRST GUESS!
I DON'T CARE WHAT'S IN THE BOX.
LIAR. YOU CARE. ALL YOU DO IS CARE. YOU CARE ABOUT EVERYTHING AND EVERYONE.
IT'S ONE OF YOUR MORE ADMIRABLE WEAKNESSES.
EITHER SHOW ME OR DON'T SHOW ME. I'M NOT PLAYING.
OH, ALRIGHT. I'LL SHOW YOU WHAT'S IN THE BOX.
READY...?
BEHOLD!
THAT'S RIGHT, RATCHET—
YOU'RE IN THE BOX!

ENERGON STICK?
MIGHT HELP YOU RELAX.
THANKS, RUNG.
HOW'D YOU SMUGGLE THESE IN?
I'M 90% SECRET COMPARTMENTS.

I THINK THERE WAS A TYREST BACK IN MY DAY—ONE OF *NOVA'S* COTERIE.
CHIEF ENGINEERING OFFICER...?
IT'S THE SAME TYREST.
HE DIDN'T REALLY MAKE A NAME FOR HIMSELF UNTIL THE WAR, WHEN HE ORGANIZED THE *EXODUS*... HE AND *DAI ATLAS* MUST'VE HELPED TEN, TWENTY MILLION NEUTRALS LEAVE THE PLANET.
AND WHAT, HE STAYED BEHIND TO FIGHT?

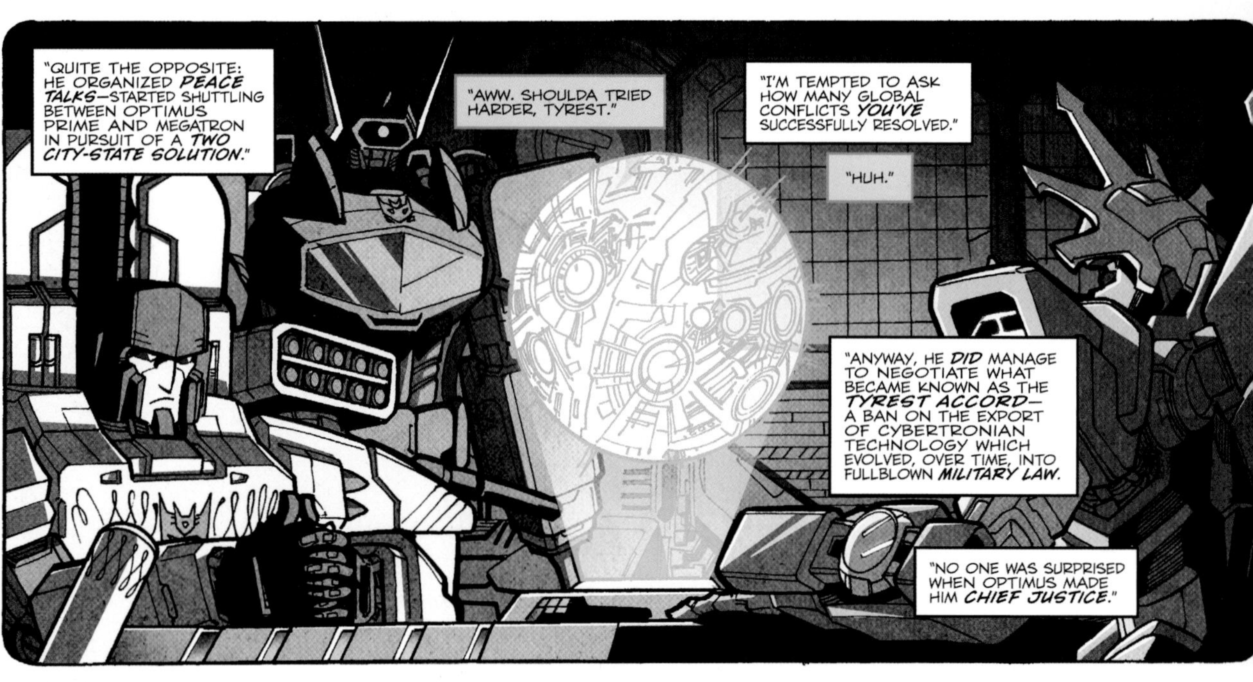

"QUITE THE OPPOSITE: HE ORGANIZED *PEACE TALKS*—STARTED SHUTTLING BETWEEN OPTIMUS PRIME AND MEGATRON IN PURSUIT OF A *TWO CITY-STATE SOLUTION*."
"AWW. SHOULDA TRIED HARDER, TYREST."
"I'M TEMPTED TO ASK HOW MANY GLOBAL CONFLICTS *YOU'VE* SUCCESSFULLY RESOLVED."
"HUH."
"ANYWAY, HE *DID* MANAGE TO NEGOTIATE WHAT BECAME KNOWN AS THE *TYREST ACCORD*—A BAN ON THE EXPORT OF CYBERTRONIAN TECHNOLOGY WHICH EVOLVED, OVER TIME, INTO FULLBLOWN *MILITARY LAW*.
"NO ONE WAS SURPRISED WHEN OPTIMUS MADE HIM *CHIEF JUSTICE*."

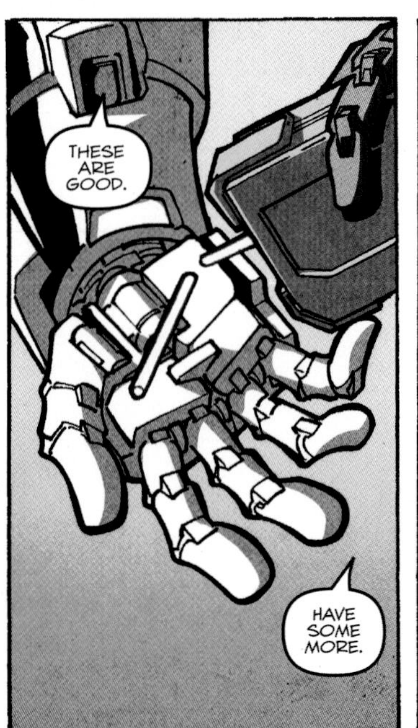

THESE ARE GOOD.
HAVE SOME MORE.

SO HANG ON—HOW DID TYREST END UP ON LUNA 1?
WHO KNOWS?
HE'S BEEN OFF THE RADAR SINCE THE *AEQUITAS TRIALS*.
ER, JUST—MAYBE JUST BE A LITTLE CAREFUL.
THOSE TRIALS ARE *TOP SECRET*...

I AGREE. IT'S NOT MY PLACE, BUT I'D STRONGLY ADVISE YOU AGAINST DISCLOSING ANYTHING CONFIDENTIAL.
YOU'RE RIGHT—IT'S NOT YOUR PLACE.
BESIDES, I'M ONLY GONNA GIVE THE *NUTSHELL VERSION*.

25 YEARS AGO, TYREST INVENTED THIS JUDGING MACHINE—"AEQUITAS"—THAT COULD CALCULATE A DEFENDANT'S GUILT WITH 100% ACCURACY.
THE LAST TIME ANYONE SAW HIM, THE AEQUITAS TRIALS WERE IN FULL SWING.
COME TO THINK OF IT, THEY WERE PUT ON HOLD AT HIS REQUEST.

YOU MUST BE WORRIED ABOUT THE REST OF YOUR CREW.
HOW MANY DO YOU HAVE UNDER YOUR COMMAND?
YOU'RE CHANGING THE SUBJECT, BUT—THREE HUNDRED.
GIVE OR TAKE.
ALL THERE FROM THE START?
YES. ER, NO. A FEW LATE ADDITIONS.
WE PICKED UP FIRST AID AND AMBULON AND SOME PATIENTS FROM DELPHI. FORT MAX...
OH, AND SKIDS, OF COURSE.

SKIDS... HE WORKS FOR THE DIPLOMATIC CORPS, DOESN'T HE?
HOW DID HE END UP ON THE LOST LIGHT?
WHY THE SUDDEN INTEREST IN SKIDS?
I'M JUST MAKING CONVERSATION...

AMBUS?
NO THANK YOU.
SURE?
REALLY, I'M FINE.
GO ON, JUST THE—

—WHOOPS!

ACCIDENT.
SORRY.

YOU'RE SHAKING THEM OUT!
SO?
SO DON'T BE SO DAMNED STUPID!

WOAH—NO NEED TO GET PHYSICAL, AMBUS...
ACTUALLY, RODIMUS, I DON'T THINK THAT'S HIS NAME.
RUNG...

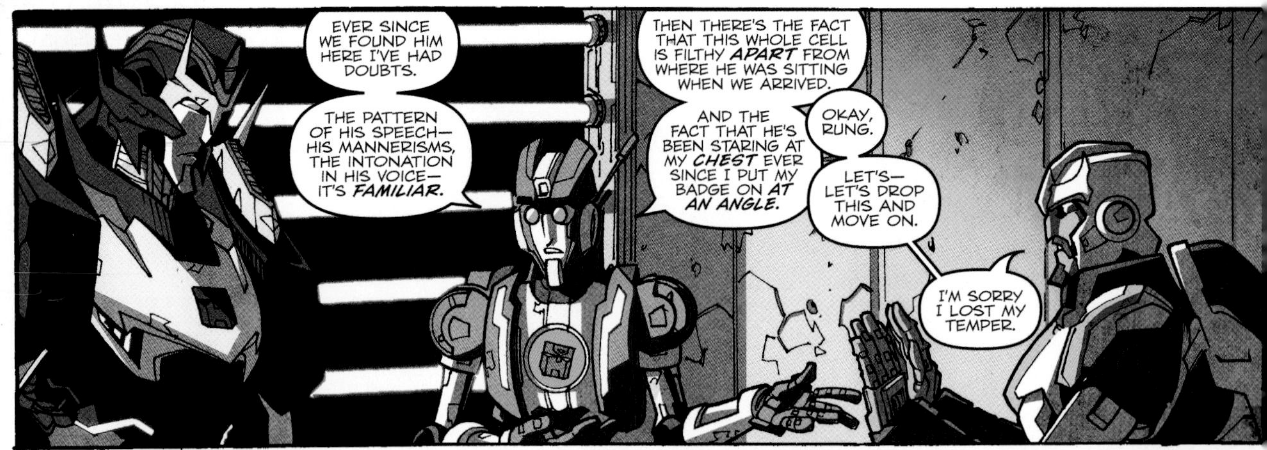
EVER SINCE WE FOUND HIM HERE I'VE HAD DOUBTS.
THE PATTERN OF HIS SPEECH— HIS MANNERISMS, THE INTONATION IN HIS VOICE— IT'S *FAMILIAR.*
THEN THERE'S THE FACT THAT THIS WHOLE CELL IS FILTHY *APART* FROM WHERE HE WAS SITTING WHEN WE ARRIVED.
AND THE FACT THAT HE'S BEEN STARING AT MY *CHEST* EVER SINCE I PUT MY BADGE ON *AT AN ANGLE.*
OKAY, RUNG.
LET'S— LET'S DROP THIS AND MOVE ON.
I'M SORRY I LOST MY TEMPER.

THE ENERGON STICKS WERE A *TEST*—I WANTED TO SEE IF HE COULD TOLERATE THE MESS.
AND HE COULDN'T, AND THAT CLINCHED IT.
CLINCHED *WHAT?*
ISN'T IT OBVIOUS?
WHY IS EVERYONE SAYING THAT TO ME TODAY?

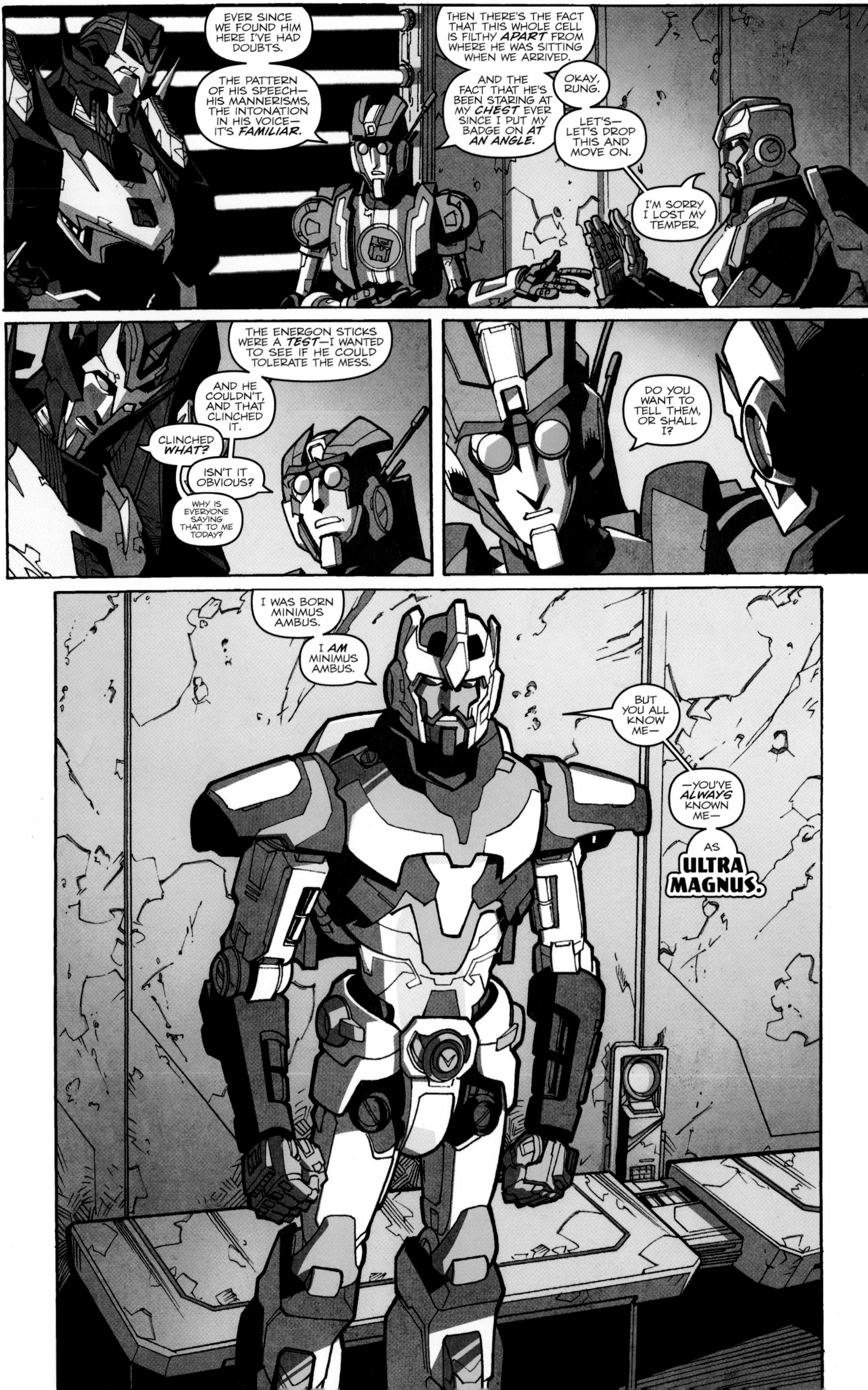

DO YOU WANT TO TELL THEM, OR SHALL I?

I WAS BORN MINIMUS AMBUS.
I *AM* MINIMUS AMBUS.
BUT YOU ALL KNOW ME—
—YOU'VE *ALWAYS* KNOWN ME—
AS
ULTRA MAGNUS.

MORE THAN MEETS THE EYE #18 COVER B

by **SEAN CHEN** Colors by **TOM CHU**

MORE THAN MEETS THE EYE #19 COVER A

by **ALEX MILNE** Colors by **JOSH PEREZ**

LUNA 1. EARLIER.
OVERLORD!
UH
...
YOU'RE AWAKE.
CHIEF JUSTICE?
HFF!
FULLY DESERVED.
REMAIN IN LIGHT 3 of 5: THE DIVIDED SELF

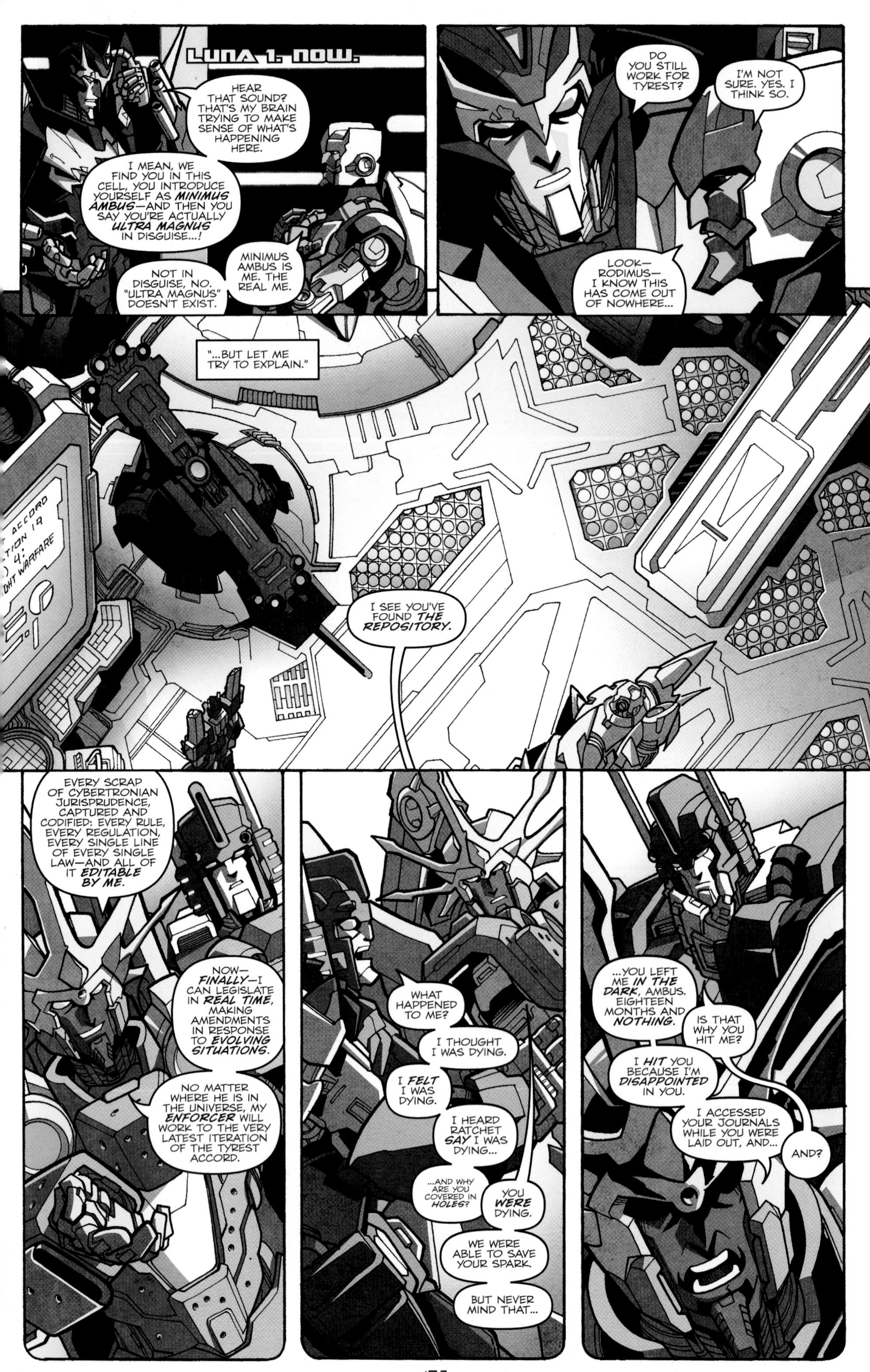
LUNA 1. NOW.
HEAR THAT SOUND? THAT'S MY BRAIN TRYING TO MAKE SENSE OF WHAT'S HAPPENING HERE.
I MEAN, WE FIND YOU IN THIS CELL, YOU INTRODUCE YOURSELF AS MINIMUS AMBUS—AND THEN YOU SAY YOU'RE ACTUALLY ULTRA MAGNUS IN DISGUISE...!
NOT IN DISGUISE, NO. "ULTRA MAGNUS" DOESN'T EXIST.
MINIMUS AMBUS IS ME. THE REAL ME.
DO YOU STILL WORK FOR TYREST?
I'M NOT SURE. YES. I THINK SO.
LOOK—RODIMUS—I KNOW THIS HAS COME OUT OF NOWHERE...
"...BUT LET ME TRY TO EXPLAIN."
I SEE YOU'VE FOUND THE REPOSITORY.
EVERY SCRAP OF CYBERTRONIAN JURISPRUDENCE, CAPTURED AND CODIFIED: EVERY RULE, EVERY REGULATION, EVERY SINGLE LINE OF EVERY SINGLE LAW—AND ALL OF IT EDITABLE BY ME.
NOW—FINALLY—I CAN LEGISLATE IN REAL TIME, MAKING AMENDMENTS IN RESPONSE TO EVOLVING SITUATIONS.
NO MATTER WHERE HE IS IN THE UNIVERSE, MY ENFORCER WILL WORK TO THE VERY LATEST ITERATION OF THE TYREST ACCORD.
WHAT HAPPENED TO ME?
I THOUGHT I WAS DYING.
I FELT I WAS DYING.
I HEARD RATCHET SAY I WAS DYING...
...AND WHY ARE YOU COVERED IN HOLES?
YOU WERE DYING.
WE WERE ABLE TO SAVE YOUR SPARK.
BUT NEVER MIND THAT...
...YOU LEFT ME IN THE DARK, AMBUS. EIGHTEEN MONTHS AND NOTHING.
IS THAT WHY YOU HIT ME?
I HIT YOU BECAUSE I'M DISAPPOINTED IN YOU.
I ACCESSED YOUR JOURNALS WHILE YOU WERE LAID OUT, AND...
AND?

WHAT'S HAPPENED TO YOU?!
IF YOU'D JOINED THE LOST LIGHT TO DO YOUR JOB, FINE!
BUT INSTEAD OF APPREHENDING CRIMINALS YOU'VE BEEN—
I CAN BARELY BRING MYSELF TO SAY IT.
BADGE INSPECTIONS! DOORFRAME AUDITS!
NANOCONS!
HUGGING!
HEDONIA!
THE DULY APPOINTED ENFORCER OF THE TYREST ACCORD IS SUPPOSED TO COMMAND RESPECT—AND YOU DO NOT.
YOU DON'T.
NOT ANY MORE. YOU'RE RIDICULOUS. OFFENSIVELY SO.
CHIEF JUSTICE, PLEASE, I KNOW WHAT'S COMING AND—PLEASE—DON'T!
YOU KNOW THE ARRANGEMENT: WHAT I GAVE I CAN TAKE AWAY.
I KNOW, SIR, I KNOW, BUT—
I'M TAKING IT AWAY, AMBUS. I'M TAKING IT ALL AWAY.
BUT IT'S MY LIFE!
KLIK
"I WASN'T THE FIRST ULTRA MAGNUS..."

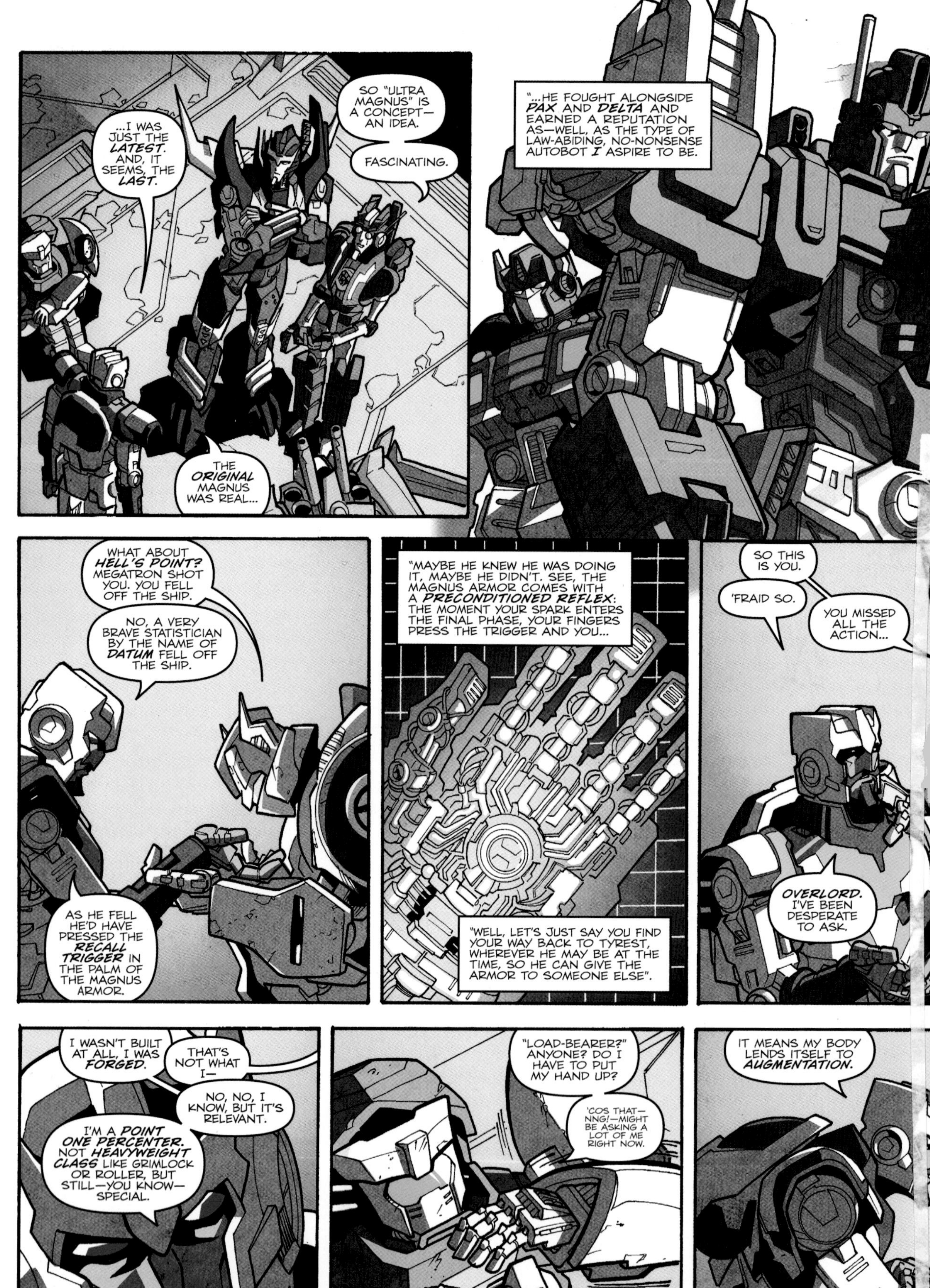

...I WAS JUST THE LATEST. AND, IT SEEMS, THE LAST.
SO "ULTRA MAGNUS" IS A CONCEPT— AN IDEA.
FASCINATING.
THE ORIGINAL MAGNUS WAS REAL...
"...HE FOUGHT ALONGSIDE PAX AND DELTA AND EARNED A REPUTATION AS—WELL, AS THE TYPE OF LAW-ABIDING, NO-NONSENSE AUTOBOT I ASPIRE TO BE.
WHAT ABOUT HELL'S POINT? MEGATRON SHOT YOU. YOU FELL OFF THE SHIP.
NO, A VERY BRAVE STATISTICIAN BY THE NAME OF DATUM FELL OFF THE SHIP.
AS HE FELL HE'D HAVE PRESSED THE RECALL TRIGGER IN THE PALM OF THE MAGNUS ARMOR.
"MAYBE HE KNEW HE WAS DOING IT, MAYBE HE DIDN'T. SEE, THE MAGNUS ARMOR COMES WITH A PRECONDITIONED REFLEX: THE MOMENT YOUR SPARK ENTERS THE FINAL PHASE, YOUR FINGERS PRESS THE TRIGGER AND YOU...
"WELL, LET'S JUST SAY YOU FIND YOUR WAY BACK TO TYREST, WHEREVER HE MAY BE AT THE TIME, SO HE CAN GIVE THE ARMOR TO SOMEONE ELSE".
SO THIS IS YOU.
'FRAID SO.
YOU MISSED ALL THE ACTION...
OVERLORD. I'VE BEEN DESPERATE TO ASK.
I WASN'T BUILT AT ALL, I WAS FORGED.
THAT'S NOT WHAT I—
NO, NO, I KNOW, BUT IT'S RELEVANT.
I'M A POINT ONE PERCENTER. NOT HEAVYWEIGHT CLASS LIKE GRIMLOCK OR ROLLER, BUT STILL—YOU KNOW—SPECIAL.
TECHNICALLY, I'M A LOAD-BEARER.
"LOAD-BEARER?" ANYONE? DO I HAVE TO PUT MY HAND UP?
'COS THAT—NNG!—MIGHT BE ASKING A LOT OF ME RIGHT NOW.
IT MEANS MY BODY LENDS ITSELF TO AUGMENTATION.

"PEOPLE LOVED AND FEARED HIM IN EQUAL MEASURE, AND THAT—THAT *FASCINATED* TYREST.

"WHEN MAGNUS DIED, HE SAW AN OPPORTUNITY TO CREATE THE *IMMORTAL LAWMAN*. HIS WORDS, NOT MINE.

"HE PUT OUT A STORY ABOUT MAGNUS FAKING HIS DEATH AND STARTED DEVELOPING THE *MAGNUS ARMOR*."

THE "ULTRA MAGNUS" WHO REAPPEARED WAS—DO YOU REMEMBER *SUTURE*?

IT WAS HIM. HE WAS THE FIRST ENFORCER.

WHAT ABOUT ALL THE *OTHER* MAGNUSES—MAGNUSI? MAGNA?—WHAT HAPPENED TO THEM?

KILLED IN THE LINE OF DUTY. CLEMENCY, SIMANZI, THE FAST-FOLDING SUN...

DON'T WORRY—WE SAW HIM OFF.

HOW DID HE GET ON BOARD IN THE FIRST PLACE?
DRIFT.
DRIFT?
HE'S EXILED.
HE'S BEEN EXILED.
I HAD TO EXILE HIM.

SO... WHAT DID YOU ACTUALLY DO BEFORE YOU BECAME *JUSTICE PERSONIFIED?*
I WAS JUST A SOLDIER.
SERIOUSLY?
'COS YOU DON'T—I MEAN, YOU'RE NOT REALLY *BUILT FOR COMBAT*, ARE YOU?

THE AVERAGE CYBERTRONIAN HAS A *LOW BREAKING STRAIN*: THEIR EXOSKELETON CAN ONLY BE *BUILT OUT* SO FAR BEFORE THE SPARK'S ANIMATING FORCE WEAKENS AND THEY FREEZE.
ONLY LOAD-BEARERS CAN HANDLE *FULLY-INTEGRATED NEUROWARE* LIKE THE MAGNUS ARMOR.

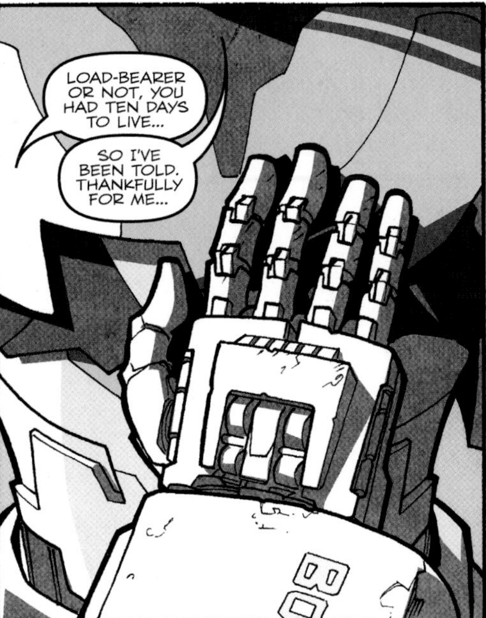

LOAD-BEARER OR NOT, YOU HAD TEN DAYS TO LIVE...
SO I'VE BEEN TOLD. THANKFULLY FOR ME...

01 : 22 : 56 : 34
...IT SEEMS THAT TYREST'S DOCTORS CAN WORK *MIRACLES*.

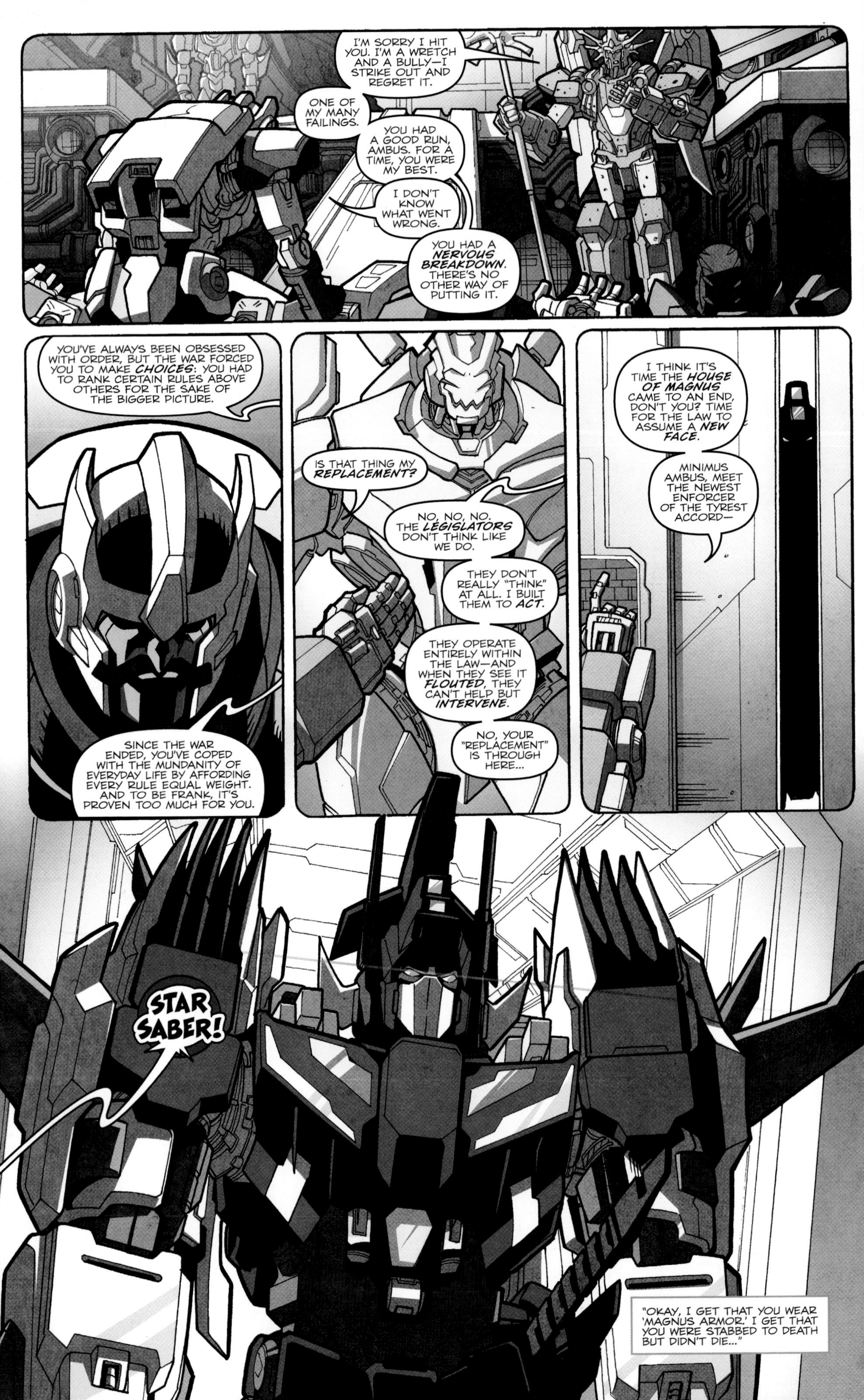
I'M SORRY I HIT YOU. I'M A WRETCH AND A BULLY—I STRIKE OUT AND REGRET IT.
ONE OF MY MANY FAILINGS.
YOU HAD A GOOD RUN, AMBUS. FOR A TIME, YOU WERE MY BEST.
I DON'T KNOW WHAT WENT WRONG.
YOU HAD A NERVOUS BREAKDOWN. THERE'S NO OTHER WAY OF PUTTING IT.
YOU'VE ALWAYS BEEN OBSESSED WITH ORDER, BUT THE WAR FORCED YOU TO MAKE CHOICES: YOU HAD TO RANK CERTAIN RULES ABOVE OTHERS FOR THE SAKE OF THE BIGGER PICTURE.
SINCE THE WAR ENDED, YOU'VE COPED WITH THE MUNDANITY OF EVERYDAY LIFE BY AFFORDING EVERY RULE EQUAL WEIGHT. AND TO BE FRANK, IT'S PROVEN TOO MUCH FOR YOU.
IS THAT THING MY REPLACEMENT?
NO, NO, NO. THE LEGISLATORS DON'T THINK LIKE WE DO.
THEY DON'T REALLY "THINK" AT ALL. I BUILT THEM TO ACT.
THEY OPERATE ENTIRELY WITHIN THE LAW—AND WHEN THEY SEE IT FLOUTED, THEY CAN'T HELP BUT INTERVENE.
NO, YOUR "REPLACEMENT" IS THROUGH HERE...
I THINK IT'S TIME THE HOUSE OF MAGNUS CAME TO AN END, DON'T YOU? TIME FOR THE LAW TO ASSUME A NEW FACE.
MINIMUS AMBUS, MEET THE NEWEST ENFORCER OF THE TYREST ACCORD—
STAR SABER!
"OKAY, I GET THAT YOU WEAR 'MAGNUS ARMOR.' I GET THAT YOU WERE STABBED TO DEATH BUT DIDN'T DIE..."

...I EVEN GET THAT A HUNDRED MICROSCOPIC ATTENTION DEFLECTORS STOPPED RATCHET SEEING THE REAL YOU INSIDE THE ARMOR.
WHAT I DON'T GET IS HOW YOU ENDED UP IN THIS CELL.
WHEN YOU LANDED ON LUNA 1, TYREST SAID HE WAS GOING TO ARREST YOU FOR HARBORING A CRIMINAL SUSPECT.

IN CONTRAVENTION OF—DON'T TELL ME, DON'T TELL ME—SECTION 17 (21) OF THE TYREST ACCORD.
SEE? ALL THOSE LESSONS PAID OFF.

ARE YOU SERIOUSLY TELLING ME THERE'S A CRIMINAL ON BOARD THE LOST LI— OH. WHIRL.
NOT WHIRL.
ATOMIZER?
LANCET?
AMMO?
SKIDS.

WHEN I HEARD YOU WERE GOING TO BE CHARGED WITH THE DEATH PENALTY, I ASKED TO BE PUT IN HERE.
WOAH, SORRY— "DEATH PENALTY"?
THAT'S NOT BEEN MENTIONED. I'D HAVE REMEMBERED THOSE WORDS. THOSE ARE MEMORABLE WORDS.

VZZZT
I HAD A PLAN: I WAS GOING TO RECORD OUR CONVERSATION AND PROVE TO TYREST THAT, LIKE ME, YOU HAD NO IDEA WHAT SKIDS DID.
BUT—NONE OF THIS IS WORKING OUT AS INTENDED. I DIDN'T KNOW ABOUT LOCKDOWN, OR THE TITANS, OR ABOUT RATCHET BEING TAKEN...

...AND I'VE NO IDEA WHY YOU'VE NOW BEEN CHARGED WITH "CRIMES AGAINST CREATION."
THAT CRIME DIDN'T EXIST 18 MONTHS AGO.

VZZZT

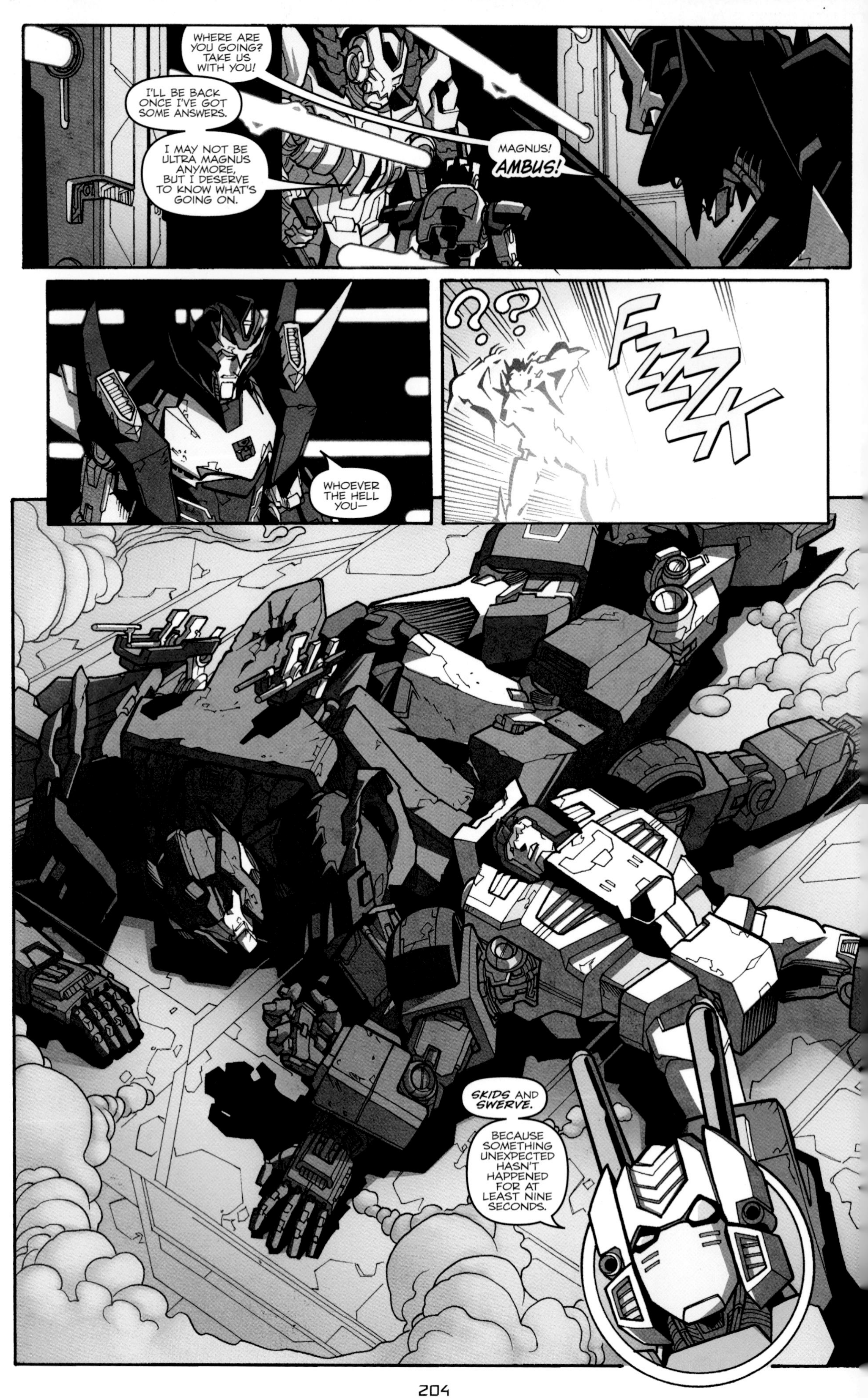

WHERE ARE YOU GOING? TAKE US WITH YOU!
I'LL BE BACK ONCE I'VE GOT SOME ANSWERS.
I MAY NOT BE ULTRA MAGNUS ANYMORE, BUT I DESERVE TO KNOW WHAT'S GOING ON.
MAGNUS! AMBUS!
WHOEVER THE HELL YOU—
??
??
FZZZK
SKIDS AND SWERVE.
BECAUSE SOMETHING UNEXPECTED HASN'T HAPPENED FOR AT LEAST NINE SECONDS.

WHIRL AND CYCLONUS. NOT FAR AWAY.
IT'S NOT LIKE I KEEP A SPREADSHEET OR ANYTHING—
—BUT THIS IS THE BIGGEST SMELTING POOL I HAVE EVER SEEN.
HOW MANY DECEPTICONS DID YOU KILL BACK THERE? Y'KNOW, OVERALL.
I WASN'T KEEPING COUNT.
...
SIX.
YOU?
DUNNO. MORE THAN SIX.
UP THERE. SOME SORT OF HABITATION BLOCK?
YOU DON'T HANG A HABITATION BLOCK OVER A SMELTING POOL; YOU BUILD A PRISON YOU CAN DUNK.
IF RODDERS AND THE GANG AREN'T DEAD THEY'LL BE UP THERE, PINNING ALL HOPES OF RESCUE ON YOU AND ME. MAINLY ME.
I SAY WE TOOL UP—THERE'S AN ARMORY NEARBY; I CAN SMELL THE ENRICHED NUCLEON—AND HAVE A LITTLE JAILBREAK.
BUT AS SOON AS WE DO THAT WE'LL HAVE TO LEAVE LUNA 1.
SO?
I'M NOT READY. I NEED TO FIND—
WHAT? WHAT WOULD SOMEONE LIKE YOU BE LOOKING FOR?
YOU WOULDN'T UNDERSTAND.
YOU'RE PROBABLY RIGHT.
NOW—FOLLOW THAT SCENT.

TYREST'S BASE OF OPERATIONS. THE MEDIBAY.

CAN YOU FEEL THAT?
CAN YOU FEEL THE— SHHH—CAN YOU FEEL THE BLADE AGAINST YOUR SPARK?
ONLY—YOU HAVEN'T SCREAMED YET, WHICH MAKES ME WONDER HOW ACCURATELY YOUR NERVECIRCUITS ARE REPORTING THE SENSATION.
I'D HATE FOR YOUR BRAIN TO BE MISINFORMED.

CAN WE TALK?
PHARMA, CAN WE TALK? I'D LIKE THAT.
YOU AND ME, EH? YOU AND ME, TALKING INTO THE NIGHT. JUST LIKE THE OLD DAYS.
HAPPY TO TALK. HAPPY TO LISTEN TO THE PANIC IN YOUR VOICE.

WHAT'S THIS ABOUT? REVENGE?
YOU DECLARED WAR ON MY BODY, RATCHET. I'M RETALIATING.
AT FIRST, I WANTED TO HURT YOU FOR RUINING THINGS AT DELPHI, BUT WHEN YOU CRASHED* I SAW THAT YOU'D STOLEN MY HANDS.
THAT TOOK THINGS TO A WHOLE NEW LEVEL.
* ISSUE 17.

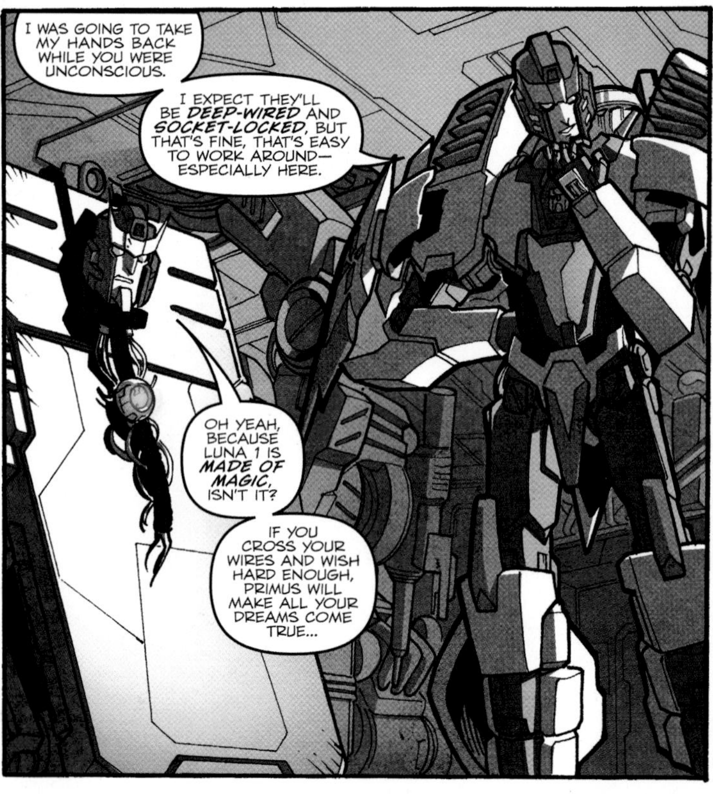

I WAS GOING TO TAKE MY HANDS BACK WHILE YOU WERE UNCONSCIOUS.
I EXPECT THEY'LL BE DEEP-WIRED AND SOCKET-LOCKED, BUT THAT'S FINE, THAT'S EASY TO WORK AROUND— ESPECIALLY HERE.
OH YEAH, BECAUSE LUNA 1 IS MADE OF MAGIC, ISN'T IT?
IF YOU CROSS YOUR WIRES AND WISH HARD ENOUGH, PRIMUS WILL MAKE ALL YOUR DREAMS COME TRUE...

TRUST ME, THE ONLY DIFFERENCE BETWEEN LUNA 1 AND LUNA 2 IS THE NUMBER.
NO, WHAT MAKES THIS PLACE SPECIAL IS THE STUFF TYREST BROUGHT WITH HIM WHEN HE ARRIVED.
THIS MEDIBAY, RATCHET—IT'S AN EMBARRASSMENT OF RICHES.
EVERY PIECE OF AVANT GARDE CYBERTRONIAN TECHNOLOGY THAT MAGNUS HAS EVER REPOSSESSED... IT'S ALL HERE.
STUFF I'VE NEVER EVEN SEEN BEFORE.

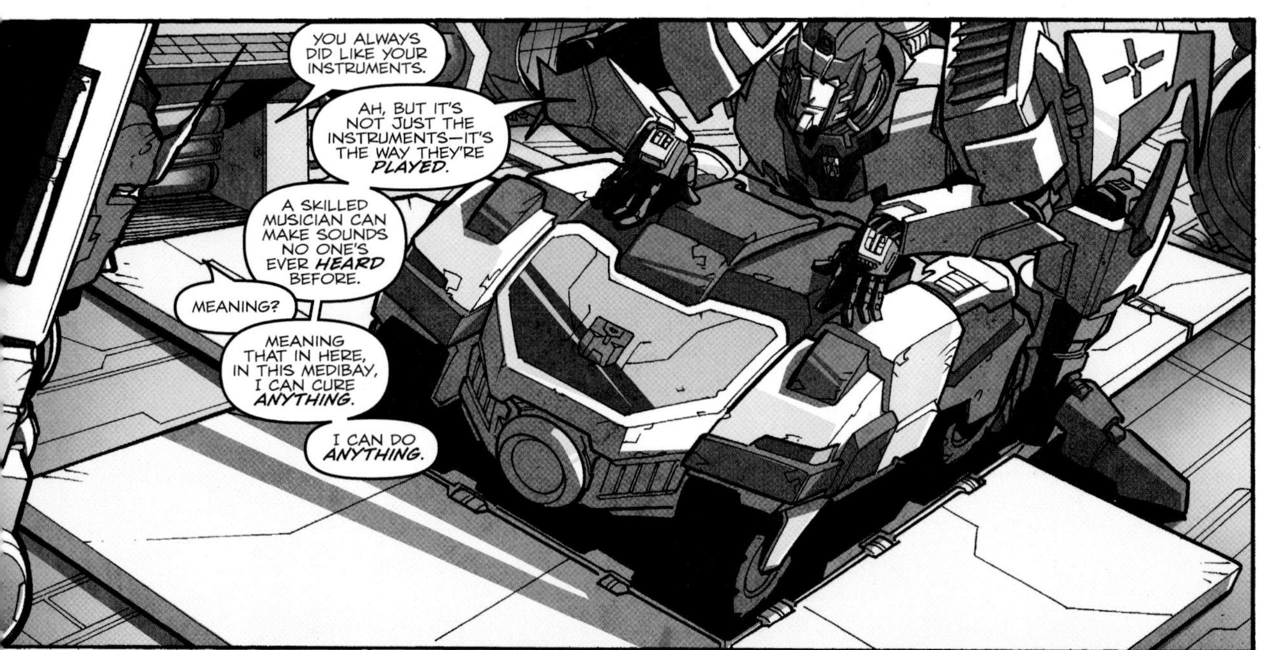
YOU ALWAYS DID LIKE YOUR INSTRUMENTS.
AH, BUT IT'S NOT JUST THE INSTRUMENTS—IT'S THE WAY THEY'RE PLAYED.
A SKILLED MUSICIAN CAN MAKE SOUNDS NO ONE'S EVER HEARD BEFORE.
MEANING?
MEANING THAT IN HERE, IN THIS MEDIBAY, I CAN CURE ANYTHING.
I CAN DO ANYTHING.

ANYTHING EXCEPT REMOVE A PAIR OF HANDS.
C'MON, PHARMA—THE TRUTH.
DEEP-WIRED, SOCKET-LOCKED... AND STILL ON MY WRISTS. WHY?
BECAUSE I'M A DOCTOR, NOT A BOMB DISPOSAL EXPERT.

YOU THINK—
WAIT.
YOU THINK I WIRED YOUR HANDS—THE ONES I ATTACHED TO MY BODY—YOU THINK I WIRED THEM TO EXPLODE?
I... THINK IT'S A POSSIBILITY, YES.

OR MAYBE... MAYBE YOU'RE SCARED OF FAILURE.
MAYBE YOU'RE AFRAID YOU WON'T BE ABLE TO PICK THE LOCK OR LOOSEN THE WIRING, SO YOU WANT HELP.
I GET IT, PHARMA.
IT TOOK ME A WHILE, BUT—IT MAKES SENSE NOW: I'M BETTER THAN YOU.

A BETTER DOCTOR? PLEASE. I OVERTOOK YOU YEARS AGO.
I DON'T NEED MY HANDS BACK TO SLAP YOU DOWN.
PROVE IT. PUT ME BACK IN MY BODY AND PROVE IT.
A RACE TO FIX THE SAME INJURY—THE BETTER SURGEON WINS THE HANDS.

ARMO
DON'T THE ALARMS BOTHER YOU?
NAH—YOU GET ALARMS WHENEVER YOU BREAK INTO A DESERTED BUILDING.
WHAT BOTHERS ME ARE THESE—FRIKKIN' STUPID FRIKKIN' HANDLES.
THEY'RE NOT EXACTLY CLAW-FRIENDLY.
LET ME.

I DON'T UNDERSTAND WHY YOU DON'T GET YOURSELF FIXED.
IF NOT THE FACE, THEN THE CLAWS.
KLIK
KLIK

YOU WANNA KNOW A SECRET, HORN-HEAD?
LIFE'S MESSED UP. I'M MESSED UP.
I'VE DONE BAD THINGS AND I CONTINUE TO DO BAD THINGS, BECAUSE THE VOICE TELLING ME NOT TO...? HE'S NOT SAID MUCH FOR A WHILE.
AND Y'KNOW WHAT KEEPS ME GOING? ANGER.

ANGER'S AN INSULATOR. STOPS LIFE GETTING TOO CLOSE.
IF I GOT MYSELF "FIXED," MAYBE THE ANGER WOULD LEAVE ME—AND THEN I REALLY WOULD BE SCREWED.
AND SINCE WE'RE GETTING PERSONAL, THOSE MARKS ON YOUR FACE...
NO.
DON'T EVEN—

HRK!

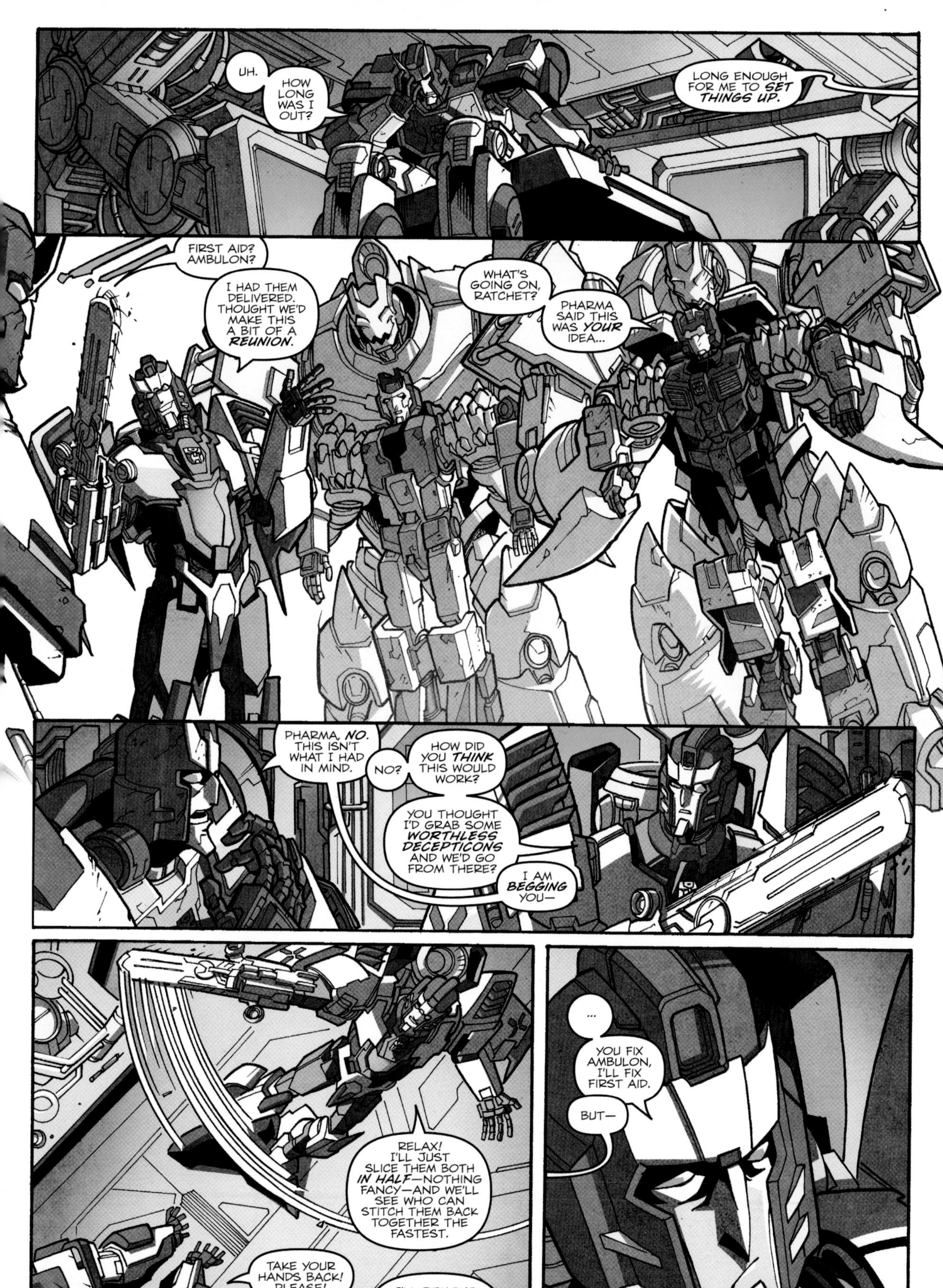
UH.
HOW LONG WAS I OUT?
LONG ENOUGH FOR ME TO SET THINGS UP.
FIRST AID? AMBULON?
I HAD THEM DELIVERED. THOUGHT WE'D MAKE THIS A BIT OF A REUNION.
WHAT'S GOING ON, RATCHET?
PHARMA SAID THIS WAS YOUR IDEA...
PHARMA, NO. THIS ISN'T WHAT I HAD IN MIND.
NO?
HOW DID YOU THINK THIS WOULD WORK?
YOU THOUGHT I'D GRAB SOME WORTHLESS DECEPTICONS AND WE'D GO FROM THERE?
I AM BEGGING YOU—
RELAX! I'LL JUST SLICE THEM BOTH IN HALF—NOTHING FANCY—AND WE'LL SEE WHO CAN STITCH THEM BACK TOGETHER THE FASTEST.
TAKE YOUR HANDS BACK! PLEASE!
YOU'RE THE BETTER DOCTOR—YOU DESERVE THEM!
I'LL REMOVE ONE AND YOU CAN REMOVE THE OTHER. WHAT DO YOU SAY? ARE WE GOOD?
...
YOU FIX AMBULON, I'LL FIX FIRST AID.
BUT—
THIS IS HAPPENING, RATCHET.
PLAY ALONG OR I'LL GET TYREST TO CUT THE LOST LIGHT IN HALF, CREW AND ALL.

LISTEN. LISTEN. BOTH OF YOU. YOU'RE JUST— YOU'RE JUST GONNA HAVE TO ROLL WITH THIS, OKAY? I'M SORRY.
YOU'RE GONNA LET DOCTOR D.J.D. CUT US IN HALF?
IF YOU RE-ROUTE YOUR NERVECIRCUITS AWAY FROM YOUR WAIST IT'LL MINIMIZE THE PAIN.
I CAN DO THIS, I CAN PUT YOU BACK TOGETHER. IT'S AN EASY FIX. DON'T WORRY.
THE WAIST? WHO SAID ANYTHING ABOUT THE WAIST?
YOU SAID YOU WERE GOING TO CUT THEM IN HALF.
YES—
—LENGTHWAYS.

I DON'T KNOW WHAT WAS MORE UNEXPECTED—BEING *STABBED* OR BEING *SAVED*.
THANK YOU.
DON'T THANK ME, THANK MY REFLEXES.
MY STUPID, INDISCRIMINATE REFLEXES.
WHERE DID YOU—*GNN!*—GET THE SWORD?
IN THE ARMORY. THERE ARE *HUNDREDS* IN THERE—AND I THINK I KNOW WHO THEY BELONG TO.
FRIENDS! PLEASE—OVER HERE!
A-HA-
"—SHALL WE SEE IF I'M RIGHT?"
THE *CIRCLE OF LIGHT*, I PRESUME?

HOW'S SKIDS?
HE'LL LIVE. IT'S SURPRISING HOW MANY STAB WOUNDS MISS THE SPARK.
I THINK IT WAS ***INTENDED*** TO INCAPACITATE. TYREST WANTS HIM ALIVE TO STAND TRIAL.

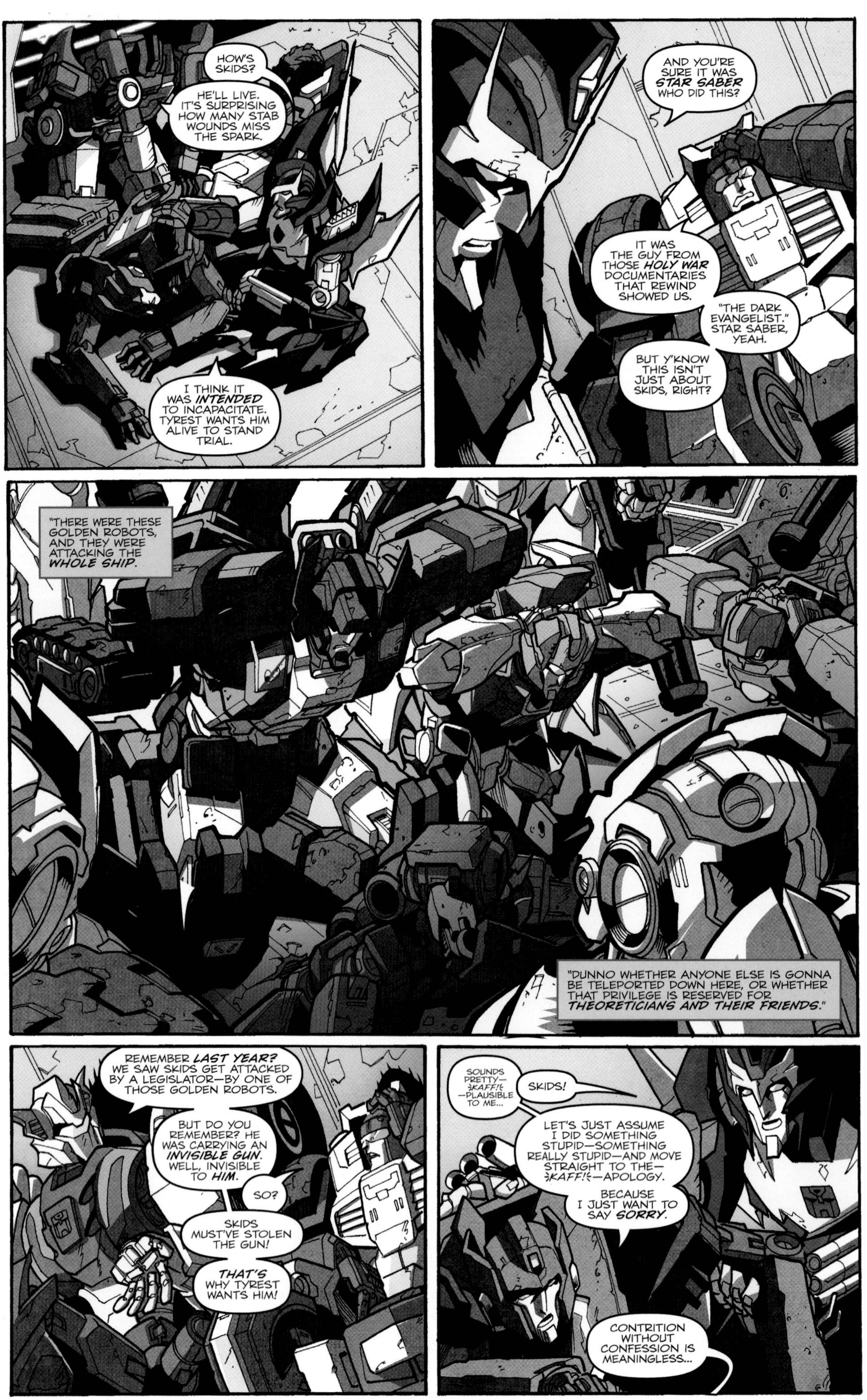

AND YOU'RE SURE IT WAS ***STAR SABER*** WHO DID THIS?
IT WAS THE GUY FROM THOSE ***HOLY WAR*** DOCUMENTARIES THAT REWIND SHOWED US.
"THE DARK EVANGELIST." STAR SABER, YEAH.
BUT Y'KNOW THIS ISN'T JUST ABOUT SKIDS, RIGHT?

"THERE WERE THESE GOLDEN ROBOTS, AND THEY WERE ATTACKING THE ***WHOLE SHIP***.

"DUNNO WHETHER ANYONE ELSE IS GONNA BE TELEPORTED DOWN HERE, OR WHETHER THAT PRIVILEGE IS RESERVED FOR ***THEORETICIANS AND THEIR FRIENDS***."

REMEMBER ***LAST YEAR?*** WE SAW SKIDS GET ATTACKED BY A LEGISLATOR—BY ONE OF THOSE GOLDEN ROBOTS.
BUT DO YOU REMEMBER? HE WAS CARRYING AN ***INVISIBLE GUN***. WELL, INVISIBLE TO ***HIM***.
SO?
SKIDS MUST'VE STOLEN THE GUN!
THAT'S WHY TYREST WANTS HIM!

SOUNDS PRETTY— *KAFF!* —PLAUSIBLE TO ME...
SKIDS!
LET'S JUST ASSUME I DID SOMETHING STUPID—SOMETHING REALLY STUPID—AND MOVE STRAIGHT TO THE— *KAFF!* —APOLOGY.
BECAUSE I JUST WANT TO SAY ***SORRY***.
CONTRITION WITHOUT CONFESSION IS MEANINGLESS...

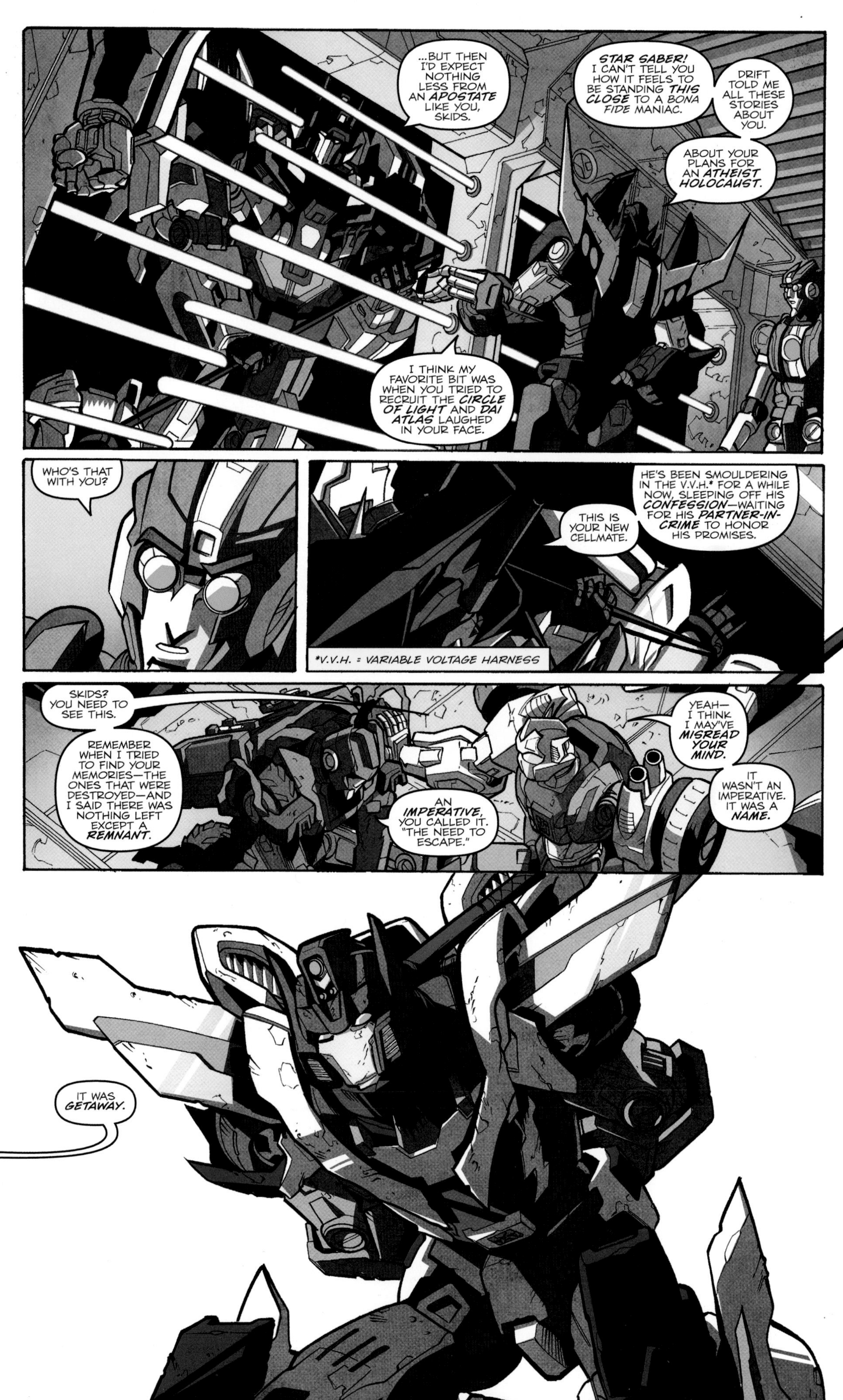

...BUT THEN I'D EXPECT NOTHING LESS FROM AN APOSTATE LIKE YOU, SKIDS.
STAR SABER! I CAN'T TELL YOU HOW IT FEELS TO BE STANDING THIS CLOSE TO A BONA FIDE MANIAC.
DRIFT TOLD ME ALL THESE STORIES ABOUT YOU.
ABOUT YOUR PLANS FOR AN ATHEIST HOLOCAUST.
I THINK MY FAVORITE BIT WAS WHEN YOU TRIED TO RECRUIT THE CIRCLE OF LIGHT AND DAI ATLAS LAUGHED IN YOUR FACE.
WHO'S THAT WITH YOU?
THIS IS YOUR NEW CELLMATE.
HE'S BEEN SMOULDERING IN THE V.V.H.* FOR A WHILE NOW, SLEEPING OFF HIS CONFESSION—WAITING FOR HIS PARTNER-IN-CRIME TO HONOR HIS PROMISES.
*V.V.H. = VARIABLE VOLTAGE HARNESS
SKIDS? YOU NEED TO SEE THIS.
REMEMBER WHEN I TRIED TO FIND YOUR MEMORIES—THE ONES THAT WERE DESTROYED—AND I SAID THERE WAS NOTHING LEFT EXCEPT A REMNANT.
AN IMPERATIVE, YOU CALLED IT. "THE NEED TO ESCAPE."
YEAH—I THINK I MAY'VE MISREAD YOUR MIND.
IT WASN'T AN IMPERATIVE. IT WAS A NAME.
IT WAS GETAWAY.

THE CONTROL ROOM.
TYREST?
I'M BUSY.
A DISTURBANCE NEAR THE SMELTING POOL.
I'M SENDING SOME LEGISLATORS TO INVESTIGATE.
WHAT HAPPENED TO "CHIEF JUSTICE"? HAVE YOU LOST YOUR MANNERS AS WELL AS YOUR ARMOR?

I'VE LOST EVERYTHING— AND I'M STARTING TO LIKE IT.
FOR THE FIRST TIME SINCE YOU CHOSE ME I FEEL... UNENCUMBERED.
UH-HUH.
THIS MAY COME AS A BITTER BLOW, BUT I HAVE PRECISELY NO INTEREST IN WHAT YOU'VE GOT TO SAY.

IS THAT WHY YOU'RE KEEPING ME OUT OF THE LOOP?
LUNA 1, THE TITANS OUTSIDE... AND DON'T THINK I HAVEN'T NOTICED THE SPACE BRIDGE PORTAL IN THE CORNER.
WHAT'S THIS ABOUT, TYREST?

IN A WORD? GUILT.
GUILT IS WHAT MAKES US DIFFERENT; IT'S WHAT MAKES US MORE THAN MACHINES.
DO LEGISLATORS FEEL GUILT WHEN THEY KILL? DO SPARKEATERS FEEL GUILT WHEN THEY FEED?
NO.
ONLY WE HIGHER BEINGS ARE TROUBLED BY OUR CONSCIENCE.

I HAVE SINNED, AMBUS. MY BODY OVERFLOWS WITH GUILT.
PLEASE. JUST TELL ME—POINT FOR POINT—WHAT'S GOING ON.
VERY WELL— BUT I WARN YOU. I'LL HAVE TO START AT THE BEGINNING.

"A CYBERTRONIAN IS CREATED IN ONE OF TWO WAYS: WE'RE EITHER FORGED OR CONSTRUCTED COLD.
"FOR THOSE OF US WHO ARE FORGED, LIFE BEGAN WHEN PRIMUS, THROUGH VECTOR SIGMA, GENERATED A PULSEWAVE.

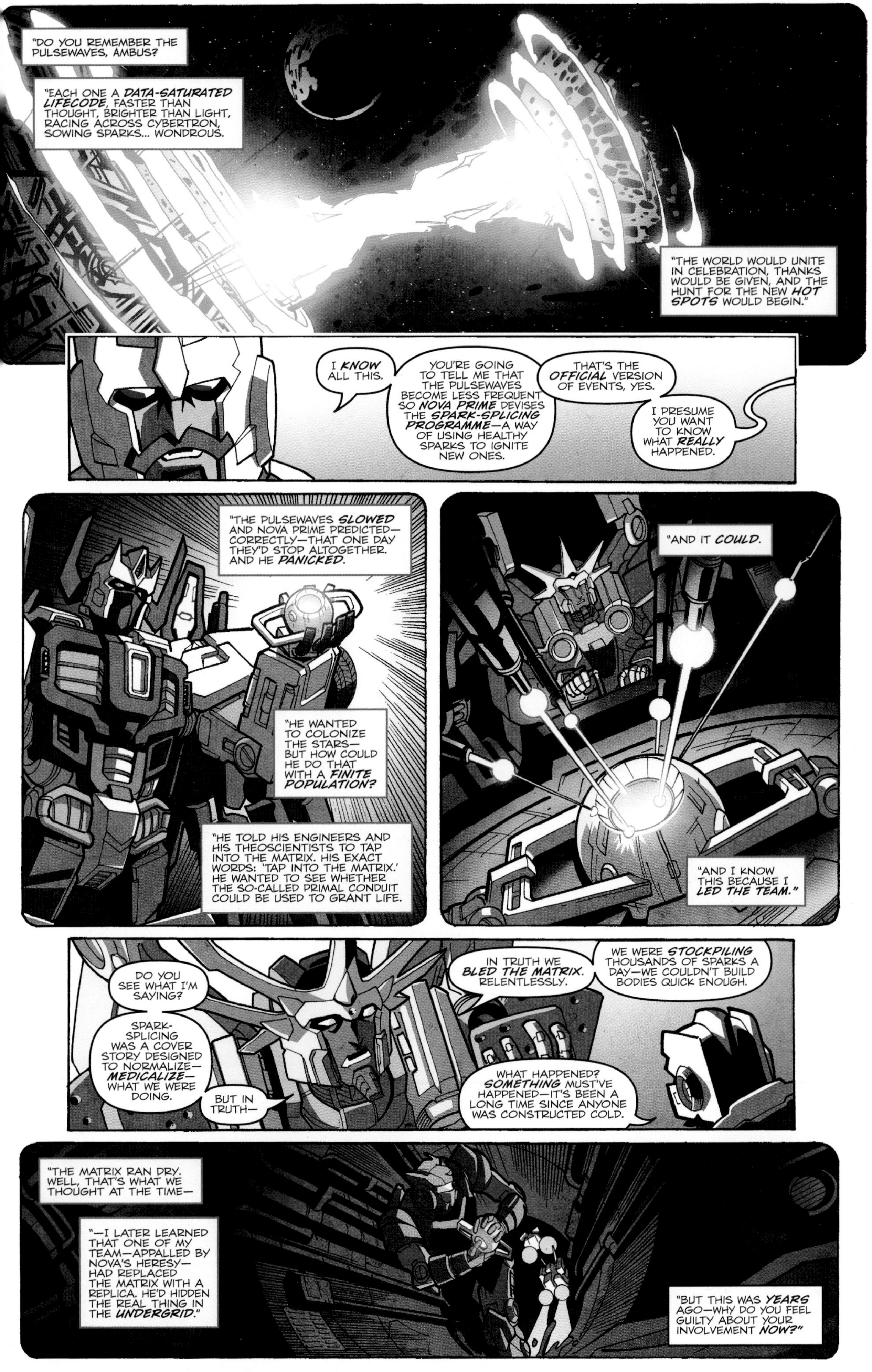

"DO YOU REMEMBER THE PULSEWAVES, AMBUS?

"EACH ONE A ***DATA-SATURATED LIFECODE***, FASTER THAN THOUGHT, BRIGHTER THAN LIGHT, RACING ACROSS CYBERTRON, SOWING SPARKS... WONDROUS.

"THE WORLD WOULD UNITE IN CELEBRATION, THANKS WOULD BE GIVEN, AND THE HUNT FOR THE NEW ***HOT SPOTS*** WOULD BEGIN."

I ***KNOW*** ALL THIS.

YOU'RE GOING TO TELL ME THAT THE PULSEWAVES BECOME LESS FREQUENT SO ***NOVA PRIME*** DEVISES THE ***SPARK-SPLICING PROGRAMME***—A WAY OF USING HEALTHY SPARKS TO IGNITE NEW ONES.

THAT'S THE ***OFFICIAL*** VERSION OF EVENTS, YES.

I PRESUME YOU WANT TO KNOW WHAT ***REALLY*** HAPPENED.

"THE PULSEWAVES ***SLOWED*** AND NOVA PRIME PREDICTED—CORRECTLY—THAT ONE DAY THEY'D STOP ALTOGETHER. AND HE ***PANICKED***.
"HE WANTED TO COLONIZE THE STARS—BUT HOW COULD HE DO THAT WITH A ***FINITE POPULATION?***
"HE TOLD HIS ENGINEERS AND HIS THEOSCIENTISTS TO TAP INTO THE MATRIX. HIS EXACT WORDS: 'TAP INTO THE MATRIX.' HE WANTED TO SEE WHETHER THE SO-CALLED PRIMAL CONDUIT COULD BE USED TO GRANT LIFE.

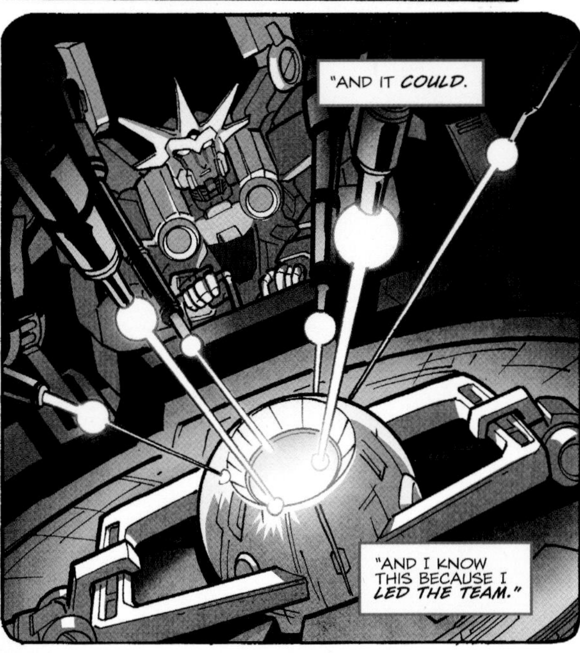

"AND IT ***COULD***.
"AND I KNOW THIS BECAUSE I ***LED THE TEAM."***

DO YOU SEE WHAT I'M SAYING?
SPARK-SPLICING WAS A COVER STORY DESIGNED TO NORMALIZE—***MEDICALIZE***—WHAT WE WERE DOING.
BUT IN TRUTH—
IN TRUTH WE ***BLED THE MATRIX***. RELENTLESSLY.
WE WERE ***STOCKPILING*** THOUSANDS OF SPARKS A DAY—WE COULDN'T BUILD BODIES QUICK ENOUGH.
WHAT HAPPENED? ***SOMETHING*** MUST'VE HAPPENED—IT'S BEEN A LONG TIME SINCE ANYONE WAS CONSTRUCTED COLD.

"THE MATRIX RAN DRY. WELL, THAT'S WHAT WE THOUGHT AT THE TIME—
"—I LATER LEARNED THAT ONE OF MY TEAM—APPALLED BY NOVA'S HERESY—HAD REPLACED THE MATRIX WITH A REPLICA. HE'D HIDDEN THE REAL THING IN THE ***UNDERGRID***."
"BUT THIS WAS ***YEARS*** AGO—WHY DO YOU FEEL GUILTY ABOUT YOUR INVOLVEMENT ***NOW?"***

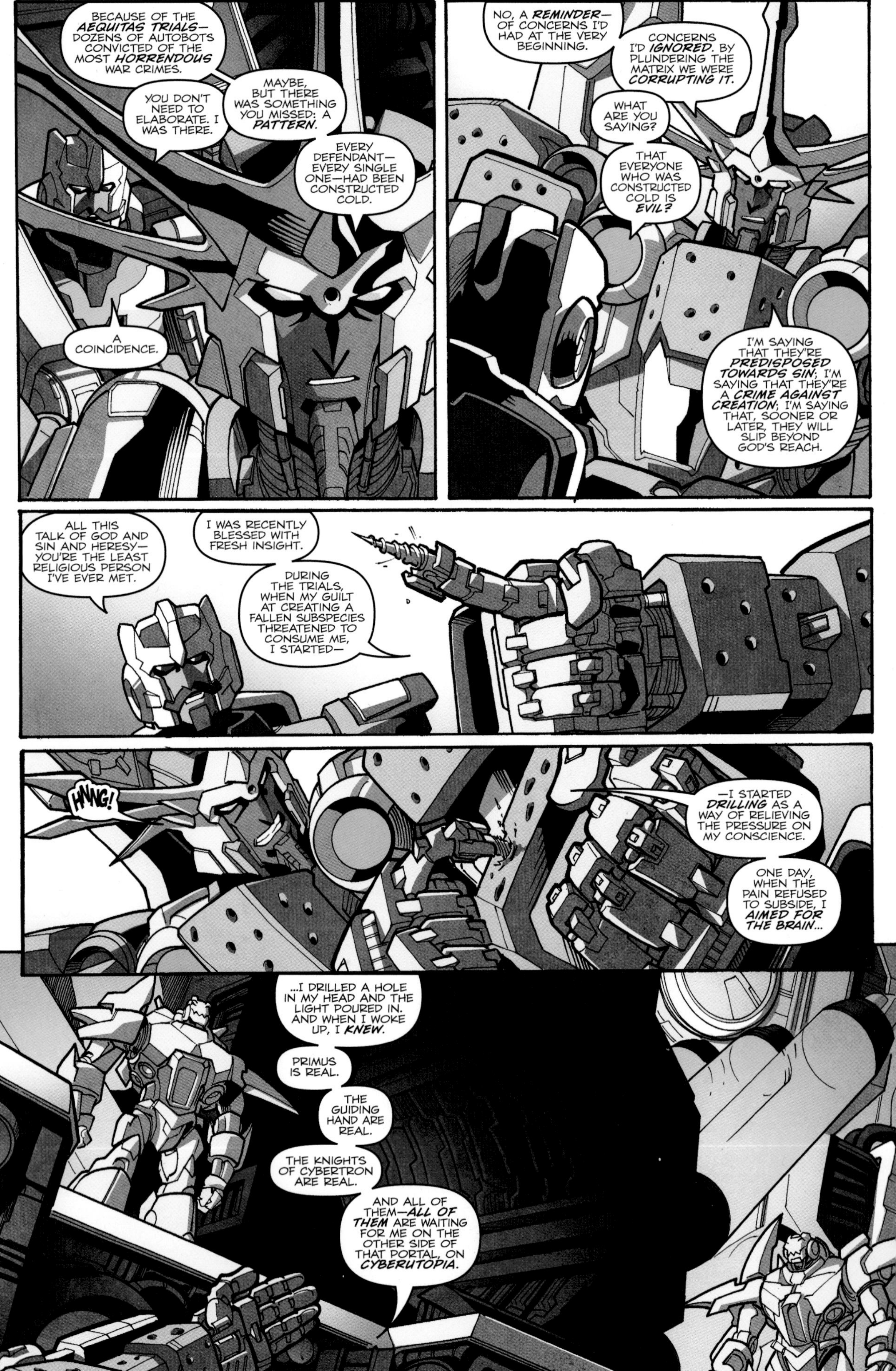
BECAUSE OF THE AEQUITAS TRIALS—DOZENS OF AUTOBOTS CONVICTED OF THE MOST HORRENDOUS WAR CRIMES.
YOU DON'T NEED TO ELABORATE. I WAS THERE.
MAYBE, BUT THERE WAS SOMETHING YOU MISSED: A PATTERN.
EVERY DEFENDANT—EVERY SINGLE ONE—HAD BEEN CONSTRUCTED COLD.
A COINCIDENCE.
NO, A REMINDER—OF CONCERNS I'D HAD AT THE VERY BEGINNING.
CONCERNS I'D IGNORED. BY PLUNDERING THE MATRIX WE WERE CORRUPTING IT.
WHAT ARE YOU SAYING?
THAT EVERYONE WHO WAS CONSTRUCTED COLD IS EVIL?
I'M SAYING THAT THEY'RE PREDISPOSED TOWARDS SIN; I'M SAYING THAT THEY'RE A CRIME AGAINST CREATION; I'M SAYING THAT, SOONER OR LATER, THEY WILL SLIP BEYOND GOD'S REACH.
ALL THIS TALK OF GOD AND SIN AND HERESY—YOU'RE THE LEAST RELIGIOUS PERSON I'VE EVER MET.
I WAS RECENTLY BLESSED WITH FRESH INSIGHT.
DURING THE TRIALS, WHEN MY GUILT AT CREATING A FALLEN SUBSPECIES THREATENED TO CONSUME ME, I STARTED—
HNNG!
—I STARTED DRILLING AS A WAY OF RELIEVING THE PRESSURE ON MY CONSCIENCE.
ONE DAY, WHEN THE PAIN REFUSED TO SUBSIDE, I AIMED FOR THE BRAIN...
...I DRILLED A HOLE IN MY HEAD AND THE LIGHT POURED IN. AND WHEN I WOKE UP, I KNEW.
PRIMUS IS REAL.
THE GUIDING HAND ARE REAL.
THE KNIGHTS OF CYBERTRON ARE REAL.
AND ALL OF THEM—ALL OF THEM ARE WAITING FOR ME ON THE OTHER SIDE OF THAT PORTAL, ON CYBERUTOPIA.

OUTSIDE.
I DIDN'T REALIZE THE CIRCLE OF LIGHT WAS SO POPULAR, DAI ATLAS.
I MEAN, YOU HEAR "KNIGHTS OF CYBERTRON CULT" AND YOU THINK TO YOURSELF, PFFT, FIFTY PEOPLE? SIXTY?
BUT THERE'S MASSES OF YOU!
GUESS SOME PEOPLE WILL DO ANYTHING TO GET A GREAT SWORD.
OUR NUMBERS ARE BUT A TENTH OF WHAT THEY ONCE WERE.
TYREST USED THE OTHERS AS RAW MATERIAL TO REPLENISH HIS LEGISLATORS.
ALL THE MORE REASON TO FIND TAILGATE AND THE OTHERS QUICKLY, BEFORE—
—BEFORE THEY ARRIVE.
SO HERE'S THE PLAN: I'LL WATCH YOUR BACK AND YOU WATCH MINE.
AND IF WE MAKE IT OUT OF THIS ALIVE, THEN ALL SCORES ARE SETTLED, OKAY?
NO MORE TRYING TO KILL ME. WHAT DO YOU SAY?
I SAY FOCUS ON THE FIGHT.

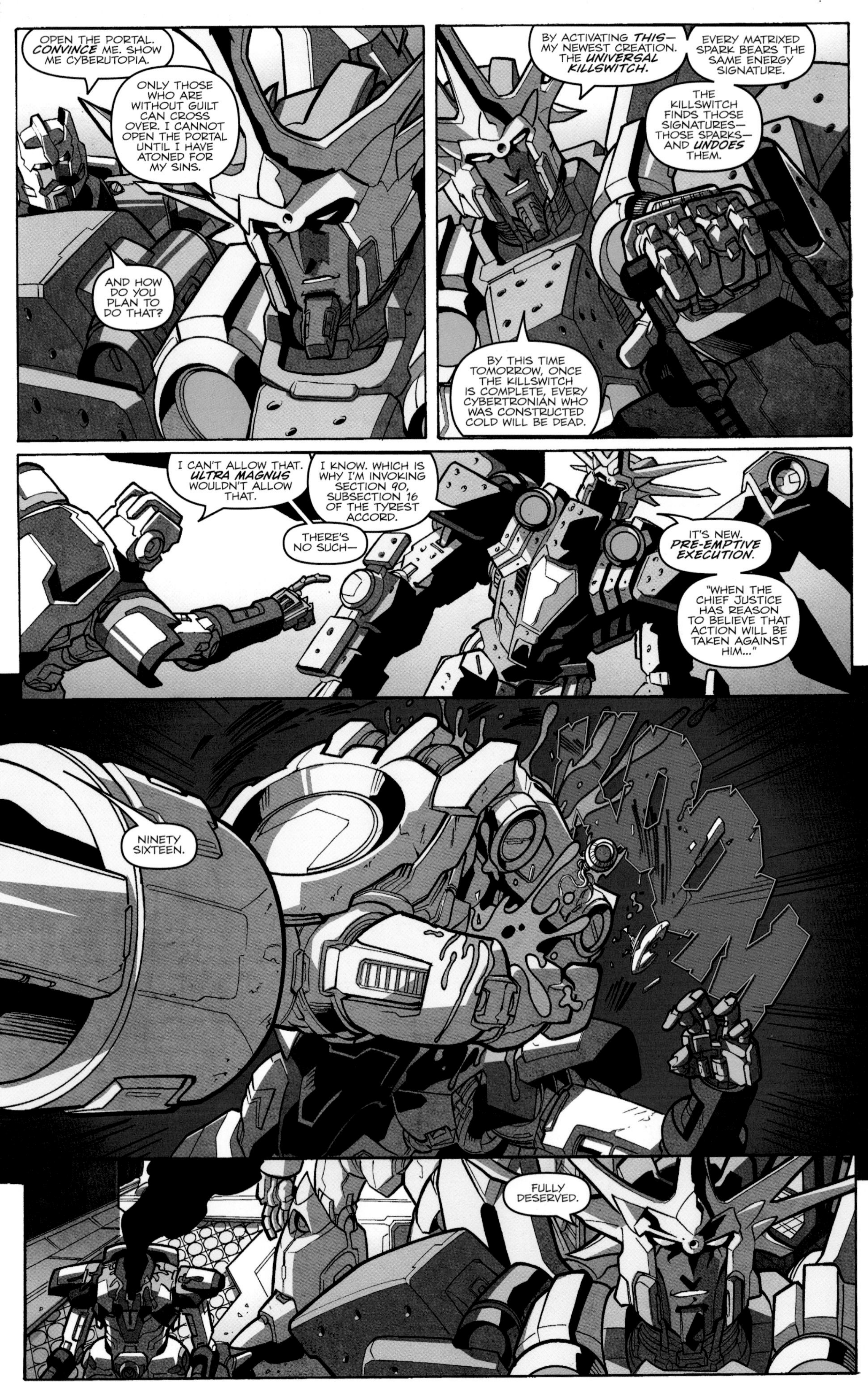

OPEN THE PORTAL. CONVINCE ME. SHOW ME CYBERUTOPIA.
ONLY THOSE WHO ARE WITHOUT GUILT CAN CROSS OVER. I CANNOT OPEN THE PORTAL UNTIL I HAVE ATONED FOR MY SINS.
AND HOW DO YOU PLAN TO DO THAT?
BY ACTIVATING THIS— MY NEWEST CREATION. THE UNIVERSAL KILLSWITCH.
EVERY MATRIXED SPARK BEARS THE SAME ENERGY SIGNATURE.
THE KILLSWITCH FINDS THOSE SIGNATURES— THOSE SPARKS— AND UNDOES THEM.
BY THIS TIME TOMORROW, ONCE THE KILLSWITCH IS COMPLETE, EVERY CYBERTRONIAN WHO WAS CONSTRUCTED COLD WILL BE DEAD.
I CAN'T ALLOW THAT. ULTRA MAGNUS WOULDN'T ALLOW THAT.
I KNOW. WHICH IS WHY I'M INVOKING SECTION 90, SUBSECTION 16 OF THE TYREST ACCORD.
THERE'S NO SUCH—
IT'S NEW. PRE-EMPTIVE EXECUTION.
"WHEN THE CHIEF JUSTICE HAS REASON TO BELIEVE THAT ACTION WILL BE TAKEN AGAINST HIM..."
NINETY SIXTEEN.
FULLY DESERVED.

MORE THAN MEETS THE EYE #19 COVER B

by **SEAN CHEN** Colors by **TOM CHU**

MORE THAN MEETS THE EYE #20 COVER A

by **ALEX MILNE** Colors by **JOSH PEREZ**

LUNA 1. THE CONTROL ROOM.
"TELL ME YOU CAN SAVE HIM.

THE CELL.
01 : 12 : 41 : 00
"RATCHET? YOU CAN SAVE HIM, CAN'T YOU?"

THE MEDIBAY.
I DON'T KNOW, FIRST AID.
I MEAN, HE'S—
—LOOK AT HIM.
LOOK AT HIM!

PHARMA SAID THAT WITH THE TOOLS IN THIS MEDIBAY HE COULD FIX ANYONE—CURE ANYTHING.

THIS IS HIS WAY OF PROVING HE'S BETTER THAN ME.
CUT AMBULON IN HALF AND RUN OFF AND LEAVE ME TO-TO-TO FAIL.
"I COULD SAVE HIM."
I CAN HEAR HIM SAYING IT: "I COULD SAVE HIM. CAN'T YOU?"

NOT FAR AWAY.
HOW ARE YOU—?
CYCLONUS! HOW ARE YOU DOING THAT?
WHAT?
YOUR SWORD. IT'S FRIKKIN' NUCLEAR POWERED.
IT'S A GREAT SWORD.
IT'S CERTAINLY IMPRESSIVE.
NO, I MEAN IT'S— THAT'S WHAT IT'S CALLED.

REMAIN IN LIGHT 4 of 5:
ARM THE LONELY
IT'S DRAWING POWER FROM YOUR SPARK TO THE NEXUS IN THE HILT AND THEN ENERGIZING THE BLADE.
I HAVE TO SAY, FOR A NOVICE, THAT'S VERY... HM.
DAI ATLAS?
THAT'S A SURPRISINGLY DEEP CONNECTION.
YOUR FRIEND IS CLEARLY DEVOUT.
SORRY, MY WHAT?

THE CELL.
SKIDS?
IT'S ME, GETAWAY. REMEMBER?
GETAWAY. CODEBREAKER. MARKSMAN. ESCAPOLOGIST.
NO? NOTHING?
...
DO I NEED TO HIT YOU?
YOU... DON'T NEED TO HIT ME.
WHY WOULD YOU HIT ME?
I DON'T MEAN HIT YOU, I MEAN—

BOMP.
WHEN YOU—BOMP—SAY SOMETHING FUNNY OR CLEVER OR BOMP, THAT'S WHAT I DO.
YOU HATE IT. YOU SAY ITS PATRONIZING. WHICH IT IS. WHICH IS WHY I DO IT.
I HAVE NO IDEA WHO YOU ARE.
OR WHY YOU KEEP SAYING "BOMP."

ANYWAY! HOT ROD.
RODIMUS.
RODIMUS.
WE'RE IN A SMIDGEN OF TROUBLE...

...TYREST HAS THIS MACHINE, THIS "UNIVERSAL KILLSWITCH," THAT ERASES SPARKS.
NOT EVERY SPARK, JUST PEOPLE WHO WERE CONSTRUCTED COLD.
HE WAS GOING TO TEST IT ON ME, BUT DECIDED THE INFORMATION IN MY HEAD—ABOUT MY "CRIME"—WAS TOO VALUABLE.

HOW CAN IT TELL THE DIFFERENCE BETWEEN FORGED AND CONSTRUCTED COLD?
THE KILLSWITCH? I DON'T REALLY KNOW.
GOING BY WHAT TYREST TOLD ME—RANT NUMBER 332—IT INVOLVES A KIND OF COMMON DENOMINATOR MATRIX CODE.
A MATRIX CODE?

HE THINKS KILLING ALL THE KNOCKOFFS WILL HELP HIM REACH CYBERUTOPIA.
WHY?
WHY WHAT?
WHY DOES HE THINK THAT?
BECAUSE, RODIMUS-NOT-HOT-ROD...

"...HE'S STARK RAVING MAD."
THERE'S A MYTH—IT'S NOT A MYTH; TO YOU IT'S A MYTH—
A TITAN CAN TAKE YOU TO THE KNIGHTS OF CYBERTRON.
AND IT'S TRUE!
PROPERLY CALIBRATED, THE SPACE BRIDGE PORTAL INSIDE A TITAN BECOMES A GATEWAY TO THE PROMISED LAND.
I FOUND MY FIRST TITAN WHEN I ARRIVED ON LUNA 1—BUT LIKE MOST OF HIS KIND, HE'D GONE ROTTEN.
HIS INNARDS HAD SPOILED. THE QUANTUM FOAM HAD CONGEALED.
SOUNDS... LOVELY...
BUT! A TINY PART OF THE SPACE BRIDGE INSIDE HIM WAS SALVAGEABLE, AND YOU KNOW WHAT THEY USED TO SAY:
<"YOU CAN USE A TITAN TO FIND A TITAN.">*
THE TITANS OUTSIDE...
DEEP INSIDE EACH ONE: ANOTHER LITTLE PIECE OF MY PATCHWORK PORTAL.
*TRANSLATED FROM OLD CYBERTRONIAN.
TYREST SAYS THE PORTAL WILL ACTIVATE ONCE THE KILLSWITCH HAS DONE ITS WORK.
FINE.
SO WE BLOW UP THE KILLSWITCH, STOP TYREST AND THEN—HOLD TIGHT, 'COS HERE IT COMES—WE GO THROUGH THE PORTAL OURSELVES.
UNIVERSE: SAVED. QUEST: OVER.
RODIMUS: DELUDED.
SORRY, CAPTAIN, BUT LIKE MOST PLANS INVOLVING FREEDOM OF MOVEMENT, YOURS IS ENTIRELY DEPENDENT ON NOT BEING IMPRISONED.
THAT'S A POINT—WHERE'S AMBUS GOT TO?
HE SAID HE'D COME BACK AND GET US OUT.
AMBUS? MINIMUS AMBUS?
YOU MAY KNOW HIM AS "ULTRA MAGNUS."
HE SAID HE WAS GONNA GET YOU OUT?
WHY, HAVE YOU SEEN HIM?
NO, IT'S— IT'S NOTHING, IT'S JUST—
LUNA 1. TYREST. THIS CELL...
ULTRA MAGNUS LURED YOU HERE.
YOU'RE EXACTLY WHERE HE WANTS YOU TO BE.

THE CONTROL ROOM.
I DON'T CARE HOW SPECIAL YOUR HANDS ARE, PHARMA— YOU DON'T TOUCH THE KILLSWITCH.
IT FASCINATES ME.
NO WONDER. IF IT WASN'T FOR THE KILLSWITCH YOU'D STILL BE ON MESSATINE—A DISEASE WAITING TO HAPPEN.
AN AMPUTEE WITH A MOUTHFUL OF SNOW.
"LET ME REPEAT HOW GRATEFUL I AM THAT YOU CAME LOOKING FOR ME, CHIEF JUSTICE."
"HOW ELSE COULD I BE SURE THAT THE KILLSWITCH COULD DIFFERENTIATE BETWEEN FORGED AND CONSTRUCTED COLD?
"AS SOMEONE FAMOUS FOR BEING FORGED, YOU WERE A PERFECT TEST SUBJECT.
"YOUR SURVIVAL PROVED THAT US PUREBREEDS WOULD BE SPARED THE CULL...
"...AND GAVE ME THE CONFIDENCE TO CONDUCT CLINICAL TRIALS ON A FAR GRANDER SCALE.
"I REASONED THAT A CITY'S WORTH OF CYBERTRONIANS WAS BOUND TO CONTAIN EXAMPLES OF BOTH CREATION TYPES.
"KIDNAPPING THE CIRCLE OF LIGHT COST ME 10,000 LEGISLATORS, BUT IT WAS WORTH IT: I WAS FINALLY ABLE TO TEST THE KILLSWITCH ON SOME KNOCKOFFS.
"IT WASN'T PRETTY."
ALL THAT WORK... STRANGE TO THINK IT ALL PAYS OFF TONIGHT.
I CAN HEAR PRIMUS SINGING IN MY HEAD: "COME CLOSER, COME CLOSER..."
TONIGHT? WHAT ABOUT GETAWAY AND SKIDS? YOU PROMISED AN EXECUTION...
I KNOW, BUT—I ALMOST REGRET ACTING AGAINST THEM.
WHEN I WAS UNSURE ABOUT THE KILLSWITCH, THEY CONVINCED ME TO PRESS AHEAD.
CHIEF JUSTICE!
STAR SABER?
OUTSIDE, SIR— THE CIRCLE OF LIGHT ARE ON THE RAMPAGE.
THE LEGISLATORS HAVE CONFRONTED THEM, BUT...
REQUEST PERMISSION TO INTERVENE.
GRANTED.
TAKE THE DECEPTICONS, TAKE THE REST OF THE LEGISLATORS, TAKE WHATEVER WEAPONRY YOU NEED—

"—AND SMITE THEM."
YOU FEELIN' ALRIGHT, PAL?
NOT PARTICULARLY, SWERVE, NO.
I'M SUPPOSED TO BE A SUPER-LEARNER—AND YET THE THING I KNOW LEAST ABOUT IS ME.

HEY!
GETAWAY! BOMP-BOT!
YOU GOT ANY DIRT ON MY FRIEND, I THINK NOW'S A GOOD TIME TO DISH IT.
PUT HIM OUT OF HIS MISERY.

YOU WORK FOR THE DIPLOMATIC CORPS.
I KNOW THAT.
UH-HUH. EXCEPT THE DIPLOMATIC CORPS IS JUST A FRONT. A NAME TO HIDE BEHIND.

THEN WHAT IS IT REALLY?
AUTOBOT SPECIAL OPS. THE WRECKERS DONE RIGHT.
GUILE, SUBTLETY... THAT'S WHAT WE'RE ABOUT. PRECISION.
BECAUSE NOT EVERY PROBLEM CAN BE SOLVED WITH BRAIN BULLETS AND BRAVADO.

"YOU AND ME—WE WERE PARTNERS. WE'RE STILL PARTNERS, I GUESS.
"WE'D BEEN SEARCHING FOR TYREST FOR YEARS. TRACING HIS FOOTSTEPS, PRESSING HIS ASSOCIATES. AND BEING CAREFUL—THE BOSS DIDN'T WANT MAGNUS TO KNOW WHAT WE WERE UP TO.
"EVENTUALLY WE TRACKED HIM HERE, TO LUNA 1...

"WE CAME PREPARED.
CONTENTS:
• "BINARY GUN" AND EXTENSIONS
• 3 X MODE LOCKS
• HOMING DEVICE

"WE SPLIT UP TO DOUBLE OUR CHANCES OF GETTING A CLEAR SHOT, AND THEN—"
"STOP STOP STOP. A CLEAR SHOT? WE WERE SENT TO ASSASSINATE TYREST?
"I COULD NEVER ASSASSINATE SOMEONE—THAT'S NOT MY STYLE. I DON'T THINK THAT'S MY STYLE. PLEASE TELL ME THAT'S NOT MY STYLE."
"HEAR ME—BOMP—OUT, OKAY?"

"YOU FOUND HIM BEFORE I DID. YOU SAID:"
GETAWAY? I'M IN POSITION.

I'M GONNA TAKE THE SHOT.

"OKAY, THIS IS DEFINITELY RINGING ASSASSINATION ALARM BELLS."
RELAX—WE WEREN'T PACKING PROPER FIREPOWER, JUST A COUPLA NUDGE GUNS.
Y'KNOW, NEW INSTITUTE TECH.

THE BINARY GUN...
BINARY GUN? OH—YEAH—TWO CHARGES. CUTE.

SEE, SKIDS, HERE'S THE THING: WHEN YOU TOOK AIM AT TYREST YOU WEREN'T ABOUT TO FIRE A BULLET—YOU WERE ABOUT TO FIRE A THOUGHT.
A THOUGHT.
AN ARTIFICIAL THOUGHT—AN IRRESISTABLE THOUGHT. BUILT IN A LAB AND DESIGNED TO BE ACTED UPON.

WHAT WAS THE THOUGHT?
RESIGN.
THAT WAS IT?
THAT WAS IT.

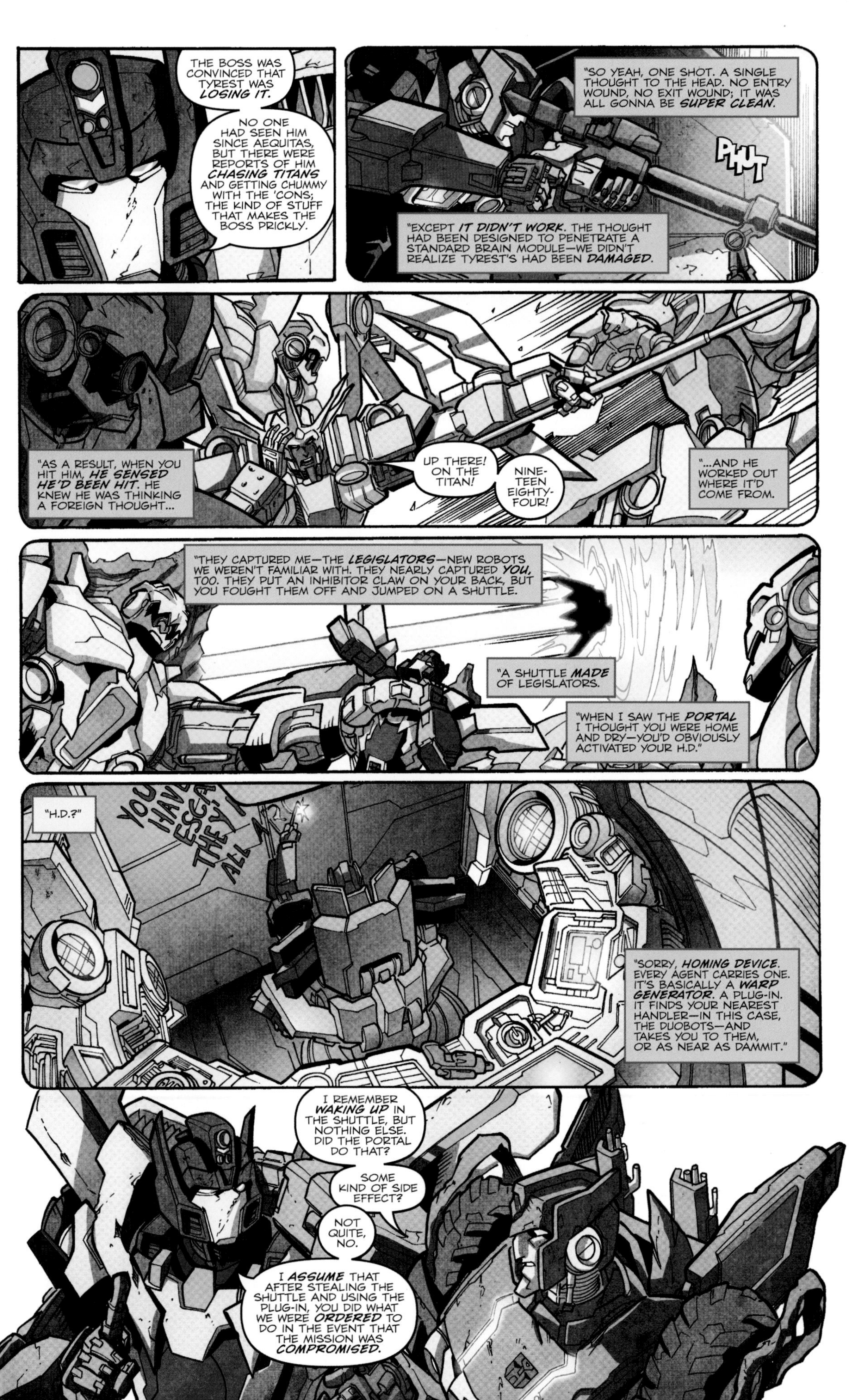

THE BOSS WAS CONVINCED THAT TYREST WAS LOSING IT.
NO ONE HAD SEEN HIM SINCE AEQUITAS, BUT THERE WERE REPORTS OF HIM CHASING TITANS AND GETTING CHUMMY WITH THE 'CONS; THE KIND OF STUFF THAT MAKES THE BOSS PRICKLY.
"SO YEAH, ONE SHOT. A SINGLE THOUGHT TO THE HEAD. NO ENTRY WOUND, NO EXIT WOUND; IT WAS ALL GONNA BE SUPER CLEAN.
PHUT
"EXCEPT IT DIDN'T WORK. THE THOUGHT HAD BEEN DESIGNED TO PENETRATE A STANDARD BRAIN MODULE—WE DIDN'T REALIZE TYREST'S HAD BEEN DAMAGED.
"AS A RESULT, WHEN YOU HIT HIM, HE SENSED HE'D BEEN HIT. HE KNEW HE WAS THINKING A FOREIGN THOUGHT...
UP THERE! ON THE TITAN!
NINE-TEEN EIGHTY-FOUR!
"...AND HE WORKED OUT WHERE IT'D COME FROM.
"THEY CAPTURED ME—THE LEGISLATORS—NEW ROBOTS WE WEREN'T FAMILIAR WITH. THEY NEARLY CAPTURED YOU, TOO. THEY PUT AN INHIBITOR CLAW ON YOUR BACK, BUT YOU FOUGHT THEM OFF AND JUMPED ON A SHUTTLE.
"A SHUTTLE MADE OF LEGISLATORS.
"WHEN I SAW THE PORTAL I THOUGHT YOU WERE HOME AND DRY—YOU'D OBVIOUSLY ACTIVATED YOUR H.D."
"H.D.?"
"SORRY, HOMING DEVICE. EVERY AGENT CARRIES ONE. IT'S BASICALLY A WARP GENERATOR. A PLUG-IN. IT FINDS YOUR NEAREST HANDLER—IN THIS CASE, THE DUOBOTS—AND TAKES YOU TO THEM, OR AS NEAR AS DAMMIT."
I REMEMBER WAKING UP IN THE SHUTTLE, BUT NOTHING ELSE. DID THE PORTAL DO THAT?
SOME KIND OF SIDE EFFECT?
NOT QUITE, NO.
I ASSUME THAT AFTER STEALING THE SHUTTLE AND USING THE PLUG-IN, YOU DID WHAT WE WERE ORDERED TO DO IN THE EVENT THAT THE MISSION WAS COMPROMISED.

"YOU TOOK YOUR GUN...
"...AND YOU TURNED IT ON YOURSELF.

"TWO CHARGES, REMEMBER? AND THE SECOND WAS A BLANK.
"A BLANK DESIGNED TO DESTROY EVERY INCRIMINATING MEMORY—EVERY MEMORY OF ME, OF THE BOSS... AND OF THE MISSION ITSELF, OF COURSE.

WHAT ABOUT THE BINARY GUN ITSELF?
SKIDS' MEMORIES OF THE GUN WOULD'VE BEEN DESTROYED, BUT IT WOULDN'T HAVE BEEN INVISIBLE TO HIM. HE'D HAVE SEEN IT IN HIS HAND BUT NOT KNOWN WHAT IT WAS FOR.
AND THE SECOND HE LOOKED AWAY, THE BLANK WOULD'VE DESTROYED HIS MEMORY OF HAVING LOOKED AT IT.
WHICH IS WHY HE NEVER LET GO OF IT—HE KEPT FORGETTING IT WAS THERE...
IF THE BLANK DESTROYS FRESH MEMORIES, HOW COME I CAN REMEMBER HIM NOW?
GETAWAY. WHEN I'M NOT LOOKING AT HIM, I REMEMBER HIM.
IT'S THAT REMNANT—THAT TRACE MEMORY.
I THINK IT'S ACTING AS A FOUNDATION FOR THE NEW MEMORIES YOU'RE BUILDING NOW.

BY ACTING AGAINST TYREST I THINK WE CONVINCED HIM OF THE RIGHTNESS OF HIS CAUSE. THE BOSS WOULD'VE CALLED IT AN UNINTENDED CONSEQUENCE.
THIS "BOSS"—IT'S PROWL, RIGHT?
C'MON, WE'RE ALL THINKING IT.
GIVE YOURSELF A BONUS POINT, HOT SHOT.

SORRY—DID YOU SAY ESCAPOLOGIST?
I MIGHT'VE DONE.
TAILGATE, GETAWAY'S BEEN A PRISONER FOR MONTHS. IF HE COULD'VE ESCAPED, HE WOULD'VE ESCAPED.

AH, BUT NOW I'M IN HERE WITH ALL OF YOU, I HAVE SOMETHING I DIDN'T HAVE BEFORE.
A FRESH SET OF KEYS.

LET ME HELP.
I CAN HELP.
IS HE STILL BEHIND US?
WHO?
THE ROBOT WITH THE—?
YEAH. WE'RE STILL TRAPPED.

LET ME HELP...!
YOU CAN'T.
DAMMIT, RATCHET, YOU THINK IT'S CHEATING?
YOU THINK YOU LOSE THE GAME IF SOMEONE ELSE HAS A GO?
DON'T BE RIDICULOUS.

THIS IS ALL YOUR FAULT.
YOU AND YOUR STUPID HANDS AND YOUR— OBSESSION WITH CARRYING ON.
"RATCHET, CHIEF MEDICAL OFFICER IN PERPETUITY."
BECAUSE NO ONE WILL EVER BE AS GOOD AS YOU, WILL THEY?
CERTAINLY NOT ME.

OH, WE'RE HAVING THAT CONVERSATION NOW, ARE WE?
I'M JUST SAYING I CAN HELP YOU FIX AMBULON!
AND I'M SAYING YOU CAN'T!
WHY CAN'T I?!

BECAUSE HE DIED HALF AN HOUR AGO.

NOW MOVE!
CHOOM
B-KOOM
AMBULON WAS DEAD BEFORE THE CHAINSAW LEFT HIS BODY—BUT TURNING A CORPSE INTO A WEAPON TAKES TIME.
RATCHET— THOSE THINGS I SAID...
WERE VERY WELL SAID.
LISTEN: IF WE SURVIVE THIS, YOU'RE TAKING OVER.
PROPER CEREMONY, PROPER HANDOVER. THE WORKS.
BUT FIRST WE FIND PHARMA AND PUT A BULLET IN HIS SPARK, RIGHT?
NO.
IF WE KILL HIM, WE'RE NO BETTER THAN HIM. IF WE KILL HIM, HE WINS.
YEAH, EXCEPT—WE ARE BETTER THAN HIM AND HE DOESN'T WIN.
HE DOESN'T ANYTHING. HE'S DEAD. THAT'S THE POINT.
RATCHET! FIRST AID!

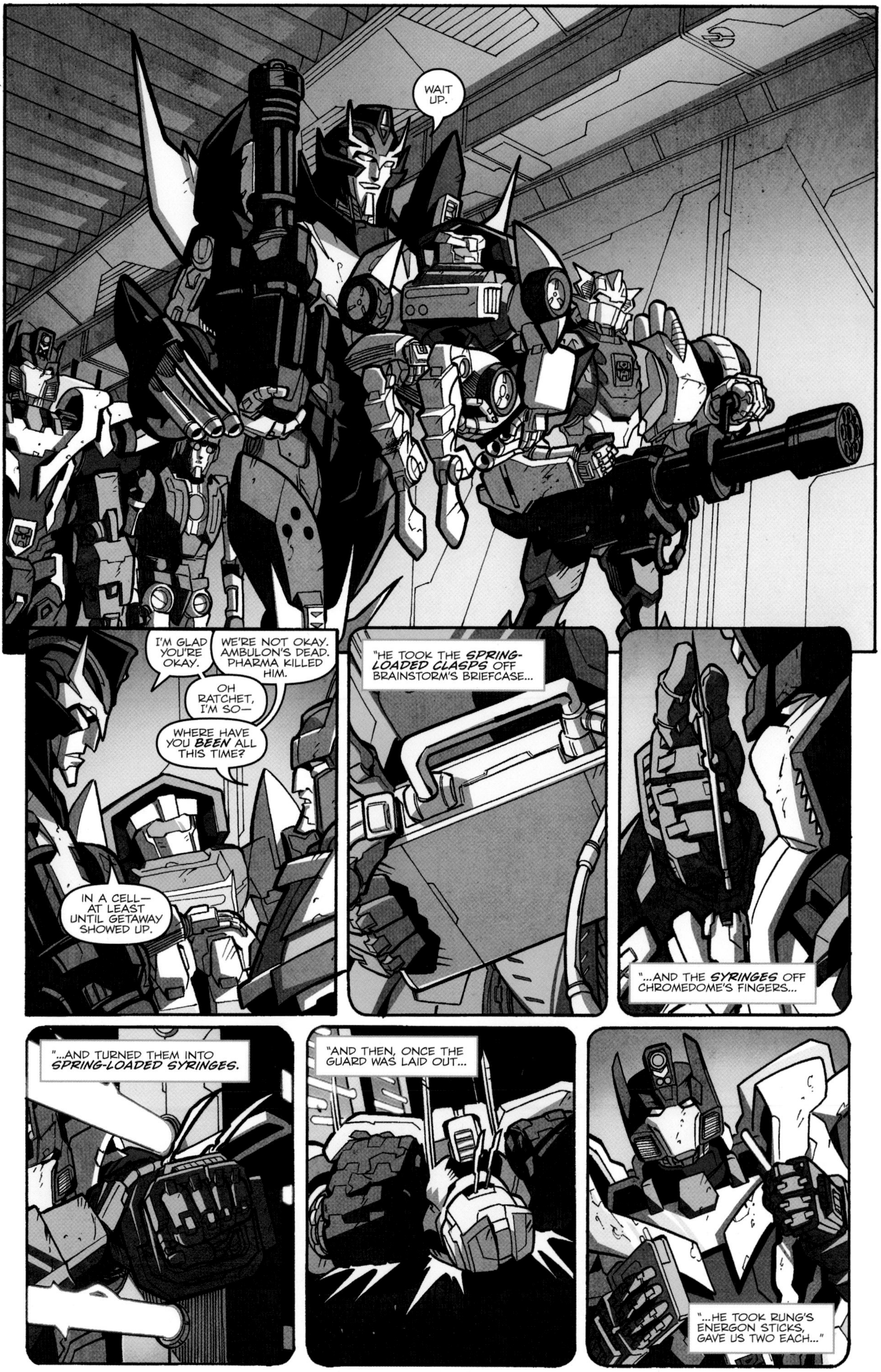

WAIT UP.

I'M GLAD YOU'RE OKAY.

WE'RE NOT OKAY. AMBULON'S DEAD. PHARMA KILLED HIM.

OH RATCHET, I'M SO—

WHERE HAVE YOU *BEEN* ALL THIS TIME?

IN A CELL— AT LEAST UNTIL GETAWAY SHOWED UP.

"HE TOOK THE ***SPRING-LOADED CLASPS*** OFF BRAINSTORM'S BRIEFCASE...

"...AND THE ***SYRINGES*** OFF CHROMEDOME'S FINGERS...

"...AND TURNED THEM INTO SPRING-LOADED SYRINGES.

"AND THEN, ONCE THE GUARD WAS LAID OUT...

"...HE TOOK RUNG'S ENERGON STICKS, GAVE US TWO EACH..."

"...AND TOLD US TO SLIDE THEM OVER THE BASE OF EVERY ELECTROBAR AT *EXACTLY THE SAME TIME*.
VZZZZ-KOOM
"AND THEN WE JUST WALKED OUT OF THERE! WELL, *MOST* OF US."

YOU OKAY, TAILGATE?
HERE, LET ME...
SERVOS IN THE LEGS SEIZING UP, THAT'S ALL. EVER GET THAT?
BIT OF SERVO TROUBLE? NO?

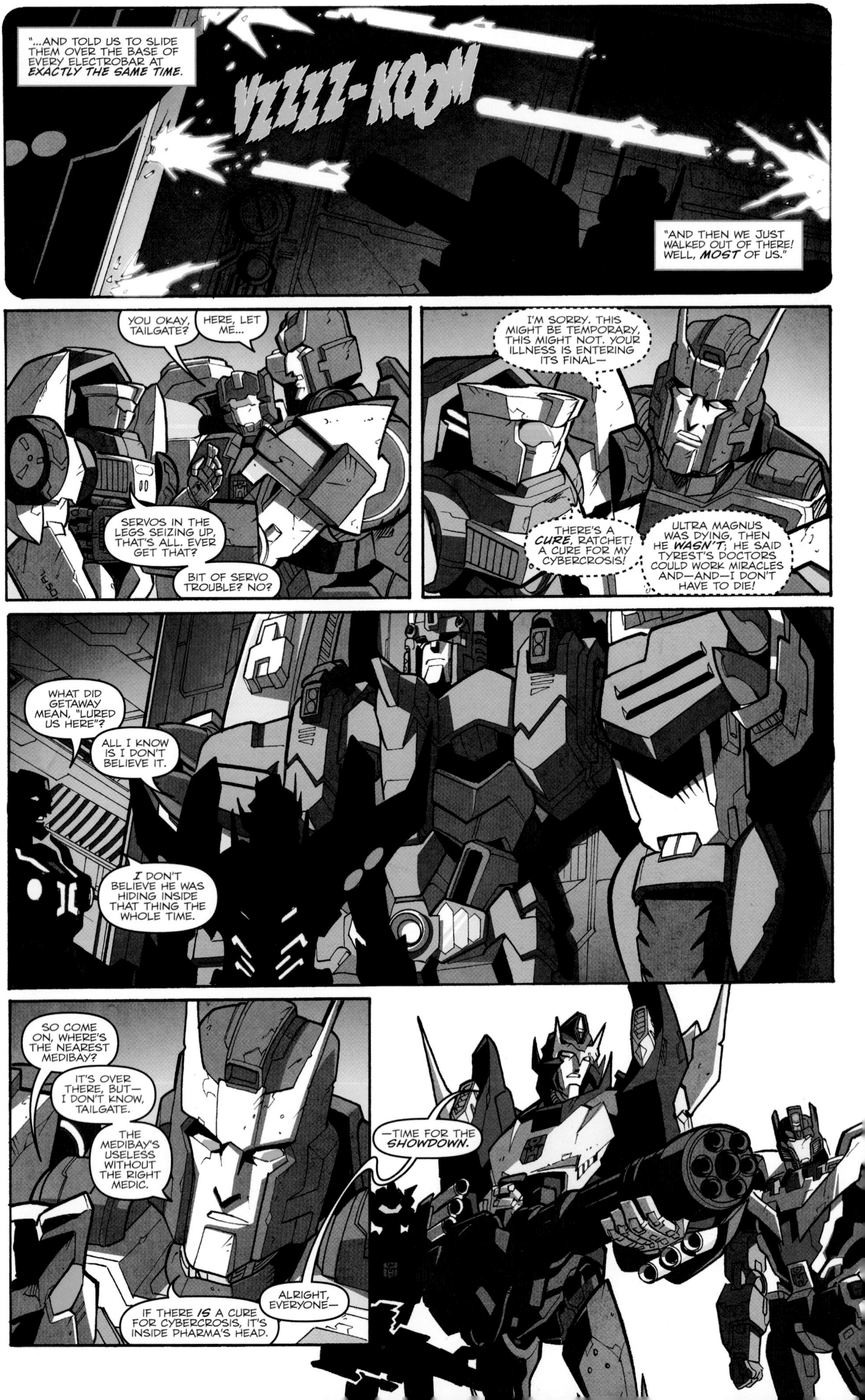

I'M SORRY. THIS MIGHT BE TEMPORARY, THIS MIGHT NOT. YOUR ILLNESS IS ENTERING ITS FINAL—
THERE'S A *CURE*, RATCHET! A CURE FOR MY CYBERCROSIS!
ULTRA MAGNUS WAS DYING, THEN HE *WASN'T*; HE SAID TYREST'S DOCTORS COULD WORK MIRACLES AND—AND—I DON'T HAVE TO DIE!

WHAT DID GETAWAY MEAN, "LURED US HERE"?
ALL I KNOW IS I DON'T BELIEVE IT.
I DON'T BELIEVE HE WAS HIDING INSIDE THAT THING THE WHOLE TIME.

SO COME ON, WHERE'S THE NEAREST MEDIBAY?
IT'S OVER THERE, BUT— I DON'T KNOW, TAILGATE.
THE MEDIBAY'S USELESS WITHOUT THE RIGHT MEDIC.
IF THERE *IS* A CURE FOR CYBERCROSIS, IT'S INSIDE PHARMA'S HEAD.
ALRIGHT, EVERYONE—
—TIME FOR THE *SHOWDOWN*.

WE'VE GOT TO FINISH THIS NOW—
—I'M NEEDED ELSEWHERE.
OH REALLY? AND THERE WAS ME DRAGGING THIS OUT FOR FUN!
I'LL JUST FINISH UP.
IS HE BEING SARCASTIC?
I DON'T THINK EVEN HE KNOWS.
THE LEGISLATORS WILL NEVER GIVE UP. THEY CAN'T. IT'S NOT IN THEIR PROGRAMMING. THE ONLY WAY TO STOP THEM IS TO KILL THEM— ALL OF THEM.
OVER THERE, BY THE SMELTING POOL...
TELEPORT FLARE.
TYREST?
WORSE.
I'LL DEAL WITH THIS.
I SHOULD HAVE DEALT WITH IT A LONG TIME AGO.

STAR SABER!

YOU!

HERETIC!

APOSTATE!

UNBELIEVER!

YOU'VE NOT CHANGED, STAR SABER. STILL CONVINCED THAT EVERYONE ELSE IS UNDESERVING OF GOD'S GRACE.

TELL ME: DOES PRIMUS SHINE HIS LIGHT ON ***ANYONE*** BUT YOU?

YOUR "FAITH" IS AN AFFECTATION. IT ALWAYS WAS. REAL FAITH ***HURTS***.

IT TWISTS LIKE A KNIFE IN YOUR SPARK AND FORCES YOU TO ***ACT***.

YOU NEVER DID ***ANYTHING***—YOU JUST SAT IN CRYSTAL CITY AND WAITED FOR THE KNIGHTS TO COME LOOKING FOR ***YOU***. SUCH ***ARROGANCE***...

IS THAT WHY YOU BETRAYED US?

THE MOMENT THE LEGISLATORS ATTACKED THE CITY YOU LOWERED OUR DEFENSES AND WELCOMED THEM IN...!

EVERYTHING I DO IS ***DIVINELY SANCTIONED***—

CHUK
—INCLUDING ***THIS***.
AH! AH! AH!
YOUR LIFE IS IN THE PALM OF MY HAND, DAI ATLAS.
BEFORE I ***SQUEEZE***, I OFFER UP ONE LAST SHINING TRUTH:

KNOCK KNOCK!
A LOT OF PEOPLE ARE LINING UP TO GIVE YOU A DAMN GOOD KICKING, TYREST.
GUESS WHO'S FRONT OF THE QUEUE?
OH *RODIMUS*. DO YOU KNOW WHAT I DID TO THE LAST PERSON WHO THREATENED ME?
I TURNED HIM INTO A *TRIPPING HAZARD.*
MAGNUS!
ARGH!
WHAT THE—?!
SHRKK
PHARMA!
PHARMA.
NO MORE SHOOTING.
WEAPON DOWN.
LET'S KEEP THIS CIVILIZED.

I'VE GOT YOUR NUMBER, TYREST. YOU THINK YOU'RE SPECIAL.
YOU'RE NOT.
YOU'RE JUST LIKE ALL THE OTHER MASS MURDERING HEADCASES WE'VE PUT DOWN OVER THE YEARS.
NO, NO, NO. YOU SEE, THIS HEADCASE—
—IS READY FOR YOU.
KLIK
OOF!
WHAT THE HELL DID YOU JUST DO?!
I CAN'T MOVE! IS THIS THE KILLSWITCH?! WHY AM I AFFECTED?!
THIS ISN'T THE KILLSWITCH.
THIS IS A NEW INVENTION— AN INVENTION MADE POSSIBLE BY GETAWAY'S THOUGHT BULLET.
I CALL IT A WEAPON OF MASS SUGGESTION.
I'M BROADCASTING A MESSAGE DEEP INTO YOUR HEADS, MAKING YOU THINK YOU CAN'T MOVE.
I CAN'T MOVE!
YOU SEE?
IT'S SO CONVINCING THAT I CAN TELL YOU IT'S A TRICK AND YOU'LL REFUSE TO BELIEVE ME.
AS FOR THE KILLSWITCH...

...IT'S OVER *HERE*.
AND BEFORE YOU SPLIT HAIRS, *YES*— GUILTY AS CHARGED— THE NAME IS MISLEADING.

KLIK
BECAUSE A NORMAL SWITCH WORKS *BOTH WAYS*, DOESN'T IT? ON AND OFF AND ON AND OFF AND ON AND OFF...
THIS *DOESN'T*.
ONCE *THIS* SWITCH IS FLICKED, IT'S FLICKED *FOREVER*.

AND WE'RE OFF!
VA-SHOOM

NNNGG!
STOP IT! YOU'RE KILLING THEM!
ARGH!
NOT JUST THEM. *EVERYONE* WHO WAS CONSTRUCTED COLD.
THE SIGNAL IS BEING CARRIED ON THE SUBSPACE NETWORK.
FROM HERE—

HUURGH!
"—IT CAN GO ANYWHERE!"
THE LOST LIGHT.

NEAR GORLAM PRIME.
WHAT IS IT, HARDHEAD? TELL ME WHAT'S HAPPENING!

CYBERTRON.
HRRGH—!

SOMEBODY HELP HIM—

M-MEGATRON?
ARRGH!

HNNNG! HNNNG!
SPEAK TO ME, KAON!
TELL ME HOW I CAN HELP!
THE PEACEFUL TYRANNY.

THE PLANET CONSTANCY.
GALACTIC COUNCIL OUTPOST 113.
TEN MILES FROM DEATH ROW.
I APPRECIATE THE RESCUE, FULCRUM.
'COURSE I DO.
WHO DOESN'T LIKE BEING RESCUED?
BUT DID YOU REALLY THINK THIS ESCAPE PLAN THROUGH?
THE PLAN WAS BULLETPROOF.
IT WENT OUT THE WINDOW, MISFIRE, WHEN YOU INSISTED ON TAKING A DETOUR...
OH, LIKE YOU NEVER GET THE MUNCHIES.

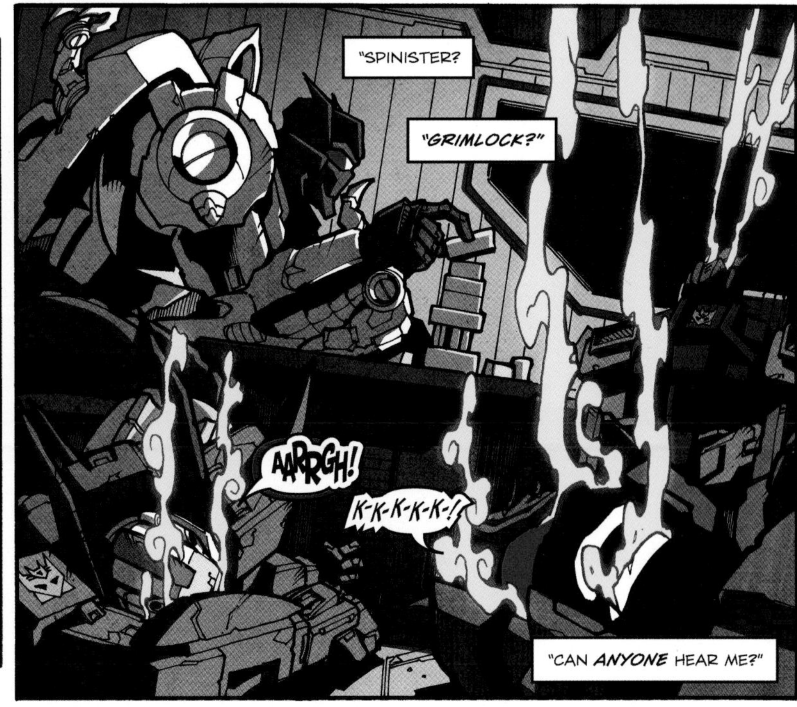

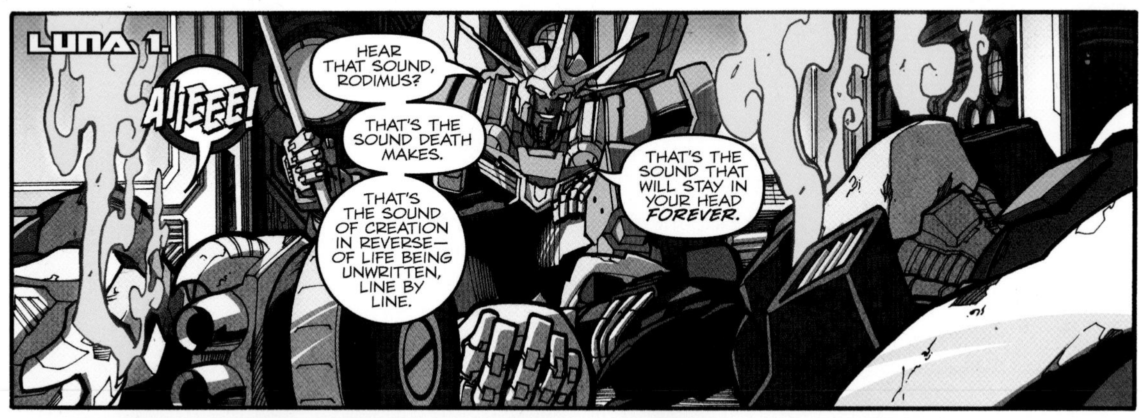

LUNA 1.
AIIEEE!
HEAR THAT SOUND, RODIMUS?
THAT'S THE SOUND DEATH MAKES.
THAT'S THE SOUND OF CREATION IN REVERSE—OF LIFE BEING UNWRITTEN, LINE BY LINE.
THAT'S THE SOUND THAT WILL STAY IN YOUR HEAD **FOREVER.**

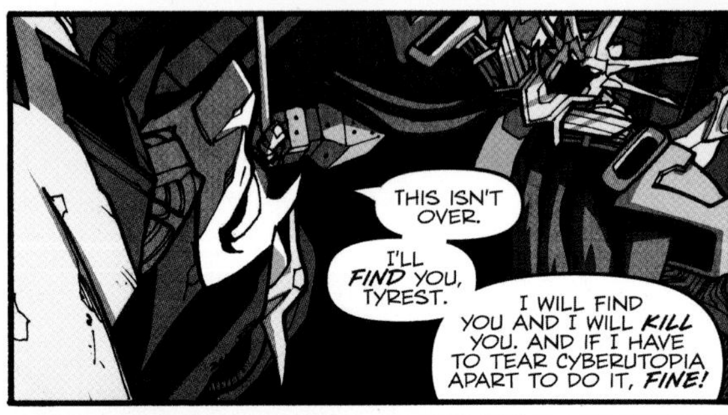

THIS ISN'T OVER.
I'LL **FIND** YOU, TYREST.
I WILL FIND YOU AND I WILL **KILL** YOU. AND IF I HAVE TO TEAR CYBERUTOPIA APART TO DO IT, **FINE!**

AH!
AND RIGHT ON CUE—

—THE **PORTAL OPENS** AND THE **PRIMAL PANTHEON** BECKONS.

PRIMUS!

THE GUIDING HAND!

THE KNIGHTS OF CYBERTRON!

CAN YOUR HEAR THEM **SINGING?**

"TYREST, COME CLOSER, COME CLOSER, COME CLOSER/ TYREST, COME CLOSER, COME CLOSER—

"—YOU'VE ***WON.*** *'"*

MORE THAN MEETS THE EYE #20 COVER B

by **NICK ROCHE** Colors by **JOANA LAFUENTE**

MORE THAN MEETS THE EYE #21 COVER A

by **ALEX MILNE** Colors by **JOSH PEREZ**

LUNA 1.

FIVE INCHES FROM ENLIGHTENMENT.

OH, NO YOU DON'T!

ARGH!

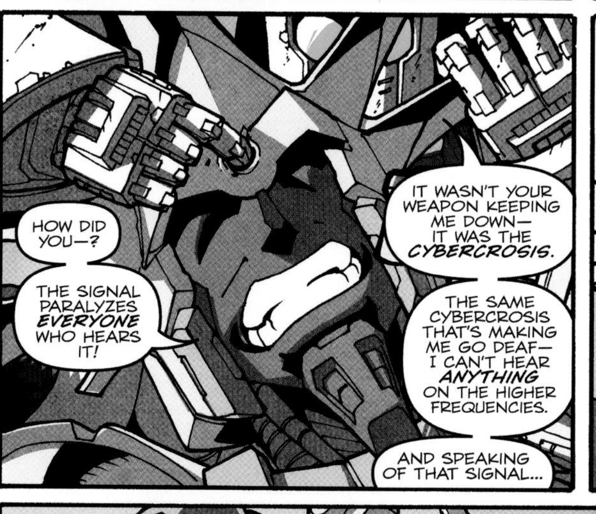

IT WASN'T YOUR WEAPON KEEPING ME DOWN— IT WAS THE *CYBERCROSIS*.
HOW DID YOU—?
THE SIGNAL PARALYZES *EVERYONE* WHO HEARS IT!
THE SAME CYBERCROSIS THAT'S MAKING ME GO DEAF— I CAN'T HEAR *ANYTHING* ON THE HIGHER FREQUENCIES.
AND SPEAKING OF THAT SIGNAL...

LET'S SWITCH IT *OFF*, SHALL WE?
KLIK

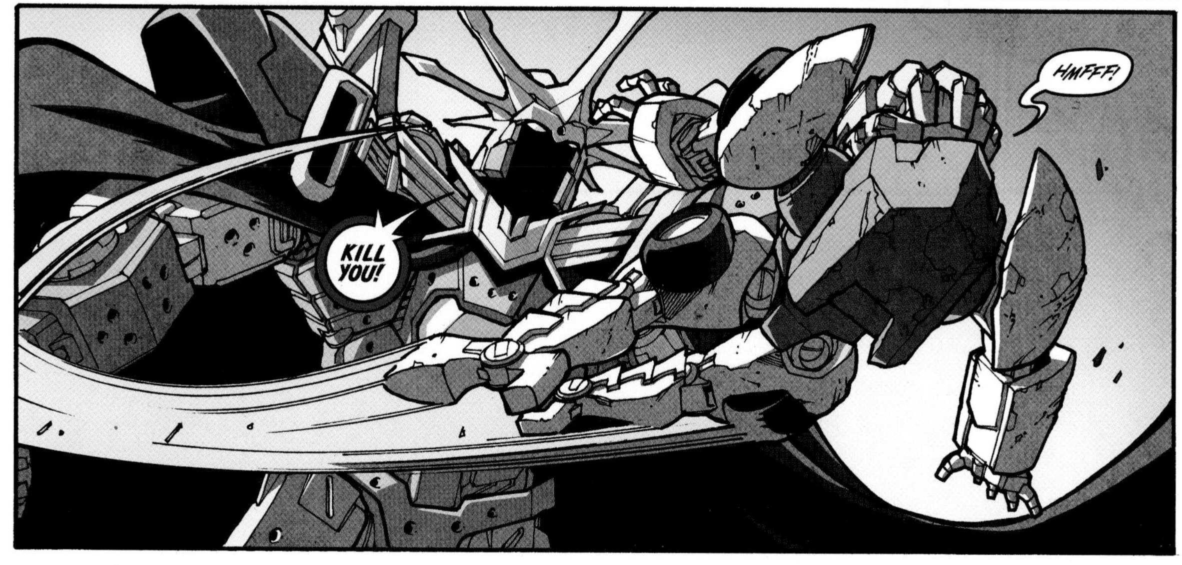

HMFFF!
KILL YOU!

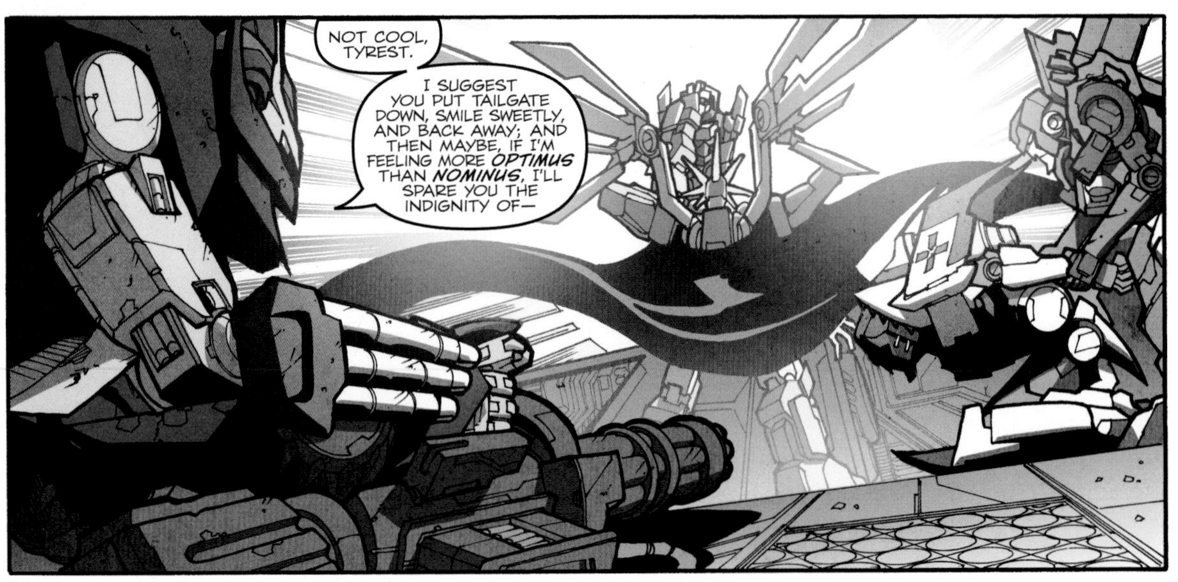
NOT COOL, TYREST.
I SUGGEST YOU PUT TAILGATE DOWN, SMILE SWEETLY, AND BACK AWAY; AND THEN MAYBE, IF I'M FEELING MORE OPTIMUS THAN NOMINUS, I'LL SPARE YOU THE INDIGNITY OF—

RODIMUS! FOCUS!
UNLESS WE TURN OFF THE KILLSWITCH, CHROMEDOME AND THE OTHERS WILL BE DEAD IN MINUTES!

I TOLD YOU— THE KILLSWITCH CAN'T BE TURNED OFF!
TEAR IT DOWN, BLOW IT UP, DOESN'T MATTER— THE DAMAGE IS ALREADY DONE!

NOW—I WANT EVERYONE WITHIN KISSING DISTANCE OF THE FLOOR. NO ONE LOOK UP 'TIL I'M THROUGH THE PORTAL.
DO IT! OR I'LL LOBOTOMIZE THE SHIP'S MASCOT.
SHOOT HIM, RODIMUS! SHOOT HIM!
TAILGATE, I—

01 : 12 : 15 : 59
I'M DYING! PROPER, FULL ON DYING!
CYBERCROSIS! THE BIG C! I'VE ONLY GOT A DAY AND A HALF LEFT!
NOW SHOOT HIM!

I DON'T THINK I NEED TO.
SHEEAAAGH!
VASHOOM
FULLY DESERVED.
AMBUS?!
REMAIN IN LIGHT 5 of 5: THIS CALAMITOUS LIFE

OUTSIDE.
PATHETIC!
ALL OF YOU!

IF GOD WERE ON YOUR SIDE YOU'D HAVE STOPPED ME BY NOW!
WILL ANYBODY PIT THEIR FAITH AGAINST MINE?

I WILL.

YOU'LL LOSE, OF COURSE.

THWOK
I FIGHT BECAUSE PRIMUS HAS ORDAINED IT.

WHY DO YOU FIGHT?
IT'S PERSONAL.
SLUTCH.
AARGH!
I'VE NEVER BOUGHT INTO THE NOTION OF PRIMAL INFALLIBILITY; I THINK THAT SOMETIMES, GOD GETS IT WRONG.
HE LETS THE BEST OF US GET SICK AND DIE WHILE DEGENERATES LIKE YOU GO ON FOREVER.
BUT I THINK PRIMUS IS SMILING ON ME TODAY, STAR SABER: HE'S LETTING ME CORRECT ONE OF HIS MISTAKES.
NO!
FZZZT

WHAT—
—THE—
—*HELL?*
I SAID I WAS A ***LOADBEARER***—I DIDN'T SAY ***HOW MANY*** LOADS I COULD CARRY AT ONCE.
BUT—
DON'T WORRY, THIS IS ME.
THE ***IRREDUCIBLE*** ME.

"WHEN THE LEGISLATOR CRUSHED MY HEAD—MY OUTER HEAD—THE FEED-BACK KNOCKED ME UNCONSCIOUS.
"WHEN I CAME TO, I HAD TO PUNCH MY WAY OUT."

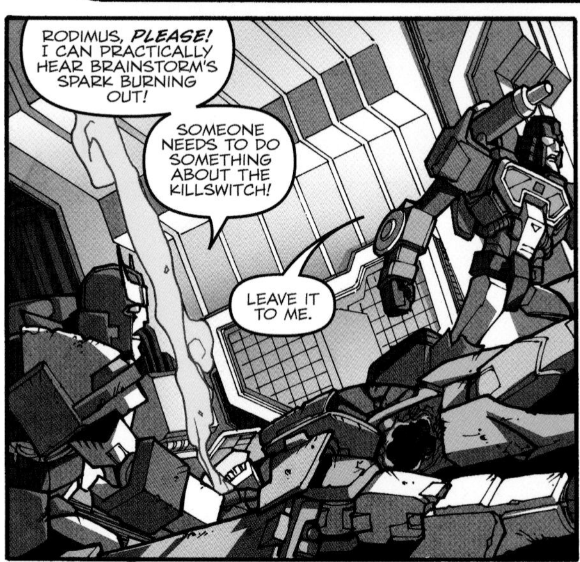

SIX MINUTES TO BRAINDEATH—ASSUMING GETAWAY'S SPARK LASTS THAT LONG...
WAIT A MINUTE—WHERE'S PHARMA?

BUT—I TIED HIM TO THE WALL! I HANDCUFFED HIM!
YOU CAN'T CUFF SOMEONE WITH HANDS LIKE HIS.
OH NO...

"...I THINK HE'S GONE THROUGH THE PORTAL!"
DON'T RUSH ON MY ACCOUNT—THERE'S NO WAY THROUGH.
TYREST SAID A GUILTY CONSCIENCE WOULD PREVENT YOU FROM REACHING CYBERUTOPIA, BUT THAT'S CLAPTRAP: IT'S JUST A FORCEFIELD.

WHOA...
HOW COME I CAN PUT MY HAND IN AND—?
RUNG. HOW COME I CAN DO THIS AND YOU CAN'T?
THE FORCEFIELD MUST—NNG!—USE SOMETHING SIMILAR TO AEQUITAS TECH: IT ONLY HOLDS YOU BACK IF IT CAN DETECT GUILT.

NOT NECESSARILY EVIDENCE OF CRIMINALITY; MORE LIKE ANGUISH OR SELF-REPROACH.
YOU MUST BE AT PEACE WITH YOURSELF.
YOU KNOW WHAT, EYEBROWS?

I THINK I FINALLY AM.

RIGHTO THEN, NURSE: ARREST ME.
TELL ME OFF AND LOCK ME UP. I'VE BEEN A BAD AUTOBOT.
YOU'RE SMILING.

EVERYTHING YOU DID AT DELPHI— ALL THOSE PATIENTS YOU KILLED—
AND YOU'RE SMILING?

I KNOW, I KNOW—
—I'M INCORRIGIBLE.

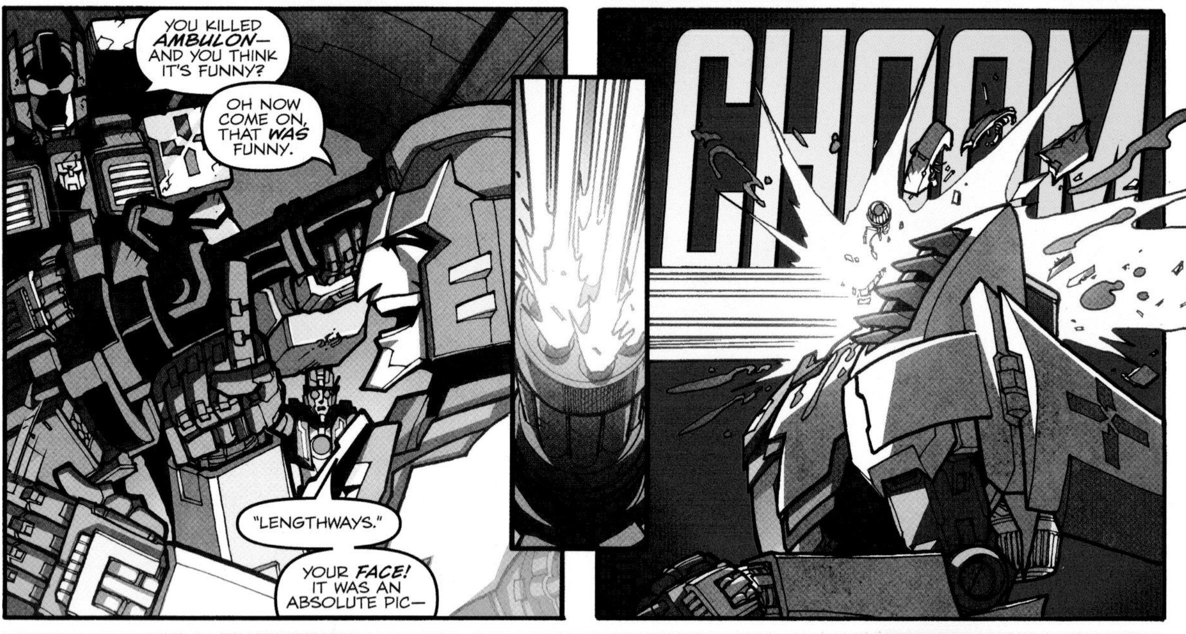
YOU KILLED AMBULON— AND YOU THINK IT'S FUNNY?
OH NOW COME ON, THAT WAS FUNNY.
"LENGTHWAYS."
YOUR FACE! IT WAS AN ABSOLUTE PIC—

IT'S NOT YOUR FAULT, FIRST AID.
IT'S NOT YOUR FAULT.
"OKAY, PERCEPTOR. RUN IT BY ME ONE MORE TIME."

EVERYONE WHO WAS CONSTRUCTED COLD HAS A SPECIAL SPARKCODE.
UNTIL TODAY, I THOUGHT THE CODE WAS A BYPRODUCT OF THE SPARK-SPLICING PROCESS, BUT IT'S NOT—IT'S COPIED DIRECTLY FROM THE MATRIX.
THE KILLSWITCH SCRAMBLES THE SPARKCODE. IF WE CAN REINSTATE THE CODE BY TAKING A NEW COPY FROM WHAT'S LEFT OF THE MATRIX, WE SHOULD BE ABLE TO REVERSE THE EFFECTS OF THE KILLSWITCH.

IS IT GOING TO KILL ME?
HONESTLY? I DON'T KNOW. IT'LL CERTAINLY TEAR THE MATRIX APART.
THERE GOES OUR MAP.

JUST GIVE ME A MOMENT TO FINALIZE THE SETTINGS.
MINIMUS—MAGNUS—C'MERE A MINUTE.

NEARBY.
I'M TELLING YOU, TYREST'S ALIVE—HE'S TRYING TO SAY SOMETHING.
HE'S SAYING...
WHAT'S HE SAYING?
SOMETHING ABOUT WINNING.

ONE

TYREST ACCORD
Part I
Section One
Immediate Vicinity
HUH.
TALK ABOUT DELUSIONAL.

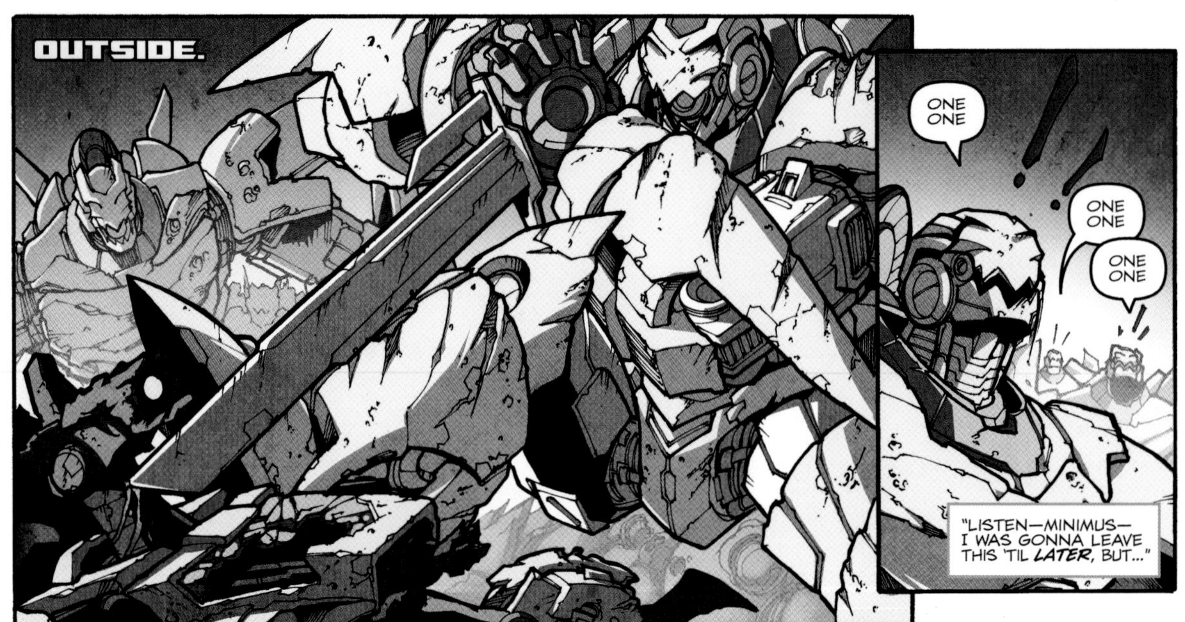

OUTSIDE.
ONE ONE
ONE ONE
ONE ONE
"LISTEN—MINIMUS— I WAS GONNA LEAVE THIS 'TIL LATER, BUT..."

...GETAWAY SAID YOU LURED US HERE.
HE THINKS THAT RATHER THAN TELEPORT HERE, YOU USED YOUR RECALL TRIGGER TO GIVE TYREST REMOTE ACCESS TO YOUR BODY, KNOWING WE'D FOLLOW YOU.
BUT IT'S AN INTERESTING WORD TO USE, ISN'T IT?
"LURED."
...
RODIMUS— CAPTAIN—I'VE BEEN UNHAPPY FOR A WHILE NOW.
WITH YOU, I MEAN. WITH YOUR LEADERSHIP.
SO YOU DID LURE US HERE!

WAIT—
MY LEADERSHIP?

I'VE HAD MISGIVINGS FROM THE OUTSET— WHEN WE WERE LEAVING CYBERTRON, AND YOU REFUSED TO SPEAK TO BUMBLEBEE.
THEN THERE WAS THE SPARKEATER, AND YOU RISKING RUNG'S LIFE, AND THEN—
AND THEN WHEN FORTRESS MAXIMUS TOOK HOSTAGES AND YOU MADE SWERVE SHOOT, EVEN THOUGH MAX HAD BEEN PACIFIED.
YOU ARRESTED CYCLONUS ON THE FLIMSIEST OF PRETEXTS, YOU ANTAGONIZED THE GALACTIC COUNCIL, AND AS FOR YOUR STAGGERINGLY IMMATURE REACTION WHEN THUNDER—
OKAY!

MESSAGE RECEIVED AND UNDERSTOOD.
ACTUALLY, NO, MESSAGE NOT UNDERSTOOD: YOU DIDN'T LIKE MY STYLE SO YOU THOUGHT YOU'D GET ME ARRESTED AND PUT TO DEATH?
YOU WERE CLOSE TO FALLING FOUL OF THE FIT PERSONS ACT!
I THOUGHT TYREST WOULD REPRIMAND YOU AND IT WOULD—I DON'T KNOW—SHOCK OR, OR, OR SHAME YOU INTO ACTING MORE RESPONSIBLY.
I DIDN'T KNOW—I OBVIOUSLY DIDN'T KNOW TYREST HAD BECOME UNHINGED.

MAGNUS—
(I'M GONNA CALL YOU MAGNUS.)
MAGNUS, IF THIS IS IT—IF I'M GOING TO DIE—I NEED TO COME CLEAN. EVERYTHING YOU'VE JUST SAID—
I'VE DONE WORSE. I'VE DONE MUCH WORSE.

I BROUGHT OVERLORD ON BOARD.

I WAS PART OF IT, WITH DRIFT AND BRAINSTORM AND THE DUOBOTS. I LET IT HAPPEN.
PROWL SAID I OWED IT TO THE AUTOBOTS. BEFORE WE LEFT CYBERTRON, HE...
WE MET IN HIS OFFICE, AND HE TOLD ME HE WANTED AN AUTOBOT PHASE SIXER—SOMEBODY AS POWERFUL AS OVERLORD, BUT ON OUR SIDE.
AND THEN HE SAID—
THESE MIGHT NOT HAVE BEEN HIS EXACT WORDS, BUT HE SAID IF I WAS SCARED OF HAVING OVERLORD ON BOARD I COULD SAY NO, WHICH...
WELL. HERE WE ARE.

WE'RE NEARLY READY TO GO.
TEN SECONDS.

I DON'T WANT TO DIE.
OF COURSE NOT. OF COURSE YOU DON'T.
NO, I MEAN—
SELF-SACRIFICE, MAGNUS—IT'S CHEAP. IT'S A CHEAP WAY OUT.
I NEED TO LIVE SO I CAN MAKE AMENDS AND—

AAAARRRGH!

ELSEWHERE.
HELLO?
ANYONE HERE?
ANYONE CARE TO TELL ME WHERE "HERE" IS?
OH!
HEY.
HI.
!
SORRY, I—
ARE YOU SPEAKING? IS THAT—
IS THAT *SOUND?*

AAAARRRGH!
KISH
LIFE SIGNS ARE GOOD. BETTER THAN GOOD.
WHATEVER YOU'RE DOING, RODIMUS, IT'S WORKING! BRAINSTORM'S GOING TO BE OKAY!
"EVERYONE'S GOING TO BE OKAY!"
ANYONE ELSE HEAR MARCHING?

HOW ABOUT THAT, CYCLONUS? WE WON!
THE LEGISLATORS HAVE GONE, LOCKDOWN'S DONE A RUNNER, AND IF YOU'RE ALIVE I'M GUESSING STAR SABER ISN'T—SO, WELL DONE US!

CLOSE ONE, THOUGH—LOOK AT THE STATE OF ME!
I'M A FRIKKIN' ENDOSKELETON!
YOU CAN'T FLY...
FLY?
I CAN BARELY STAND.

NOW, ABOUT OUR LITTLE DEAL...
REMEMBER?
I SAID THAT IF WE SURVIVED THIS, YOU AND I, WE'D PUT OUR HILARIOUSLY VIOLENT PAST BEHIND US AND START AFRESH.
SO WHADDYA SAY?
ARE WE COOL?

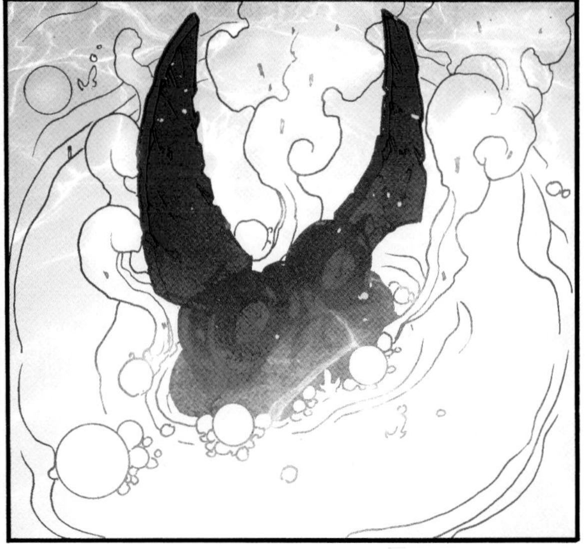

I SAID, ARE WE COOL?
WE'RE "COOL."
SKIDS!
ONE ONE
A LITTLE HELP IN HERE!
ONE ONE
SKIDS!

ONE ONE
WHAT'S ALL THIS "ONE ONE" BUSINESS?
THE LEGISLATORS ARE PROGRAMMED TO ENFORCE THE LAW—SO I'M GUESSING SECTION 1 (1) HAS SOMETHING TO DO WITH PROTECTING THE CHIEF JUSTICE...
"GUESSING"? I THOUGHT YOU WERE AN EXPERT.
IT'S NEW. TYREST WAS USING THAT COMPUTER TO AMEND THE LAW.
THAT COMPUTER OVER THERE?
WISH ME LUCK!

PLEASE TELL ME YOU'VE NOT CHANGED SECTION 500...
TAP TAP TAP
THERE!
HUH?
WHY ISN'T IT WORKING? WHAT HAVE I MISSED?
OF COURSE!
THE SEMI-COLON!
THEY'VE STOPPED!
THEY'VE ALL JUST— STOPPED!
OF COURSE THEY'VE STOPPED!
THEY HAVE TO DO WHAT THE LAW SAYS— AND I'VE JUST REPEALED THE LAW!
ALL OF IT!
I FIGURED THAT WITHOUT ANYTHING TO ENFORCE, THEY'D JUST... THEY'D JUST...
01 : 11 : 58 : 01

00 : 00 : 14 : 30

YOU STOPPED SINGING.

I'LL, UH, GIVE YOU TWO SOME TIME...

YOU DRIFTED OFF.

I WENT TO SEE RATCHET. THEY'RE ALL IN PHARMA'S MEDI-BAY, LOOKING FOR A CURE.

AND...?

...

KAFF!

NEARLY FORGOT—

—I MADE YOU A PRESENT.

IT'S IN OUR HAB SUITE, UNDER THE WINDOW SILL—AND YOU'VE *GOT* TO WEAR IT.

NO EXCUSES.

00 : 00 : 11 : 30

DID YOU EVER VISIT RIVETS FIELD?
ON CYBERTRON? YES, I WATCHED IT IGNITE. WHY?
I WAS BORN IN RIVETS FIELD.
BUT THAT WAS—RIVETS FIELD IGNITED TWO WEEKS BEFORE ARK 1 TOOK OFF.
TWO WEEKS BEFORE YOU WERE TRAPPED UNDERGROUND...

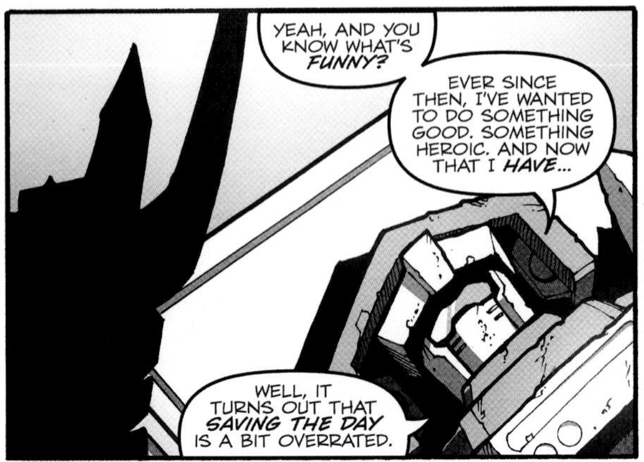

YEAH, AND YOU KNOW WHAT'S FUNNY?
EVER SINCE THEN, I'VE WANTED TO DO SOMETHING GOOD. SOMETHING HEROIC. AND NOW THAT I HAVE...
WELL, IT TURNS OUT THAT SAVING THE DAY IS A BIT OVERRATED.

GIVE ME ANOTHER MOVIE NIGHT INSTEAD.
GIVE ME ANOTHER AFTERNOON IN SWERVE'S, OR—OR A NIGHT IN.
JUST A NICE NIGHT IN, DOING NOTHING.

HAVE YOU THOUGHT ABOUT WHAT I SAID EARLIER?
YES.
AND THE ANSWER IS STILL NO.
BUT WITH CYBERCROSIS, THEY SAY THE END—THE VERY END—IS *AGONIZING*.
AND I DON'T— I DON'T WANT TO DIE *SCREAMING*.
IF YOU COULD JUST SHOOT ME, OR TEAR MY HEAD OFF... SOMETHING *QUICK*.
I'M NOT KILLING YOU.
NOT *YET*, OR NOT AT ALL?
BZZZT
I'M SORRY. I SHOULD'VE DOUBLE-CHECKED THE RESULTS BEFORE CALLING YOU.
BUT YOU *HAVE* FOUND A CURE?
WELL, YES— THANKS TO SWERVE'S INTERPRETATION OF PHARMA'S NOTES—BUT IT'S TOO LATE TO TREAT TAILGATE.
THE ANTI-CORROSION AGENTS NEED TO BE SEEDED MUCH EARLIER, BEFORE THE SPARK REACHES THE FINAL STAGES OF CONTRACTION.

I'M SORRY.
...
...
THANK YOU FOR TRYING.

CYCLONUS, I—
NOT NOW.
BUT—
NOT NOW!

CYCLONUS?
I THINK THIS IS IT.
00 : 00 : 01 : 59
SHUNK

EPILOGUE.
WELL?
WHAT DO YOU THINK?

YAY, THE ARMOR'S BACK. NOW THERE'S THE ULTRA MAGNUS WE ALL KNOW AND LOVE...
WELL I DON'T KNOW ABOUT THAT.
ANYWAY. GAVE IT A GOOD CLEAN. STILL FITS.

YOU WEREN'T AT SWERVE'S "GRAND REOPENING."
YEAH, I DUNNO. NOT REALLY IN THE MOOD. STILL SMARTING FROM THE KILLSWITCH.
AND—Y'KNOW—THINGS ON MY MIND.
WAS I MISSED?
YOU WERE TALKED ABOUT... PEOPLE ARE SURPRISED THAT WE LEFT LUNA 1 SO QUICKLY.

TYREST'S PORTAL BURNT ITSELF OUT DURING THE FIGHT WITH THE LEGISLATORS, THE HOT SPOT WOULDN'T REIGNITE—PROBABLY BECAUSE THE MATRIX IS DUST—
—AND RATCHET TOOK WHAT HE WANTED FROM PHARMA'S MEDIBAY.
SO WHY STICK AROUND?

ANYWAY, I THOUGHT PEOPLE WOULD BE GLAD TO MOVE ON!
LUNA 1 WASN'T EXACTLY A LIFE-AFFIRMING EXPERIENCE, WAS IT?
AMBULON'S DEAD, HALF THE SHIP IS IN RUINS, FIRST AID'S NOT TALKING TO ANYONE...

"...AND BRAINSTORM'S LOCKED HIMSELF AWAY IN HIS WORKSHOP."

SO MUCH FOR THE "MIRACLE MOON." AT THE END OF THE DAY—AFTER BEING LOST FOR 12 MILLION YEARS—IT WAS JUST... A MOON.
ALL THE SAME, I REGRET NOT ASKING MORE QUESTIONS OF TYREST.
HE SAID HE JUST FOUND IT, DIDN'T HE?
YES, JUST HAPPENED TO STUMBLE UPON IT A COUPLE YEARS AGO.
WHICH BEGS THE QUESTION...

"...HOW DID IT MANAGE TO GO UNDISCOVERED FOR SO LONG?"

HAB SUITE 14. LATER.
I'VE JUST HEARD ABOUT TAILGATE. IS HE...?
HE'S STILL IN THE MEDIBAY. IT'LL TAKE A FEW WEEKS BEFORE HE'S BACK TO NORMAL.
THE TREATMENT TAKES TIME.

CYCLONUS, A LOT OF PEOPLE—
A LOT OF PEOPLE ARE TALKING ABOUT THE *STABBING* AND THE *RECOVERY*, AND... THE WORD "MIRACLE" IS BEING BANDIED ABOUT.
A MIRACLE, YES— IN THE FORM OF ***INSTANTANEOUS SPARK TRANSFUSION***.

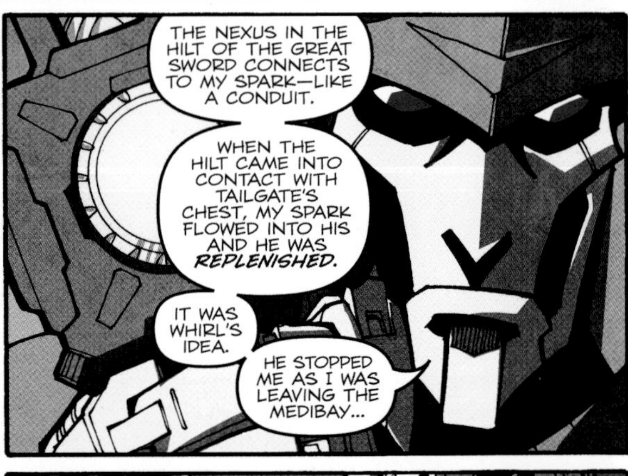

THE NEXUS IN THE HILT OF THE GREAT SWORD CONNECTS TO MY SPARK—LIKE A CONDUIT.
WHEN THE HILT CAME INTO CONTACT WITH TAILGATE'S CHEST, MY SPARK FLOWED INTO HIS AND HE WAS ***REPLENISHED***.
IT WAS WHIRL'S IDEA.
HE STOPPED ME AS I WAS LEAVING THE MEDIBAY...

"...AND TOLD ME SOMETHING *DAI ATLAS* HAD SAID TO HIM WHEN WE WERE FIGHTING THE LEGISLATORS."
HE THOUGHT YOU HAD THE SPARK OF A ***NEWBORN***— THAT'S WHY YOUR CONNECTION WITH THE SWORD IS SO ***FREAKISHLY INTENSE***.
SO?
SO WHY NOT ***USE*** THAT EXCESS ENERGY?

I THINK THAT WHEN VECTOR SIGMA RESURRECTED ME— WHEN HE GAVE ME A NEW LEASE ON LIFE*— IT ***SUPERCHARGED MY SPARK***.
NONETHELESS LETTING YOUR SPARK FLOW INTO TAILGATE— THAT WAS A ***MASSIVE GAMBLE***. YOU PUT YOUR ***OWN*** LIFE AT RISK.
NO MATTER.
CYCLONUS, I KNOW I'M A LITTLE LATE IN SAYING IT, BUT...
*SEE ***MTMTE*** ISSUE 1.

...WELCOME ABOARD.

MORE THAN MEETS THE EYE #21 COVER B

by **NICK ROCHE** Colors by **JOANA LAFUENTE**

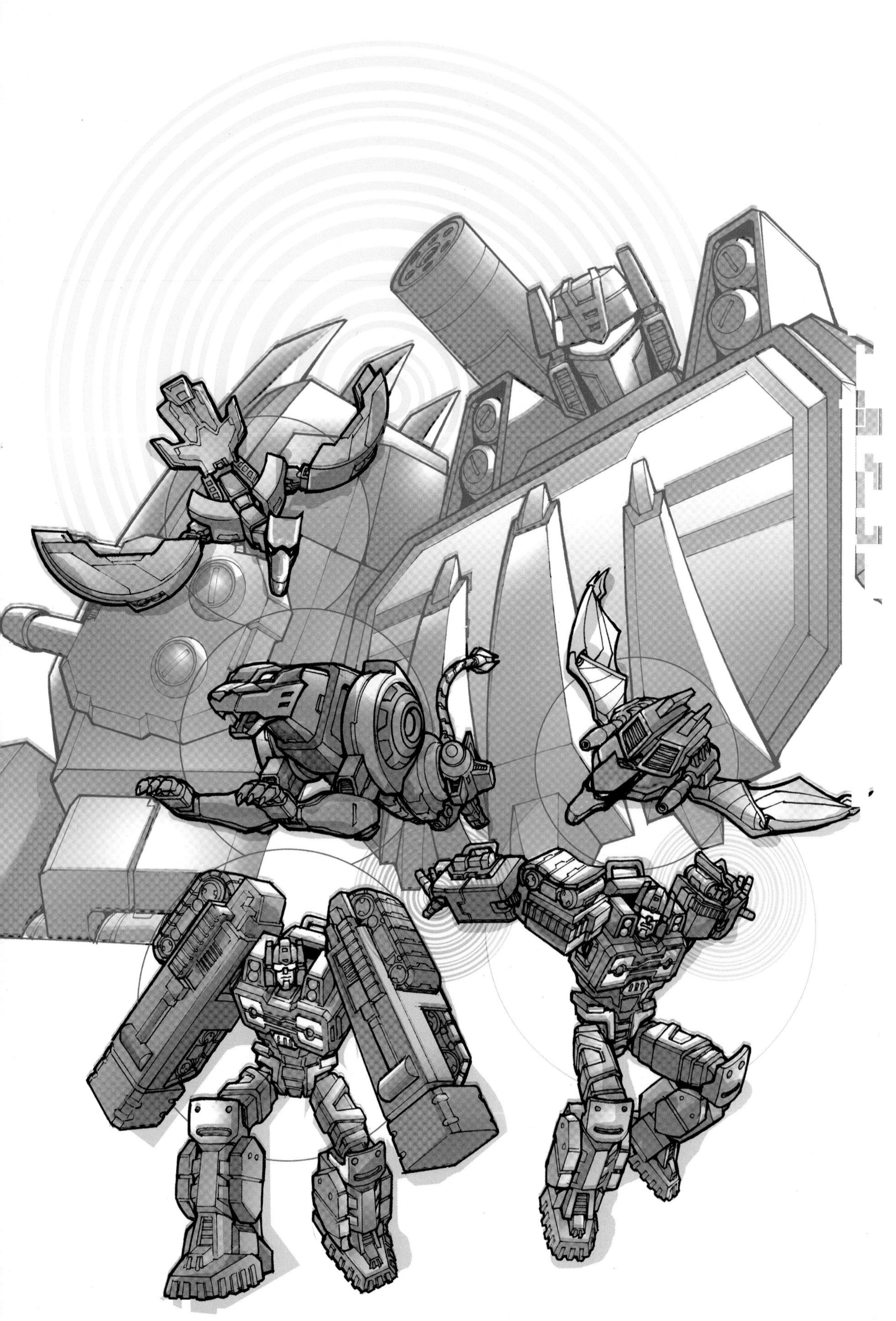

ROBOTS IN DISGUISE #21 COVER A

by **ANDREW GRIFFITH**

I HEAR THE COLOR OF MY BROTHERS' EMOTIONS.
THE SOUND OF FAILURE.
OF LOSS.
CYBERTRON. MONTHS AGO.
IT THREATENS TO OVERWHELM ME... BUT ONLY FOR A MOMENT.
WE SURRENDER! UNCONDITIONALLY!
I IGNORE THE SOUNDS, THE COLORS, THE SMELLS—BLOCK THEM, USING TECHNIQUES I LEARNED LONG AGO.
FOCUS ON RATBAT—HIS BLUSTER THE GROWLING FLAVOR OF AN UNSCRATCHABLE ITCH.
ALL DECEPTICON FORCES! AS YOUR RANKING OFFICER, I ORDER YOU—
—LAY DOWN YOUR WEAPONS!
JUST— AUTOBOTS, PLEASE, GO EASY ON ME—
—ER—
—DO NOT HARM MY PEOPLE.
RIGHT, RIGHT. COME ON, FLAPPY.
I CANNOT IGNORE THE PRIDE—THE ARROGANCE—OF THE AUTOBOTS. IT BURNS MY EYES WITH THE STENCH OF SULFUR.
I AM ONE OF YOU—
—A SENATOR—
—SENATOR RATBAT.
YEAH, I KNOW, YOUR HIGHNESS. NOW, MOVE.
I SHUT OUT THE ACRID, GRUNTING BLUE THAT COMES WITH LOSING AN EONS-LONG WAR...

...IN FAVOR OF THE CHAOTIC MELANGE OF DREAMS BURNING IN BOMBSHELL'S MIND.
DO... RUN?
DO... HIDE...?
WE WILL NOT FIGHT A BATTLE WE CANNOT WIN.
THE VOICE COMES FROM NOWHERE. I CONCENTRATE, FOCUS, STRAIN MY SENSES...
...AND SEE HIM.
SHOCKWAVE— THE PERFECT CYBERTRONIAN.
ARRANGEMENTS HAVE BEEN MADE. WE SHALL ALLOW THE GOOD SENATOR TO PROVIDE A DISTRACTION.
I TRUST YOU WILL FIND RESONANCE IN THAT, SOUNDWAVE.
AH. YOUR RUINED VOCAL PROCESSOR PREVENTS YOUR REPLY.
NO MATTER, YOUR QUESTIONS WILL WAIT, AND YOU HAVE... OTHER MEANS OF COMMUNICATION.
THAT IS WHAT WE HAVE NEED OF.
LORD MEGATRON LIVES.
I SENSED MEGATRON'S FOOTSTEPS— A SCENT AT THE EDGE OF HEARING.
BUT FROM SHOCKWAVE HIMSELF... NOTHING.
MY OPTICAL PROCESSORS TELL ME HE STANDS BEFORE ME. MY AUDIO RECEPTORS RELAY HIS WORDS.
BUT IN ALL OTHER WAYS, HE IS INVISIBLE TO ME. HE BETRAYS NO SECRET, NO EMOTION.
SOON, THOUGH...

...SHOCKWAVE WOULD BETRAY US ALL.
HUH. NOW THAT, BOSS...
THE CRYSTAL CITY, CYBERTRON. TODAY.
...THAT IS REALLY SOMETHING.
MY WOUND'S JUST— JUST—
—CLOSIN' RIGHT UP!
STILL WISH YOU'DA GIVEN A WARNING BEFORE YOU SHOT ME, BUT, WELL.
IT'S, WHAT—THESE CRYSTALS DOIN' IT?
IT IS AN ORE, DREADWING...
...ORE-14. NOW— SILENCE. I HAVE BUSINESS.
MORE THAN JUST BUSINESS, MY STUDENT.

JHIAXUS. YOUR SITUATION?
I ORBIT GORLAM PRIME. I AWAIT THE ARRIVAL OF ORION PAX.
IT IS... AN ODD FEELING TO RETURN TO THIS WORLD, AFTER THE YEARS I SPENT...
YOUR FEELINGS ARE IMMATERIAL...

...RESULTS MATTER. CONTACT ME WHEN THE MISSION IS COMPLETED, JHIAXUS.

I NEVER DID TRUST A GUY I COULDN'T SMELL...

THE SURFACE OF CYBERTRON. SOME DISTANCE AWAY.

...BUT SHOCKWAVE HASN'T EVEN GOT A NOSE. THAT'S A LOT WORSE.

I WAS WRONG TO CONVINCE YOU TO FOLLOW HIS LEAD, RAVAGE.

YEAH, PRETTY MUCH.

EH. WE ALL MAKE MISTAKES.

"WE ALL MAKE MISTAKES"? SERIOUSLY? THAT MAKES THINGS OKAY?
LOOK AT US. WE LOOK LIKE... LIKE...
LIKE THE LAST TIME YOU AND SHOCKWAVE HATCHED A PLAN.
WHEN WE STARTED EATING EACH OTHER FOR ENERGON.

MEGATRON'S GONE. TURMOIL'S DEAD. STARSCREAM'S TURNED TRAITOR. SKYWARP IS BARELY HANGING TOGETHER.
NOBODY KNOWS WHERE THE CONSTRUCTICONS ARE.
THE DECEPTICON JUSTICE DIVISION IS OUT THERE SOMEWHERE—WHAT DO WE DO WHEN THEY SHOW UP?!

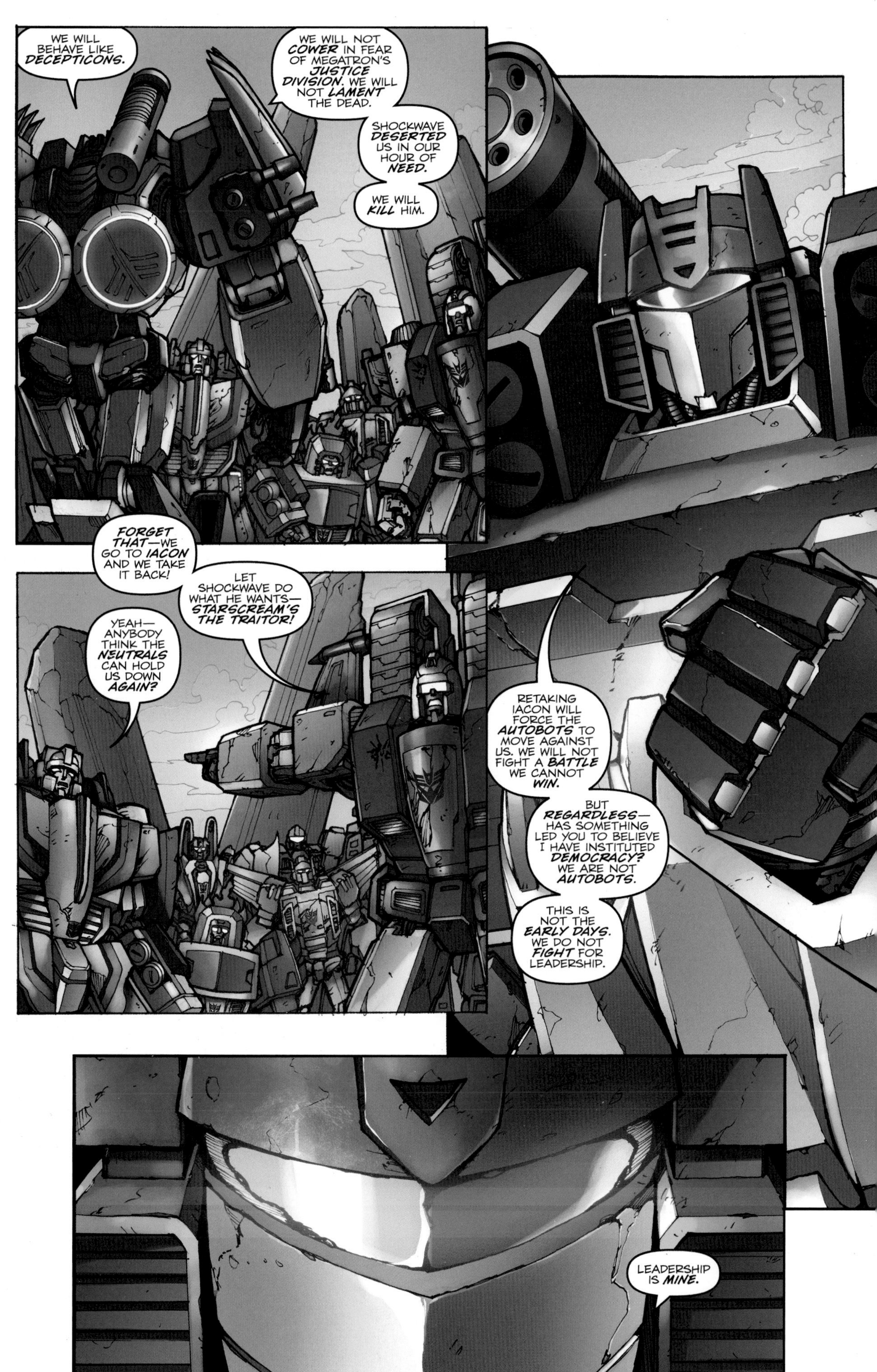
WE WILL BEHAVE LIKE DECEPTICONS.
WE WILL NOT COWER IN FEAR OF MEGATRON'S JUSTICE DIVISION. WE WILL NOT LAMENT THE DEAD.
SHOCKWAVE DESERTED US IN OUR HOUR OF NEED.
WE WILL KILL HIM.
FORGET THAT—WE GO TO IACON AND WE TAKE IT BACK!
LET SHOCKWAVE DO WHAT HE WANTS—STARSCREAM'S THE TRAITOR!
YEAH—ANYBODY THINK THE NEUTRALS CAN HOLD US DOWN AGAIN?
RETAKING IACON WILL FORCE THE AUTOBOTS TO MOVE AGAINST US. WE WILL NOT FIGHT A BATTLE WE CANNOT WIN.
BUT REGARDLESS—HAS SOMETHING LED YOU TO BELIEVE I HAVE INSTITUTED DEMOCRACY? WE ARE NOT AUTOBOTS.
THIS IS NOT THE EARLY DAYS. WE DO NOT FIGHT FOR LEADERSHIP.
LEADERSHIP IS MINE.

YEAH, RIGHT!
POW
HANDS OFF THE BOSS!
RAARGH!
SMAK!
YEAH!
YOU CAN'T HIDE BEHIND YOUR CASSETTES FOREVER, SOUNDWAVE!
COMMAND OF THE DECEPTICONS ISN'T SOMETHING YOU GET FROM A SET OF RULES!
IT'S SOMETHING YOU EARN!
CHAKKA
CHAKKA

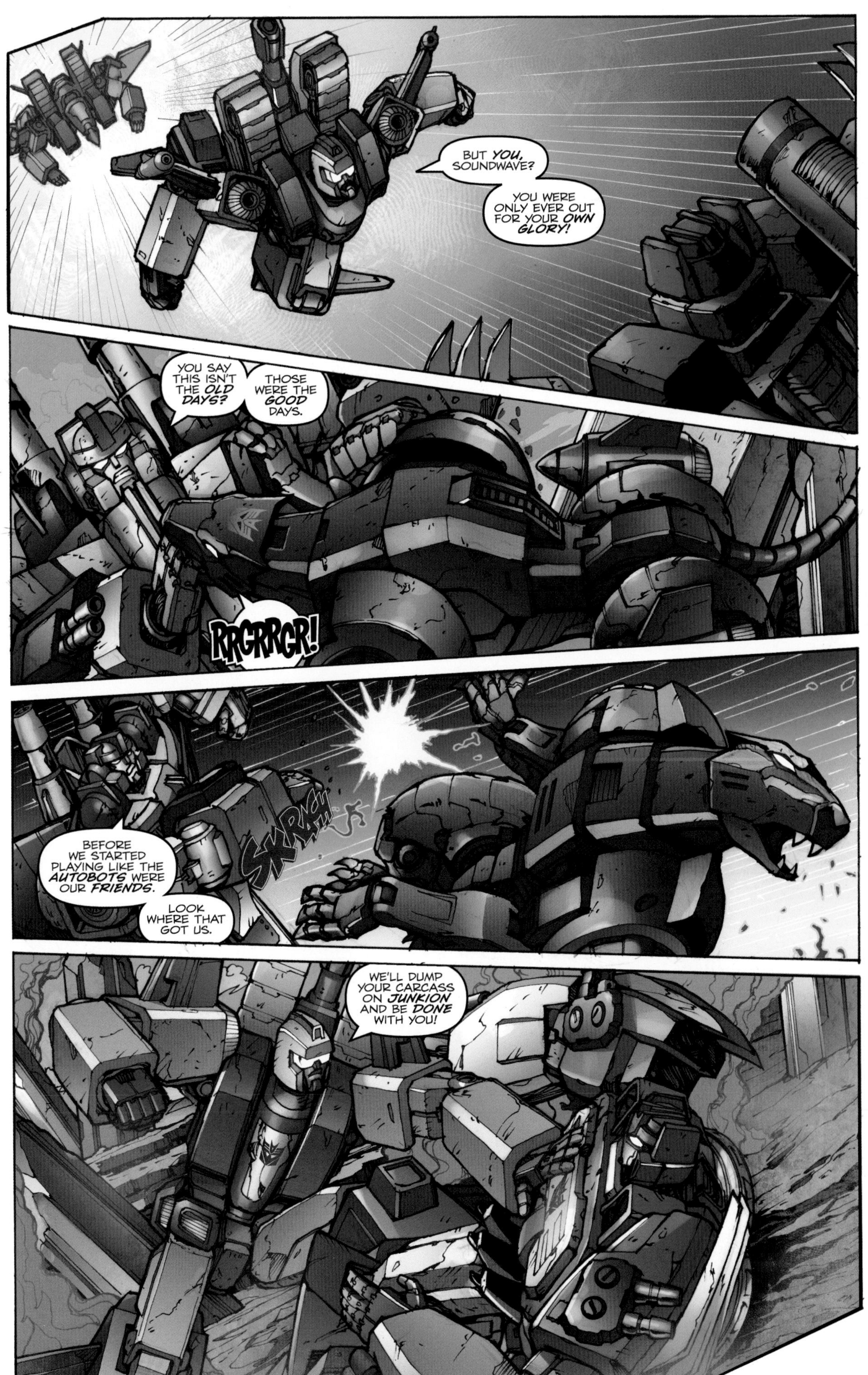
BUT YOU, SOUNDWAVE?
YOU WERE ONLY EVER OUT FOR YOUR OWN GLORY!
YOU SAY THIS ISN'T THE OLD DAYS?
THOSE WERE THE GOOD DAYS.
RRGRRGR!
SKRATCH!
BEFORE WE STARTED PLAYING LIKE THE AUTOBOTS WERE OUR FRIENDS.
LOOK WHERE THAT GOT US.
WE'LL DUMP YOUR CARCASS ON JUNKION AND BE DONE WITH YOU!

ENOUGH FIGHTING!

BACK IN IACON, YOU TOLD US SOMETHING WAS GOING TO HAPPEN, AND WE DIDN'T ASK QUESTIONS.
WE TRUSTED THE CHAIN OF COMMAND.
LUCKY SHOT, LITTLE MAN...
WE HAD A CHANCE AT PEACE, AND YEAH, I KNOW THE AUTOBOTS WERE LYING TO US AGAIN...

...BUT WE COULDA GOT WHAT WE WANTED. WE COULDA BEEN A PART OF SOMETHING!
INSTEAD, WE LOST IT ALL.
THOSE NEUTRALS... THEY WERE RIGHT, WEREN'T THEY?
ALL WE ARE IS A FORCE OF DESTRUCTION, FIGHTING ANOTHER FORCE OF DESTRUCTION.

WE CAN TELL OURSELVES IT ALL MEANT SOMETHING, BUT WHAT DID IT GET US? WE FOUGHT FOR FOREVER, AND WE LOST.
I MISS MY LIFE BEFORE THE WAR. I MISS SELLING CHIC CHIPS. I MISS HORRI-BULL.
YOU WANT TO KILL SHOCKWAVE? MAYBE YOU GOT YOUR REASONS.
BUT YOU'RE GONNA HAVE TO DO IT YOURSELF...

...BECAUSE YOU'RE ALL OUT OF SOLDIERS.

SOLDIERS.
ONCE, WE WERE LABORERS, FIGHTERS, INTELLECTUALS... ONCE WE ALL HAD LIVES.
LIVES WE WALKED AWAY FROM...
...FOR A SHARED BELIEF—THAT INEQUALITY COULD NOT BE ALLOWED TO STAND.

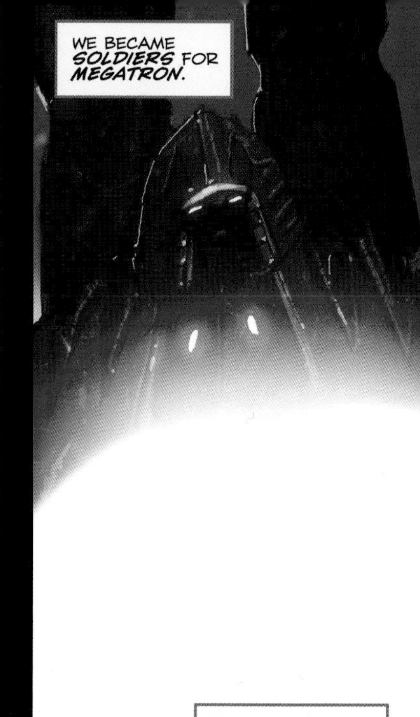

WE BECAME SOLDIERS FOR MEGATRON.
WE FOLLOWED COMMANDS THAT BURNED LIKE AN ANCIENT WAR SONG.

WE FOLLOWED HIM— TO BATTLE THE MAD ANCIENT CALLED GALVATRON.
GALVATRON: HERO OF THE FIRST CYBERTRONIAN CIVIL WAR, VANQUISHER OF THE ANCIENT HEADMASTERS.
GALVATRON, WHO UNLEASHED PRIMORDIAL ENERGIES THAT TWISTED OUR UNITY OF PURPOSE...

...PERVERTED IT INTO SOMETHING EVIL.

ONLY ONE STOOD HIS GROUND:

MEGATRON OF TARN, WHO FORMED THE DECEPTICONS IN THE FACE OF AUTOBOT OPPRESSION.

WHO GAVE ME PURPOSE.

AS HE GAVE TO US ALL.

AGAINST HIM... AGAINST OUR VERY PURPOSE...
...WE WERE DRAWN TOGETHER.
DRAWN INTO ONE UNSTOPPABLE FORM.
STRIPPED OF OUR FREE WILL, WE COULD ONLY WATCH, LISTEN, FEEL—AS WE WERE TURNED AGAINST THE OBJECT OF OUR LOYALTY.

AND WHERE NO ONE COULD POSSIBLY SUCCEED—MEGATRON STOOD HIS GROUND.
FROM WITHIN THE MONSTER I COULD WATCH—HEAR—FEEL EVERYTHING.
I COULD NOT BLOCK OUT THE SHRIEKING OF MY BROTHERS' SPARKS.
NOR COULD I IGNORE THE COLD, FLUID HEROISM OF HIS.
MY BROTHERS, TOGETHER—WE HAD THE POWER TO SHATTER A WORLD.
AND MEGATRON STOOD HIS GROUND.

THE FATE OF ALL CREATION HELD IN HIS HAND, MEGATRON DID NOT FALTER.

HE STOPPED THE UNSTOPPABLE.
BUT ONE OTHER STOOD APART.

ONE OTHER POSSESSED A VISION SO UNIQUE, SO PERFECT...
...A VISION SO SINGULAR, THAT HE COULD NEVER BELONG WITH US.

AND SHOCKWAVE WATCHED IT ALL.
ALONE, PLANNING...

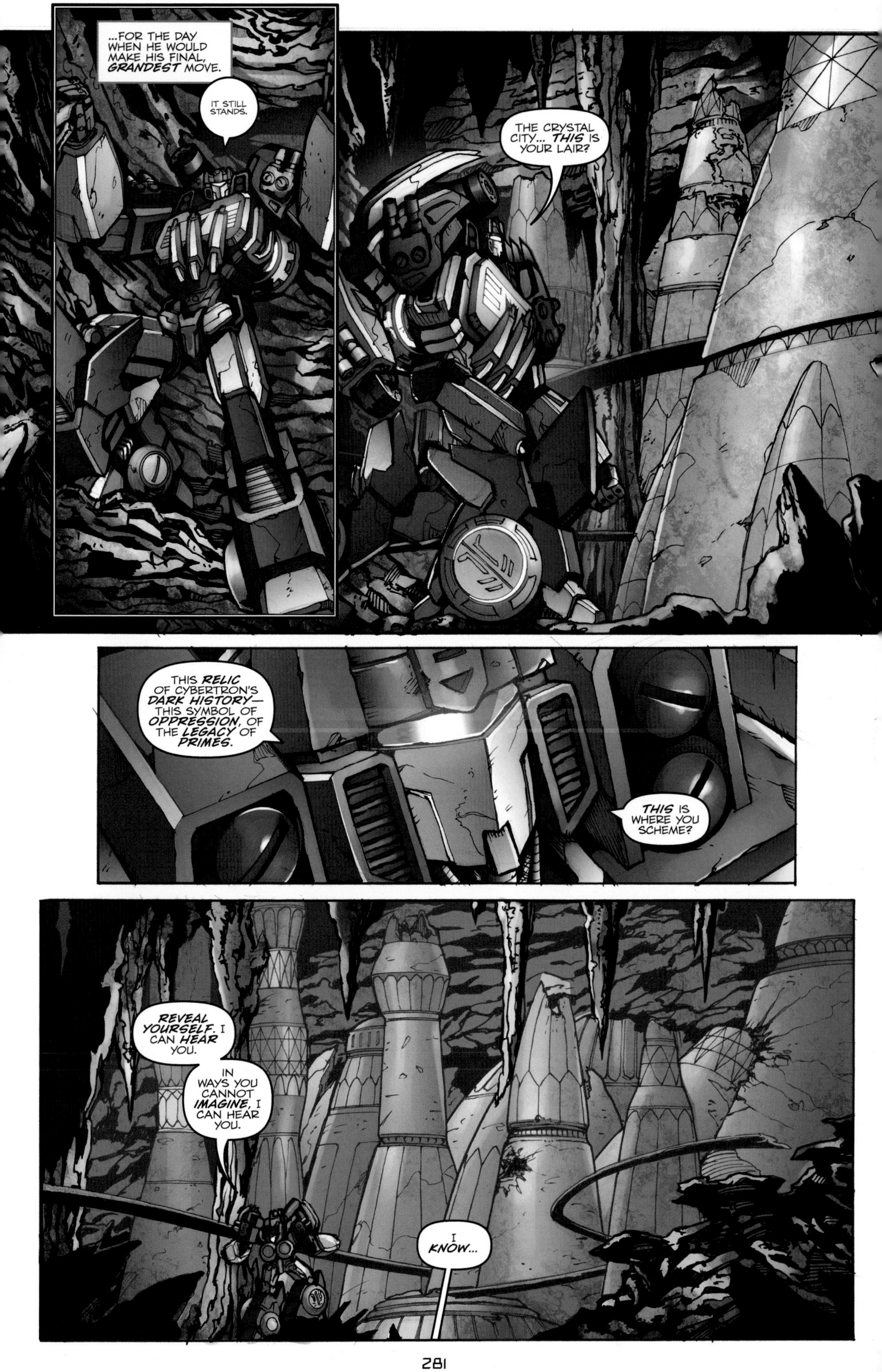

...FOR THE DAY WHEN HE WOULD MAKE HIS FINAL, ***GRANDEST*** MOVE.

IT STILL STANDS.

THE CRYSTAL CITY... ***THIS*** IS YOUR LAIR?

THIS ***RELIC*** OF CYBERTRON'S ***DARK HISTORY***— THIS SYMBOL OF ***OPPRESSION***, OF THE ***LEGACY*** OF ***PRIMES***.
THIS IS WHERE YOU SCHEME?

REVEAL YOURSELF. I CAN ***HEAR*** YOU.
IN WAYS YOU CANNOT ***IMAGINE***, I CAN HEAR YOU.
I ***KNOW***...

...I JUST WANTED TO MAKE A COOL-ASS ENTRANCE.
CRUNCH

DREADWING!
KRACT

HEH. DON'T WEAR IT OUT, SOUNDWAVE.
NICE PUNCH— FOR A LAME-O.
YOUR FORM MIMICS THE BODY I DESIGNED FOR GREAT MEGATRON...

...YOU WEAR IT TO HONOR OUR FALLEN LEADER.
I AM HERE TO STOP SHOCKWAVE FOR THE SAME REASON. WE HAVE NO QUARREL.

CHRAK
SORRY, SOUNDY— SHOCKWAVE TOLD ME TO KILL YOU.
AN' MEGATRON'S HONOR DON'T NEED YOUR HELP!

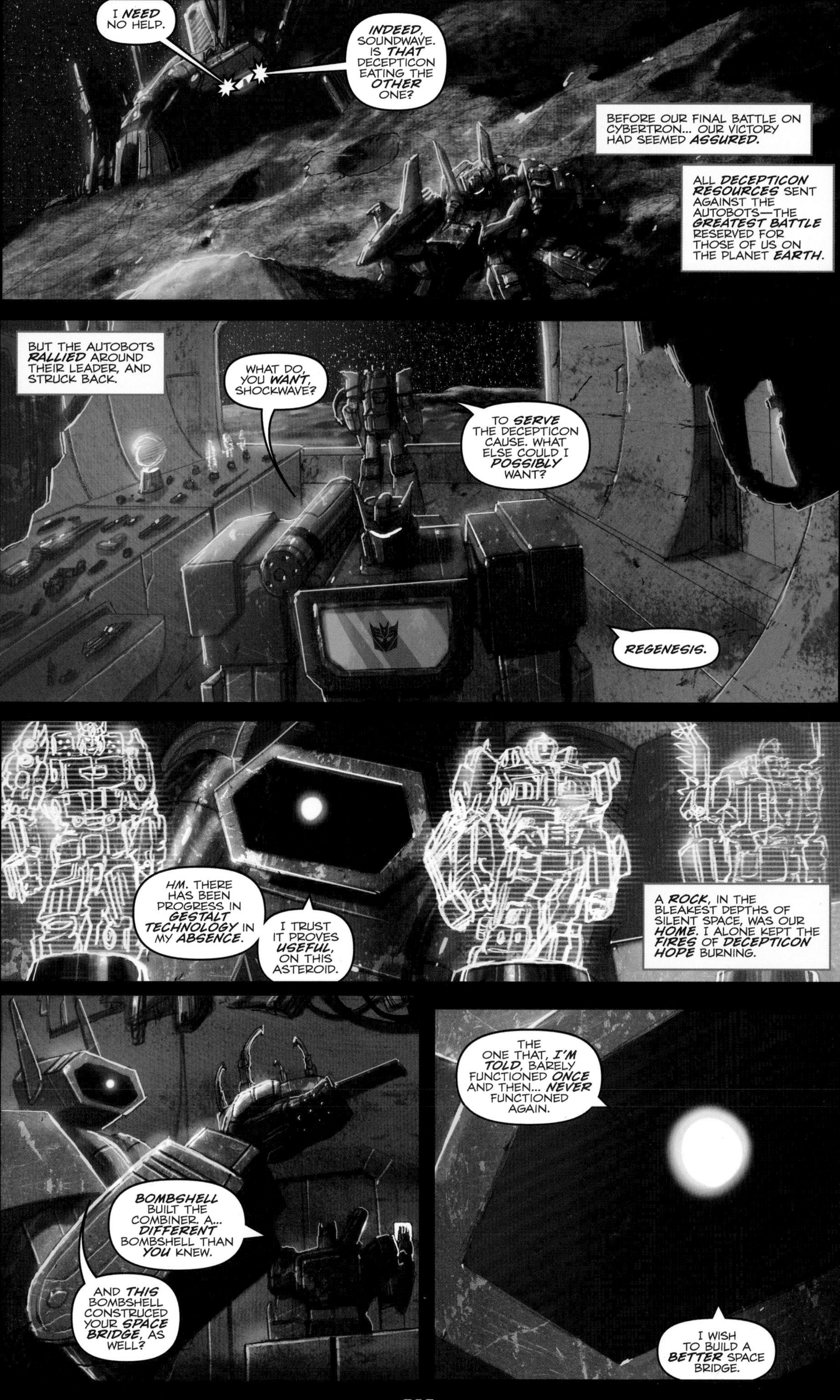
I NEED NO HELP.
INDEED, SOUNDWAVE. IS THAT DECEPTICON EATING THE OTHER ONE?
BEFORE OUR FINAL BATTLE ON CYBERTRON... OUR VICTORY HAD SEEMED ASSURED.
ALL DECEPTICON RESOURCES SENT AGAINST THE AUTOBOTS—THE GREATEST BATTLE RESERVED FOR THOSE OF US ON THE PLANET EARTH.
BUT THE AUTOBOTS RALLIED AROUND THEIR LEADER, AND STRUCK BACK.
WHAT DO, YOU WANT, SHOCKWAVE?
TO SERVE THE DECEPTICON CAUSE. WHAT ELSE COULD I POSSIBLY WANT?
REGENESIS.
HM. THERE HAS BEEN PROGRESS IN GESTALT TECHNOLOGY IN MY ABSENCE.
I TRUST IT PROVES USEFUL, ON THIS ASTEROID.
A ROCK, IN THE BLEAKEST DEPTHS OF SILENT SPACE, WAS OUR HOME. I ALONE KEPT THE FIRES OF DECEPTICON HOPE BURNING.
BOMBSHELL BUILT THE COMBINER. A... DIFFERENT BOMBSHELL THAN YOU KNEW.
AND THIS BOMBSHELL CONSTRUCED YOUR SPACE BRIDGE, AS WELL?
THE ONE THAT, I'M TOLD, BARELY FUNCTIONED ONCE AND THEN... NEVER FUNCTIONED AGAIN.
I WISH TO BUILD A BETTER SPACE BRIDGE.

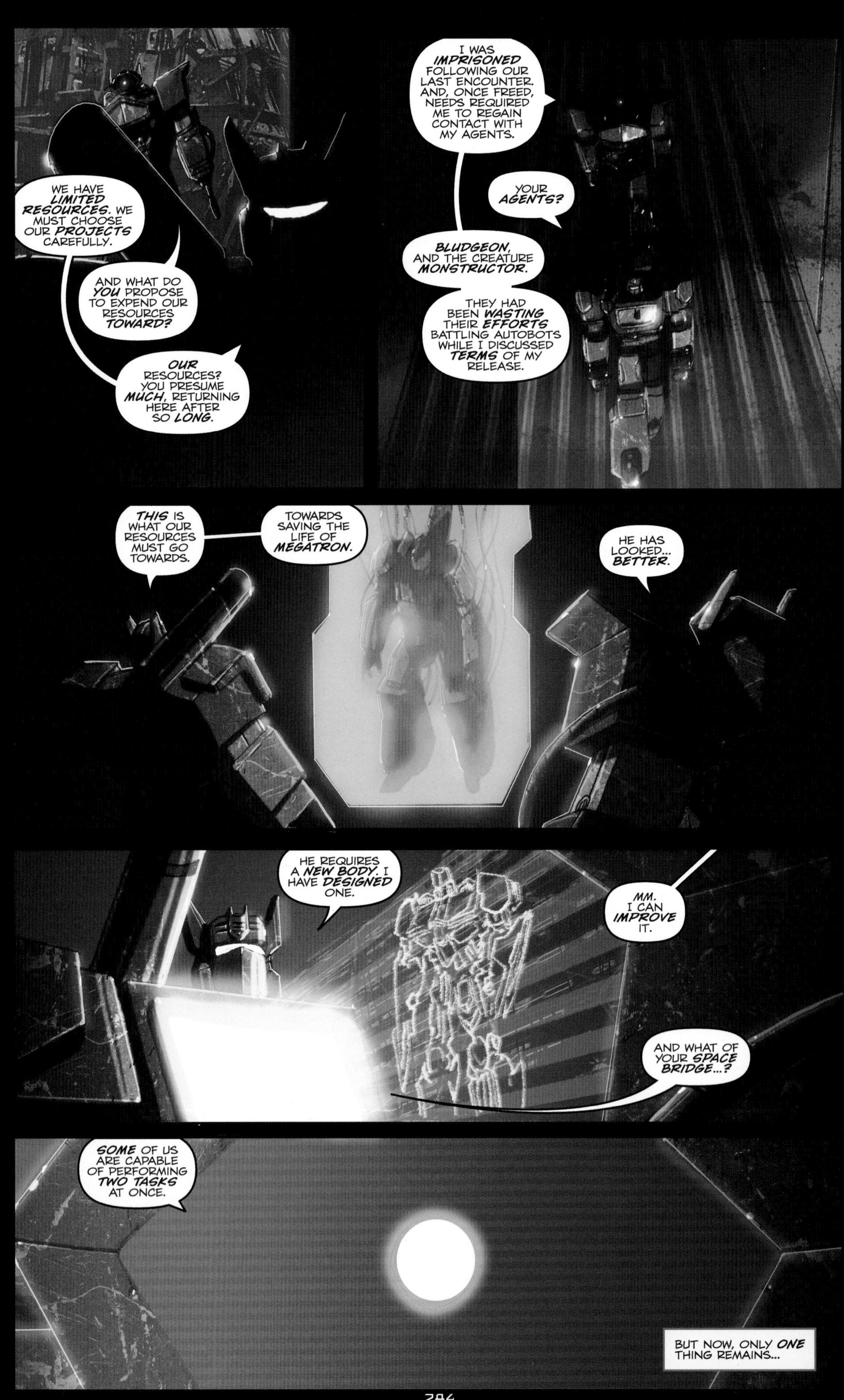

WE HAVE LIMITED RESOURCES. WE MUST CHOOSE OUR PROJECTS CAREFULLY.
AND WHAT DO YOU PROPOSE TO EXPEND OUR RESOURCES TOWARD?
OUR RESOURCES? YOU PRESUME MUCH, RETURNING HERE AFTER SO LONG.
I WAS IMPRISONED FOLLOWING OUR LAST ENCOUNTER. AND, ONCE FREED, NEEDS REQUIRED ME TO REGAIN CONTACT WITH MY AGENTS.
YOUR AGENTS?
BLUDGEON, AND THE CREATURE MONSTRUCTOR.
THEY HAD BEEN WASTING THEIR EFFORTS BATTLING AUTOBOTS WHILE I DISCUSSED TERMS OF MY RELEASE.
THIS IS WHAT OUR RESOURCES MUST GO TOWARDS.
TOWARDS SAVING THE LIFE OF MEGATRON.
HE HAS LOOKED... BETTER.
HE REQUIRES A NEW BODY. I HAVE DESIGNED ONE.
MM. I CAN IMPROVE IT.
AND WHAT OF YOUR SPACE BRIDGE...?
SOME OF US ARE CAPABLE OF PERFORMING TWO TASKS AT ONCE.
BUT NOW, ONLY ONE THING REMAINS...

...AND SHOCKWAVE MUST BE STOPPED.
NO CASSETTES, HUH?
WHAT'CHA GONNA DO, SOUNDWAVE?
THUGGA
THUGGA
TRY TA TALK YOUR WAY OUTTA THIS?
CHAGGA CHAGGA
NO.
IMPRESSIVE...
...DREADWING HARDLY STOOD A CHANCE.

YOU DO NOT STAND A CHANCE.
TRAPPED IN THIS FORM, YOUR LAST RESERVES OF POWER FAILING...
...BUT I CAN HELP YOU.
IF YOU CALL OFF YOUR BEASTS.
I HAD BEEN PARTIALLY RESPONSIBLE FOR SHOCKWAVE'S IMPRISONMENT, PRIOR TO OUR TIME ON THE ASTEROID.
I ENABLED HIS DOWNFALL, AT THE VERY LEAST.
SHOCKWAVE CAME TO ME, IN MY TIME OF NEED—WHEN I WAS TRAPPED IN AN UNFORTUNATE EARTH DISGUISE BY A WEAPON OF HIS DESIGN.
THEY... ARE NEITHER BEASTS... NOR MINE TO CALL OFF.
BUT, FOR THE FIRST TIME, I SENSED SOMETHING WITHIN SHOCKWAVE. SOMETHING IN HIM...
...BUT NOT OF HIM. SOMETHING PLACED INSIDE.
NEVERTHELESS. RAVAGE... DOWN.
WHAT... WHAT DO YOU PROPOSE... SHOCKWAVE?
IN EXCHANGE FOR FREEING YOU FROM THIS... MODE IN WHICH YOU FIND YOURSELF TRAPPED...
...I REQUIRE YOU TO INTERCEPT AND DECRYPT A CODE.
THE DETONATION SIGNAL FOR... THE BOMB THE EARTHLINGS... HAVE IMPLANTED IN YOUR HEAD.
I WILL HELP YOU... IF YOU TELL ME OF... REGENESIS.
AH.

I HAD THOUGHT THE TRAIL WOULD HAVE ENDED WITH BLUDGEON.
WHAT DO YOU KNOW OF REGENESIS?
IT IS THE PROCESS BY WHICH YOU CREATED... WHAT STARSCREAM CALLS... ORE-13.
OF COURSE HE DOES. STARSCREAM... HAS A WAY OF KNOWING THINGS.
I CAN SENSE IT ALL AROUND THIS PLANET. LIKE ENERGON... BUT VOLATILE. POWERFUL, YET UNSAFE.
BUT REGENESIS... IS MORE THAN AN ENERGON SUBSTITUTE.
MUCH.
TELL ME... OR I WILL NOT HELP YOU.
NO.
WHAT?
NO. IF YOU DO NOT HELP ME, I WILL DIE. THUS, THE INFORMATION WILL BE LOST. YOUR ONLY GOAL WILL BE LOST.
IT IS NOT INFORMATION THAT I...
...I BELIEVE IN THE DECEPTICON CAUSE, SHOCKWAVE.
THEN YOU HAVE ALL THE MORE REASON TO WORK WITH ME.
THE FIRST OF SO MANY PACTS, BORN OF MISTRUST.
THE FIRST, BUT I VOW...

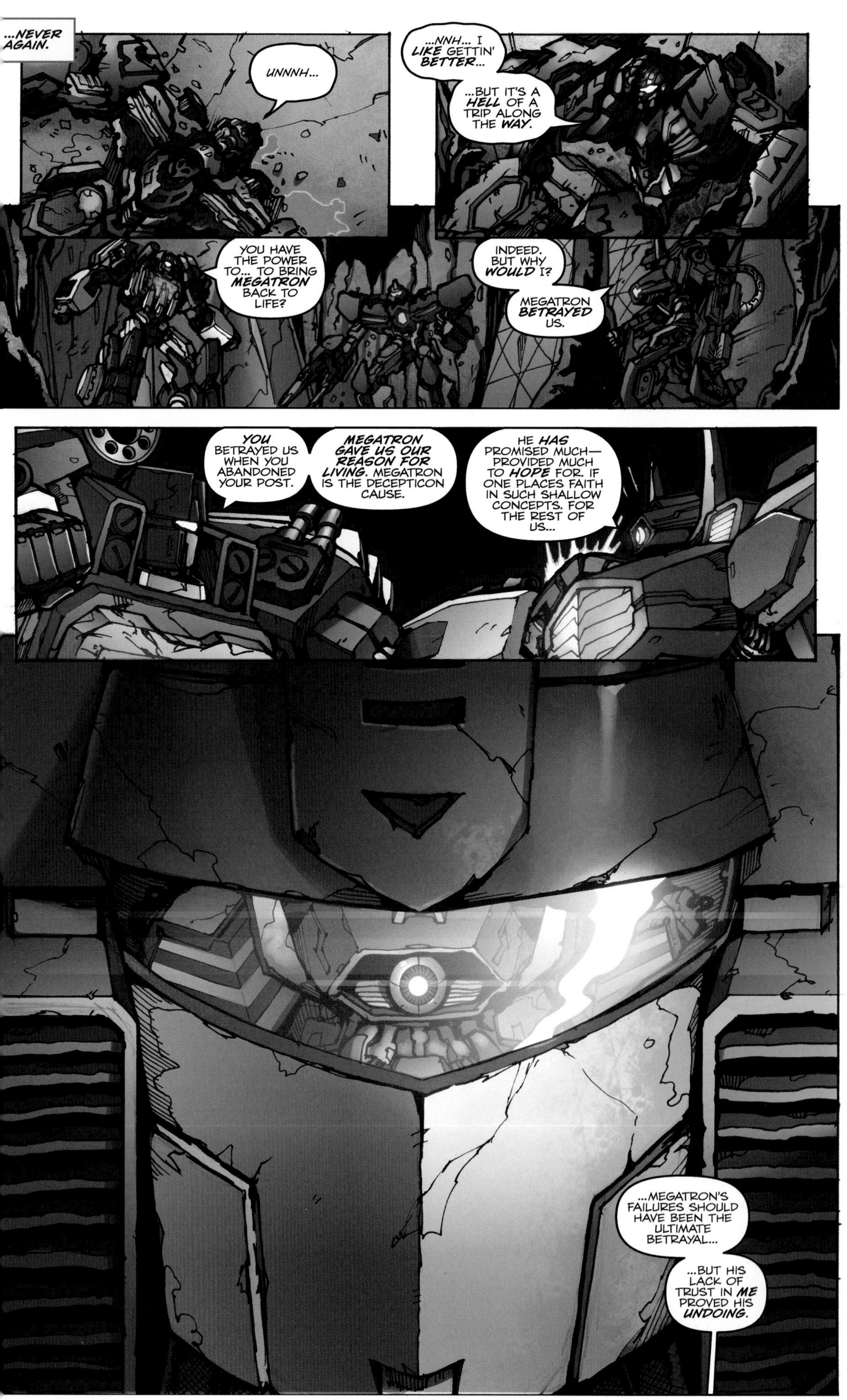
...NEVER AGAIN.
UNNNH...
...NNH... I LIKE GETTIN' BETTER...
...BUT IT'S A HELL OF A TRIP ALONG THE WAY.
YOU HAVE THE POWER TO... TO BRING MEGATRON BACK TO LIFE?
INDEED. BUT WHY WOULD I?
MEGATRON BETRAYED US.
YOU BETRAYED US WHEN YOU ABANDONED YOUR POST.
MEGATRON GAVE US OUR REASON FOR LIVING. MEGATRON IS THE DECEPTICON CAUSE.
HE HAS PROMISED MUCH— PROVIDED MUCH TO HOPE FOR. IF ONE PLACES FAITH IN SUCH SHALLOW CONCEPTS. FOR THE REST OF US...
...MEGATRON'S FAILURES SHOULD HAVE BEEN THE ULTIMATE BETRAYAL...
...BUT HIS LACK OF TRUST IN ME PROVED HIS UNDOING.

A LACK OF TRUST... IS EXACTLY WHAT LED ME TO BE STUCK ON EARTH...
YOU MUST DEFEND THE CAUSE THIS DAY, BLUDGEON.
YOU WILL CONDUCT A FULL AND PAINSTAKING INVESTIGATION, INTO ALL SHOCKWAVE'S CURRENT AND ARCHIVED PROJECTS.
I WANT TO KNOW EXACTLY WHAT HE WAS WORKING ON. DO YOU UNDERSTAND?
OH... COMPLETELY.
VERY WELL. YOU ARE DISMISSED.
SOUNDWAVE...
...KEEP AN OPTIC ON HIM.
YES, LORD MEGATRON. ONLY ONE?
YOU FIND HUMOR IN THIS SITUATION?
MY APOLOGIES. I ONLY MEANT...
I KNOW WHAT YOU MEANT. YOU NEVER TRUSTED SHOCKWAVE. AND WHEN HE DISAPPEARED...
HE HAD SOMETHING PLANNED.
OF COURSE HE DID.
WHATEVER SHOCKWAVE HAS CREATED, WE WILL USE IT FOR THE GOOD OF THE DECEPTICON CAUSE.
EQUALITY FOR ALL. FREEDOM THROUGH TYRANNY, MY FRIEND.

YOU WILL FOLLOW WHATEVER DIRECTION THE CLUES MAY POINT, AND YOU WILL FIND WHAT SHOCKWAVE HAS FORGED ACROSS THE COSMOS.
I TRUST YOU IN THIS MISSION, MY FRIEND. YOU WILL MAKE SHOCKWAVE'S CREATION OURS.
I WILL NOT FAIL YOU, MY LORD.
I HAD NO ILLUSIONS—I COULD SEE THE SOUNDS OF HIS FEELINGS. I COULD TASTE HIS MISTRUST.
BUT I FOLLOWED ANYWAY.
I UNDERSTOOD THE BETRAYALS MEGATRON HAD ENDURED. I FELT THE LIFE HE LIVED. I SAW THE HONESTY WITHIN HIS SPARK.
IT IS NOT TRUST THAT DRIVES ME.
AS SHOCKWAVE SAYS... IT IS HOPE. BUT HE DOES NOT UNDERSTAND THE POWER THIS GRANTS ME.
IF SHOCKWAVE STANDS IN THE WAY OF MEGATRON'S DREAM, IT IS THE SPARK OF HOPE THAT WILL DEFEAT HIM.
THE SPARK OF MY HOPE.
SHOCKPOINT

ROBOTS IN DISGUISE #21 COVER B

by **CASEY W. COLLER** Colors by **JOANA LAFUENTE**

ROBOTS IN DISGUISE #22 COVER A

by **ANDREW GRIFFITH**

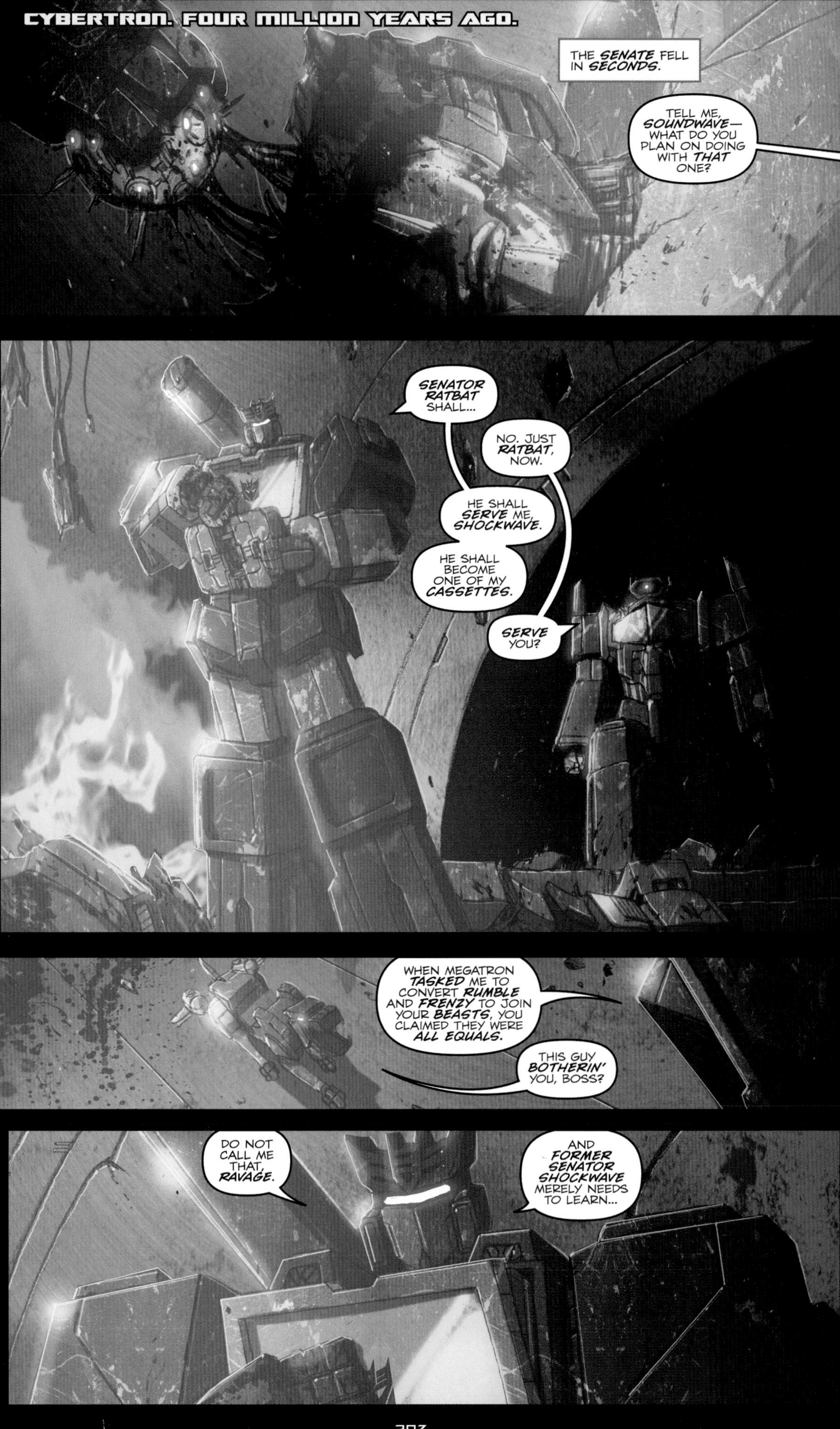
CYBERTRON. FOUR MILLION YEARS AGO.
THE SENATE FELL IN SECONDS.
TELL ME, SOUNDWAVE— WHAT DO YOU PLAN ON DOING WITH THAT ONE?
SENATOR RATBAT SHALL...
NO. JUST RATBAT, NOW.
HE SHALL SERVE ME, SHOCKWAVE.
HE SHALL BECOME ONE OF MY CASSETTES.
SERVE YOU?
WHEN MEGATRON TASKED ME TO CONVERT RUMBLE AND FRENZY TO JOIN YOUR BEASTS, YOU CLAIMED THEY WERE ALL EQUALS.
THIS GUY BOTHERIN' YOU, BOSS?
DO NOT CALL ME THAT, RAVAGE.
AND FORMER SENATOR SHOCKWAVE MERELY NEEDS TO LEARN...

...SOME ARE MORE EQUAL THAN OTHERS.
THE CYBERTRONIAN SENATE, LURED TO THE CITY OF KAON—
—AND MURDERED.
BY US. BY DECEPTICONS.

THIS IS THE GREATEST ACT OF CIVIL DISOBEDIENCE IN HISTORY.
THE UNIVERSE IS A LARGE PLACE, SOUNDWAVE, AND HISTORY LOOMS LARGER.
STILL... IT WILL SERVE AS A STATEMENT OF PURPOSE.

NO—THIS IS THE END OF AN ERA, AND THE BEGINNING OF A PROCESS.

WE WILL TEACH THE PEOPLE OF CYBERTRON—PROVIDE THEM THE INFORMATION THEY NEED TO CREATE A WORLD BASED IN EQUALITY.

INDEED? YOU MAKE MUCH OF YOUR ABILITY TO HEAR THINGS. I HAD ASSUMED YOU WERE ABLE TO UNDERSTAND, AS WELL.

MEGATRON BATTLES SENTINEL PRIME EVEN NOW. KAON IS IN FLAMES. THIS IS WHAT WE HAVE ACHIEVED.

COME, SOUNDWAVE. I HAVE AN IDEA FOR RATBAT'S NEW BODY. THE DECEPTICON CAUSE WOULD DO WELL TO HAVE MORE FLIERS.
TO SHOCKWAVE, LOYALTY—LIKE ALL EMOTION—EXISTED TO BE MANIPULATED...

...BUT AT LEAST HE WAS HONEST ABOUT IT.
YOU DO NOT UNDERSTAND LOYALTY!
KRAMN

INDEED.
THERE... YOU DO HAVE SOME SENSE OF ME.

DREADWING'S HOPELESS CONFRONTATION WITH YOU CONFIRMED YOUR CASSETTES ARE ABSENT.
HOPELESS?
EVEN ALONE, I KNOW YOU CAPABLE OF OUTFIGHTING HIM...

...BUT NOT ME. YOU SHOULD NOT HAVE COME ALONE, SOUNDWAVE.
CHOOM

A DECEPTICON IS NEVER ALONE.

BUZZSAW—
—LASERBEAK—
—RUMBLE—
—FRENZY—
—RAVAGE—
—EJECT.
YOU MADE THE MISTAKE, NO-NOSE—
—TIME FOR YOU TO LOSE!
CHOMP

LOSING IS NOT AN OPTION, SOUNDWAVE.
ONE DAY HE WOULD IGNITE THE FLAME OF HOPE UNDER A POPULATION TERRORIZED AND TRAMPLED UPON.

BUT FIRST, MEGATRON NEEDED AN ALLY... AS DID I.
YOU ARE A THORN IN THE SIDE OF SENATOR PROTEUS' GOVERNMENT, MEGATRON.
NOT ENOUGH OF ONE. THEY IGNORE US.

YOU KNOW MY EMPLOYER SEES POSSIBILITIES.
YOUR SENATOR RATBAT DOES NOT UNDERSTAND THE CAUSE. HE THINKS WE CAN BE... BARTERED.
HE SENDS YOU, HIS SERVANT—
I AM NO ONE'S SERVANT.

...
I STAND CORRECTED, SOUNDWAVE. NOW THAT YOU HAVE... PULLED YOURSELF TOGETHER, YOUR PRIDE—
YOU MISUNDERSTAND.

I LISTEN. I HEAR EVERYTHING.
EVERY TRANSMISSION, EVERY VOCALIZATION, EVERY FLASH OF LIGHT, EVERY HOLOGRAM.
I HEAR IT ALL. AND NOW THAT I AM ABLE TO... FOCUS MY ATTENTION... I KNOW HOW TO USE THE SENATOR TO FURTHER YOUR CAUSE.

IF THE STAKES WERE HIGH ENOUGH, SENATOR RATBAT WOULD CALL AN EMERGENCY ASSEMBLY OF THE CYBERTRONIAN SENATE HERE, IN KAON—IN HIS DISTRICT.
ALLOW YOURSELF TO BE CAPTURED.
AND WHAT STAKES COULD BE THAT HIGH?
MYSELF? HA.
WHY WOULD THEY NOT SEND ME TO IACON?
FOR THAT MATTER—SENATOR PROTEUS' PUPPET PRIME, THE ONE CALLED SENTINEL.
WHY WOULD HE NOT MERELY PUT A BULLET IN MY SPARK?
NOT "YOU," MEGATRON...
..."YOU," THE DECEPTICONS.
ALL OF YOU. TOO MANY TO MOVE, AND TOO IMPORTANT TO IGNORE. THE SENATE WOULD CONVENE IN KAON, AND YOU COULD KILL THEM ALL.
I WOULD ELIMINATE ALL EVIDENCE OF WHO WAS THERE.
INDIVIDUALLY, YOUR DECEPTICONS WOULD REMAIN FREE...
...BUT EVERYONE WOULD KNOW THAT, AS A GROUP, THE DECEPTICONS ARE A FORCE TO BE RECKONED WITH.
THE WORLD WOULD BE YOURS, MEGATRON.
YOU COULD REBUILD THE STATE—WITH EQUALITY FOR ALL.
OURS, SOUNDWAVE.
THE WORLD SHALL BE OURS.
SOME QUESTION MY LOYALTY TO MEGATRON. NONSENSE. I WANTED TO GIVE HIM CYBERTRON...

...BUT *DESIRE* IS NEVER ENOUGH TO DECIDE THE FATE OF A WORLD.
THIS WORLD BELONGS TO THE DECEPTICONS— NOT TO *YOUR SCHEMING*.
RAHRR
NNG.
CHOOM

GOTCHA, YOU—
CHAKK
AGGK!

RAAGH!
FOR ONE WHO *HEARS* SO MUCH—

—YOU HAVE ALWAYS UNDERSTOOD SO *LITTLE*.
NO!

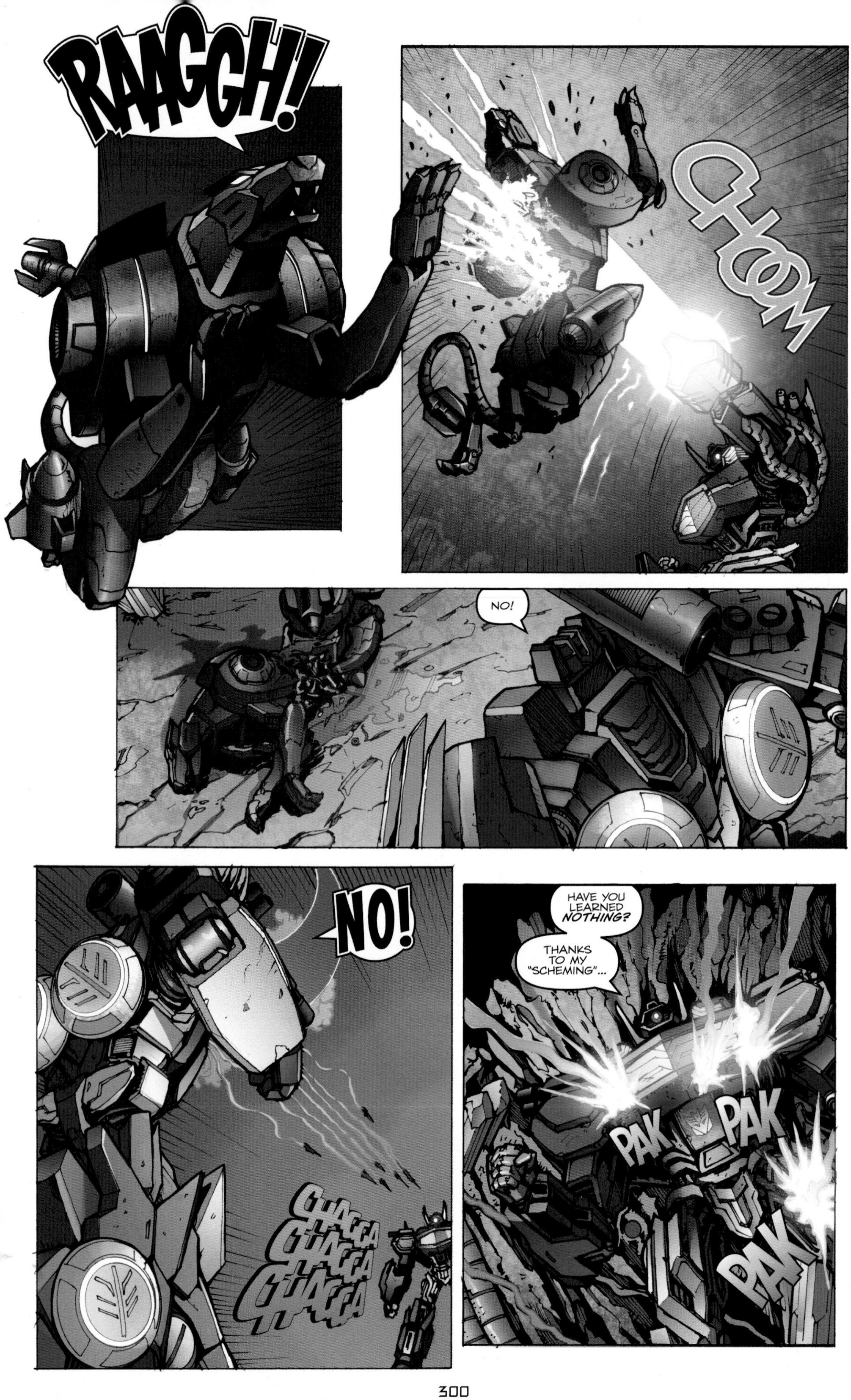

RAAGGH!

CHOOM

NO!

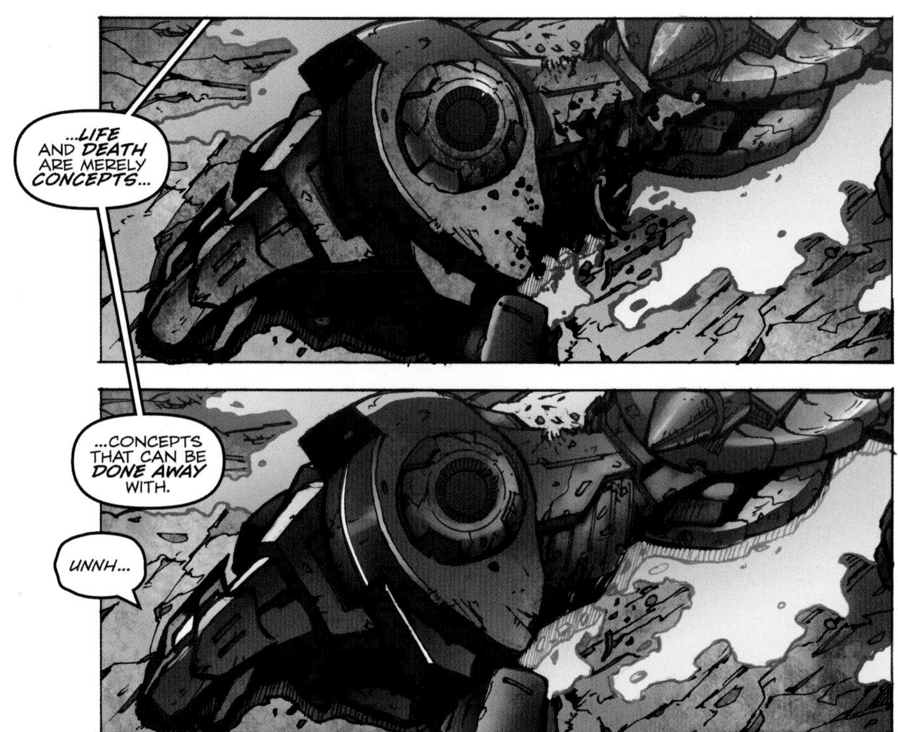
...LIFE AND DEATH ARE MERELY CONCEPTS...
...CONCEPTS THAT CAN BE DONE AWAY WITH.
UNNH...

...HNNNH.
INFORMATION IS ALL THERE IS.
LIFE, DEATH, TIME, PLACE—MERELY INFORMATION, DATA TO BE MANIPULATED.
HOPE IS MEANINGLESS, SOUNDWAVE.

YOU WILL LIVE.
AND YOU WILL SEE THE POINT OF ALL THIS. I WILL SHOW YOU WHAT A PURITY OF INFORMATION WILL REVEAL.

I WILL SHOW YOU WHAT YOU STAND AGAINST.

...YOU DO NOT STAND WITH PROTEUS.
YOU'RE USING THE SENATE FOR YOUR OWN ENDS, BUT THE SENATE HAS VERY LIMITED RESOURCES WHEN IT COMES TO WHAT YOU WISH TO ACCOMPLISH.
BEFORE THE SENATE... BEFORE THE REVOLUTION...
...I HAD A REVELATION.
SHOCKWAVE WAS THE FIRST CYBERTRONIAN I HAD EVER ENCOUNTERED WHOSE THOUGHTS, WHOSE EMOTIONS I COULD NOT FEEL.
I HATED HIM IMMEDIATELY.
YOU STUDIED UNDER JHIAXUS.
I WANT A COMBINER. I WANT A COMBINER OF MY OWN, LIKE MONSTRUCTOR— EXCEPT CONTROLLABLE.
THAT... MAY TAKE A WHILE.
I HAVE TIME. I AM PLAYING A LONG GAME, SENATOR SHOCKWAVE.
NOW, YOU HAD BEST RETURN TO YOUR SENATE. SOUNDWAVE WILL BE YOUR CONTACT.
"SOUNDWAVE"...
...YES. I KNOW YOU.
YOU SERVE SENATOR RATBAT.
I SERVE NO ONE. I HAVE SKILLS, AND THE SENATOR EMPLOYS ME FOR THEIR USE.
HIS LACK OF EMOTION WAS THE RESULT OF EMPURATA, A PUNISHMENT FOR HIS CRIMES AGAINST THE SENATE.
LIKE HIS FACE, HE WAS BLANK.
AH.
THEN I SHALL SEE YOU, SOUNDWAVE.
SHOCKWAVE WAS PERFECTION.
YOU ARE TROUBLED, MY FRIEND.
I DO NOT TRUST HIM.
I KNEW IMMEDIATELY...

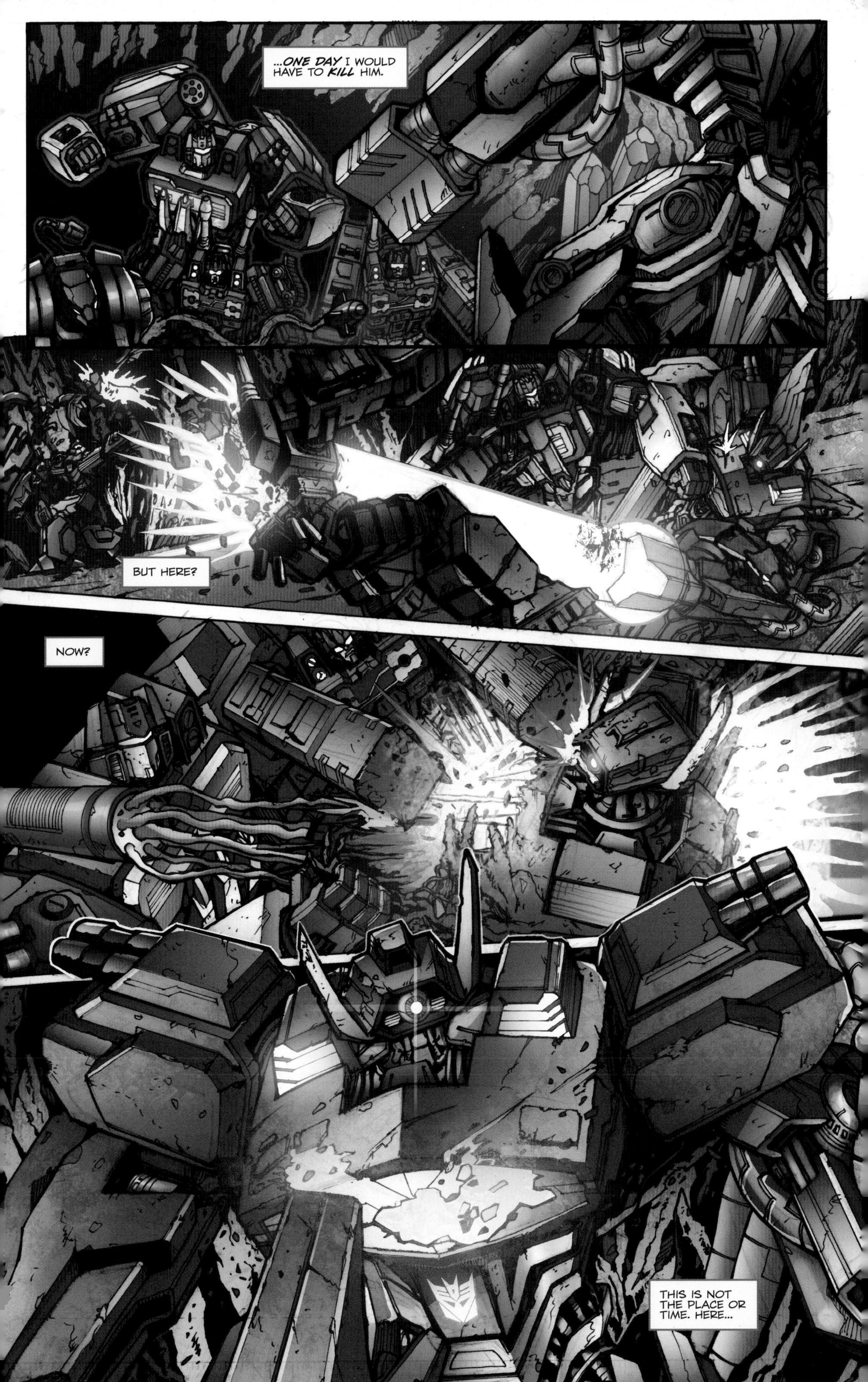
...ONE DAY I WOULD HAVE TO KILL HIM.
BUT HERE?
NOW?
THIS IS NOT THE PLACE OR TIME. HERE...

...JUSTICE IS BEYOND MY POWER.
IT IS POWER, MY FRIEND...
...YOUR MASTER SUPPLIES US WITH WEAPONS. HE PROFITS FROM THE CHAOS WE CAUSE...
...AND YET CYBERTRON IS DAMAGED IN THE PROCESS.
UNDER ORDERS OF MY EMPLOYER, SENATOR RATBAT, I HAD APPROACHED MEGATRON. RATBAT SAW AN OPPORTUNITY.
AND I DID NOT EXPECT TO BE IMPRESSED.
DOES THIS BOTHER YOU?
I... TRY...
...I TRY NOT TO LET IT.

YOU SEEM DISTRACTED, AS ALWAYS. YOUR EMOTIONS GET IN THE WAY.
THEY... SOMETHING.
SOMETHING LIKE THAT. THEY... ARE NOT MY EMOTIONS.
AND YOUR... CREATURES HERE?
THESE ARE... THEY ARE FRIENDS. CYBERTRONIANS. NOT...
...CREATURES.
I KNOW.
I MERELY WONDERED IF YOU DID, AS WELL.
HE TOLD THE TRUTH. AS HARD AS IT WAS, THEN, FOR ME TO SHUT OUT THE SOUNDS AND SIGHTS OF THE WORLD, I KNEW...
...HERE WAS A CYBERTRONIAN WHO TOLD THE TRUTH.
THE SENSE... THE EMOTION... WAS UNLIKE ANYTHING I HAD EVER EXPERIENCED.
HE LOOKED AT RAVAGE, LASERBEAK, AND BUZZSAW— AND HE SAW BROTHERS. NOT SLAVES.
HERE WAS SOMEONE WHOSE EMOTIONS—WHOSE THOUGHTS— I DID NOT WANT TO BLOCK.
YOU KNOW WHAT THE RATIOISTS, THE FUNCTIONALISTS, WOULD DO WITH YOUR FRIENDS.
"EACH A COG IN THE GREAT MACHINE."
DECIMUS. HE... HE SAYS THAT. HE SERVES WITH MY EMPLOYER.
"SERVES." THE SENATE SHOULD SERVE CYBERTRON... INSTEAD, THEY RULE US.
WHAT DOES RATBAT WANT FROM US?

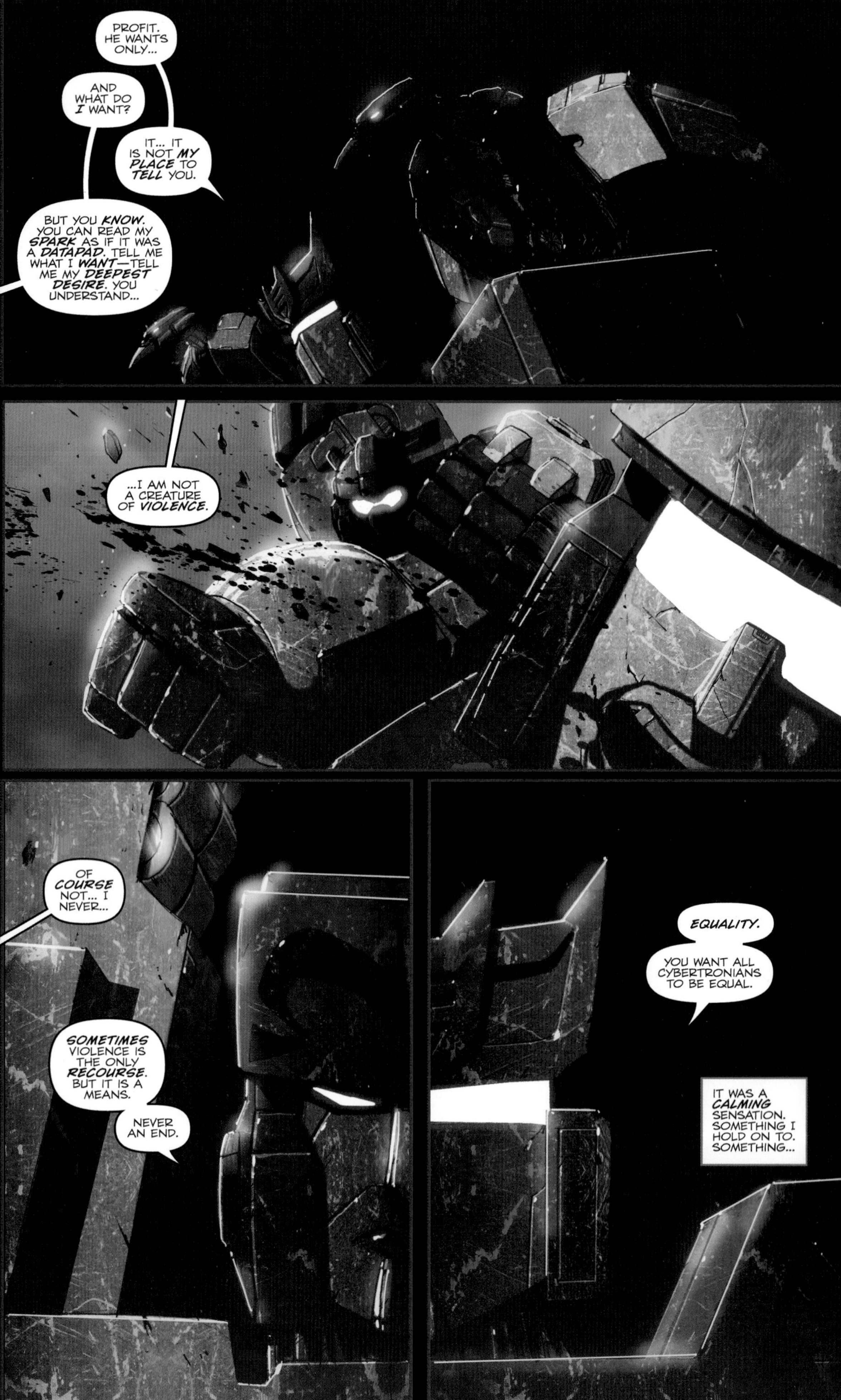
PROFIT. HE WANTS ONLY...
AND WHAT DO *I* WANT?
IT... IT IS NOT *MY PLACE* TO *TELL* YOU.
BUT YOU *KNOW*. YOU CAN READ MY *SPARK* AS IF IT WAS A *DATAPAD*. TELL ME WHAT I *WANT*—TELL ME MY *DEEPEST DESIRE*. YOU UNDERSTAND...
...I AM NOT A CREATURE OF *VIOLENCE*.
OF *COURSE* NOT... I NEVER...
SOMETIMES VIOLENCE IS THE ONLY *RECOURSE*. BUT IT IS A MEANS.
NEVER AN END.
EQUALITY.
YOU WANT ALL CYBERTRONIANS TO BE EQUAL.
IT WAS A *CALMING* SENSATION. SOMETHING I HOLD ON TO. SOMETHING...

...I COULD BELIEVE IN.
I CAN'T BELIEVE IT, BOSS—

—YOU'RE LETTING THEM GO!
NONE CAN DIE HERE. THE ONLY POSSIBLE OUTCOME IS A STALEMATE.
THE LOGICAL COURSE IS TO AVOID DELAY.
JHIAXUS. HAS THE TIME ARRIVED?
INDEED—

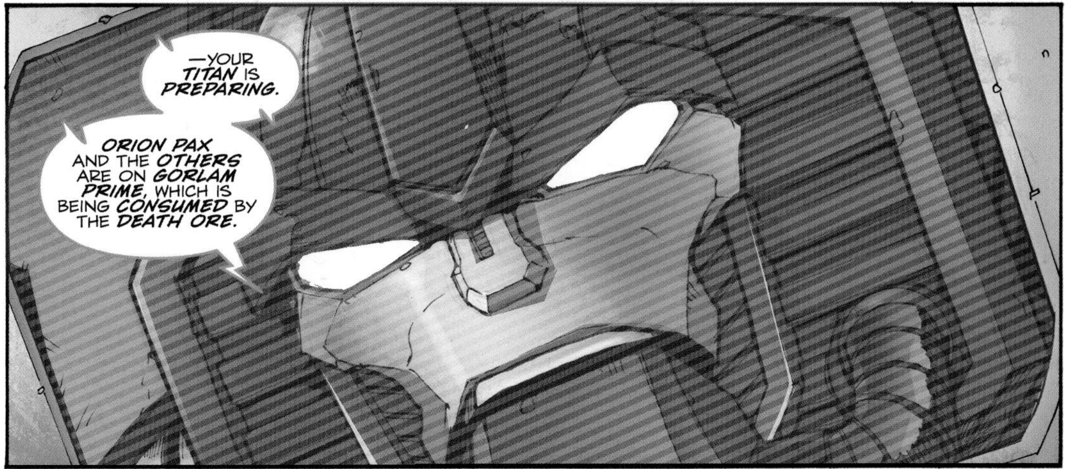
—YOUR TITAN IS PREPARING.
ORION PAX AND THE OTHERS ARE ON GORLAM PRIME, WHICH IS BEING CONSUMED BY THE DEATH ORE.

YET THEY LIVE?
AS YOU ASKED.
I DID NOT ASK, JHIAXUS...

...I COMMANDED.

YOUR REPUTATION COMMANDS ATTENTION, SOUNDWAVE.
I HAVE HEARD OF YOU. THE 'BOT WHO CAN LISTEN TO ANYTHING, ANYWHERE...
...THOUGH— CLEARLY—YOU ARE SOMETHING OF A MESS. WHERE DO YOU LIVE? SURELY NOT ON THESE FILTHY STREETS.
I FIND IT DIFFICULT... TO FOCUS MY ABILITIES... BUT I AM LEARNING. THANKS TO THE AID OF SOME FRIENDS...
WELL. PERHAPS I COULD BE OF HELP. IN EXCHANGE FOR YOUR SERVICES, THAT IS.
YOU SEE, LISTENING TO THINGS IS SOMETHING OF A HOBBY OF MINE, AS WELL.
IT IS... IT IS NOT A HOBBY. WHO... WHO ARE YOU?
RATBAT. SENATOR RATBAT.
PERHAPS, TOGETHER, WE COULD THINK OF SOMETHING YOU COULD CONCENTRATE ON.
I SUSPECT YOU WOULD THRIVE IN A NEW LIFE, AWAY FROM ALL THIS. LEAVE BEHIND THE... BEASTS YOU CONSORT WITH.
HIS WORDS. VILE, FUNCTIONALIST WORDS. THE TASTE OF SCORCHED CHROME.
YOU CAN DO BETTER, SOUNDWAVE. YOU CAN STAND WITH A HIGHER CLASS OF CYBERTRONIAN.
I HATED THEM. I HATED HIM.
I FOCUSED ON RATBAT, ON HIS WORDS. AND EVERYTHING ELSE FELL AWAY.
HM. A NEW LIFE?
CONSIDER IT DONE.
I FELT DENIGRATED. THE WORLD SMELLED CALLOUS. BUT I COULD THINK.
THINK FOR LONG ENOUGH...

...TO GET WHERE I NEEDED TO BE.
TO MY BROTHERS.

BROTHERHOOD HOLDS ME TOGETHER. THE BROTHERHOOD OF DECEPTICONS.
WHAT HAPPENED?

I SAW THE PURSUIT OF INFORMATION WITHOUT LIMIT, AND FOUND IT WANTING.
A LESSON I HAD LEARNED LONG AGO.

UH. OKAY...
ENOUGH OF THIS— DID YOU STOP HIM?

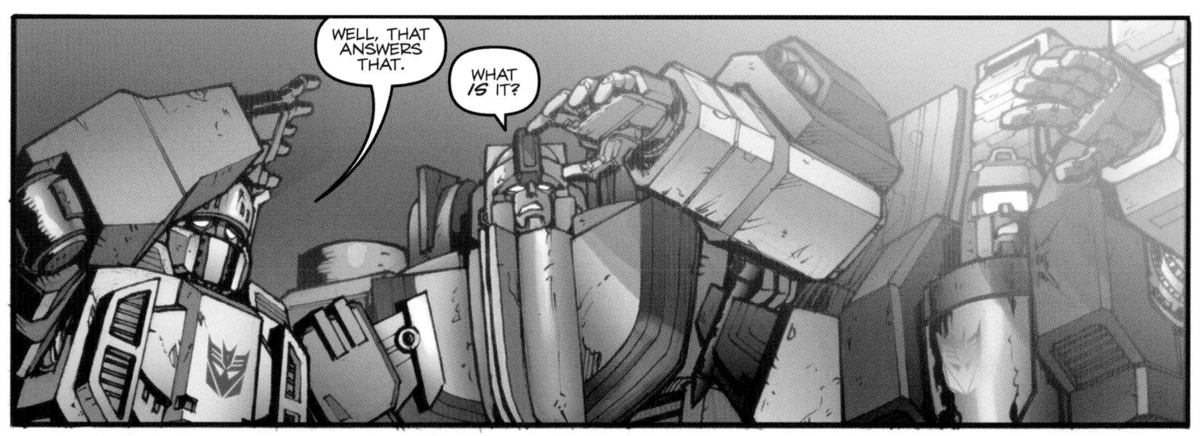
WELL, THAT ANSWERS THAT.
WHAT *IS* IT?

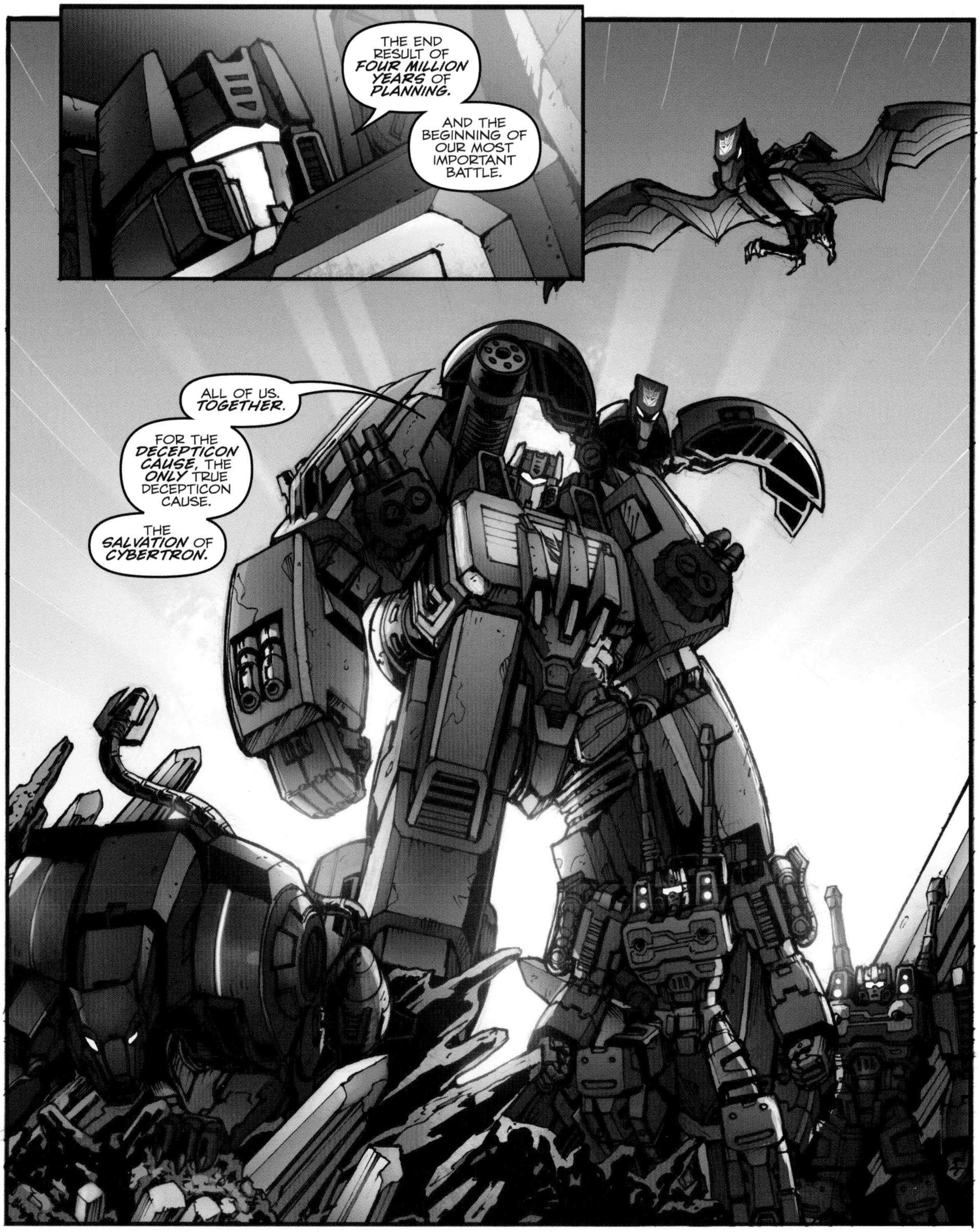

THE END RESULT OF ***FOUR MILLION YEARS*** OF ***PLANNING.***

AND THE BEGINNING OF OUR MOST IMPORTANT BATTLE.

ALL OF US. ***TOGETHER.***

FOR THE ***DECEPTICON CAUSE,*** THE ***ONLY*** TRUE DECEPTICON CAUSE.

THE ***SALVATION*** OF ***CYBERTRON.***

SO I SAID, "CYBERTRON'S SALVATION? YEAH, RIGHT.
"YOU WANT THE ENERGON, SENATOR—GET IT YOURSELF. I'M NOT GOING BACK IN THERE, NOT TODAY."
NO YOU DIDN'T.
THE COUNCIL WOULD HAVE YOUR SPARK EXTRACTED.
BIRDS. NEVER TELL A STORY TO A BIRD.
THE POINT ISN'T WHETHER OR NOT IT HAPPENED, BUZZSAW. THE POINT IS—
SNIFF SNIFF
—HOLD UP.
WHAT DO YOU SMELL? POLICE?
NO. I SMELL FEAR.
ARE YOU OKAY?
SOUNDS. LIGHTS. TASTES. SMELLS. EVERYWHERE.
SO MANY...

WHO ARE YOU?
I... I DO NOT KNOW... SO MANY...
RAVAGE. YOUR... NAME IS RAVAGE.
YEAH, HOW—?
I CAN SEE... I CAN HEAR... EVERYONE. I CAN SEE EVERYTHING ABOUT EVERYONE.
HOW'D YOU WIND UP ON THE STREET, NOT IN THE INSTITUTE?
SEEMS LIKE THE FUNCTIONALISTS WOULD HAVE A FIELD DAY WITH YOU.
WHERE... WHERE ARE...?
WHO AM I...? I AM... CAN'T... SHUT ANYTHING OUT...
...SO MUCH, SO MANY... SO TERRIBLE... ALL THE VOICES... SO TERRIBLE...
CHARMING. OKAY, I CAN SEE WHY YOU WOUND UP IN THE GUTTER WITH THE REST OF US DREGS.
I... I DIDN'T MEAN...
...IT'S... EMOTIONS... SO STRONG DOWN HERE.
LOOK. YOU... YOU SMELL LIKE AN ALRIGHT GUY. I CAN SMELL THINGS LIKE THAT, THINGS MOST PEOPLE CAN'T.
BUT I HAD TO LEARN TO FOCUS MY SNOUT. TO FIX ON ONE THING AT A TIME.
MAYBE THAT'S WHAT YOU GOTTA DO.
FOCUS... ON WHAT...?

ANYTHING YOU CAN.
RAVAGE SAVED ME THAT NIGHT, BUT IT WOULD TAKE TIME TO FIND THE FOCUS HE SPOKE OF.
SHOCKWAVE'S LACK OF EMOTION BLINDS HIM TO OUR POWER.
TO HIM, DECEPTICONS ARE THE MEANS TO HIS END... ONLY HE CAN FATHOM.
BUT IT DOES NOT MATTER IF I UNDERSTAND SHOCKWAVE.
IT MATTERS ONLY THAT I STOP HIM.
SOUNDWAVES

ROBOTS IN DISGUISE #22 COVER B

by **CASEY W. COLLER** Colors by **JOANA LAFUENTE**

MORE THAN MEETS THE EYE #22 COVER A

by **ALEX MILNE** Colors by **JOSH BURCHAM**

INTRODUCE MYSELF?
WHY HAVE I GOT TO INTRODUCE MYSELF?
EVERYONE *KNOWS* WHO I AM.

THEY CALL ME *ULTRA MAGNUS*, DULY APPOINTED ENFORCER OF THE TYREST ACCORD.

RODIMUS.
RODIMUS *PRIME.*
COMMANDER OF OUR STARSHIP, THE *LOST LIGHT.*

"*SKIDS*," APPARENTLY.
I'M A FORGETFUL THEORETICIAN.
LET'S JUST LEAVE IT AT THAT.

FIELD COMMANDER, ALPHA CLASS.
RECIPIENT OF THE *DISTINGUISHED SERVICE ORDER* AND THE *NOVIC MEDAL FOR OUTSTANDING VALOR.*

SWERVE? HELLO...?
WHAT IS IT, *NERVES?*
JUST PRETEND I'M NOT FILMING, OKAY? LOOK AT ME, NOT AT THE CAMERA.

THE *RODIMUS STAR?*
ER—
YES, I'VE RECEIVED THAT, TOO. BUT...

A film by
Rewind of Lower Petrohex

TAILGATE.
RECIPIENT OF SEVEN *NOVICS*, THREE *DSO'S*, THE GALACTIC CREST FOR GALLANTRY AND THE *HERO OF HEROES AWARD.*
FAVORITE COLOR: BLUE.

MY REAL NAME IS *TUMBLER* BUT EVERYONE—
—*STILL*—
—CALLS ME *CHROMEDOME.*
EVEN *YOU.*

OKAY, NOT "PRIME"— NOT *YET*— BUT—
NOM*MUS*, OPTI*MUS*, RODI*MUS*.
PATTERN'S A PATTERN.

RUNG. SHIP'S PSYCHIATRIST.
R-U-N-G.
(YOU'D BE SURPRISED.)

CYCLONUS OF TETRAHEX.
I AM NOT A DECEPTICON. I WANT THAT ON SCREEN.
NOT A DECEPTICON

IT'S WHIRL, SPELLED:
KER-KLICK!
CHOOM!

BRAINSTORM.
WEAPONS ENGINEER AND—ACCORDING TO PERCEPTOR—SHIP'S GENIUS.
ARE YOU INTERVIEWING HIM TOO?

lost/cam | 2819 rec)))
BRAINSTORM!
I TOLD YOU TO STAY OUT OF MY LAB!

YOUR NAME... DEFINES YOU. IT'S YOUR SOUL EXPRESSED IN SYLLABLES.
HM?
OH, YES, SORRY. IT'S DRIFT.

CHIEF MEDICAL OFFICER RATCHET—
—AND SOMEONE WHO HAS A DOZEN "BETTER" THINGS TO DO THAN "SIT" HERE AND BE "INTERVIEWED."
YEAH, ABOUT THESE AIR QUOTES...

FIRST AID, CHIEF MEDICAL OFFICER...
...
...IN TRAINING.

HOLD STILL.
YOU'VE GOT DIRT ON YOUR LENS.

YES, SORRY, RETIRING CHIEF MEDICAL OFFICER.
I THOUGHT I'D MADE THAT...
OBVIOUSLY NOT.

AND—JUST TURN THE CAMERA AROUND—ME! REWIND!
NOW, LET ME TAKE YOU BACK TO THE BEGINNING: THE DAY BEFORE WE TOOK OFF.

YOU'RE GONNA SHOW SOME OF THE SPEECH?
'S NOT EMBARRASSING, IT'S JUST—
I REALLY GAVE IT MY ALL.

TOMORROW, THIS PATCH OF LAND BECOMES A LAUNCH PAD.
TOMORROW, I WILL BOARD THE *LOST LIGHT* AND SET OFF IN SEARCH OF OUR ANCESTORS.
THEY WERE KNOWN AS THE ***KNIGHTS OF CYBERTRON.*** THEY'RE REAL. I'M GOING TO FIND THEM.
AND I WANT YOU ALL TO COME WITH ME.
"A FILM? AS IN A ***FILM*** FILM?"

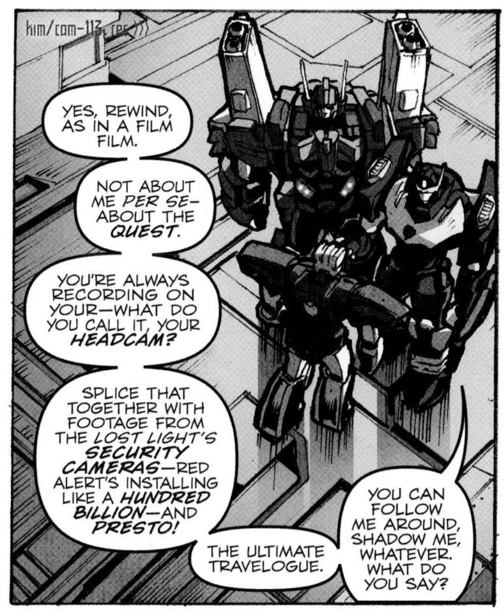

YES, REWIND, AS IN A FILM FILM.
NOT ABOUT ME *PER SE*— ABOUT THE ***QUEST.***
YOU'RE ALWAYS RECORDING ON YOUR—WHAT DO YOU CALL IT, YOUR ***HEADCAM?***
SPLICE THAT TOGETHER WITH FOOTAGE FROM THE *LOST LIGHT'S* ***SECURITY CAMERAS***—RED ALERT'S INSTALLING LIKE A ***HUNDRED BILLION***—AND ***PRESTO!***
THE ULTIMATE TRAVELOGUE.
YOU CAN FOLLOW ME AROUND, SHADOW ME, WHATEVER. WHAT DO YOU SAY?

AUDIO RANGE >>> MAX
ARE YOU SURE YOU KNOW WHAT YOU'RE DOING, RODIMUS?
"NEVER TRUST AN AUTEUR"—IT'S NOT IN THE ***AUTOBOT CODE,*** BUT IT ***SHOULD*** BE.
REWIND'S AMIABLE BUT MISCHIEVOUS; WE COULD END UP LOOKING ***RIDICULOUS.***
HOW?
HE COULD— I DON'T KNOW...
...HE COULD LET ME VOICE THIS TYPE OF CONCERN AND THEN CUT AWAY TO A SHOT OF ME DOING SOMETHING WHICH, TAKEN OUT OF CONTEXT, LOOKS STUPID.

FOOTAGE REMOVED BY ORDER OF THE DULY APPOINTED ENFORCER OF THE TYREST ACCORD

AUDIO RANGE >>> MAX
WHAT IF I LET YOU CLEAR THE FINISHED PRODUCT FOR RELEASE?
HM?
BECAUSE I HONESTLY THINK YOU'RE WORRYING ABOUT ***NOTHING.*** WE'RE GOING ON A QUEST!
AUTOBOTS IN SPACE!
IT'LL BE NON-STOP ***FIGHTS*** AND ***EXPLOSIONS*** AND ***CHASES!***
WE WON'T JUST BE LYING AROUND...

SORRY, I MUST HAVE ***DRIFTED OFF...***

TAILGATE? REWIND? WHAT DID I MISS?

HAVE WE FOUND THE KNIGHTS OF CYBERTRON YET?

HAR HAR. WE WERE JUST TALKING ABOUT ***RODIMUS.***

WHAT ABOUT HIM?

HE'S GOT A COOL ***ALT MODE.*** MAGNUS, TOO. AND CYCLONUS...

I MEAN, YOU WOULD, WOULDN'T YOU?

YOU'D WANT THOSE ALT MODES.

AN ALT MODE DISCUSSION AND NO ONE'S MENTIONED ***RUNG?***

WHAT DOES RUNG TURN INTO?
A BUGGY OR A UNICYCLE OR SOMETHING.
HE'S GOT THAT WHEEL ON HIS BACK. ISN'T THAT RIGHT, REWIND?
NO, THE WHEEL'S PART OF HIS BACKPACK, WHICH HE USES AS A TROLLEY.
NO ONE KNOWS WHAT HE TURNS INTO.
"AND THAT'S WHEN YOU SAID—WHAT WAS IT, A HUNDRED SHANIX?"

YEAH, A HUNDRED BIG ONES TO THE FIRST PERSON WHO FOUND OUT RUNG'S ALT MODE.
BUT WITHOUT ASKING HIM. YOU COULDN'T ASK HIM OUTRIGHT.
THAT WAS THE RULE...

"...ASIDE FROM THAT, ANYTHING WAS FAIR GAME."

KONK
OW!

lost/cam-0788.rec >>>
SORRY, RUNG—WAVERIDER AND I WERE PLAYING HAND GRENADE TAG.
Y'KNOW, SOME PEOPLE SAY THAT A BLOW TO THE NEURAL CLUSTER CAN TRIGGER INVOLUNTARY MODE CHANGE.
OBVIOUSLY NOT.
HM.

lost/cam-0788.rec >>>

lost/cam-0788.rec >>>
KONK
OW!

SEE, I DON'T THINK HAVING WAGERS AND DOING STUFF LIKE THAT IS IMMATURE.
WE ALL NEED HOBBIES.
BRAINSTORM'S GOT HIS BRIEFCASE, RUNG'S GOT HIS COLLECTION OF SPACESHIPS...
ULTRA MAGNUS HAS GOT HIS MUSIC—NOT TO MENTION HIS AND HIS FRANKLY BIZARRE OBSESSION WITH —WHICH RATCHET SWEARS CAN LEAD TO PREMATURE DEATH AND, EVEN WORSE,

AUDIO SOUNDTRACK CENSORED BY ORDER OF THE DULY ELECTED ENFORCER OF THE TYREST ACCORD

HOBBIES?
NAH.
I GET INTO SOMETHING, MASTER IT, THEN KIND OF LOSE INTEREST.
IT GETS KINDA BORING...

ARK 1, ARK 2, ARK 3, ARK 4...
(ARK 5'S BROKEN.)
ARK 6, ARK 7, ARK 8, ARK—

MEETING NEW PEOPLE, DOES THAT COUNT?
LIKE THE STENTARIANS. THE ONES WE MET ON HEDONIA, WHILE WE WERE ON SHORE LEAVE.
THE AMMONITES AND THE TERRADORES—THE TWO WARRING FACTIONS. THE STENTARIANS.
YOU WERE THERE, REWIND, REMEMBER? YOU WERE FILMING IT ALL...

ALWAYS NICE TO MEET ANOTHER RACE OF MECHANICALS.
I'M SKIDS.
"SKIDS."
WHAT A STRANGE NAME.
I'M 16444/9.
I'M A FIELD COMMANDER WITH THE **AMMONITE ARMY**. WE'RE AT WAR WITH THE ACCURSED **TERRADORES**.
AT WAR, EH?
WAR.
"WAR."

FORGIVE MY, ER—
FRIEND?
—**CREWMATE**. OUR OWN WAR WAS SO—
AWESOME?
—**PROTRACTED** THAT IT—IT KIND OF TOWERS ABOVE THE REST.
BY COMPARISON, OTHER CONFLICTS ARE ESSENTIALLY—
SKIRMISHES?
SPATS? TIFFS?
TAKE YOUR PICK

SO YOU THINK YOU'RE BETTER AT WAR THAN US? HOW LONG WERE YOU FIGHTING?
FOUR MILLION YEARS. YOU?
SIXTEEN.
SIXTEEN YEARS.
SIXTEEN MILLION.
SIXTEEN MILLION YEARS?! SIX-**TEEN**?
THAT'S RIDICULOUS. THAT'S A RIDICULOUS NUMBER.

WELL, I BET YOU HAVEN'T BEEN **BLACKLISTED** BY THE **GALACTIC COUNCIL**.
PLEASE. THE COUNCIL WAS FORMED IN RESPONSE TO **OUR WAR**.

WE'RE **BIMODAL**. WE CAN TURN INTO VEHICLES, MACHINERY, AND WEAPONS.
SO?
SOME OF US HAVE **THREE** MODES.
I ONCE WENT TOE-TO-TOE WITH A **SIX-CHANGER**.
JET!
BEAST!
TANK!
GUN!
AND SOMETHING ELSE I CAN'T REMEMBER!
WE'VE GOT **DECABOTS**—TEN MODES **EACH**.
THAT'S BASICALLY SIX—THE MOST YOUR RACE CAN DO—PLUS FOUR MORE.

GESTALTS!
BEG PARDON?
WE'RE *THIS FAR* FROM PERFECTING *COMBINER TECHNOLOGY*— SOON, GROUPS OF US WILL BE ABLE TO MERGE INTO A SINGLE 'BOT.
WE'RE *ALREADY* COMBINERS. *ALL* OF US.
IN FACT, WE MIX AND MATCH. WE'RE *OMNICOMBINATIONAL*.

PROVE IT.
WHAT, NOW?
RIGHT NOW, *RIGHT* HERE. PROVE IT.

READY?
ON MY COUNT.
THREE, TWO, ONE...

TSCHE-CHU-CHU-CHU-CHU-TSCHE

HAPPY NOW?

SO HOW GOES THE WAR?
FOR ME PERSONALLY? FOR ME AND MY MEN?
NOT GOOD, SKIDS.
NOT GOOD.
WE'RE BEING PURSUED BY THE TERRADORIANS' IMPERIAL GUARD, AND THEY'RE *RELENTLESS*.
THEY'VE CHASED OUR FLIGHT SIGNATURE HALFWAY ACROSS THE ARGON NEBULAE—AND THEY'RE *GAINING*.

SO WHY HEDONIA?
WE NEED TO BUY A NEW SHIP; THROW THE TERRADORES OFF OUR TAIL.
AND THE MEN DESERVE A FEW HOURS' REST AND RECUPERATION.
WE JUST NEED TO KEEP A LOW PROFILE.

HEY, MONDO!
YOU EXPECTING A DELIVERY OF WEAPONS-GRADE NUCLEON?
BECAUSE A *TERRADORIAN WARCRUISER* THE SIZE OF THE *RAGING PRISM* JUST LANDED ON YOUR DOORSTEP!

IT'S THEM! THE IMPERIAL GUARD! THEY'VE FOUND US!
SIGH
LEAVE THIS TO ME.

WHAT'S HAPPENING OUT THERE? WHAT'S GOING ON?
YOUR ARCH-ENEMIES—THESE TERRADORES. DESCRIBE THEM TO ME.
ER— THEY TEND TO CARRY STAFFS.
THEY WEAR THE ROYAL CREST ON THEIR FOREHEAD. AND CLOAKS—THEY'RE REALLY INTO CLOAKS.
AND SCALE-WISE?
SAME AS US.
SO KNEE-HIGH.

WHY, WHAT'S YOUR CREWMATE DOING?
HE'S TALKING TO THIS GUY WITH A COWL AND A GOLDEN STAFF.
THAT'S ***IMPERIUS DRAX!***
THE ***ETERNAL SOVEREIGN!***
THE LEADER OF THE TERRADORES! BY THE ***GREAT SHATTERING,*** THIS IS ***SERIOUS!***

IT'S GETTING HEATED.
OH, WHIRL. DON'T TELL ME YOU'RE GOING TO—

CHOOM
CHOOM
KER-CLICK
CHOOM

I THINK SIXTEEN MILLION YEARS OF WAR JUST CAME TO AN END.

AND ***THAT,*** MY ITTY-BITTY FRIEND, IS HOW THE ***EXPERTS*** DO IT.
"I TELL YOU, REWIND— THESE ***QUESTIONS...***"

..."ARE YOU HAPPY?"
HOW AM I SUPPOSED TO ANSWER THAT?

I'M HAPPY WHEN I'M WORKING, YES.

I DON'T UNDERSTAND THE QUESTION.
NOT A DECEPTICON

WHAT IS THIS, A *THERAPY SESSION?*
BECAUSE I'VE BEEN TRICKED LIKE THAT BEFORE.

...
TODAY, I'M HAPPY.
WITH YOU, I'M HAPPY.

NO ONE'S EVER ASKED ME THAT BEFORE.

EVERYONE ASSUMES THAT IF YOU MAKE JOKES YOU'RE HAPPY.
WHY?
WHY IS THAT?

ARE *YOU* HAPPY?
IS THAT A NOD...?
AND... WE HAVE A THUMBS UP.

SOON.
NOT YET.
SOON.

CAN I LOOK STRAIGHT AT THE CAMERA?
I'VE NEVER BEEN HAPPIER.

DEFINE "HAPPY."

RUNG!
RUUU-UUNG!

TAILGATE?
IS THAT YOU?

lost/com-1159. rec >>>
SURPRIIIISE!
WHAT'S GOING ON?
WHAT DOES IT LOOK LIKE?
WE'RE HAVING AN ALT-MODE PARTY! COME AND JOIN US!
AN ALT-MODE PARTY?
THEY WERE ALL THE RAGE BACK IN MY DAY...
...AND, ER, THEREFORE YOUR DAY.

lost/com-1157. rec >>>

lost/com-1157. rec >>>
HOW DO YOU REACH YOUR DRINKS?

...
...
GOOD POINT.

Lost/bridge-com-0002. re)))
SORRY, BLASTER, I CAME AS QUICKLY AS I COULD.
I THOUGHT YOU DIDN'T LIKE HATS.
THEME NIGHT AT SWERVE'S: "PEOPLE YOU'D LIKE TO PUNCH."
I WAS A LONE MEGATRON IN A SEA OF WHIRLS.
ANYWAY, WHAT IS IT?
YOU SOUNDED EXCITED. IS IT THE KNIGHTS? HAVE WE MADE CONTACT?

BETTER THAN THE KNIGHTS.
LOOK WHO WANTS TO COME ON BOARD.
OH.
HIM.

A FINE AUTOBOT. A FINE AUTOBOT.
VERY FIRM HANDSHAKE.
VERY STRAIGHT BADGE.

I...
...WAS IMPRESSED.
NOT A DECEPTICON

YOU WANT TO HATE HIM, BUT—
YOU JUST CAN'T.

HAVE YOU ASKED RODIMUS ABOUT HIM?
ASK HIM. ASK HIM AND WATCH HIS FACE.

I HEARD—
—THIS IS JUST WHAT I HEARD—
—BUT I HEARD THAT OMEGA SUPREME GOES TO HIM FOR ADVICE.

I GOT HIS AUTOGRAPH.
CAN YOU BELIEVE IT?
A DATAPAD SIGNED BY—

THUNDERCLASH!
WHAT ARE THE CHANCES? DESPITE THE TRILLIONS OF PEOPLE IN THE UNIVERSE THAT AREN'T YOU—
—WE MANAGE TO RUN INTO YOU.
IT'S AMAZING, ISN'T IT?
IT'S UNBELIEVABLE. THAT'S THE WORD.
IN FACT—I REALLY CAN'T DESCRIBE WHAT I'M FEELING RIGHT NOW.
I KNOW. IT'S BEEN TOO LONG.
HAS IT?
I MEAN, YES, OF COURSE IT HAS. FAR TOO LONG.
LOOK—HANDS UP—CARDS ON THE TABLE.
I DON'T SEE IT.
THE HERO WORSHIP, THE BLIND ADULATION— I DON'T SEE IT.
IN FACT, THE WHOLE CULT OF PERSONALITY—I ACTUALLY FIND IT DISTASTEFUL.
AND IF THAT'S UNFASHIONABLE— IF THAT'S "UNCOOL"— WELL, I'M SORRY, I DIDN'T BECOME CAPTAIN BECAUSE I THOUGHT IT WAS COOL.
YOU KNOW, I'M NOT UP HERE—I'M NOT MAKING ALL THESE SACRIFICES AND LEADING THESE GUYS INTO BATTLE AND BEING INSPIRATIONAL—I'M NOT DOING THAT BECAUSE IT MAKES ME LOOK GOOD.
I TAKE IT YOU'RE STILL THE CAPTAIN OF THE VIM AND VIGOR?
THE VIS VITALIS, YES. BUT THEN I DON'T HAVE MUCH CHOICE IN THE MATTER.
OF COURSE, OF COURSE...
BUT THAT LEVEL OF DEPENDENCY. YOU'RE VERY BRAVE.
NOT AT ALL. IT'S MY CREW— THEY'RE THE BRAVE ONES, CHOOSING TO TRAVEL WITH ME.
ALL THOSE FIGHTS, EXPLOSIONS, AND CHASES. IT'S NON-STOP.

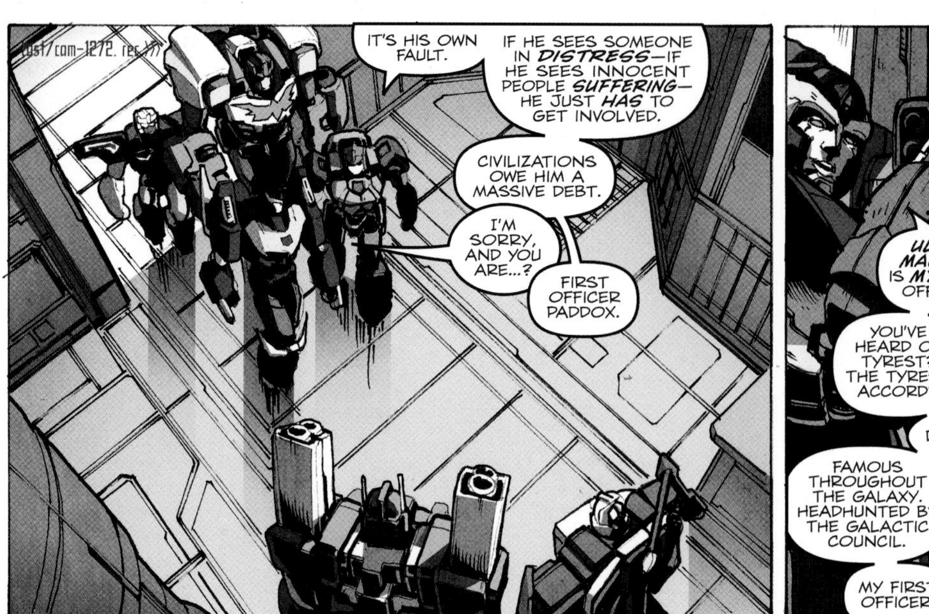
IT'S HIS OWN FAULT.
IF HE SEES SOMEONE IN DISTRESS—IF HE SEES INNOCENT PEOPLE SUFFERING—HE JUST HAS TO GET INVOLVED.
CIVILIZATIONS OWE HIM A MASSIVE DEBT.
I'M SORRY, AND YOU ARE...?
FIRST OFFICER PADDOX.

ULTRA MAGNUS IS MY FIRST OFFICER.
YOU'VE HEARD OF TYREST? THE TYREST ACCORD?
HE'S THE DULY APPOINTED ENFORCER.
FAMOUS THROUGHOUT THE GALAXY. HEADHUNTED BY THE GALACTIC COUNCIL.
MY FIRST OFFICER.

MAGNUS!
I WAS ALREADY A HUGE FAN OF YOUR WORK AS TYREST'S MOST TRUSTED, AND THEN I READ YOUR ARTICLE ON THE AUTOBOT CODE—THE ONE ON TYPEFACES.
BRAVO, SIR—BRAVO.
I HAD CONSIDERED MYSELF AN EXPERT ON THE INTERRELATIONSHIP BETWEEN TYPOGRAPHY AND MILITARY JUSTICE, BUT YOU TOOK IT SO MUCH FURTHER.
I'M SORRY IF I'M MAKING YOU UNCOMFORTABLE. PEOPLE REACT TO COMPLIMENTS IN DIFFERENT—

—WAYS.

DRIFT'S AN EX-DECEPTICON. I SORT OF REHABILITATED HIM.
REHABILITATED ME?
SORT OF. YOU KNOW WHAT I MEAN.
SHH.

THE CALL OF THE WAVELENGTH?
BUT HOW DID YOU KNOW—
THAT YOU WERE A PRACTICING SPECTRALIST?
YOU'VE BEEN ADJUSTING THE COLOR OF YOUR EYES TO REFLECT THE FLUCTUATING LEVELS OF EMOTIONAL DISCOMFORT IN THE ROOM.
(AND I AGREE: THIS IS ABSOLUTELY A MAGENTA MOMENT.)

lost/com-1272. rec
HEY, THUNDERS! AREN'T YOU FORGETTING SOMEONE?
RATCHET!
WHAT THE—? NEW HANDS!

SORRY I'M LATE.
I WAS ORGANIZING THE WELCOME PARTY.
YOU TWO KNOW EACH OTHER?
HE TAUGHT ME EVERYTHING I KNOW.
A GROSS EXAGGERATION— I JUST HELPED HIM PASS HIS MEDICAL EXAMS.

SORRY, "THUNDERS," BUT WHY EXACTLY ARE YOU HERE?
IT'S WONDERFUL TO SEE YOU—I'M SURE THE OTHERS WILL TESTIFY TO THAT—BUT WE'RE A BIT BUSY.
OH?
WE'RE ON A QUEST. NOTHING TOO IMPORTANT— THE FATE OF OUR ENTIRE RACE HANGS ON THE OUTCOME, THAT'S ALL.
WELL, IF YOU'RE IN CHARGE THEN OUR RACE IS IN SAFE HANDS.

lost/com-1272. rec
AM I THE ONLY ONE WHO THOUGHT THAT SOUNDED SARCASTIC?
REALLY?

NO, NO, I WAS BEING SINCERE.
I'M SMILING BECAUSE WE'RE ON OUR OWN QUEST.
WE'RE LOOKING FOR THE KNIGHTS OF CYBERTRON.

I... THINK I HANDLED IT PRETTY WELL, ALL THINGS CONSIDERED.

WHAT?!
THAT'S MY QUEST!
YOUR QUEST?
OUR QUEST!
THAT'S OUR QUEST!

FINDING THE KNIGHTS HAS ALWAYS BEEN AN AMBITION OF MINE—SOMETHING TO DO WHEN THE WAR WAS OVER.
BUT YOU HAVEN'T GOT A MAP...!
THERE'S A MAP?
IN THE MATRIX. THE MATRIX WAS BROKEN—I'M SURPRISED YOU DIDN'T HEAR ABOUT THIS—I MEAN, THIS WAS BIG STUFF—AND INSIDE THERE WAS A STAR MAP LEADING TO CYBERUTOPIA...

WE NAVIGATE BY INSTINCT AND FAITH.
FROM TIME TO TIME THUNDERCLASH ENTERS A TRANCE-LIKE STATE, DURING WHICH HE RECEIVES DIVINE DIRECTION.
I CARRIED THE MATRIX FOR OPTIMUS WHEN HE TOOK HIS FIRST SABBATICAL.
KEPT IT WARM FOR HIM.

THEY SAY IT HAD TO BE SURGICALLY REMOVED. LIKE IT DIDN'T WANT TO BE TAKEN OUT.

SORRY—BEFORE THE LOVE IN THE ROOM OVERWHELMS ME—I'M STILL NOT SURE WHY YOU'RE HERE.
IT'S MY SHIP.
"OKAY, REWIND, I THINK I CAN EXPLAIN THIS..."

...THE VIS VITALIS IS A LIFE-SUPPORT MACHINE.
A GIANT, WIRELESS, LIFE-SUPPORT MACHINE.
THUNDERCLASH IS THIS FAR FROM TOTAL SHUTDOWN—AND THAT'S NO SECRET; HE'LL HAPPILY SHOW YOU HIS WOUND.

AS LONG AS HE STAYS WITHIN A CERTAIN DISTANCE OF THE V.V., HE'S SAFE.
HE TURNED HIS LIFE-SUPPORT MACHINE INTO A "SPACESHIP" SO HE COULD CARRY ON DOING WHAT HE DOES BEST: ROAMING THE GALAXY, BEING—WELL, YOU'VE MET HIM. YOU CAN IMAGINE.

HE'D TRACKED US DOWN BECAUSE THE V.V. WAS LOSING POWER—IT HAD BEEN DAMAGED RESCUING SOME ORPHANS FROM AN EXPLODING SUN.
THAT'S WHAT RODIMUS SAID, ANYWAY.
BUT BASICALLY, YEAH, HE WANTED A SHIP-TO-SHIP JUMPSTART.
PERCEPTOR WAS SKEPTICAL AT FIRST, BUT...

I STAND CORRECTED—THERE *IS* A WAY TO USE THE QUANTUM ENGINES TO REPLENISH THE V.V.'S POWER SUPPLY.
THANK YOU FOR YOUR ASSISTANCE, THUNDERCLASH.
IT'S... BEEN A LONG TIME SINCE SOMEONE TAUGHT ME SOMETHING.
I'LL HOOK UP THE TRANSFER CABLES.

I VOTE WE *PAUSE* A MOMENT.
ANYONE WHO DISAGREES CAN WATCH THUNDERCLASH LOSE HIS HEAD.
AND IF HE DIES, THE *VIS VITALIS* AUTOMATICALLY EXPLODES. ALL HANDS LOST.
PADDOX?! WHAT ARE YOU *DOING?!*

WELL, *EXACTLY.*
THERE'S "OUT OF NOWHERE" AND THERE'S "OH, COME *ON*."
(AND THE BIT ABOUT THE EXPLODING SHIP WAS NONSENSE, BY THE WAY.)

HE'S A *DECEPTICON SECRET AGENT!* ALL THIS TIME YOU'VE HAD A DECEPTICON SECRET AGENT ON BOARD AND YOU DIDN'T KNOW IT! HOW *EMBARRASSING!*
WE ARE NOT A DECEPTICON.
"WE"?
WE'RE *AMMONITES.*

FUNNY, ISN'T IT, THE WAY ONE *ASSUMES* THINGS.
TURNS OUT THAT THE AMMONITES THAT WE MET ON HEDONIA WEREN'T ACTAUALLY THAT NICE.
"THE *EVIL AMMONITES* AND THE *HEROIC TERRADORES.*" THAT'S WHAT EVERYONE CALLS THEM, APPARENTLY...

BUT—YOU AND I HAVE BEEN SHIPMATES FOR *YEARS!*
I'VE SAVED YOUR LIFE ON—
—WAIT A SECOND—
—FOURTEEN SEPARATE OCCASIONS!
WHY ARE YOU *DOING* THIS?

WE'VE BEEN FIGHTING THE TERRADORES FOR SO LONG WE THOUGHT WE'D REACHED AN ETERNAL STALEMATE.
AND THEN— THREE WEEKS AGO—THEIR LEADER, IMPERIUS DRAX, WAS ASSASSINATED ON HEDONIA.
HIS SUCCESSOR IS DETERMINED TO WIN AT ANY COST—EVEN IF IT MEANS REACHING OUT TO THE DARK CYCLOPS.
EVEN IF IT MEANS OUR PLANET IS DESTROYED IN THE PROCESS.

WE'VE BEEN SPYING ON YOU AUTOBOTS FOR YEARS, PASSING ALL YOUR SECRETS BACK TO OUR WEAPONS ENGINEERS.
BUT IN THE LAST FEW DAYS, EVERY UNDERCOVER AGENT HAS BEEN RECALLED AHEAD OF THE BIG PUSH—AND WE'VE BEEN TOLD TO STEAL ANYTHING THAT MIGHT GIVE US AN EDGE.
YOUR QUANTUM ENGINES WOULD GIVE US THAT EDGE: OUR SCATTERED FORCES WOULD BE REUNITED IN DAYS IF OUR WARSHIPS COULD TRAVERSE THE ARGON NEBULAE IN THE BLINK OF AN EYE.

Lost/engine.com-6255.rec)))
I THINK HE'S DOWN HERE SOMEWHERE... I HEARD SWOONING.
I CAN'T BELIEVE YOU'RE BEST FRIENDS WITH THUNDERCLASH.
SECRET BEST FRIENDS; SUBTLE DIFFERENCE.
NOW, RUNG, THIS AUTOGRAPH... YOU REMEMBER THE DEAL, RIGHT?
YOU GET THUNDERCLASH TO SIGN MY DATAPAD IF I PROVE TO YOU THAT MY TRANSFORMATION COG IS WORKING.
WAIT. LOOK OVER THERE...

WE HAVE TO DO SOMETHING.
LIKE WHAT? I'M THE SECOND WEAKEST PERSON ON THIS SHIP AND YOU'RE THE FIRST— AND WE'RE BOTH COMPREHENSIVELY UNARMED.
PERHAPS NOT...

THIS DOESN'T NEED TO GET MESSY, RODIMUS.
ORDER EVERYONE OFF THE LOST LIGHT AND I'LL BE ON MY W—

Lost/engine.com-6255.rec)))
THWUNK!

Lost Engine Cam-6258. Rec
YOU CAN CHANGE BACK NOW, RUNG.
DID IT WORK?
"I DON'T KNOW WHAT I TURN INTO, IS THE SIMPLE ANSWER. NO ONE DOES."

WHEN THE FUNCTIONISTS CAME TO POWER THEY SUBJECTED ME TO EVERY EXAMINATION YOU CAN IMAGINE.
I DON'T BLAME THEM: THE BASIS OF THEIR ENTIRE PHILOSOPHY WAS FLAWED UNLESS THEY COULD WORK OUT WHAT I WAS FOR.

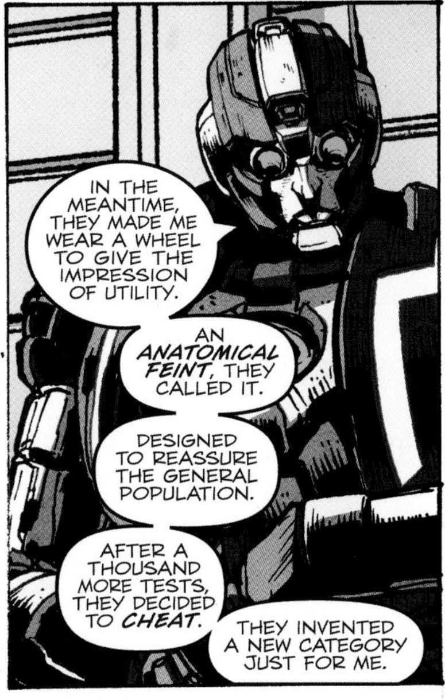
IN THE MEANTIME, THEY MADE ME WEAR A WHEEL TO GIVE THE IMPRESSION OF UTILITY.
AN ANATOMICAL FEINT, THEY CALLED IT.
DESIGNED TO REASSURE THE GENERAL POPULATION.
AFTER A THOUSAND MORE TESTS, THEY DECIDED TO CHEAT.
THEY INVENTED A NEW CATEGORY JUST FOR ME.

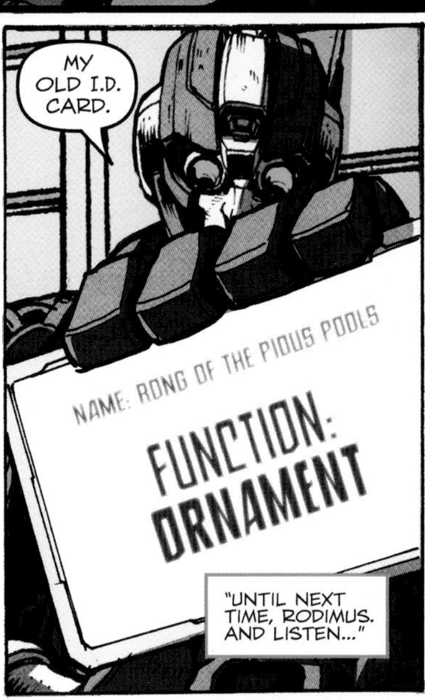
MY OLD I.D. CARD.
NAME: RUNG OF THE PIOUS POOLS
FUNCTION: ORNAMENT
"UNTIL NEXT TIME, RODIMUS. AND LISTEN..."

...PERCEPTOR TOLD ME THAT USING YOUR QUANTUM ENGINES TO RE-ENERGIZE THE V.V. HAS SET YOU BACK MONTHS—FROM NOW ON YOU'LL BE JUMPING LESS OFTEN, AND COVERING SHORTER DISTANCES.
IF I FIND THE KNIGHTS BEFORE YOU DO, I HOPE FUTURE GENERATIONS REALIZE THAT IT WAS ONLY POSSIBLE BECAUSE OF YOUR SELFLESSNESS AND INTEGRITY.
YOU WERE AN AUTOBOT IN NEED—WHAT ELSE COULD I DO?

I TELL YOU, REWIND, I'M STARTING TO REGRET THE WHOLE "FULL ACCESS" THING...
WHY, WOULD YOU HAVE ACTED DIFFERENTLY HAD I NOT BEEN FILMING?
WHAT? DON'T BE RIDICULOUS.
BOR-ING!

LUNA 1.
THE ENTERTAINMENT SUITE.

TURN IT OFF!
IT'S RUBBISH!
HEY!
FOR MISSIONARIES AND INTELLECTUALS YOU'RE A PRETTY ROUGH CROWD, YOU KNOW THAT?

YOU PROMISED US AN INSIGHT INTO LIFE ON BOARD THE LOST LIGHT!
YES, IN THE HOPE THAT YOU'D JOIN US ON OUR QUEST. THE MORE MEMBERS OF THE CIRCLE OF LIGHT THAT SIGN UP, THE BETTER.
WHY?
WHAT'S THE PROBLEM?
WHAT'S THE PROBLEM?
EVERYONE ON BOARD THE LOST LIGHT IS CRACKED IN THE HEAD!

YEAH, DYSFUNCTIONAL ISN'T THE WORD! THERE ISN'T A NORMAL 'BOT AMONG YOU!
AND THAT WOULDN'T BE SO BAD IF YOU ACTUALLY MADE PROGRESS— BUT AS FAR AS I CAN MAKE OUT, ALL YOU DO IS ARGUE, CRACK JOKES, AND GET SIDETRACKED DOING POINTLESS, SILLY THINGS THAT ONLY YOU FIND AMUSING!
I JOINED THE LOST LIGHT AFTER THE QUEST HAD BEGUN... IT'S LIKE HOME TO ME.
"SILLY"? I GUESS YOU DON'T SEE IT IF YOU'RE PART OF IT...

DON'T WORRY. AS A RECRUITMENT TOOL, YOUR LITTLE FILM HAS WORKED WONDERS.
IT HAS?
SURE. I JUST HOPE IT'S NOT TOO LATE TO GET IN TOUCH WITH THUNDERCLASH.
YEAH, AT LEAST HE KNOWS WHAT HE'S DOING.

WHAT'S NEXT?

ONCE WE FIND THE KNIGHTS, THEY EITHER RESTORE CYBERTRON TO ITS FORMER GLORY OR WE START AGAIN ON CYBERUTOPIA.
THAT'S ALWAYS BEEN THE OBJECTIVE.

I HAVE THIS THEORY—
(DON'T GIVE ME THAT LOOK.)
I HAVE THIS THEORY THAT WE'RE THE KNIGHTS OF CYBERTRON.

PFFT.
HEY, DID YOU HEAR THAT?
PFFT.
I'VE BEEN TRYING TO MAKE THAT SOUND FOR EVER.

I THINK DRIFT'S RIGHT, IN A WAY.
THIS HAS NEVER BEEN ABOUT THE KNIGHTS. IT'S ABOUT US.
YOU, ME... ALL OF US.
I THINK THAT'S WHY I'M HERE.

LITTLE VICTORIES, REWIND.
LITTLE VICTORIES.

I'M HOPING FOR MORE MASSIVE, RAMBLING DIVERSIONS.
WHO WANTS CLOSURE? LET'S REALLY STRETCH THIS SUCKER OUT.

RETIREMENT?
OF COURSE.
EVENTUALLY.

IN THE FUTURE, I'D LIKE TO SEE A WORLD WITHOUT GUNS.
HA!
NO.
JOKING.

LONGER TERM... FOR ME, I DON'T REALLY KNOW. NOT REALLY THOUGHT ABOUT IT.
FOR EVERYONE ELSE—FOR MY CREW—I'D SETTLE FOR HAPPY EVER AFTER.
THEY DESERVE IT.

WE HAVEN'T EVEN GOT STARTED!
WHO KNOWS WHAT'S AROUND THE CORNER?

GROUP SHOT, EVERYONE! GROUP SHOT! EVERYONE OVER HERE!
COME ON, CHOP CHOP!
YOU TOO, CYCLONUS...
...I DON'T CARE WHERE EVERYONE STANDS...

"...SO LONG AS WE'RE ALL IN IT *TOGETHER*."

MORE THAN MEETS THE EYE #22 COVER B

by **NICK ROCHE** Colors by **JOSH BURCHAM**

THE SOUND OF BREAKING GLASS

By James Roberts

"That is *pungent*," said Minimus Ambus, tapping the side of his nose and recalibrating his olfactory sensors. "Is that the spacebridge?"

"The greater the distance covered," said Rodimus, "the stronger the smell. That's what Wheeljack says, anyway."

They were standing in Tyrest's Control Room, watching Brainstorm, Grapple, and Inferno sift through the wreckage of the spacebridge.

"Do you think Tyrest did it?" said Minimus. "A doorway to Cyberutopia?"

Rodimus tried to shrug, but his body—still tender after being pulverized by the Killswitch—was having none of it. "Dunno about Cyberutopia, but Skids says the portal took him *somewhere*. He's not making much sense, admittedly; it's all, 'I saw a giant spark and it spoke to me in feelings…'" He snapped his shoulder hydraulics back into position. "Rung thinks he experienced a form of trans-lingual synesthesia, whatever that is. In time, perhaps he'll—careful, Grapple! Set it down gently!"

"You're busy," said Minimus, stepping away. "We'll talk later."

Rodimus pressed his communicator to his ear. "Just let me make a few calls…"

Call 1: "Actually, Perceptor, I think finding Tyrest's communications room is a priority. He had a computer that would have—no, hear me out. If he could reach his Enforcer wherever he was in the galaxy, surely we can reach Cybertron?"

Call 2: "No, still no sign of… Ratchet, if we find Pharma's body I will tell you. I will call you. Yes. Yes, obviously. And what about Tailgate, any news? No, no, I understand. Keep me posted."

Call 3: "Just land outside, Max. Anywhere! What sacred ground? Oh, the hot spot. Okay, see the big tower by the smelting pool? Park alongside that."

Call 4: "I'm smiling. I am! I'm getting—Minimus is giving me a funny look because I'm standing here smiling. Nice one, Perceptor. Let me know as soon as you get it working."

It occurred to Minimus that Rodimus had given more orders in the space of three minutes than he had in the last 12 months. "You look like you're about to fall apart," he said, as Rodimus finally turned off his communicator.

"I'm fine."

Minimus tapped his leader's bicep. A hunk of machinery and buckled plating slid to the ground.

"Well I'm not about to bother Ratchet *now*, am I?" said Rodimus, stepping delicately out of the pool of his own body parts. "Not when he's got Tailgate to worry about."

In the 40 minutes since Tailgate's collapse, the team of engineers, medics and mechanics in Pharma's well-stocked medibay had discovered the cure to four infamous Cybertronian diseases. Under normal circumstances, an Autobot who solved the problem of form fatigue or static spark syndrome would have punched the air and yelped with delight. Today, with Tailgate's death clock creeping towards zero, they merely smiled, put the latest miracle formula to one side, and got back to work.

"You are tired, though," insisted Minimus. "Mentally, you're exhausted."

"I'm tired; other people are dead. Have you seen outside? There are hundreds of corpses out there—we're talking half the Circle of Light. Now, if I can't help them I can at least try to fix the spacebridge."

Rodimus rocked on his heels as Inferno barged past and fired foam into a section of the spacebridge that had caught fire. When the foam ran out Inferno stamped on the flames, and with a sad thud another chunk of Tyrest's precious patchwork portal hit the floor.

"Maybe it's better that the spacebridge isn't fixed," said Minimus slowly, seeing the look of horror on Rodimus's face. "If it was fixed, it might make people think that our losses were worthwhile: 'The ship was overrun and people died, but at least we found a way to get to Cyberutopia.' I don't want that. Do you?"

There was a sudden squeal of excitement, and Rodimus and Minimus turned to see Brainstorm skipping around the remains of the Killswitch, holding his briefcase above his head. Beaming behind his faceplate, the weapons engineer jogged out of the Control Room, pausing only to tug playfully at Minimus Ambus' moustache.

"Whatever happened to priorities?" muttered Rodimus, frowning with disapproval. "Now Minimus—sorry, Magnus—what was it you wanted?"

"I was, um, wondering if you'd found my outer shell?"

"The one without a head?" Rodimus pointed across the room. "Storage locker. I thought you'd come looking for it."

"Thank you," said Minimus, turning to leave.

"Magnus, wait. Listen. When it was all kicking off—when I was being wired into the Killswitch—you and I, we…" Rodimus paused to test the depth of a newly discovered dent in his forehead. "We came clean, didn't we? I told you about Overlord and… yeah."

Minimus waited for him to continue.

"I am going to do something about it, you know. I'm going to—"

"Make amends. So you said."

Rung looked up from the table at the sound of breaking glass and saw Fortress Maximus pulling his boot from the remains of a displaced engex canister. Max wasn't really to blame: it was impossible to walk across Swerve's ransacked bar without treading on something breakable.

"Thank you for seeing me," said Fortress Maximus, sitting down opposite Rung. He tilted his head and realized that the shards of tinted glass in front of the ship's psychiatrist bore a strong resemblance to Ark 5. "You know I'd have been happy to meet you in your office."

"My office is full of dead Legislators," said Rung, pushing a drink across the table.

Fortress Maximus swirled the room-temperature engex around the glass, watching the luminous pink liquid crest and collapse. "I've been made an offer. A new position. Rodimus was impressed by my handling of the Legislator invasion—which is ridiculous, frankly, because all I did was let them take over the ship..." He sipped his drink; it tasted bad. "Anyway. Yes. A new position."

"Congratulations. I'm pleased for you."

A second sip. "I don't know whether to accept."

Rung turned his friend's empty glass on its side; it made a decent rear thruster. "You don't think you've earned it?"

"Oh, I know I haven't 'earned' it. This isn't about 'earning' it. This is about whether I'm cured or not. The shooting spree—that's in the past. I mean—hell—it's easy for *me* to say that, but..." He slumped a little in his chair. "I feel like myself again. Like I did before Overlord attacked Garrus 9."

Rung swept the mosaic aside and put his elbows on the table. "You're not 'cured' because you were never diseased. But the fact you're asking these questions—of me, of yourself—is good, Max. It's really good."

"But do you think I might come unstuck again?"

"I think you're ready for whatever is around corner. As ready as the rest of us." Rung reached across the table and unclenched his friend's fist. "But promise me: if your thoughts run away with you, come find me. Ten floors down."

"Ten floors down?"

"My office is ten floors below the Bridge. I assume that's where you'll be, if you're going to be third in command?"

"Who said anything about being third in command? Rung, this new position—it means I have to leave the Lost Light."

As Rodimus stepped into his office he shielded his eyes—literally put his hand to his face—to avoid catching sight of the flames he'd had painted around the doorframe. As soon as he'd sorted out the current mess he'd ask Atomizer to help him redecorate. No more fire-rimmed entrances, garish pink walls or self-aggrandizing plaques: just a desk, a chair, some subdued lighting and a memorial to crewmembers killed by Sparkeater, Legislator, or Overlord.

Overlord.

When his guard was down—when he wasn't showing off or doodling or spray-painting—the name made him think of the people who had died or lost loved ones because he'd been too scared to say no to Prowl. Overlord made him think of Pipes and Rewind and Chromedome and Lockstock and Lancet, but one face—Drift's face—kept crowding out all the others. It had been here, in his office, that they'd had their last proper conversation.

"An inquiry?" Drift stood in the doorway, looking incredulous. "An *inquiry?*"

Rodimus dragged him inside and locked the door. "I had to do *something!* People were asking questions! And what do you do if you want to stall things? You launch an inquiry." He slumped into his chair. "An inquiry into something *I'm* responsible for. Oh god. Oh god, I feel sick. I've messed up big time."

"I can sort this out, Rodimus. Honestly, I can fix this."

"This is my fault, not yours. We were standing in Prowl's office, and he was trying to convince me that bringing Overlord onboard was 'right and proper', and you called me an idiot for even considering it."

"Was I that blunt?"

"I don't know why he even let you in on those discussions in the first place. It's not like he trusts you."

"I'll tell you exactly why he wanted me there: it was in case something like this happened. Need a scapegoat? Get an ex-Decepticon."

"Well it's not gonna happen. I'm taking the fall for this one. Your name doesn't have to come into it. It's taken you years to win back people's trust, and you're not throwing it all away on my behalf."

"Rodimus, if you tell the crew what you've done, then that's it. The quest's over. We'll never find the Knights."

"No, it just means someone else will take over. You, maybe? Ratchet? I dunno. Someone."

"But someone *doesn't* take over!"

Rodimus looked up sharply. "'Doesn't'?"

"Won't."

"You said 'doesn't.' What d'you mean, 'doesn't'?"

"It's hard to explain what I mean." Drift unclipped his Great Sword and placed it on the desk. "You remember when I nearly died, back on Cybertron? I was within feet of Vector Sigma."

"Yes..." said Rodimus slowly, unsure where this was going.

"When I put this sword through my spark, I saw something."

"What, like a vision?"

"Kind of. More a sense of how things would play out. It was abstract and it was fleeting, and every time I call it to mind it becomes harder to interpret, but something is around the corner, Rodimus—and a year from now, or 50 years from now, that something will arrive, and we won't be able to stop it unless we find the Knights. And I don't care if you think, 'Oh, that's just Drift being Drift,' because I'm convinced that you need to remain in charge. People can come and go—they can die—but you have to be here, otherwise we will fail. And so the simple solution—the only solution—is that I take the blame for this."

"I won't let you do this for me."

"I'm not doing it for you. I'm doing it for everyone else."

"Hey, what are you two doing in here? Are you... looting? I expected it of you, Fort Max, you light-fingered rogue, but *Rung?!*"

A grinning Swerve skipped across the room and went to vault over the bar. He caught his boot on an engex pump and fell face-first into the serving space on the other side. A second later, a solitary wheel rolled out from behind the bar, circled Rung's leg three times, and toppled over.

"Save your innermost energon," said Swerve, clambering to his feet. "I am unharmed!"

"You seem... reinvigorated," said Fortress Maximus.

"Saved a life, Max, saved a life. Tailgate! Lives! On!" He threw an energon goodie into the air and almost caught it in his mouth. "Who says you can't be a metallurgist *and* a bartender?"

Swerve's grin left his face as he saw a silhouette in the doorway: head, legs, arms, briefcase.

"I'd like a word with Chatterbot in private," said Brainstorm, fishing a barstool from the wreckage and sitting down. "You gonna do this place up, Swerve?"

"That's the plan, yeah."

"Good. Because people come here and they talk, and I need you to keep your ears open."

"For what? What am I listening out for?"

"I think..." Brainstorm looked over his shoulder to check that Rung and Fortress Maximus had left. "I think someone's tampered with the briefcase. It looks like someone's opened it, and I want to know who."

"Easy. Just look for the guy with no head."

Brainstorm laughed and clapped Swerve on the shoulder, agitating an old injury and making the bartender flinch. Brainstorm continued to laugh until Swerve joined in, at which point he grabbed him by the back of the neck and pulled him close. "It's not funny. Opening the briefcase when I'm not around is very far from being a sensible thing to do." He climbed off the stool. "So... any idle chatter and you come to me. Are we clear?"

Swerve nodded—but not, Brainstorm realized, in agreement. The nod was directing his attention downwards, to the green light escaping from his chest plate. Before Swerve could say anything, Brainstorm smothered the leaking light with his briefcase and fled the room.

Satisfied that the energon transfusion was having the intended effect and that the key points of articulation—waist, knees, elbows—were responding to his touch, Ratchet left Tailgate sleeping on the circuit slab. With the stab wounds in his chest and back patched up, the Waste Disposal Expert looked freshly forged. Sadly, that was just on the outside; before the anti-corrosives had forced it into remission, his rampaging cybercrosis had caused so much internal damage that when he'd collapsed in Tyrest's Control Room, it had sounded like someone punching a bucket of nails.

Before administering the anti-corrosives, Ratchet had bled Tailgate's body, opening the vents and traps designed to keep energon, oil and petrolex from escaping. Swerve had laid claim to the slops, saying he intended to run some tests. (It was nice that he was taking an interest, thought Ratchet, even if he wasn't prepared to give up his day job.) Now, all that was left was to wait for Tailgate's resurgent spark to build itself up until it could sustain him without the assistance of a life support machine.

Ratchet walked into the morgue, went to open one of the body-lockers, and stiffened as he sensed someone behind him. Minimus Ambus was standing in the doorway wearing the bottom section of the Magnus Armor, his wrist-thin legs plugged into a pair of massive kneecaps.

"Hello, Ratchet," said Minimus sheepishly, tottering into the room as if on stilts. "The armor's easy to take off but hell to put on, especially by yourself. I wondered if you could help. I can talk you through the process, give you instructions."

"I'm impressed you were able to sneak up on me," said Ratchet, kneeling down to examine the point where Minimus' right leg disappeared into the Magnus Armor. He tapped 13 hidden pressure pads in quick succession and the armor rose up and wrapped itself more tightly around Minimus's limb.

Minimus watched a confident Ratchet do the same—13 taps—with the other leg. "How long have you known?" he said quietly.

"About you and the armor? Ooh, quite a while now."

"But how? The armor is filled with these attention deflectors..."

"That work for all of five seconds." Ratchet climbed to his feet and wiped his hands. "You might as well use smoke and mirrors. And quite frankly, I'm a little insulted that you'd think I'd be fooled."

"You never said anything..."

"Why would I say anything? 'Hey, Ultra Magnus, I know your secret.' Why would I say that? What would that achieve? I didn't say anything to the others, either."

"You knew the other Magnuses?"

"Suture, Datum, Ramp, Blockus—all the way back to the original."

"What was he like?"

"He wasn't like you, that's for sure."

Minimus looked hurt. "Well, thanks for the assistance. I think I can put the rest on by myself."

"No two Magnuses are alike," continued Ratchet, worried that he'd said the wrong thing. "But because people assume they're the same person, they make allowances without realizing it. I've known you longer than any of your predecessors, and maybe that's why, to me—and I know this sounds strange—you're the true Ultra Magnus."

Minimus gave a nod of—what? Understanding? Gratitude? He wasn't sure, but he left the medibay feeling ten times taller, and it had nothing to do with the armor on his feet.

Ratchet turned back to the body-locker, slid a key in the lock, and braced himself. The body inside was different to all the other bodies in the morgue: it was alive.

"Anything?"

Rodimus pressed his foot gently against the lunar landscape as if testing the temperature of bath water. "No. Nothing." He pushed down harder—with his heel, this time. "Still nothing."

"Are you sure this is the place?" asked Getaway, who was standing on a Mobile Autobot Repair Bay that was hovering a few feet off the ground.

"Mountain range to the left," muttered Rodimus, flicking a thumb towards the horizon. He dropped to his hands and knees and pressed his cheek against the silver surface, hoping to detect weak heat or distant movement. "Last time, this whole place lit up the moment I stepped off the M.A.R.B. Millions of sparks, from here to the horizon. This—this sea of electric blue. VOMPF!"

"I'm no expert," said Getaway, "but hot spots don't normally blink in and out of existence. They ignite, they stay ignited."

"True, but they're not normally ignited by someone treading on them." Rodimus sat on the edge of Getaway's M.A.R.B. and scanned the resolutely un-illuminated landscape; the hot spot's stubborn dormancy registered as yet another personal failure. "Then again, you have to harvest surface sparks quickly, otherwise they... evaporate isn't the right word, but you know what I mean. Maybe we just missed our chance."

Getaway jumped to the ground, gave it a quick tap (why pass up an opportunity to find out if you were a Matrix-Bearer-in-waiting?) and sat down next to Rodimus. Sensing his despondency, he gave him a playful jab—"bomp"—on the upper arm. "What now, then?"

Rodimus reached into a compartment in his waist and pulled out the remains of the Matrix. "I don't know if this is the right thing to do," he said, scattering the cloudy fragments over the ground, "but I feel we should do something mark the passing of Luna I's lost generation."

"I hope I don't have to arrest you for littering," came a new voice, and Rodimus and Getaway turned to see a second M.A.R.B. heading their way.

"Arrest me?" said Rodimus. "Does that mean what I think it means?"

Fortress Maximus skidded to a mid-air stop and smiled. "The newly-appointed Enforcer of the Tyrest Accord, reporting for service."

"Good decision, Max, good decision. Just because Tyrest lost the plot it doesn't mean there's not work to be done."

"Thank you for your faith in me."

"Happy to accept the thanks, but it was Magnus who wanted this to happen. He said his successor should..." His voiced trailed off as someone stepped out from behind Fortress Maximus.

"Red Alert?"

"Captain, I want to apologize for—"

"Stop right there. No apologies. Not on my ship."

"But I can't imagine the inconvenience I caused by my decision to, um, remove myself from the field of play."

"Nonsense. You were under tremendous pressure. Okay, so you didn't feel able to confide in me, but that says more about my failings as a leader than anything else." He pictured Ultra Magnus listening to him and nodding sagely at his words.

"Ratchet's brought me up to speed," said Red Alert. "I know that some of the Circle of Light are staying behind, and that you intend for Tyrest's body to remain here too, and I—"

"We've built a secure room in the medibay," interrupted Rodimus, pointing vaguely in the direction of what had been Tyrest's base of operations. "We've stabilized Tyrest but he won't be resuscitated until I've spoken to High Command—if I ever get to speak to High Command—and they've decided what to do with him."

"My point, Rodimus, is that I'd like to stay here." He held up a hand to forestall Rodimus's protests. "We all know there are pockets of rogue Decepticons out there. I can help the Circle of Light prepare for the possibility of attack. I'm already thinking that we could reprogram the... what are they called, Legislators? We could reprogram the Legislators to act as the moon's protectors."

"I think with you and Fort Max, Luna I is going to be in safe hands. Just promise to stay in touch!"

"Actually, Rodimus, that's why we're here. Perceptor's been trying to reach you."

Rodimus turned his communicator back on and nodded towards the hot spot. "Sorry, I was expecting to be busy with the..." He looked up. "What did Perceptor want?"

"You said you wanted to contact Cybertron as soon as I got this working," said Perceptor, gesturing to a monitor screen took up an entire wall of the Communications Room.

Rodimus craned his neck. "That. Is. Massive." He beckoned Getaway, Red Alert and Fortress Maximus over. "Who else wants one of these on the Lost Light?"

"I intend to replicate the comms system *without* the oversized monitor," said Perceptor, taking his seat at the operating console. "But first... dialing Kimia now, captain."

Rodimus clapped his hands. "Right! Good! Let's surprise Bumblebee!"

"I hope he's alright," said Red Alert, as the screen filled with static.

"'*Course* he's alright! I bet within 48 hours of us leaving Cybertron he'd talked the NAILs 'round, taught the 'Cons the error of their ways, and become Cybertron's first democratically-elected postwar leader. You'll see—any second now he'll be waving his little cane at us, telling us about the New Golden Age..."

Getaway was the first to detect a picture amongst the static. "What's that? Some kind of emblem? It's not an Autobot symbol, that's for sure." He read the words underneath the emblem as soon as they appeared. "'Welcome to the Republic of Cybertron.'"

"You see?" Rodimus turned to the others. "*You see?* He's brought the whole planet together. Good old Bee. Good old brilliant Bee."

"That's not Bumblebee," said Fortress Maximus.

"Don't tell me Prowl is screening his calls..." Rodimus muttered, turning back to the screen.

Starscream looked down at him and grinned. "Well, well, well. What a *lovely* surprise."

POSTSCRIPT

Being entirely mechanical, Outrigger had never experienced breathlessness before, but running down half a mile of corridor and cutting across the hot spot put such a strain on his aging servos that when he crashed into Red Alert's office it took him a moment—bent in half and clamoring at the doorframe—before he was able to speak.

"He just moved!"

Red Alert helped Outrigger to his feet. Weren't members of the Circle of Light were supposed to be prime physical specimens? Weren't they supposed to be high-shine, chrome-coated überbots, their bodies and minds sharper and more deadly than the Great Sword they carried on their backs?

"Sorry, Red. I'd have called you, but I know you don't like using your communicator because you think it interferes with your—"

"Brainwaves, yes, yes. Forget that. *Who* just moved?"

"Tyrest!"

"I'm not saying I don't believe you," said Red Alert as they approached Luna I's medibay a few minutes later. "But unless someone repairs him properly, Tyrest's going to be paralyzed forever. Maybe you saw the shadows move?"

"There are no shadows in the medibay," said Outrigger, pointing at the locked room in the corner. "Take a look. Tell me I'm seeing things."

Red Alert took a step closer, suddenly wary. "*How* did he move, exactly? Did he twitch? Was it a spasm?"

"No, nothing like that. It was very... *considered*."

Red Alert checked the door—still locked—and then put his eye against the peephole.

"It was his fingers," continued Outrigger. "The fingers on his right hand. It looked he was going to clench his fist."

"Get Fortress Maximus," said Red Alert, face still pressed against the door.

"Why? What should I tell him?"

"Tell him Tyrest has gone."

TRANSFORMERS

THE IDW COLLECTION • PHASE TWO, VOLUME 5